W9-BRP-306

Acknowledgements

I want to thank Heather Webb for seeing a story where any rational person would have only seen bad writing.

I would also like to thank the members of the Northern Connecticut Writers Workshop for their countless hours of critiquing and guidance.

This book would not be in its current form without the efforts of Donna Smith a good friend and insightful critic. Thank you, Donna.

And finally, I want to thank Jennifer Harrington, a professional writer who gave generously of her time.

Chapter One
Among Peasants

**"It is not the man who has little, but the
man who craves more that is poor."
Lucius Annaeus Seneca**

"Chevalier, only you will I miss."

The chestnut stallion lowered his head, offering his ears and neck to the boy's touch. Jean-Marc pressed his face to the horse's. He breathed in, enjoying, trying to memorize the big stallion's scent. The animal nudged his face forward and exhaled.

How long will I be gone? Will I ever see you again? Damn my father, and brother.

They nuzzled while the horse was saddled. Then the boy, small for sixteen and wiry strong, leapt on his horse's back and shouted, "Run, Big Boy." Chevalier reared and galloped across the yard, easily clearing a hedge. They rode as one, until they were both exhausted, then returned to the stable. The sweat-covered animal gasped for breath. Jean-Marc's soaked shirt clung to his body.

Sliding from the saddle, he walked to Chevalier's front. They both sucked for air. He pressed his face to the stallion's again.

Can you understand, Big Boy? Who will ride you when I am gone? Who would you let ride you?

He hugged the animal one last time and scratched between his ears. Then he turned to the stable boy, "See to him."

Walking to the house, he wiped his hands across his face.

Three large chests were strapped to the back of the carriage that would carry him to the Seine. The team of white horses and the driver's red and white uniform looked smart against the dark blue carriage. The gold crest of the Comte d'Artois on the coach's doors completed the image.

In his room, his dresser helped him change into clothing fitting his rank. Putting on his long brown wig he thought, *Now, to see Mother one last time. I am sent away but she acts the victim.*

He walked to his mother's drawing-room. Through the open door, he could see Marie sitting on a blue and gold brocaded chaise. A servant filed her nails. He walked in without knocking.

"Adieu, Mother. Since Francois refuses to meet his obligations to the family, I leave for Acadia, in America."

Marie pulled her hand from the servant's and turned to face him. "Francois has many responsibilities." She motioned for him to sit beside her.

"But none to his family." He ignored the invitation to sit.

"You know Francois had to pay the king to ensure his title. Now he pays a yearly tax just to retain it and Louis requires him to have fifty armed men at the ready–"

"And his mistress must have her estate."

"Jean-Marc, don't be unpleasant. I may not see you for years." Marie patted the chaise again. He walked to the window.

"Why would I be unpleasant? Francois has Father's wealth and lives as if he were Louis, while I must go to the wilderness and be a merchant among savages."

"Don't be this way." Marie stood and smoothed her dress. "Kiss me before you leave."

He left without kissing his mother. He did not see her wipe a tear from her eye.

*****

For two hours, the coach rode through a rolling countryside of forest, vineyards and an occasional peasant's cottage. The boy sat behind drawn drapes and fumed. He saw nothing. When they reached the Seine, he waited while the coachman hired a boat to take him to Le Havre.

Speaking through the drapes the driver said, "The boatman tells me the journey will take five days, my Lord. He assures me there are fitting inns along the way. He will stop each night and arrange for your accommodations."

"And in Le Havre?"

"There he will see to a room for you at an inn, and he will hire an agent to secure your passage to Acadia on a fitting ship."

The boy pulled back the drape and nodded. His luggage was already being loaded onto a cart to be moved to the boat.

"Let us hope this boatman is worthy of your trust." Jean-Marc walked the few yards to the gangplank where he was greeted by a peasant dressed in rags.

The boatman bowed low. With a toothless smile he said, "Welcome aboard, my Lord. We've made a comfortable seat for you under an awning."

Jean-Marc looked around the craft. The unpainted *galiot* was fewer than thirty feet long. A small hatch led under its deck to the single compartment where he could see the boatman's family.

These people must live down there, with their cargo. Is the stench from the cargo or the peasants?

On the river bank, a small boy sat on a horse waiting to pull the barge down the shallow river.

I will not travel on a freight barge. The coachman will have to find appropriate accommodations.

He turned to scold the driver but the coach was already headed away at a hurried pace.

"*Salaud!*" (Bastard!) Jean-Marc shouted at the coach.

He wasted no time making his escape. The salaud knew this was unacceptable. Now, I am left to cope!

He sighed and said to the boatman, "I fear we have different understandings of what is comfortable. A wooden chair under an old sail falls far short of comfort. Bring me an upholstered chair and a clean awning."

"Unfortunately, my Lord, this is our only chair. Perhaps if you sat in it, you would—"

"I would discover that wood has become soft?" He sighed again. "Very well, this will have to do. Bring cushions and pillows for the chair."

The man bowed again, bringing his clasped hands toward his mouth. "Again, forgive me, my Lord. I am but a poor man. I have no pillows or cushions. My family sleeps on the same straw we use for the animals. I could pile some straw on the seat for you."

Jean-Marc sighed again. *I had no idea the wilderness would begin in France.* He waved his hand and said to the boatman, "No, no straw. This will suffice. Bring some wine." He stepped over tools and ropes lying on the deck and sat on the hard chair, directing a thousand silent curses at his mother and brother.

The boatman returned with a crude wooden cup filled with white wine. Jean-Marc decided not to comment on the cup. He raised it to his nose and sniffed.

Has the fool brought vinegar by mistake?

Again, he chose not to comment. He sipped the wine and tried not to show his distaste.

Please God, speed us to a comfortable inn with a proper chair and decent wine.

The day was hot and unpleasant. The stench from below deck seemed to grow worse. The old sail protected him from direct sun but was not cooling. He drank little of the inferior wine. The boatman tried to engage him in conversation, but he had no interest in befriending a tradesman.

As the sun sank behind the trees that lined the river, the boat stopped near an inn. The boatman went inside to make arrangements.

"They are prepared for you now, my Lord. They have not served supper yet. The seat at the head of the table is saved for you."

What, am I to be entertainment for the riff-raff? I have no intention of eating among them. Jean-Marc said, "Bring my luggage to my room."

He was greeted at the door by the innkeeper who bowed low and said, "Welcome to the Saint Louis Inn, my Lord. Supper will be served in a few minutes. Would you like some wine while you wait?"

"No. Have my luggage brought to my room. I'll take my meal there. And send me a dresser. I'm quite tired."

The innkeeper straightened and saw the boatman and his son pulling one of Jean-Marc's large chests out of the hold. He said, "My Lord, if we put such a large chest in the room, there will be no room for the others to move or to use the chamber pot."

"Others?"

"Yes, my Lord. We are quite full tonight. You share a room with three other travelers."

"That is impossible! Put them somewhere else."

"There is nowhere else to put them, my Lord." The innkeeper nervously wiped his hands on the dirty apron covering his immense stomach. "We have three rooms. All of them are full."

"Tell the others they are leaving. I require the room tonight."

"Where are they to go, my Lord?" He raised his hands from his apron. "The next inn is a day's journey away."

Jean-Marc walked past him. "Their problems are not mine. Show me to my room and send the dresser to me."

"For an additional fee I could arrange the private room for you, my Lord, but I have no servant to dress you."

I have no intention of negotiating with peasants.

"So be it." He pulled a silver coin from his purse and flipped it to the innkeeper. "I trust this covers everything. Now show me to my room."

"As you wish, my Lord." The innkeeper bowed again. He led Jean-Marc up a steep set of stairs and opened a door to a small room, almost completely filled with an immense bed.

"Where am I to sit while I eat?"

"I have no bench small enough to fit here, my Lord. Perhaps you could sit on your chest? I will bring a small table for you to eat from." The innkeeper bowed again as he backed out of the room.

Jean-Marc shook his head and sighed.

Even peasants must have better beds than this.

He pulled back the woolen cloths. The bed had a wooden frame. Ropes threaded between the sides supported a large mattress which was apparently filled with wool. He pulled back the mattress.

But of course ... lice. Every bed has lice, but I did not expect every louse in Artois to be in one bed.

The boatman's son knocked and brought one of Jean-Marc's chests into the room.

"There is no need to bring the others," he said, looking around the room. "There is no space for them."

"Yes, my Lord." The young man wedged the chest between the bed and wall then bowed before leaving.

Minutes later the innkeeper knocked at the door and brought a small table into the room. He was followed by his wife. Her over-filled green dress was covered with flour and large grease stains. She attempted a curtsy as she placed a tray filled with a large bowl of watery stew, a loaf of bread, a wooden mug and pitcher of wine on the table. They both bowed as they fumbled backward saying they hoped he would enjoy his meal.

Jean-Marc sniffed the stew. *This must be what rancid smells like. I'll not enjoy this.* If anything, the wine was worse than he had on the boat. He ate little of the food. *I'll keep my clothes on for protection from the lice and fleas.*

He took off his wig and placed it on the chest. Then he stretched out on the bed and lay fully clothed for hours before he slept.

Early the next morning, there was a knock at the door.

Already awake, he called, "Enter."

The innkeeper's wife brought a loaf of bread, some cheese and more wine on another tray. She wore a clean red dress. Her hair was held back with a tortoise-shell comb. As she cleared away his uneaten supper, she nervously said, "The boatman bid me tell you that he leaves within the hour. You'll need to be onboard by then."

Now I'm being dictated to by fat women and tradesmen? Jean-Marc nodded. He ate some cheese, the loaf of bread and managed to drink most of the wine before walking to the boat. He told the boatman, "Send someone for my chest. In the future see that you arrange for me to have my own room. I have no intention of bargaining with another innkeeper." He reached into his purse and handed the boatman four silver coins. "Use these to make the necessary arrangements."

Without waiting for a reply, he went to his chair and sat.

I fear the next four days will be very long.

*****

In Le Havre, the boatman arranged for a private room at a small inn. Jean-Marc walked to the harbor to book his passage to Acadia.

I'll insist on the finest accommodations. This, at least, Francois is paying for.

To his horror all the ships headed to Acadia or Quebec were merchant ships. The few passengers they carried were indentured servants who would be quartered below deck with the cargo and travel like cattle.

"You cannot tell me gentlemen travel in this fashion."

The ship's officer replied, "Monsieur, few gentlemen travel to the colonies, so few ships are equipped for them. Perhaps if you inquire with Jacques La Chappelle, he may be able to help you find appropriate accommodations." The officer pointed to a nondescript building across from the wharf. "He's a shipping agent. He may be aware of a ship with something suited for a man of your rank."

Jean-Marc thanked him and walked to the door under the painted sign "Jacques La Chappelle Shipping Agent." Without knocking he walked through the door.

"Are you Jacques La Chappelle?" he asked a young man in a cheap suit who sat writing in a thick book.

The man took off his spectacles and looked up. "Monsieur La Chappelle is very busy. May I help you?"

Jean-Marc explained his situation.

"One moment, please." He left his desk and walked through a door into another room. In a few minutes, he followed a well-dressed, fat, older man back into the room. The younger man hurried into the street.

"I believe Marcel said you are Monsieur Bompeau?"

"I am."

"Please allow me to introduce myself. I am Jacques La Chappelle." he smiled and bowed. "If they are still available, I believe I may have just the accommodations you seek. I sent Marcel to see if they are spoken for."

"And these accommodations would be?"

"For one hundred écus we can book a private cabin aboard *Le Griffon.* You will take your meals at the Captain's table."

Jean-Marc blanched. *That's outrageous. With a hundred écus a man could support a family for more than a year.* Then he thought, *Of course, the price concerns Francois not me.*

He smiled. "What must be must be. The passage will be billed to my brother, the Comte d'Artois. I am no peasant. I will not live like one."

"Very well, this is easily arranged. It is my understanding that *Le Griffon's* hold is only half full. So, she remains in port until her hold is—"

"What? You expect me to wait while they load the ship?"

"This, my Lord, is necessary. But it will provide time for your brother to confirm the purchase before she sails. Until then, we should be able to hold the cabin for you."

"How long am I to wait?"

"This, I am afraid, we never know. Ships cannot afford to sail with less than a full load. We must wait until the shipper has enough freight to fill his hold." La Chappelle held his hands together and tried to look sympathetic.

"At a hundred écus for one passenger, it would seem the ship would sail when he is ready."

"So, it would seem, my Lord, but it is not so."

The young man returned to the office. Both men looked at him.

"The cabin has not been taken, Monsieur La Chappelle. The shipper will hold it pending payment before she sails."

La Chappelle turned back to Jean-Marc. "Then we should waste no time. I can send a messenger to the Comte tonight."

Jean-Marc swore then nodded. *I cannot believe I am to wait until a merchant is ready.* Fearing there would be no better alternative he nodded again. "Secure the cabin, Monsieur La Chappelle." *My brother will pay dearly to be rid of me.*

"Keep me informed as to where you are staying. I will send a boy to tell you the day before the ship is to sail and a teamster to move your luggage for you."

La Chappelle wrote down the name of the inn where Jean-Marc was staying and bowed again as he turned to leave.

*****

Jean-Marc returned to the inn and went directly to his room. *There is no lock on this door. It may be good that my luggage will not fit in here. I hope it will be safe in their cellar.* The bed almost filled the room. The low ceiling dropped sharply over a small window which admitted little air when the door was closed. Under the window was the chamber pot. He tried to imagine how he could use it in so small a space. He decided the gray walls were once white. A stenciled red fleur-de-lis pattern was barely visible beneath the grime. *I cannot eat in here.*

This meant eating with the other guests. The inn served meals at seven each morning and evening in the dining-room. A bell notified him dinner was served. The keeper's fat wife greeted him at the door.

"Monsieur Bompeau, we are honored to have such a gentleman stay with us. I have reserved the seat at the head of the table for you."

She seated him at a large, uncovered wooden table. A number of other guests filled the side benches. They rose, as if by command, and bowed to greet him. He returned a slight nod of his head and sat.

The innkeeper's wife placed a large bowl of stew beside Jean-Marc's plate. "Please serve yourself, Monsieur."

He looked into the bowl. Then he looked around the table at the hungry peasants. *This stringy meat will not make it even half-way around the table. The people sitting at the other end will be left with nothing but turnips and onions.* Glad to be seated where he was, Jean-Marc filled his bowl to overflowing with meat and vegetables. He looked at large loaves of a coarse brown bread on the table. *They will be glad to fill their stomachs with bread.*

When the bowl approached the foot of the table one man shouted at the man next to him, "You pig! You're taking everything and leaving me nothing but broth!" Pushes were exchanged.

Those waiting for the stew intervened. "If you idiots spill the stew, none of us will eat!" The pushing ended.

Good, they're quick to turn on each other, but none dare to question me.

Much clear broth was soaked up by bread that evening. The innkeeper brought several large pottery pitchers filled with cheap wine. Jean-Marc's wooden cup was filled before the pitchers were passed around the table.

He sniffed the wine before sipping. *Can it be? The wine on the boat was better. There's little meat, but there'll be no shortage of bad wine at this meal.*

The commoners amazed Jean-Marc. The only peasants he had ever known were servants. This would be the sixth night he spent in a public inn, but the first time he ate among them. *Mon Dieu. They wear rags. They stink. Now I must eat with them? Have I already fallen so far?* He cursed Francois and his mother again.

During dinner, a louse crawled from a merchant's hair and paraded back and forth between the man's eyebrows throughout the meal. Neither the merchant nor the other guests seemed to notice.

Jean-Marc shook his head. *Can they not even feel lice? Has this become my life?*

*****

Nothing in Jean-Marc's life prepared him to wait for anything. Yet nine days passed and *Le Griffon* was still tied to the wharf. He sat alone in the inn's great room in the early afternoon.

"Would Monsieur like more wine?" the innkeeper's pretty, fourteen-year-old daughter asked.

"Perhaps Monsieur would prefer something sweet," he said, reaching to wrap his arms around her waist.

Chantel, prepared by a lifetime of dealing with drunken customers, took his left hand with her right, lifted it high, ducked under his grasp and turned for the safety of the kitchen. She laughed nervously. "Perhaps Monsieur would like to visit the women who work near the wharves."

Jean-Marc stood and said, "Perhaps Monsieur is tired of whores. Perhaps today he chooses a maiden." He stepped toward Chantel. "Things would be much more entertaining in my room." He wrapped his left arm around her waist and pulled her against his body. He threw his right arm over her shoulder, thrust his hand inside her bodice and grabbed her left breast.

Chantel cried out, "Papa! Papa!"

Her father was experienced at dealing with drunks who bothered the girls working for him. He raised a meat cleaver over his head and ran into the great room shouting, "Touch my daughter again and I'll geld you."

The innkeeper was a large, powerful man. He expected that by the time he got into the great room, his daughter would be released and the drunk would be stumbling backward in fear. He would push the drunk to the floor, kick him a few times and chase him from the inn. The drunk's possessions would be taken and sold to cover his bill, usually with a bit extra to reward the innkeeper for his effort. No drunk would dare appeal to the authorities. The innkeeper paid them well to protect his family and the inn.

However, Jean-Marc was no drunken merchant. He had trained in combat techniques since he was a small boy. The innkeeper's shouting drew his attention. He released Chantel. Reacting to the knife, Jean-Marc stepped backward, grabbed a half empty wine bottle from his table, stepped toward the innkeeper and crashed the bottle into the on-rushing father's face. Red wine, mixed with blood, spewed across the room as the bottle broke against the man's nose, crushing it into his sinuses, dislodging several front teeth, and embedding broken glass into his face and eyes.

Chantel ran from the inn screaming that her father was being murdered.

The innkeeper dropped the cleaver. He raised both hands to his shattered face. As if he planned it, Jean-Marc tripped the man backward, grabbed the cleaver and ran it across the man's throat. Blood spurted from the innkeeper's neck.

In a moment, Chantel burst into the room with Inspector-General Laflamme. "What is the meaning of this?" he called out.

Laflamme knew Jean-Marc. It was his job to know any nobles in his city.

Jean-Marc fixed his eyes on the Inspector-General as he used a cloth to clean blood from his hands and face. "This man assaulted me. When he saw I was alone in the room, he attacked me with this knife and tried to rob me."

Chantel looked at her father's body, "He's lying! He tried to rape me. When my father came to save me, he murdered him!"

Jean-Marc glared at her. *If she hadn't made this fuss her father would still be alive.* He said to the Inspector-General, "Why would I need to rape this gutter tramp? She'll lift her skirt for anyone who'll throw her two sous."

Chantel could not believe what she was hearing. *Papa pays Laflamme to protect us. No one dares talk to us like this.*

"I could go to any brothel in this city and pay for its best whore. For a few sous more I could buy a virgin. What need have I for this pox-ridden tramp?"

Laflamme looked at his feet. Then he turned to Chantel. "Quiet yourself girl. Monsieur Bompeau is of a noble family. You'll gain nothing lying about him."

"Lying?" Chantel was hysterical.

Jean-Marc smashed the back of his right hand into her face, knocking her to the ground. "I'll not have my reputation besmirched by a whore for defending myself from a thief. Have her flogged. Or must I send to my brother for satisfaction?"

"There's no need for that, my Lord. I'll see to it at once." Laflamme bent over and pulled Chantel to her feet. "Now come peacefully. You don't want to make things worse."

Chantel wailed as he dragged her away. Jean-Marc followed them to the square in front of the cathedral and watched as Laflamme stripped her to the waist and tied her wrists to a post. A crowd of sailors, local toughs, merchants and their wives jeered while Laflamme whipped her. Flesh tore from her back with every lash. She passed out after the fourth lash, never feeling the last six.

While Chantel hung from the post, Jean-Marc said to Laflamme, "Have my things moved to another inn and see that nothing gets lost along the way. I hold you responsible. I'll wait at Monsieur La Chappelle's office until my things are moved. I trust you to select a more reputable establishment. And cover that whore. Decent women pass through this square."

He turned and left for his agent's office without looking back.

Chapter Two
At Sea

"My pride fell with my fortunes"
William Shakespeare

Two weeks later, Jean-Marc received word *Le Griffon* would sail with the morning tide. He was to board that evening. A teamster came to bring Jean-Marc and his luggage to the dock. From there his trunks would need to be carried into his cabin.

The teamster steered his wagon to the wharf, helped Jean-Marc down from the wagon's seat and began unloading the luggage.

Am I really to live on this, for weeks on end? The ship was nothing like the splendid river barges he so often cruised on as a boy. *At least it's an improvement on that poor excuse for a barge that brought me here.*

Le Griffon was a mid-sized, Dutch-built *fluyt*, a merchant ship designed to carry as much cargo as possible at the least cost. Painted black with yellow trim, she was short and broad, widest at the waterline, narrowing as she rose from the sea. This made her slow, even under full sail, despite her three masts. Just eighty feet long, she carried no cannon. *Le Griffon* could be comfortably manned with a crew of twenty to thirty able-bodied seamen. For this voyage, she had a crew of twenty-nine.

He walked up the gangplank, looking for someone to show him to his cabin. Busy men hurried in all directions. A tall man, with graying brown hair and a pock-marked face, stood near the middle of the deck. He shuffled through a thick stack of papers and shouted directions to the crew. In spite of the poor quality of his clothing, Jean-Marc decided this man must be in charge. He could read.

"You appear to be an officer. My luggage is being unloaded now," he pointed to the teamster. "Have it taken to my cabin."

The officer looked at Jean-Marc, to the three large trunks being unloaded, then back at his pile of papers, which he rolled up in his hand. "Your cabin? How do you expect to fit all of that into your cabin?"

"They can be moved after the servants unpack them.*"*

The officer sighed and said, "You must be one of the passengers who'll be eating at the Captain's table. What's your name, Sir?"

"Jean-Marc Bompeau."

The man looked at his papers, then at Jean-Marc. "Sir, there are no servants on this ship. If you'd like to book passage for a servant, you're welcome to bring one. But it doesn't look like you've done that and none are provided with your fare. Servants aside, there's no room for those trunks in your cabin, and there's nothing to unpack them into. Pick out what you intend to wear, and one of my men will stow your chests below."

"But won't it be inconvenient for them to bring me clean clothing when these are soiled?"

The officer laughed. "How long do you expect this trip to take? With any luck, we'll be in Acadia in seven weeks." He signaled for one of the deck hands. "If you're comfortable in those, you can wear them the whole way. But you're better dressed for one of His Majesty's grand balls than an ocean voyage." He gestured toward Jean-Marc's clothing. "You'll probably want simple, warm clothes. The ocean's rough and cold in April. Get something warmer, and I'll have the rest of your things stowed away until we're in Acadia."

"You can't expect me to wear the same clothing for seven weeks!"

"I expect nothing of you, Sir. But with everything else stowed away, you'll get pretty cold if you don't wear them. We don't often see naked men on deck." He signed for the deck hand to wait. "Come with me. I'll show you your cabin. Then you can pick out your clothes."

He followed the man across the main deck to his cabin. At the door, the officer said, "This is your cabin, one of three here, in the fore-castle." He pointed to another door and said, "There's another passenger booked in this cabin next to yours. He'll likely be your main companion." Then he pointed to a third door. "This is the crew's cabin. They'll not bother you."

The man turned and pointed to the ship's rear. "The captain's quarters and his dining cabin, where you'll be eating, are there, in the aft-castle, below the quarter-deck." He looked at Jean-Marc, who nodded his understanding, before continuing. "The main deck's between. You'll spend most of your time there. Do your best to stay out of the crew's way. They'll have work to do. And stay away from the hatch in the main deck's middle. You've no need to go below. That's where the freight and common passengers go."

The officer turned back and opened the door to the cabin. Jean-Marc's face whitened. "You cannot expect me to sleep in there! I've seen bigger closets." The cabin was, perhaps, three feet by six feet, maybe less. "There's no bed."

"At sea, we sleep in hammocks."

Jean-Marc looked back in. A hammock, with a thin, dirty blanket, hung between once- white walls. Light came through a porthole. It had no glass. A wooden shutter could seal the hole, but that would also seal out all light. He said, "I see no stand for a lamp. How am I to see at night?"

The officer shook his head. "Too much risk of fire."

"All lamps have fire. We still need them to see."

"You're going to sleep in there. That means your eyes'll be closed, so you won't be needing a lamp. "

Looking around the tiny cabin, Jean-Marc said, "There's not even a chamber pot."

"That's right. You piss in pissdales. They're fore, aft and amid ship, port and starboard. There's seats over holes in the grating of the beaks-head." The officer pointed to the front of the ship, "They're the seats of ease. You shit there."

"The beaks-head?"

"The beaks-head's in the very front of the ship, off the fore-deck. Oft as not's too cold and wet to spend long there, but know the crew uses them too. Be about your business and be gone."

"This is unacceptable." Jean-Marc snapped, "I shall discuss this with your captain."

"You should do that." The sailor chuckled.

Jean-Marc thought *Does this man dare laugh at me?*

"Captain Lafarge'll be surprised to find out we don't supply chamber pots. He's only been captain for nine years. He'll be on board sometime tonight. You keep a quick eye out for him. He'll be happy to learn of the conditions on his father-in law's ship."

Jean-Marc said, "I'll not sleep in this poor excuse for a cabin."

"You paid for it. You don't have to use it."

"I'll also report your insolence to the captain. For now, one chest can be placed beneath the hammock. I'll show your man which one to bring in."

"As you'll have it, Sir." The officer told the sailor to follow Jean-Marc. On the wharf, he opened his trunks and moved things he thought he would need into the smallest. To no one in particular he said, "I'll not wear the same clothing for seven weeks." *Perhaps I can hire one of the women traveling below deck to launder my things.*

The sailor just managed to wedge the trunk into the cabin. It covered over a third of the floor. The other trunks were taken below.

Jean-Marc had the run of the main-deck, but no one to talk to. He saw a few peasants come aboard. They were hurried below deck. When the sun set, he went into his cabin. He was cold and alone.

Undressing in the dark, he stepped on his trunk and climbed into the hammock. As soon as he pulled up the blanket he felt lice. He fell out of the hammock, hitting his head on the trunk. He swore as he tumbled out the door and on to the deck, then ran to the ship's side and threw the lousy blanket overboard.

"Perhaps a peasant will live like this but not the brother of the Comte d' Artois!" Jean-Marc swore and stomped around the deck expecting someone to hurry to his assistance. *This must be corrected at once.* To his amazement, the busy crew ignored him.

He was furious, but he was also cold. He returned to his cabin and again climbed into the hammock. Without the blanket, there were fewer lice. He itched everywhere. It took hours for him to fall asleep.

Jean-Marc woke shivering. Without a blanket, he couldn't cover himself. All he had on was his long, silk shirt. *What time is it? How long was I asleep?* He got out of the hammock and felt around for his clothing. He managed to dress and get back in the hammock but was still too cold to sleep. He got out of his hammock, opened his trunk and groped about for another shirt and pair of breeches. He put them on but was still cold. Little by little he put on everything he had in his cabin. The clothing felt tight but at least he wasn't cold. He climbed back into the hammock but couldn't sleep. The night seemed endless. A few times he dozed off, but woke after a few minutes, less comfortable, more tired, and more frustrated.

I can't stand this for seven weeks. If every night is like this, I won't survive.

At last, the sky began to lighten. He went out on the deck, into the cold April morning. Walking to stay warm, he stopped to look down the hatch near the middle of the main deck.

A sailor approached him, "You'll not want to go below, Sir. It'll smell down there already anyway."

"Why would that be?"

"First deck below's where the cheapest cargo's stowed. Gets soaked in every storm. This trip, we've commoners there. We make 'em stay down there, except to use the piss-dales or seat of ease." The sailor looked down the hatch, then back at Jean-Marc. "Truth be told, we can't have 'em movin' about the deck. They get in our way. We make it clear they're to just stay below. They can piss on a wall, or farther down, in the ballast or bilge water. The stench's already started. You'll be happiest away from that hatch, Sir." The sailor bowed and returned to work.

An older man, possibly the captain, shouted to cast off. The ropes to the wharf were untied and pulled on-board. The large kedging anchor was lowered into a dinghy and six men rowed toward the center of the channel. There they lifted the anchor and dropped it into the water.

On the fore-deck, a group of sailors watched as the anchor's rope ran over the ship's side. When the rope stopped running, they knew the anchor was on the bottom. Sailors wound slack rope around the capstan and manned each spar. Walking around the capstan, they drew in the rope and that pulled the ship's bow toward the channel. When the anchor reached the surface, it was lowered into the dinghy again and the process was repeated until the ship was pointed out to sea.

The captain ordered the anchor secured on board, and the dinghy returned to the ship. The receding tide pulled the ship to sea. Several small sails were opened. They caught the wind and *Le Griffon* entered the choppy sea.

Jean-Marc was exhilarated. For the first time, he was leaving France. He was off to Acadia, to make his fortune trading furs. He thought about coming back to France in a few years and smiled. *Then, I will be wealthy and treated with respect. And then, I'll settle accounts.* He leaned over the rail, watching the waves slip under the ship.

He tried to remember what the officer called the thing he would use to relieve himself. "Excuse me," he called to one of the men. "Where does one relieve himself in the morning?"

The man smiled. "Oh, you need a pissdale. I'll take you to one, Sir. They're all around the ship." He led Jean-Marc to a funnel mounted to the ship's side-rail. A tube ran from the funnel, several feet down the side. "You piss in there, Sir. And remember, when you need it, the seat of ease is in the beaks-head."

Jean-Marc found urinating into a small funnel on a pitching ship more difficult than it seemed. He got as much on his hands, clothing and the deck as he did into the pissdale. To his irritation, there were no linens to clean himself. He wiped his hands on his wet breeches, swore, and continued to walk about the ship.

A short time later, a young boy approached. "Monsieur Bompeau, Captain Lafarge told me to bring you to his cabin for breakfast."

The boy led him to a small dining room in the aft-castle. The room appeared recently painted white. Captain Lafarge and a priest were seated at the table, which creaked as it moved to stay level, while the ship pitched front to back and side to side. Lafarge was a large man, whose trimmed beard covered part of his pock-marked face.

This is how the captain dresses, in a gentleman's wig, but merchant's clothing? I expected better.

The clean shaven young priest wore clericals and no wig.

At least he dresses for his station. But who am I to talk? I'm wearing four layers of clothing, and no wig. My hair isn't even combed.

"Welcome, Monsieur Bompeau." Captain Lafarge rose and greeted him with a smile. "This is Father Montcalm, who will join us for our meals. Sit. We can enjoy our breakfast together. The first day's meals are always the best of the voyage. Everything is fresh. We'll worry about sea biscuits and salt cod another day. Now we have mutton, cheese, and fresh bread. We also have hot coffee and fresh cream for it. Have you tasted coffee?"

"I have," Jean-Marc said. "It was served at the masked ball held for His Majesty's last birthday. I am told it comes from Turkey."

The priest's eyebrows shot up. "Have you met the King?"

Jean-Marc laughed. "I have done that, too. My father was the Comte d' Artois. We were often at Court."

"I think it's safe to say neither the good Father nor I have ever met anyone who knew our King," Lafarge said. "We are honored."

Jean-Marc replied, "The honor is mine." He sat. The ample supply of cold mutton, cheese and bread pleased him. He enjoyed the coffee, considering it a kingly drink. He enjoyed the conversation more.

When they were done eating, Jean-Marc said, "My cabin is quite small, and has no lamp."

Lafarge nodded. "We can take no chance of a fire at sea and our limited supply of oil is for cooking. None of our cabins have lamps. And all of them are small. Space used for sleeping is not available for cargo. This is a merchant ship. In fair weather, we spend our time on the deck, except to take our meals or to sleep." Lafarge went on to explain what to expect on the voyage.

He makes the voyage sound like torture. He must be exaggerating. Jean-Marc sipped his coffee and stopped listening.

*****

Jean-Marc passed a boring day, feeling quite alone. The captain was busy overseeing the ship's complex operations: taking in one sail, letting out another, calculating speed, and correcting course. The priest was nowhere to be found. The endless day dragged on.

I see no women. One lonely night was enough. What will I do for seven weeks ... And with no women who will wash my things? He grimaced. *It matters not. I'm wearing my entire wardrobe.*

Near noon, he needed to use the seat of ease. There were two on opposite sides of the narrow beaks head, separated by a short screen. The many thick ropes and the wooden screen gave some privacy. Choosing the one to the left, he unbuttoned the front of each of the pairs of breeches he was wearing and untucked the three shirts. An outhouse bench was bolted above a hole in the meshwork. As the ship rose and fell, water splashed through the meshwork, often coming through the hole in the bench. Given no alternative, Jean-Marc sat and relieved himself into the sea. Spray wet both his exposed buttocks and his clothing. There were no linens to clean himself. He used the water splashing through the mesh. "My clothes may be wet," he muttered, "but at least I didn't piss all over myself again."

*****

The scenery changed little. The waves seemed endless with only some unidentified piece of land in the distance. The sun rose and set. At dusk, the same boy came to summon him for dinner.

Good. I'm hungry. It was a long day. It'll be good to talk to someone.

He was greeted by the Captain and the priest. He smiled, until he looked at the food.

"We had this for breakfast!"

"This is true, Monsieur Bompeau. We eat all the mutton and cheese before we open the salted foods. Soon you will wish for a meal such as this." The Captain took a pot and poured three cups of steaming coffee. "Also, we should enjoy coffee while we are able. The fresh water will soon turn bad. Then it will be impossible to brew good coffee. On these voyages, we must drink beer when we are thirsty. But," he smiled, "now we have coffee and we will always be able to have wine with dinner and some brandy after."

"The mutton was excellent this morning," the priest said. "I look forward to it again."

Lafarge served each man generous helpings of mutton and cheese. Jean-Marc was hungry. The meal and conversation were both good.

*****

The sun was setting when they left the dining cabin. Rather than trip about a dark deck, Jean-Marc retired to his cabin. Before dawn, bad weather set in. The seas grew rough. Soon, he was vomiting over the ship's rail.

Hours crept by. Dense fog ensured a sunless day. He vomited until his stomach was empty. Then he heaved, but nothing came. Hours passed without relief.

The sailors still had to sail the ship. Jean-Marc curled up against the fore-castle's wall, groaned and wished he would die. From time to time, he ran to the side-rail and heaved again. Sailors cursed when they tripped over him in the fog. He crawled into his cabin and lay on the floor.

When the hard floor bothered him more than the nausea he climbed into his hammock and lay there groaning. He passed two days and a night this way. Sometime during the second night, the seas calmed. His stomach settled. He slept.

He woke near noon. Still feeling weak and somewhat queasy, he stumbled onto the deck, into the clear, cold air. The cold felt good. He wasn't hungry although the high sun told him he had missed another breakfast. He wondered if he would ever be hungry again, but he was thirsty.

There's beer ... Ugh ... Just thinking about beer sickens me. Should I risk drinking water? Peasants drink it, but it carries disease ... Have to drink something.

He found a large wooden water barrel mid-ship, tied to a mast. He lifted the lid and drew the ladle from the barrel. In most circumstances, he would be repulsed at the idea of sharing a ladle with commoners. Today, he did not notice. He drank until his thirst was gone. The water tasted strange, perhaps from the barrel, perhaps not. Whatever the taste, he drank the water throughout the day. Then it began to taste bad. For the first time, he noticed it had a green tinge. Insects swam on its surface. He spat and again was wracked with dry heaves.

By late afternoon, he had to relieve himself. He walked slowly to one of the pissdales and began unbuttoning his layers of breeches. This time he managed not to wet himself or his clothing, which was more than he could say about the deck.

As evening approached, he felt he could eat and went to the captain's table for his first meal in several days.

"Good evening, Monsieur Bompeau. Feeling better?"

"I am. Thank you."

"You'll get your sea legs soon enough, although you may have another bout or two of sickness before you're completely over it. You missed little. It was too rough for the cook to light the stove, so we all made do with sea biscuits. You'll get your introduction tonight. I know I'll welcome a hot meal."

The cabin boy brought in a bowl of boiled salt cod, similar to what Jean-Marc ate on Fridays at home. As Father Montcalm entered, Lafarge ladled out bowls of the cod, peas, and onions in a light broth. It was poorly prepared, but after so long without eating, Jean-Marc appreciated it. In the place of bread, the captain introduced his guests to sea biscuits.

"Gentlemen, sea biscuits are a sailor's only dependable food. As long as we keep them dry, they seem to last forever. But you would break a tooth if you bit into one without first soaking it." Lafarge poured three tankards of warm, dark beer, passing them to his guests. "We drink beer on board because it doesn't spoil, the way water does. It also softens the biscuits. Please pick up a biscuit."

Both men complied. Demonstrating as he spoke, Lafarge continued, "Now, tap the biscuit in its side." As he did this, several weevils and a maggot fell from the biscuit. "Turn the biscuit several times, rapping it each time. This will rid it of most weevils. Now dunk it in your beer and wait for it to soften."

He thinks I will eat wormy food?

The priest followed Lafarge's example. Each of the men ate several spoonsful of their cod. Then the captain pulled his biscuit from the beer and ate it. The priest did the same. Jean-Marc made do with his bowl of cod. He wasn't very hungry anyway. Lafarge and Father Montcalm each ate several of the biscuits. Jean-Marc's floated in his beer.

After supper, the captain poured a small glass of brandy for each of them. They enjoyed a pleasant hour's conversation. As the cabin darkened, Lafarge said, "Please excuse me, gentlemen. I have pressing matters to which I must attend."

Jean-Marc and Father Montcalm continued their conversation on the pitching deck.

"What takes you to Acadia," the priest asked.

"I had but little choice. My father was killed at the Battle of Boyne."

"I will pray for his soul."

"Prayers I am certain he needs. Long before his death, he'd arranged good marriages for my sisters. When he died my oldest brother, Francois became the new Comte."

Montcalm nodded. "All as it should be."

"But he made no provision for me."

"Are you saying he left no will?"

Jean-Marc leaned on the rail and looked at the waves. "I'm saying he left me out of it. He bought his second son a position in the army. His third he bought a priesthood. He even bought mercantiles for his bastards, but I was forgotten."

"I'm sure he would have remembered you, if not for his unexpected death," the priest said, also leaning on the rail.

"You think better of my father than I do. No death in war can be unexpected."

"I've learned how often people do harm without intention. Your mother and brothers must have made provisions for you?"

"My dear mother said she could do no more on the allowance Francois gives her, and Francois gave me nothing but fare to Acadia. I'm to earn my fortune or die."

"You have been wronged."

"And you?"

"As in your family, my older brothers inherited the title and estates. But I was called to priesthood long ago. In his will, my father purchased a position in the Church for me."

"And yet, you are here. What's the use of being a priest if you have to go to Acadia anyway?"

Montcalm looked surprised. "I'm going to Acadia because I'm a priest. There aren't enough priests to perform the Sacraments for the Frenchmen there, and there are natives to convert."

Jean-Marc shook his head. "My father endowed a chapel with a large vineyard at St. Lo for my brother, Philip. His peasants produce the wine that supports Philip, his woman, and their bastards."

"There are many such priests in France. I am called to live otherwise."

"Otherwise?"

"My Lord calls me to servanthood."

"Servanthood? Is that why I see you coming out of that stinking hold every day?"

"Jean-Marc, you should see the conditions these men endure—"

"No, I should not. I have seen such as them in the public inns. I paid my fare so I don't have to associate with their type."

"I cannot believe you don't care about their suffering."

"If the voyage is suffering for them, they should have stayed in France."

"These men are all to be indentured servants. Most of them were sold into servitude to repay their debts. They—"

"They could have lived within their means. Or they could have paid their debts. I am going to Acadia to earn my fortune so that I do not become indebted. Unlike you, my friend, no one bought my way into the priesthood." His voice was angry. "Like those in that stinking hold, I have to support myself. Unlike them, I have not sold myself to do so. That they lack discipline and ambition is no problem of mine."

The priest thought, *How do I respond to such ignorance?* He said, "It is already cool and becoming dark. We should retire."

Each man went to his small cabin. In the dark, Jean-Marc thought, *Well, here I am. The accommodations are terrible. The Captain feeds us wormy biscuits and promises the food will get worse. For company, I have a fanatical priest who would have me to worry about peasants. Has it occurred to him that no one worries about either of us? In France, he would have found these conditions unacceptable. Now we live like this. Never did I dream things could be this bad.*

He climbed into his hammock and closed his eyes. Sleep was slow in coming. Over and over, he cursed Francois and his mother.

*****

Weeks passed. The food indeed became worse. Somehow, Jean-Marc managed to eat the infested sea biscuits. There was inferior wine with dinner every night, but at no other time. Otherwise, he drank the warm beer that was always available.

This beer disgusts me. If people didn't die from it, I'd be tempted to drink the water. What I would not give for wine such as we had at home.

Even if he decided to drink water, the so-called fresh water was now a deep green and filled with insects. Jean-Marc leaned against the ship's rail when Father Montcalm, whom he now called Andre, joined him.

"My friend, I don't know how they do it." The priest shook his head when he leaned on the rail next to Jean-Marc.

"Do what?"

"You need to see it below."

"Why would I need that?"

"Thirty-nine people eat, sleep and do everything else in that small space." Andre looked at the waves running beneath the ship, then out toward the horizon. "The smell in there is sickening."

"I know. I smell it every time I walk past the hatch."

"You can't know. You've never gone down there. I go there every d—"

"Anyone who stands near you knows that. Do you think the stench doesn't come back with you?"

"You wouldn't believe it—"

Jean-Marc straightened and exhaled, "Trust me. I believe you."

"And you would not believe the lice and fleas—"

"You were raised a gentleman! Why do you go near them?" Jean-Marc was angry. "No amount of perfume will cover their stench. That they are infested should surprise no one. Why do you—"

"Because I must!" Now Andre was angry too. "It seems you cannot understand."

"So, it seems."

Without a mirror, Jean-Marc had no idea how much his appearance had deteriorated. Like everyone else, his beard and hair were now long and shaggy. He'd now worn the same clothing every day for five weeks. In France he had a few lice, but now he was infested. His constant scratching left him with rashes and open sores. He would be appalled if anyone told him, but he looked little different from the captain and crew, just a step above Andre. No human should look like those in the hold.

Every day he saw one or two dead rats on the deck. He kicked them overboard and thought, *So much the better, one less rat.*

*****

Jean-Marc was standing near Lafarge when Andre and the officer he spoke with his first night on board approached. Both were upset.

The officer spoke first. "Sir, there's ship-fever among those below. The Father's been caring for them without telling anyone, but now three've died."

"Ship-fever, are you certain, Georges?" The concern in Lafarge's voice was obvious.

"Aye, sir. Their piss is black. It's ship-fever. We're all at risk now."

"Five weeks out." Lafarge was almost talking to himself. "If we turn about now, even with the current, we're still three weeks from land. There's no choice but to continue for Acadia. We should make landfall in two weeks." He sounded decisive. "Throw the bodies over the side and see to it that the people below stay there. We can provide them enough sea biscuits and beer to feed those that survive until—"

Andre interrupted. "Captain, their bodies can't be thrown overboard! Without a Christian burial, in consecrated ground, their souls could never rest. I'll not permit it." The priest's voice grew threatening. "To commit such an act would be a mortal sin."

Lafarge was shaken. "All right, Father." He paused. "Georges, have the bodies stored with the ballast if there's room ... or put them in bilge if necessary."

"You know that's where they piss," Georges replied.

"I know that, but we can't leave them rotting among the others." After another moment's thought, the Captain turned to the priest and added, "More are bound to take sick. Father, I'll leave their care to you." Turning to Georges, he said, "We have to keep them away from the crew. After the good Father goes down there ..." He turned again to the priest. "I assume you are going below. Am I right?" The priest hesitated then nodded. Lafarge looked at Georges again. "After he goes below, board the hatch shut. See that no one gets out!"

Georges hurried off, calling several men to move the bodies.

"You're going to board us in?" Andre sounded incredulous. "They'll all die! Why not just kill them now?"

Lafarge shook his head. "Father, I doubt anyone can save the poor bastards below. No one would blame you for not going down there. They're beyond help."

"But—" Andre protested.

Lafarge raised his hand to the priest's face cutting him off. "Father, if the fever gets into my crew, everyone will die. No one you save below will live if my crew can't man the ship." He looked down and shook his head. "My duty is to try to save any that I can. God help us."

Andre tried to argue, but Lafarge just raised his hand again and walked away. The priest took a step to follow, then stopped. He turned toward the hatch. Then he noticed Jean-Marc standing nearby, listening in shock. He called out, "Jean-Marc, you're the only other man on board without regular duties. I need your help caring for the sick."

Jean-Marc stepped back. "No, you don't! I'll not set foot into that pestilent hellhole."

"I can't care for them all alone. There're already five more with fever."

"Then don't care for them. They'll die ... or they won't. You can die with them if you want, but I'll not."

Jean-Marc turned and walked away. The captain, still near enough to hear the exchange, turned and said, "There you are, Father. The sick are yours. As they die, it would be good if you could arrange to have their bodies hauled to the ballast. My men will board up the hatch as soon as you go in. We have to try to keep the fever below. If it starts taking the crew, we'll all be lost at—"

The captain was interrupted by shouting from the hatch. The three men ran to the tumult. Georges stood at the opening with six armed sailors. They were forcing commoners back below deck. Several wounded men lay at their feet. One had been stabbed with a half pike. Several were slashed by cutlasses. One man's arm was almost severed. Bone protruded from the wound. The right side of another's face was cleaved away from his skull. Men looked up from below, cowed by the seamen's weapons.

One shouted. "We'll all die down here!"

A seaman shouted back, "God'll decide that, not me."

"God'll damn you," a man in the hold shouted. "You're killing us."

"He may damn me, but I'll sure kill you if you set foot on this deck!"

Lafarge stepped to the front. He turned to Georges. "Seal this hatch! Kill any of them who come within five feet of it. Father, if you are going below, go now!"

Jean-Marc watched as Andre stooped to help the injured men. "These men are dying! I need help!" No one moved. The others below were afraid of the sailors. The armed sailors made no attempt to help the wounded. Two seamen began to lower barrels, one with sea biscuits and three with beer onto the deck below. The frightened men crowded as near the hatchway as they dared.

Andre looked up from the dying and cried out, "Georges, they'll need more to eat and drink than that."

"No, they won't, Father." Georges shook his head. "There won't be enough of them to finish this."

"For the love of God, have you no mercy?"

"Love and mercy are God's, not mine. Maybe when we open the hold you'll all walk out, even the dead restored. My guess is, in His mercy, God'll make their passing quick. Either way mercy's not mine to grant." Georges turned to his men. "Board 'er up boys. Make it strong so that the boards can't be kicked loose."

Father Montcalm just lowered his head and returned to the wounded.

Jean-Marc remembered being told about the great deaths that had swept across France, time and again. No one knew what caused plagues. Most agreed they were punishments God visited on sinful people. He remembered his father telling him that during the great deaths, plagued families were boarded up in their houses. City gates were locked, some from inside to keep the plague out and some from outside to keep the plague in.

God's judgment is God's judgment. Everyone knows the only hope for the well is to keep away from the sick. How could Andre, a priest, object to sealing them below?

He also remembered his father said that none of it seemed to matter. Plagues did what plagues do, until God's anger was quenched. Only then would He lift His hand and allow people to rebuild.

Andre's stupid to interfere. Who benefits from his death? Who benefits from anyone's death? What could these men have done to bring God's judgement on us all?

Father Montcalm might pity the infected, but Jean-Marc did not. At supper that night, he asked the captain what would happen.

"It would have been better to throw the bodies over the side. Truth be told, it would have been better to throw the sick over with them but Montcalm would have had nothing to do with that either. And I'm no man to confront a priest. I've seen what comes of that." Lafarge sounded resigned. "We're all in peril now. If fever gets into the crew, we may not be able to man the ship." Lafarge paused. "That's where ghost ships come from. Fever takes so many of the crew that the ship can't be managed. She just drifts until everyone on 'er dies. Then she'll drift until she runs aground."

Lafarge chuckled. "More than once locals scavenging a ghost ship have brought the plague on themselves. If you're a praying man, I suggest you pray. That's more hope in prayer than I can give you." He paused and looked at Jean-Marc. "I never thought you really wanted to go to Acadia." He smiled. "Your problem may be solved."

Jean-Marc was struck dumb. He got up from the table and went to his cabin and passed another sleepless night.

At dawn, he heard a commotion. Men stood over a feverish crewman. Georges said, "We can't do anything for him anyway. If we don't throw him over, we'll all die."

A heated argument followed. Lafarge came from his cabin and ended it, "Georges' is right. His piss's black. He's a dead man. The only question is how many of us die with him. There's a bottle of brandy in my cabin. Give him a good-sized draught and throw him over." Lafarge looked at his men. "Others who get the fever will have to be thrown over, too. God have mercy on us all."

He took a few steps toward the quarter-deck then turned around. "We'll be short-handed now. We can't spare an able-bodied man to cook. It'll be sea biscuits until we reach shore." He pointed at one of the sailors. "Claude, take our passenger, Monsieur Bompeau, and teach him as much as you can about the running of the ship. If we're going to get off it alive, we're going to need the labor of every man we've got."

Jean-Marc protested, "Captain, I'm no commoner. My father was Jean Louis Bompeau, Comte d' Artois. I'll not work like a common seaman. I paid handsomely for this passage, not so that I could do a commoner's—"

Lafarge cut him off. "You are right, Monsieur Bompeau. You booked passage to Acadia aboard my ship. And if you hope to get there, learn your seamanship well. Ships don't carry extra men and like as not we'll have fewer tomorrow than today. On every voyage, a crew has some men without experience. They learn enough to help in a day or two. Put your mind to doing that or we all might die." Jean-Marc tried to interrupt, but Lafarge raised his hand and went on. "Besides, under these circumstances, if you refuse my order, I'll have you thrown over-board. We have no time for pampered gentry and no hands to spare. Learn well, my friend. All of our lives depend on it."

He attempted to argue, but the captain interrupted him again. "Georges, see to it that Claude teaches Monsieur Bompeau well ... and, Georges, if he proves to be a reluctant student, you have no need to speak with me about this. Throw him overboard. There will be trouble enough on this passage without useless distractions." Lafarge turned back to Jean-Marc, "Monsieur Bompeau, I trust I have made myself clear. The choice is yours. Learn how to sail a ship or learn how to swim. I don't care which you choose but choose you will. I will not be bothered with this again."

The captain turned and began giving orders for the running of the ship. A seaman returned from the captain's cabin with the bottle of brandy. He poured a good-sized draught into a mug and pressed it to the sick man's lips. The man made no attempt to drink. The other sailor stood and said, "No use wasting good brandy." He downed the amber fluid in one swallow.

Two sailors lifted the sick man to the rail and dropped him into the sea. He made no attempt to struggle as he slipped beneath the surface.

Good! That's no loss. Perhaps he'll take the fever with him, Jean-Marc thought.

Crewmen stared at the empty sea. Then, a few at a time, they moved from the side-rail to return to their work.

Claude approached Jean-Marc. No peasant was ever comfortable approaching a gentleman, but it was harder for Claude. He looked much the younger of the two. His forced smile showed that, unlike the rest of the crew, he still had most of his teeth. Baby fine hair covered the sides of his face. He led Jean-Marc to the ship's rigging and taught him how to tie several knots. Each had a specific use. He tried to show him how to take in and let out sail but Jean-Marc could not climb the rope ladders to the masts. Claude said, "Practice climbing, Sir. If you're ordered to climb a mast, it will mean there is no one else to do it, and so you must. I'll come back later to see how you're doing. Then I'll show you how to adjust the sails."

Jean-Marc looked down and saw another dead rat. He kicked it overboard and swore.

He began trying to climb the ropes. Afraid of falling overboard, he stayed on the ropes toward the middle of the ship. As the day wore on, he could manage them. Late in the afternoon Claude returned. "Please come with me, Sir. I'm going to show you how to adjust the ropes at the bottom of the sails when they're brought in or let out." Tying the large ropes into knots while the sail was filled with wind was difficult, but after several tries even Jean-Marc could tie them.

"Each sail weighs hundreds of pounds," Claude said. "It takes many men to pull it up. Only two men are needed on deck to adjust the knots. You can do this now. That's a start. If more die, you may need to climb to the top and help bring in the sails. For today, being able to tie off the sails from below's enough."

As darkness neared, Jean-Marc found himself eating sea biscuits and drinking beer with the men of the ship.

I've never associated with such people in this way. They're crude, but I smell no better.

There was a dark humor in their joking that night. All were sure more of them would die before reaching Acadia.

Jean-Marc retired to his cabin. Exhausted, he slept until Claude pounded on his door at dawn. "Are you awake, Sir? You have to get up and get your sea biscuits. Today we have to work the top masts together."

Jean-Marc climbed out of his hammock and opened his door. Sore from climbing the ropes the day before, he began to protest, but Claude interrupted him. "No, Sir! Please stop it! There's no time. It looks like Georges and another man have the fever. Cold as it is, they're soaked with sweat. Both say they're fine. They're not. We need every man to do his share."

He thought about arguing. Then he thought about being thrown overboard and held his tongue. He joined the others as they climbed and re-climbed masts, bringing up sail and letting sail out. By mid-day he was exhausted. "The sails can't really need to be changed this much. Are we doing all this just to teach me?"

"This is the life of a sailor, Sir," Claude said. "The life is hard, but the pay is good. On this passage alone, I'll earn more than double what I would in a year at home, if I live to be paid." He smiled. "If I survive several voyages, I'll not have to live in the poverty I knew as a boy."

Throughout the day, Claude taught him the endless tasks of a mariner. At sunset they came down from the masts. There was a great commotion. Georges and two others lay on the deck, semi-conscious, soaked with sweat. Their pants were black at their groins.

One man shouted, "Georges himself insisted on it yesterday. They can't be saved, but we can be lost."

The debate continued a short time longer, until the captain approached, bottle in hand. "Here's the brandy. Give them each a good portion and throw them over. They're dead men. We are not."

The bottle was held to the men's lips but none of them drank. Several men lifted the sick sailors and dropped them overboard. The sick did not seem to notice.

That night there was no dark humor. The men ate their sea biscuits and drank their beer. They didn't sit together. Each man wanted to separate himself, as much as possible, from the others. Tempers were short. Several fights broke out. At dark, Jean-Marc retired to his cabin alone. The crew had no such luxury. Except for Jean-Marc and Captain Lafarge, the men had hammocks in one common room. Some men wrapped themselves in blankets and tried to sleep on the pitching deck.

There were twenty-eight in the crew. Four are dead in two days. That leaves twenty-four to man the ship. Counting me, there's twenty-five. The cook and captain can work. Twenty-seven can man the ship. But we lost four men in two days. They say it's still twelve days to Acadia? How many men does it take to sail this ship? Am I on a ghost ship?

Tired as he was, he did not sleep. He tossed and turned, now blaming his father and then his brother, cursing them both.

A noble's son has no business on such a ship in the first place. My father should have provided for me, so it would not come to this. And surely, Francois should have corrected our father's error.

Men were being thrown overboard when Jean-Marc came out of his cabin the next morning. There were no arguments, no brandy. Four more men were dropped into the ocean without ceremony.

Frightened men do shameful things.

When the journey began, no crewman would have felt himself capable of throwing a living shipmate overboard. One could only hope that time brings forgetfulness to those who live. The crew was now twenty-one.

The day was hot. Men neared exhaustion trying to sail the short-handed ship. Sweaty sailors looked at each other, wondering who would be next. And, as night follows day, by day's end, another man was lying on the deck, his pants black from piss. There were no arguments. The fevered man said nothing. His friends took his hands and feet and threw him over.

The crew was now at twenty. With good winds, they hoped to reach Acadia in eleven days. No one said it. No one actually expected to get there. They were dead men walking.

The next morning, Lafarge did not come out of his cabin. The cabin boy was sent to fetch him but found him already dead. His body was thrown over.

With Lafarge and Georges gone, they had no experienced navigator. Several men claimed they could navigate. No one believed them. Senior sailors claimed command. Others disputed their claims. Violent fights broke out.

Yves, the oldest and most experienced crewman tried to bring order. "So, things aren't bad enough yet?" he shouted. "Have we all gone crazy? If we—"

"Shut up, old man," Charles, a muscular, younger man interrupted, pushing Yves to the deck. "We're all dead anyw—"

Yves scrambled to his feet and charged the younger man, slamming his shoulder into Charles' middle, driving him to the deck. His head snapped backward, slamming into the ship's side, opening a large gash. Yves jumped on the bleeding man, grabbing at his throat.

Jean-Marc joined the semi-circle of men who formed around the fight, swearing and goading them on.

Struggling to breathe, Charles clawed at the other's eyes. Grasping at anything, he grabbed an ear and tore at it, ripping it away from Yves' head. Yves screamed. He released Charles' throat and grabbed the side of his head. Charles grabbed him by the hair, yanking a fistful out by the roots, pulling them face to face. Lifting himself upward, he bit the older man's nose off, spitting it out as he pushed him away. Blood spewed from Yves face. Charles struggled to get to his feet. Reaching out for anything he could use to pull himself up, his hand fell on a spar. Managing to get to his knees, he raised the spar above his head and dove toward Yves, slamming it into Yves' head again and again. He dropped the spar and grabbed Yves by the hair. Struggling to his feet, he dragged the injured man to the side rail. Grabbing Yves' shirt at the throat, he put a hand between his legs and lifted him to his feet. With a loud shout, he pulled Yves up and pushed him backward, over the side, before dropping to his knees in the blood that covered the deck.

The shouting men fell silent. They looked in shock as they watched Yves struggle. His bleeding body slipped beneath the surface as the ship sailed away. One man handed Charles a rag to cover his bleeding head. The crowd dispersed. Men argued about the fight.

That night two more feverish men were thrown over.

At least ten days from shore, without a leader, all seemed lost. At best, the remaining crew could keep the ship headed to the setting sun. Dead rats were everywhere. No one bothered to kick them over the side anymore.

The next morning was more promising. No more crewmen seemed sick. Spirits rose. One of the men went into the captain's cabin and brought out several bottles of brandy.

"I'll have mine while I can still drink it," he said, pulling the cork from the bottle and drinking. Others pulled the bottles from his hands and passed them around. Within the hour, all the brandy on the ship was gone and they broke into a cask of the captain's wine. One of the men tied the tiller in place, to keep the ship headed west.

They drank throughout the day, opening cask after cask of wine and helping themselves to the ship's supply of rum. One by one, the men passed out drunk on the deck.

*****

When they began to wake, men covered with vomit lay everywhere. The ship smelled worse than ever. One of the bleary-eyed men noticed the tiller had slipped its knot. No one knew how long the ship was adrift. There was now no pretense that the remaining men knew where they were or when they would find land.

Worse, two men on the deck weren't waking up. Their pants were blackened at their groins. Without discussion, members of the hung-over crew dragged the sick men to the side-rail and managed to drop them into the sea. Another man fell over in the process. He thrashed in the water, but by the time the still half-drunk crew was able to respond to the cries of "Man overboard!" he was gone.

Even with a captain and first mate, no crew of thirteen could manage *Le Griffon.* The exhausted crew was unable to bring in or let out the heavy sails. When the wind turned, the crew tried to tack into it, without success. The ship drifted. From time to time, another man was found with ship-fever and thrown over. There had been no sounds from below deck for days.

Time passed unnoted.

Five men were left alive: Pierre, Louis, Charles, Philippe and Jean-Marc. They stopped trying to sail the ship. Cooperation was a thing of the past. Small misunderstandings became reasons for bloody fights. The most recent death had occurred when Philippe beat a man to death in a fight over a sea biscuit, although there were whole, unopened casks of them. The exhausted men laid about the deck, waiting to die.

One evening, just at dusk, Charles shouted, "Land ho!"

The men ran to the rail. Louis ran to find the glass which was somewhere on the ship. Several minutes later he returned, placed the glass to his eye and peered. "He is right. I see land; no buildings or people, just trees above a rocky shore. I think the current's pulling us past. We're not getting any closer."

The men passed the glass around, each agreeing with Louis. Pierre said, "We can't just sit here and hope we run aground. The current might pull us back out to sea."

"We've got to fill a dinghy with supplies and row to shore." Jean-Marc shouted.

"It takes eight men to launch a dinghy. Only an idiot would try with five men," Charles said.

In the end, they decided using the dinghy was their last hope. Each man went his own way, gathering whatever valuables he could scavenge from the ship's supplies or the Captain's cabin, a musket, powder and shot, a cutlass, some food.

Charles and Philippe fell into quarrelling over a pistol. The argument was ended when Charles grabbed the pistol and beat Philippe over the head with its handle until Philippe's body stopped twitching.

No one dared open the hold to see if there was anything of value below. The dead priest and peasants were silent guardians over anything there, and none of the remaining men were willing to tempt them or the fever.

Jean-Marc found something of a pack which he filled with bags of powder and shot. He had some gold that he found hidden among the captain's things, and none of the others tried to take his fat purse, which he always kept tied around his neck. He grabbed a blanket, some sea biscuits, a cutlass and musket, then made for the boat.

The others were gathering, each stowing his treasures. Under normal circumstances, two men would climb into the boat while six pushed it over the side and lowered it to the sea. The two men would use oars to hold the boat against the side of the ship while the others climbed down a rope ladder.

With only four men, no one could be lowered with the boat. They would have to lower the boat and hope the hooks held fast while they climbed down the ladder. Pierre pushed the long boat over the side. Charles, Louis, and Jean-Marc tried to hold the lines. The dinghy dropped. Rope ripped through their hands, tearing skin as the boat crashed into the sea.

It landed upright!

The ropes' hooks slipped and the boat began floating away. There was no time to climb down the ladder. Beginning with Pierre, man after man jumped over the side hoping to grab the boat.

These were acts of pure desperation. None of the men could swim. Jean-Marc thrashed until his hand brushed a rope hanging over the boat's side. He grabbed it and pulled himself to the boat. Charles somehow found himself in contact with the boat, grabbed the side and held on.

Louis fought to stay above water just beyond their reach. He slipped below the surface, emerged once and slipped below again. They called his name and reached for him. He was gone.

Neither man saw what happened to Pierre.

The men tried to climb into the boat, but its sides were too steep. Shivering in the cold water, they clung to the dinghy for hours. Fighting to stay awake, each lost hold and began to sink several times. Each time the other pulled him back.

Charles heard it first. "Waves! I hear waves."

Jean-Marc roused himself from the cold-induced stupor and listened. "I hear them too! They're on the other side."

Hand by hand, they moved around the boat. Listening, they both heard surf pounding on the shore. "There it is. I see it, maybe a couple of hundred yards away!" Charles shouted.

Jean-Marc squinted his eyes and nodded. "You're right, but, neither of us can swim. It might as well be a hundred miles."

They peered into the night. Were they drawing nearer, or were they just hoping?

Charles, the taller of the two, cried out, "My foot hit something! There, again. I'm touching bottom."

Minutes later Jean-Marc's foot brushed bottom.

Charles released the dinghy and pulled on its rope. "Help me. We can pull it in from here."

When Jean-Marc found firm footing he moved next to Charles and pulled the boat through the surf to dry land. There was no sand on this rocky coast but both men threw themselves on land for the first time in over two months and slept.

Chapter Three
A New World

**"We are much beholden to Machiavelli, who wrote what
men do and not what they ought to do."**
Francis Bacon

Charles buried his foot into Jean-Marc's ribs. "Bompeau, roll
over!"

The searing pain jolted Jean-Marc awake. Curling his body to
protect his ribs, he looked up. Charles kicked him in the face. His
head snapped backward. Blood spewed from his nose.

Scrambling to his feet, Jean-Marc dove forward, driving his
shoulder into Charles' knee, wrapping both arms around the leg
before he could kick again. Jean-Marc slammed his fist upward into
Charles' groin, then grabbed and twisted. Charles doubled over and
bellowed in pain. Clawing downward to gouge at Jean-Marc's eyes,
Charles caught two fingers inside his left cheek and pulled upward,
tearing open the side of Jean-Marc's mouth. Jean-Marc turned his
face and bit into the fingers, his mouth filling with a mixture of their
blood. Charles dropped from his feet to his knees, slamming his free
forearm and the full weight of his body into the back of the smaller
man's neck. Jean-Marc released his bite and fell forward onto his
face, spitting out blood. Charles climbed to his feet, holding his
mangled right hand in his left. He kicked Jean-Marc in the face again
and again, until he was sure Jean-Marc was unconscious.

Charles fell to his knees and sobbed, holding his throbbing
fingers. Jagged pieces of bone protruded from the torn flesh of his
fingers. Jean-Marc began to groan as he came to. Charles struggled
to his feet and kicked him in his face. Jean-Marc lost consciousness.

Charles looked around for something to wrap around his injured
hand. He found a shirt in the boat and wrapped his painful hand. He
picked up the pack Jean-Marc brought from the ship. Using his good
hand, he filled it with supplies he thought he would need. Then he
threw everything he did not intend to take as far into the forest or the

ocean as he could. He limped over to Jean-Marc and kicked him in the ribs, rolling his body over.

"I'll take that gold you worthless lout." Charles reached down with his left hand and yanked the purse from Jean-Marc's neck. "I put up with you on the ship, but I don't have to now."

As if to emphasize the point, Charles again kicked him in the ribs. He threaded his injured hand through the pack's strap, pulled the pack on, picked up a musket with his left hand and walked into the forest.

Jean-Marc lay unconscious for many minutes. When he came to, he was covered with dried blood. His face throbbed. He could just see through his swollen eyes. Breathing hurt.

"What now?" he moaned. *How did I come to this? Was supposed to earn my fortune. Now I'm stranded in a wilderness ... without money. Where do I go? How do I get there?"*

Still bleeding, his ribs throbbing, he curled up and passed out.

When he regained consciousness, thirst forced him to move. Struggling to his feet, he saw Charles had left nothing but the boat, which was far too big for him to handle alone.

So ... I have nothing.

Without hope, but driven by his thirst, he held his painful ribs and stumbled into the forest.

Somewhere, there must be something to drink.

After only a few moments, he noticed a cutlass in the brush.

So, what he didn't take he threw into the forest. Now, at least, I'm armed.

Looking for anything else Charles left, he found two sea biscuits. He sat and sucked on them but his mouth produced no saliva. Struggling to his feet, he limped to the water's edge. Dropping to all four, he held the biscuits in the cold water until they softened enough to chew with his loose teeth and swallow. The salt water in the biscuits felt good in his dry mouth. He used the water to scrub off the worst of the coagulated blood that covered him.

Resuming his search, he found a musket and then a bag of powder and another of shot.

With this, I can defend myself. I can hunt.

He continued to search but found nothing he could use for shelter. Neither did he find money, clothing, additional food, or water.

Without thinking, he walked south, fumbling to carry the musket, cutlass, powder, and shot.

I have nothing, and I can't even carry that.

He stopped and threaded the cutlass through his belt. He filled one pocket with powder and the other with shot. Removing one of his shirts, he fashioned a crude wrap to hold the rest of his powder and shot. Using the sleeves, he slung the shirt over his neck.

I should load the musket.

He poured powder down the barrel, then realized he had nothing to use for wadding. After a moment's thought, he took off the sling and tore some cloth from the shirt to use as wadding. He stuffed a piece of the cloth down the barrel and the rest in his pocket with the shot. Using the musket's ramrod, he tamped the cloth onto the powder. Then he dropped in a ball, another piece of cloth and tamped it again.

There, that's done.

Replacing the sling, he took the musket in his right hand and went south along the forest's edge, looking for water.

An hour later, he came to a small stream. He leaned the musket against a tree and took the shirt from around his neck, so that his powder would stay dry. Then he lay on his stomach and drank. Sitting back, he thought, *It took too long to find this. I need to find a way that I can carry water.* He searched for several minutes, but he saw nothing he could use. *If I leave the stream, I'll be without water until I find another ... But, without food or shelter, I'll die if I stay here.*

He lay back down and drank as much as he could. Then he put the sling back over his neck, picked up the musket and continued southward, looking for game as he went. Finally, he saw a squirrel. He aimed and fired. The squirrel scampered away, unhurt. The shot hit ground far to the right. *How did I miss so easy a shot?*

He re-loaded. A short time later, he saw a rabbit. Taking aim, he tried to adjust after missing to the right with his last shot. He fired. Again, he missed. This shot struck a tree well above the rabbit.

He shoved his finger into the barrel. "*Sacrament*! Smooth bore!" he shouted. Unlike his rifled hunting piece, still in the hold of *Le Griffon*, there were no grooves cut into the barrel of this gun. Without grooves in the barrel to spin the shot, aiming this smooth-bored piece was haphazard at best. A shot could pull wide to the right of the target, and then the next shot pull just as far to the left.

This may do well for firing at lines of infantry, but for hunting? This is useless. Jean-Marc reloaded. *I'll never hit anything small with this, but I'll be ready if I'm attacked by something big. It's anyone's guess what manner of animals roam this wilderness.*

Still looking for food, he walked past bushes covered with small red berries. *Can I eat them? Have I a choice?* He picked and ate a few handfuls. They were tasty enough but did nothing to curb his hunger. With the sun lowering in the sky, he came to another small stream.

It'll soon be dark. I'll stay here tonight.

Exhausted, he sat against a tree.

Getting cold. I need a fire ... But how to start one? Servants always saw to this. Fire was always just there. Why didn't I ever watch to see what they did? The temperature dropped rapidly after sundown. *Cold. No blankets or extra clothing. Have to do something!*

He covered himself with some leaf debris from the forest floor. Shivering and staring into the dark, he listened in fear to the sounds of the forest at night. And cursed himself for not knowing how to start a fire.

Numb with cold, Jean-Marc watched as dawn broke, revealing a heavy frost on the ground around him. Ice formed on the edges of the stream.

In this cold, I won't last long without fire.

Forcing his stiff legs to move, he struggled to his feet, stamping them to warm himself. He was thirsty, but in the cold he could not bring himself to drink from the frigid stream. He was hungry, but there was nothing to eat except more berries. He walked south.

He pulled his cutlass from his belt and walked, musket in his left hand, cutlass in his right. *Perhaps I'll get close enough to an animal to kill it with the sword.*

The wilderness seemed unchanging. Trees followed trees. There was a stream every few miles. The animals he saw ran away long before he got close.

Jean-Marc stopped walking early in the day on the bank of another small stream. He said, "If I can't build a fire, at least I can make a shelter." Then he shook his head. "This is not good. Already, I'm talking to myself."

He used the cutlass to cut small branches from the surrounding trees. With these, he managed to build a small frame on the ground, barely big enough for him to climb into. Over the frame, he piled as much moss and leaves as he could gather. At sunset, he drank and climbed into his improvised shelter. It was dark. He was hungry. The night noises frightened him. But he slept.

Again, there was a heavy frost in the morning, but he was not as cold as the day before. He stayed in his shelter until sunlight filled the clearing in the woods, then he climbed out and stood in the warm light.

He drank some water and ate some berries. Then he walked, slower now, to the south. About noon, he saw a massive animal grazing in a stream. It raised its head and looked at Jean-Marc. The monster stood six to seven feet at the shoulder. Its head supported a huge rack of broad, flat antlers. Jean-Marc froze. The animal grunted and went back to its grazing.

Even with this smooth bore, I won't miss a target that big.

Lying down his cutlass, he raised the musket. With as little noise as possible he lowered to one knee and took careful aim at the animal's chest. He fired, striking the animal on its right foreleg. The shot left a long crease on the animal's leg and shoulder. Rather than turning to escape, as one might expect a wounded animal to do, it bellowed and charged Jean-Marc. Dropping the musket, he got up to run. The behemoth was almost on him. Jean-Marc threw himself to the ground to avoid the animal's antlers. It charged past, just missing him but stomping on his left leg as it ran by. The animal turned to make another charge. Scrambling to escape, Jean-Marc's hand landed on the cutlass. He grabbed it and flailed at the charging animal. The cutlass opened broad cuts on the beast's snout and chest. Blood flowed from both wounds. The animal turned to charge again.

So, this is to be a fight to the death.

Years of sword training took over. He faced the mighty beast, twirling the cutlass in his right hand. It charged. Jean-Marc stepped to the side, slashing at its face as it passed. A cut opened across its left eye.

It has to be blinded.

The enraged animal turned to attack. Jean-Marc moved to his right, trying to stay on its blind side. He side-stepped the charge and slammed the cutlass up, under the beast's chin, slashing into its throat. It bellowed and turned to charge but fell. The dying animal struggled to its feet, only to fall again.

Jean-Marc stood back while the animal thrashed in pain. When it stopped, he walked forward and put the animal out of its misery, with another blow to its throat.

Now, I have more than I need. This would feed a family for weeks. But how do I gut or skin it? I have no knife ... I'll have to hack at it with the cutlass.

First, he hacked out the gut and dragged the intestines and other organs away from the carcass. Next, he hacked through the skin into the animal's muscles, cleaving out huge chunks of meat. Then he had a sudden realization.

Mon Dieu, I have no fire. I'll have to eat this raw.

The idea sickened him but ravenous from days without food, he bit into the animal's warm flesh, and tore off a mouthful. Blood ran from his mouth. Gagging, he chewed, and managed to swallow. He dropped the meat and fought to avoid vomiting. Then he picked up the meat and tore out another mouthful. With each mouthful, it became less sickening. He ate his fill, then lay back and fell asleep.

He awoke with a sudden realization. *I have meat enough for a week ... but I cannot carry it. I have to stay here. I need shelter.*

Moving a short distance from the carcass, Jean-Marc used the cutlass to chop small branches from trees. He leaned them against a rock to form a shelter tall enough to sit in. He covered the branches with leaves and moss, then put more branches over the leaves so they wouldn't blow away.

This, I think, is good.

As the sun fell, he ate as much of the raw meat as he could, then he climbed into the shelter and covered himself with leaves.

The forest sounded different. *A howling dog?* He heard growling. *A dog fight?* Jean-Marc looked out from his shelter. In the pale light of a quarter-moon he saw a pack of wolves feeding on the dead animal's carcass.

In terror, he climbed out of his shelter and ran as fast as he could away from the clearing. Running in the dark, he fell, got up, ran, and fell again. When he could run no more, he dropped to the ground, bruised and bleeding. He shivered in the cold but he could not hear the wolves.

In the morning, he limped back to the stream to see if the wolves had left him anything. Bones and torn flesh were strewn about the clearing. Over half of the meat that he expected to eat for weeks was gone.

The wolves'll be back for the rest tonight. I can't stay here.

He cut a large piece of meat, wrapped it with leaves and stuffed it into his makeshift pack. Then he gathered the rest of his things and walked south, not even knowing why.

I'm alone in a wilderness ... Where am I going? Will I find anything?

He walked, because he walked. What else was there to do?

Then something felt different. He had a strange sensation. It was as if he almost heard something behind him. He spun to see if wolves were following him. Nothing. He started walking. The feeling returned. *Something's behind me.* He turned but saw nothing.

He could not rid himself of the feeling he was being followed. Several times he went back to see what or who was following him, but there was never anything there.

Charles would not bother coming after me. Or would he? The thought of another fight made him feel more vulnerable. He walked faster. *In an empty forest, who would follow me?*

After several hours, he heard a voice say, in French, "Answer Papisse Conewa or your scalp hangs in my lodge this night.*"

Jean-Marc cried out, "Don't hurt me. I mean you no harm. I'm alone. Please help me. Don't hurt me."

A man stepped from behind a tree. *Is this one of the savages?* His skin was dark. The sides of his head were shaved. The bright red hair in the center of his head stood on end. A long black braid hung down the back of his neck. He wore animal skins that appeared cut to fit him.

"What my French brother do here alone? Papisse Conewa think you English. I thought to kill English dog."

Jean-Marc looked at the arrow notched on something similar to an English long-bow and at what appeared to be a stone hatchet hanging from the native's bright, red, and white belt. "No, no, I'm French. I was stranded on a beach days ago. I need help to get to Acadia."

Somehow Jean-Marc had stumbled onto the path of a native allied with France in its North American wars against England. He should have felt relieved. He was terrified.

"Papisse Conewa help. Come to village. We clean and feed you before our raid on English. After raid, take you Acadia. Come."

Jean-Marc had a thousand questions, starting with, "How do you know French?" Most of the questions were answered with, "Come". The others were ignored.

Still in pain from his fight with Charles, he struggled to keep up with the slender native. He followed the man for several hours before they entered a small encampment. Papisse Conewa led Jean-Marc to an older man and said something in the native language. To Jean-Marc it sounded like a series of incomprehensible grunts.

Then Papisse Conewa turned to Jean-Marc and said, "This my father. He Conewa, Great Bear. He Great Chief of Abenaki people. Me Papisse Conewa, Child of Great Bear. Conewa say we go on warpath against English who steal our land and kill our children. French soldiers promise us many gifts, many guns from our great French Father Louis after we kill the English in village. You come fight with us. After we kill English, we take you to Acadia to see French brothers."

Jean-Marc protested, "But I'm not here to fight. I'm here to get rich and return to France, to live as a gentleman."

"Good! Get rich in raid on English, then go home France."

"I'm not here to fight. I'm here to trade furs."

"Not want come on raid, go Acadia by self."

"But I'll never find Acadia by myself. I've been lost for days."

"Good! Then come on raid. Then we take you Acadia. Go clean self by stream. Then we eat."

Realizing he would not win this argument, Jean-Marc looked around for something he could use to clean himself. "Do you have linens that I can use?"

"What linen?"

"Linen is a cloth. You rub it on your skin. It draws out the dirt."

The native looked confused. "Not have linen. Have water. Rub on skin. Dirt come off."

"But water will make me sick—"

"No, water make clean. Dirt make sick. Go to stream. Papisse Conewa take rags you wear. Burn them. Kill bugs."

Jean-Marc felt trapped. *I need this savage's help. I'm cold and hungry.* He went to the river and removed his clothing. Without comment Papisse Conewa took all of his clothing. Holding them at arm's length, he carried them to a fire and threw them in.

Using as little water as possible, Jean-Marc began to dab at the dirt covering his face and hands. Papisse Conewa came to the water and splashed at him. "Have much dirt. Use much water." He began to rub his wet hands on Jean-Marc's hands, which began to come clean. "Even small boy know how to wash. How you not know this? Rub much water on skin. You be clean. After clean, Papisse Conewa give clothing that not have bugs. You wear. Be warm. Not itch."

Standing naked at the stream, Jean-Marc rubbed the cold water on his skin. When he believed he had done this long enough, he walked back to the village in hopes of being given clothing. Twice, he was told that he was still dirty and had to clean himself better. On the third try, Papisse Conewa pronounced him clean enough and gave him deer-skin leggings, loin-cloth, shirt, and moccasins. Jean-Marc needed help dressing in the native clothing but for the first time in weeks, felt warm and comfortable.

A small woman, with black hair parted in the middle and pulled back into a braid, brought Jean-Marc what appeared to be dried meat and a hollowed gourd filled with some form of porridge made of something that looked like beans and large yellow grains he had not seen before. *No idea what this is ... Hot food! It's been so long.*

When he finished, Conewa came and said something in the native language. Without waiting for his son to translate, he walked away.

Papisse Conewa said, "Now rest, then eat more. Sleep tonight. In morning come on war-path. You sleep in my lodge. In morning, we attack English."

Jean-Marc was taken into a low, long, wood and bark building. He was shown to a mat and bearskin, where he was to rest. The natives left him, although he felt that he was being watched all the while. Near sundown, natives began to gather in small groups to eat. The same woman brought Jean-Marc another meal of dried meat and the strange porridge. After everyone ate, they retired for the night. Jean-Marc returned to his mat and slept better than he had since leaving France.

Before dawn, a small a boy shook Jean-Marc awake and signaled for him to follow. Conewa was standing with a group of older men. He seemed to be giving instructions to the younger ones.

Papisse turned to Jean-Marc and said, "Conewa say no bring musket. Not good. Not hit anything. Bring long knife. Stay with me. Not make noise. I show you how to fight."

After making all of their preparations, a group of about twenty natives walked into the forest. As they moved, Papisse often turned to explain to Jean-Marc that he could not just thrash his way through the forest.

"Watch what touch." "No make sound." "Walk on toes." "Be quiet." "Watch where you put foot." "Break one twig, you leave sign others use to track us."

For several hours, they walked in silence, except for Jean-Marc's heavy tread and Papisse Conewa's frequent reminders to make less noise. Making as little noise as possible with Jean-Marc among them, they approached three buildings surrounded by fields. Conewa signaled for everyone to stop. The natives crouched and concealed themselves in the woods. Papisse pushed a hand down on Jean-Marc's shoulder and whispered, "Get down. Don't let the English see you."

Two young warriors crept forward, moving from furrowed row to fence post. They seemed to disappear into the clearing. A short time later they returned and made signs to Conewa, who in turn made signs to the others. They crept across the fields without a sound.

Soon a farmer came from the crude log cabin, walking toward an out-building. One of the young warriors gave a loud shout, and charged the farmer, striking him in the neck with a tomahawk before the man could raise a hand to defend himself. Screaming, the other warriors ran into the cabin, killing a woman and three small children.

The natives removed the scalp from each of the dead.

Jean-Marc was horrified. "What are they doing? They're desecrating the dead!"

"We bring scalps to Acadia. French give us tools, rifles, shot, and powder for English scalps," Papisse said, smiling.

The natives searched the house for anything of value. Two of the young warriors were sent back to their village with a milk cow and two oxen. The cabin and out buildings were set on fire, and the natives resumed their silent passage through the forest. Twice more before dark, they came to isolated English farms which were attacked and looted for property and scalps. Jean-Marc was a wide-eyed bystander during the massacres.

Women? Children? Never have I seen whole families killed this way.

As night fell, the men sat to eat something made from the same beans and yellow grain they ate in their village. Now it was pressed with animal fat into cakes. Papisse told Jean-Marc, "We sleep here. Warriors return from village by morning. We attack English village then. Now sleep." The other warriors disappeared into the forest.

Anyone happening this way would see nothing. The woods looked deserted.

Jean-Marc climbed into a niche beneath a fallen tree and tried to sleep. *I've seen horrible things. In Acadia, they cannot know what these savages are doing.* Sleep would not come.

Before dawn, he heard a stirring in the forest. Warriors from another Abenaki village, led by the war-chief Agamagus joined them. The men who took the captured animals back to Conewa's village were back too. Jean-Marc estimated there were as many as a hundred warriors. They ate without talking. Then Agamagus signaled. The men picked up their war clubs, bows and arrows, and walked in single-file through the forest.

Near dawn they approached a large settlement of perhaps as many as sixty houses on either side of a road along the coast. This would be no sudden attack to kill the lone man on a farmstead followed by the easy killing of his wife and children. These houses had two stories. They were built like individual stockades. From the windows of one of these houses men with hunting pieces could shoot warriors attacking the house across the narrow street.

Jean-Marc had trained to fight from the time he could walk, but this would be his first battle. His hands shook.

The natives spread out and disappeared into the fields that stretched away from the settlement. Warriors crept from the fields, going into each barn and out-building in the village. In a few minutes, they returned, crouched and waited. To Jean-Marc the few minutes seemed like hours before flames began to show around the doors of one barn and then another. Fires grew throughout the village. A man ran from one of the buildings and cried, "Fire! Fire!"

He ran to a bell and began ringing it, still shouting, "Fire! Fire! Fire!"

Men and boys rushed into the street pulling on breeches and shoes. They attempted to form a bucket brigade. Fire was everywhere they looked. They had no idea where to start. The fires grew. Men ran back and forth in the street accomplishing nothing.

Agamagus stood and screamed. This was echoed by a hundred other voices. The Abenaki set upon panicked Englishmen, killing a score of them before the town's men even knew they were under attack.

The English began to fight back. Buckets became cudgels. Women ran from burning houses carrying loaded muskets, powder, and shot for their men. Pitch-forks and shovels became lances and maces. Nothing in this battle was noble.

As the melee raged, Jean-Marc tried to find a place to hide. *English or not, I'll not help these savages kill Christians.*

The Abenaki had surprise on their side, but the English had numbers. They fought with the same savage fury as the natives who attacked them. Women surged from their houses swinging hoes, axes, anything that would pass as a weapon. One of the women saw Jean-Marc crouching behind a shed. With a wooden rake for a weapon, she charged him. He stood, confident he could pull the rake from her hands and be done with her. Fighting for her life, she slammed the rake down on his head. He fell backward throwing his arms over his face for protection. Over and over she swung the rake at him, tearing at his face and head. Protecting his face with his left arm, he pulled the cutlass from his waist and slashed at her feet while she pummeled him. He felt the blade find bone. The woman screamed. Grabbing for her leg, she fell at his side. His eyes half blinded with blood, he raised himself to one knee and slammed the cutlass into her head.

Jean-Marc struggled to stand. He was charged by a boy of ten or twelve holding a wooden pitch-fork like a lance. He struck Jean-Marc in the chest driving him to the ground and knocking the wind from him. The boy raised the pitch-fork over his head. Jean-Marc lifted the cutlass and drove it into the boy's stomach. The pitch-fork fell to the ground.

Jean-Marc pulled his weapon from the lifeless body and swung it upward, just in time to deflect a musket being swung at his head like a club. The musket glanced off his sword, opening a gash above his left ear. The blow spun him to his right. The musket's momentum carried it high over the Englishman's left shoulder. The man tightened his grip and swung the musket again. Jean-Marc threw himself under the musket toward the Englishman's feet and drove his cutlass into the man's groin. He twisted and stood, driving the sword deep into the man's abdomen. The man fell to the ground. Jean-Marc put a foot on the man's leg to pull the sword free.

He turned and faced a blood-covered Englishman, who brought a blacksmith's hammer down on Jean-Marc's neck and shoulder. For Jean-Marc the battle was over. He lay unconscious between his victims. The Englishman who struck him fell on top of Jean-Marc, his head cleaved by a tomahawk.

The carnage lasted, hand to hand, for almost twenty minutes. Then spent Abenaki began to fall back to the forest. They had lost many brave warriors. Although they killed many English, this raid brought no scalps to trade with the French.

The Abenaki disappeared into the fields and then into the forest. Behind them they heard the sounds of the English assembling as a militia to chase them down. Exhausted Englishmen followed exhausted Abenaki. Using swords and muskets as firearms or as cudgels, they hunted the natives, who turned and fought back with arrows and tomahawks. Many more brave men died that day. When they could fight no more, the English broke off their pursuit and struggled back to the remnants of their town.

A small fraction of the Abenaki returned to their villages to tell the women their husbands had died as men.

In the village they called Wells, people numbed by fatigue and loss went on. Captain Converse, who had organized the counter-attack, ordered that the Christian dead be gathered and given funerals. Women tended to the Christian wounded. Converse ordered wounded Abenaki be dispatched without mercy. Dead natives were scalped and buried in a mass grave. Indian scalps would draw a handsome price in England. The money brought by several score of scalps would help pay to rebuild the town. Every barn, out-building, and many of the homes in Wells were destroyed.

Riders were sent to near-by villages to warn them of possible attacks. Others were sent to Boston to ask that the militia be mustered to avenge their losses.

In time, Jean-Marc came to. He couldn't move his left arm. He struggled from under a dead Englishman's body and to his feet. A townsman charged him, to run him through.

"*Non! Non! Anglais! Non!*"

The man recognized this as French. He noticed Jean-Marc's reddish blond hair. He realized Jean-Marc was white. Holding his injured arm at the wrist, the prisoner was brought to Captain Converse. "Look here, John; we've a French frog, masquerading as an Indian."

"Well, well" the captain said. "What have we here. He must be a spy of some kind."

"Should we kill him?"

"No, papist though he is, he'll be a Christian. We'll question him and decide what to do after we know why he's here."

Questioning the prisoner proved harder than expected. He spoke little English and no one in Wells spoke French. Jean-Marc winced as his arms were tied behind his back. He was taken to one of the undamaged houses.

An overwhelmed older woman hurried from one of the wounded to the next, attempting to administer healing to those who would recover and mercy to those who would not. Understanding little that was spoken, Jean-Marc knew what was taking place.

Other women entered. The older woman would say something, and they would set about treating the wounded. Hours passed before anyone tended to Jean-Marc. When one of the women did come to treat him, she angrily shouted something at the man standing guard over him. The man shrugged and untied Jean-Marc's hands.

His shoulder throbbed from being forced into a painful position by his tied hands. He grimaced and gave an involuntary yelp when the man yanked the rope from his wrists. The woman said something. She knelt beside him, gently touching his arm. Then she called another woman. They talked. The women noticed that Jean-Marc was supporting his left wrist with his right hand. They fashioned a sling for his injured arm, then washed blood from his head, face, neck, and hands. They dressed his wounds, and after additional discussion, decided that French or not, they would not leave a

Christian dressed in a savage's clothing. Jean-Marc gritted his teeth as the shirt Papisse Conewa gave him was stripped off along with the rest of his deerskin clothing. The women threw these into the fire.

Jean-Marc chuckled to himself. *They must not do laundry in America. They just burn everything.*

He winced as his arms were threaded into the sleeves of a coarse, white wool shirt before his sling was replaced. A heavy young woman led Jean-Marc up a flight of stairs and helped him settle into a bed. Its feather-filled mattress was supported by a mesh of ropes in a wooden frame. She brought him a bowl of stew, a thick wedge of black bread and a tankard of beer. Using his good right arm, Jean-Marc ate, finished his beer and soon fell asleep.

He awoke when a pregnant woman shook him and said something he did not understand. She placed another bowl of stew, piece of bread and tankard of beer on the table next to his bed. He looked out the window and decided that it must be morning. His shoulder throbbed. His cuts and bruises hurt little by comparison.

A man entered the room and shouted at him, but Jean-Marc could only shrug and sign that he did not understand. He remembered so little from the English lessons his mother insisted he take.

This pattern continued for a week. Kind women tended his wounds and brought him food. Angry men came and shouted at him. To his surprise, Jean-Marc began to remember some English. He understood some of what was being said to and about him.

Captain Converse decided Jean-Marc would be taken to Boston as a prisoner of war and be sold as an indenture to help fund the town's rebuilding. He was impatient for Jean-Marc's injuries to be healed enough for him to travel. The captain had to go to Boston to plan a campaign to punish the Abenaki for their attack, and he wanted to be rid of the Frenchman.

Chapter Four
To Boston

**"When sorrows come, they come not single
spies but in battalions."
William Shakespeare**

On the ninth day after the attack, Converse decided, injured or not, Jean-Marc was well enough to travel.

"You two hold his arms. I'll tie him."

What's happening?

Jean-Marc struggled against the three powerful men. He clenched his teeth as his hands were pulled behind his back and his wrists tied. The men dragged him from the house where he had been recovering and threw him on the hard, wooden bed of an ox-cart.

Is this the cart to the axman? Jean-Marc shook in the pre-dawn cold.

The Captain climbed into the saddle on Belam his gray, ten-year-old plow horse. He turned Belam toward his men. "Hezekiah, get in the cart with the prisoner. Be sure he can't reach your weapons. The rest of you position yourselves around the cart. Look lively." He took the time to look each man in the eye. "Keep your pieces locked and loaded. For all we know his redskin friends'll come for him."

More stepping than jumping into the high cart, Hezekiah flipped his heavy pack into the cart with one hand. Several of the other men shook their heads and smiled as they hefted their smaller packs into the cart. Hezekiah steered the ox into position behind the Captain.

Years of fighting had left their mark on Converse. Ever wary of others, he was named captain of the militia nine years ago, in 1682, while fighting the Abenaki during Castin's War. His cold, gray eyes, leathery skin, and tall sinewy build intimidated other men. No one felt Converse was their friend. He wore black, knee-length breeches, off-white woolen stockings and shirt, suspenders, and a black hat. A heavy black woolen coat and leather gloves were tied behind his saddle.

Converse's men all dressed like him, yet differently. Their breeches and coats were a variety of sad colors, russets and greens. They did not presume to imply equality with their commander by wearing black. Their coats were bundled in the ox-cart with Jean-Marc.

Four men walked on each side of the cart, their eyes scanning the surroundings against an Indian attack. The man behind the cart often walked backward to guard against attack from the rear. These men knew Abenaki tactics. They were experienced fighters. For a colonial militia, they were well trained.

Flies that seemed to ignore the militia swarmed Jean-Marc. They flew into his mouth, eyes, and nose. He clamped his eyes shut, blew his nose, spat, and sputtered. Tied as he was, he couldn't shoo them. He shouted in frustration.

"Hold a minute, Captain. The black flies are choking the frog." Hezekiah reached into his pack for a jar filled with a light brown, odorous ointment. "Learned this from the redskins. Squaw root, bear fat, and piss. Nothing like it," he said as he smeared it on all Jean-Marc's exposed skin. The swarm began to thin.

The cart lurched from side to side, across deep ruts in the road. Jean-Marc bounced on his injured shoulder. His mind raced. *Some of these are the same men who tried to question me ... Where are they taking me? Why now? Why didn't the women stop them this time?* He tried to ask, but no one understood him or cared.

The day grew hot. One of the men called out, "Captain, a drink would be good."

Converse turned his horse to look at his men, pulled its head back to look at the trail ahead then back toward his men. "You're right, Amos. The day's hot and the trail's dusty. We'll rest. Then another man can ride in the cart. That'll keep you all fresh."

Although he could see no one else on the trail, Hezekiah pulled the cart to the side, picked up his hunting piece and jumped out. Amos reached into the cart and pulled out a cloth bag. "Martha made us some biscuits for the trip," he said, passing the bag. Micah drew cider from a small cask. A few soft, blond hairs on his cheeks reflected the sunlight. He passed the cask to the others.

Jean-Marc tried to show that he was thirsty too. He shouted *"L'eau se il vous plait!"* He made a slurping noise and smacked his lips. The men either did not understand or did not care. *How do you ask for water in English?* He squinted and tried to remember.

After the short break, Amos climbed into the cart. Gray hair stuck out from under the thin man's hat. "Don't try anything," Amos said, giving Jean-Marc a light kick as he walked to the front of the cart. He steered the cart behind Converse. The others took up their positions, straining to see past the edge of the woods along the trail.

The militia rested every few hours. Each time Jean-Marc strained to remember how to ask for a drink in English. *They speak no French. Asking for de l'eau is useless.* The noises he made to tell the militia that he was thirsty had no effect. Then a new man would climb into the cart and give Jean-Marc a light kick or rap with the butt of a musket to ensure he understood they would tolerate no mischief, and the cart would move on.

Just before dusk the party approached the Oliver Cromwell Inn. Captain Converse was greeted at the door by the inn-keeper. "Good eve to you, squire. Will your men be staying with us this night?" He bowed his head in deference to the Captain.

"That we will keeper. I require supper and beds for my ten men, my prisoner and for me, then feed and water for the animals."

"A fine kettle of stew is ready on the fire. You'll not go hungry. I've three sleeping chambers each with a bed that'll sleep six, but none are empty. I can bed your men, but they'll have to sleep with the others, divided up between the rooms."

Converse shook his head. "That's not acceptable, keeper. We've a prisoner to keep secure."

"Come in, come in. You'll not find a better meal on the Post Road, and not another place to stay for a day's journey in any direction. You can tie your prisoner in the barn. One of your men can sleep in the cart with him." He reached out an arm as if to lead Converse into the inn. Converse raised his arm to block it and stepped back. The inn-keeper continued. "I'll only charge for the meals of those in the barn with no charge for bedding. You and your other men can pick the beds you'll share. Then come downstairs for a fine bowl of stew, a loaf of bread, and a tankard of beer."

"And what choice have I?"

The inn-keeper smiled. "None, squire, but you'll be the happier if you chose it to be so and not that it must be so."

Captain Converse thought then called out, "Hezekiah, lead Belam and the ox into the barn. Don't unyoke the ox until inside. Take the prisoner out of the cart and tie him to a post. Stay with'm. I'll have food brought out for both of you. The rest of you follow the keeper to your beds. Then come eat." He turned back to the inn-keep. "See that the animals are fed and watered."

"Josiah, show this man to the barn, then feed and water his animals. Get him clean straw that he can use for bedding in his cart," the inn-keeper called over his shoulder.

A boy in his early teens stepped from behind his father, took Belam by the bridle and told Hezekiah to follow him. He led them into a large, unpainted post and beam barn surrounded by a fenced yard. Hezekiah pulled Jean-Marc from the cart, pushed his back against a post and without loosening his bonds, tied another rope around him securing him to the post.

To this? Not for the night. Not even these peasants would do this, would they? He pleaded with Hezekiah, "*Non.* No." *That's it. No is English. How do I say don't do this?*

Ignoring him, Hezekiah double checked the knot.

Josiah led Belam to a stall, watered and gave him a large bucket of oats. Then he unyoked the ox and led it to a watering trough next to a trough filled with hay. "The well's in the yard," he told Hezekiah. "There's a bucket and a ladle there. How'll your man eat, tied like that?"

Hezekiah curled his lip, revealing his brown picket-fence teeth. "After I eat my fill, my guess is I'll have to spoon-feed him like a babe."

"As you'll have it, sir. I'll bring out your bowls together."

Hezekiah went to the well and dropped the bucket. He drew cool, clear water, and drank from the ladle. Taking a ladle of water to

Jean-Marc, he said, "Here you be, frog, drink. Thought we should have finished you like we would a redskin, myself."

Hezekiah held the ladle to Jean-Marc's lips. He sucked in as much as he could, spilling as much as he swallowed. When his guard turned to walk away, he cried out, "*De l'eau*", made a slurping noise, nodded and indicated with his head and eyes that he wanted more. Hezekiah went to the well, brought back the bucket, and held ladle after ladle for him.

Josiah returned with two large bowls of thick, steaming stew, two loaves of dark bread and two tankards of beer, on a wooden tray. After eating and drinking his fill, Hezekiah snarled, "I'm not spoon-feeding you. I'll untie you from the post and you can feed yourself. Try to run and I'll end your misery right quick."

What does he say? What does this mean? Why can't I remember?

He untied Jean-Marc's hands behind his back, pulled them to his front and retied them. Then he untied him from the post and stepped back. The prisoner fell on the food eating as rapidly as his tied hands would permit.

They give me nothing all day, then this? A full bowl of stew. A whole loaf of bread!

The tankard was filled with strong, dark beer. He ate until he was full. He drained the tankard. Then he looked around the barn and saw horses eating from troughs filled with oats. The ox stood eating from a trough filled with hay.

Can there be so much food in America? Even the animals are over-fed. At home, peasants eat not so well. Perhaps they would do well here. But me? Francois should rot in Hell for sending me to this place.

Hezekiah noticed Jean-Marc was finished eating. "Now then, frog, back against the post."

Does he mean to tie me to the post again? I must relieve myself.

He protested, and gestured, trying to show that he needed to relieve himself. Hezekiah understood, and pushed him toward the outhouse behind the inn. At the door, he grabbed his prisoner by the shoulders and spun him so that they were face to face.

"I'm not doing this for you either," Hezekiah said, untying his hands. "Try to escape and I'll kill you."

Aha! I know what he said! Where would I run? Whatever your plans for me, returning to the wilderness would be worse. With the ropes removed, he flexed his arms and wrists, moved his painful left shoulder and neck, then stepped into the outhouse.

When he emerged, Hezekiah pushed his face against the small building. He tied Jean-Marc's hands again and shoved him toward the barn. Inside, Hezekiah pushed him into a sitting position and tied him against the post.

He expects me to sleep like this? He looked around to see if there would be any alternative.

Hezekiah left to visit the outhouse himself. When he got back, he filled the ox-cart with clean straw for his bedding.

Josiah returned. "Just come for the dishes, sir. I thought you might like a bit extra." He handed Hezekiah another tankard of beer and a large piece of gingerbread.

"Nothing for the frog?" Hezekiah asked.

"The others told me about him. Don't know if I hate him for being French or for acting red. He's already had too much." He picked up the dishes and left.

Hezekiah enjoyed his bread and beer. Without undressing, he lowered the lamp's flame, climbed into the cart and slept. He snored loudly. Jean-Marc's chin dropped to his chest. He slept tied to the post.

Inside, Captain Converse and his men ate, and retired to their rooms. Two or three people, more men than women, already sleeping in each room. The newcomers elbowed and squeezed their ways into the beds and under the quilts.

Toward dawn Hezekiah heard someone enter the barn. He pointed the barrel of his cocked rifle over the cart's wall. "Not another step if you value your life."

The innkeeper's boy called out, "'Tis only me, sir, with your breakfast."

Hezekiah lowered his rifle, climbed from the cart, stretched and groaned. Then he headed for the barn door.

"Porridge looks good. I've got to use the outhouse. You stay with him, boy, 'til I get back,"

Josiah sat on the back of the cart and glared at Jean-Marc until Hezekiah returned.

"I got'm now, boy."

"Enjoy your meal, sir," Josiah jumped from the cart and hurried back to the inn.

Hezekiah sat in the cart and ate. When he finished, he untied Jean-Marc and took him to the outhouse. When they returned, Hezekiah said, "Get over to the cart. I'll help you in. That way you can eat sitting up, 'stead o' off the floor like an animal." He bent then straightened his knees and made a lifting motion with his hands to sign his meaning.

Jean-Marc was shocked as Hezekiah helped him into the cart and placed food beside him. He said, "Merci ... Sank you."

Hezekiah laughed. "Well, well, well. Our Frencher knows some of the king's own English. You eat. I'll leave the straw in the cart for you to lay on today."

Jean-Marc smiled, nodded, and ate.

When he was finished, Hezekiah tied him and pushed him into the cart.

Never thought I'd be happy for straw.

Captain Converse came out with his other men a short time later. "Caleb, you start in the cart." The small carpenter, known for his powerful hands and arms, stepped on the cart's axle and lifted himself into the cart. "The rest of you form up," Converse ordered as he saddled Belam.

Complaining about their poor night's sleep, the men positioned themselves around the cart. Converse climbed into the saddle. "Keep an eye out for the red devils." He rode out in the lead.

Several hours passed. Behind them, the men heard a rushing noise.

What is this? Are we being attacked?

Amos shouted, "Pigeons!"

Jean-Marc looked up. He saw a flock of large, red-breasted, gray birds flying over. The men in the militia raised their rifles and fired.

The rustling sound grew louder, like a mighty wind. The birds thickened, blocking out the sky.

Converse's men turned their rifles and used them to club low-flying birds from the air. He shouted, "Stop and reload! You're defenseless now! Reload! Reload!"

The frenzied men ignored their commander. He shouted over the noise of countless flapping wings. Still the birds came.

Above, Jean-Marc could see no sky, only birds.

Amos, the oldest, was the first to stop. "Hold, boys. We've more than we can use now."

Converse, fearing an Abenaki attack, shouted to reload. The others kept swinging.

Another shouted, "We can't clean what we have now." He stopped.

Others still swung their rifles at the endless flock of passenger pigeons filling the sky, east to west, north to south. The men attacked the birds until they were too tired to swing their rifles. Still, the birds came.

In the cart, Jean-Marc looked up wide-eyed. *There's no end to them! Can this be real?*

Under skies darkened by countless birds in flight, above the deafening sound of their flapping wings, Converse screamed, "Reload, damn you! Reload! We're all defenseless! Reload!"

At last, his men reloaded. Then they began collecting the birds they killed.

"How do you expect to clean all of these?" Converse demanded.

"We'll clean what we can and leave the rest," Caleb shouted over the din from above.

The men threw birds into a great pile by the cart. They stopped collecting them at two hundred, leaving the many more where they fell. The sky was still blocked from view. Converse dismounted. Caleb gathered wood and started a fire. The others sat to gut and pluck birds.

Hezekiah pulled Jean-Marc from the cart. "You'll eat your fill today, frog."

The men plucked pigeons until their fingers ached. Scores more lay on the ground. Over a dozen roasted over the fire. More were hung from the sides of the cart and when there was no more room, they were thrown into it.

"Leave the rest. I can't pluck anymore."

"Shame we can't save 'em for our hogs."

Caleb passed around roasted pigeons. Jean-Marc was untied and handed one. He pulled off a leg and bit into dense, moist meat. *In America, the air is filled with food!*

Still the birds came. The men ate their fill and more before continuing on their way. They took with them more birds than they could use. They left many on the ground.

Jean-Marc could not believe what he saw. For the rest of that day, birds blocked out the sky. The men had to shout over the noise of their flapping wings. At sunset, the flocks began to thin. Still there were more birds in the sky than Jean-Marc had ever seen before. That night they stopped in a clearing, built a fire and ate pigeons for supper, sleeping under the stars. In the cart, Jean-Marc shivered without a blanket, trying to cover himself with straw.

*****

After days on the trail, Jean-Marc noticed the militia took fewer precautions. At inns, a different man slept in the barn to guard him every night. Some treated him better, some worse. They all seemed to appreciate his attempts to speak English, so he kept trying.

On the fourth day, they came to a river still swollen by the spring snow melt. "Would that there was a ferry. We'll have to ford it. Let's go, Belam." Converse's horse stepped into the water. The cart followed.

"Hold a moment, Captain," called Caleb from beside the cart. "We'll need to truss up our powder and shot."

Converse pulled Belam to a halt while the men secured their ammunition. One by one they finished and waded into the chest-deep water, holding their weapons over their heads. A few yards into the river, Micah, the shortest, slipped and went under. He got right up.

He wasn't hurt, but his wet powder would be useless for several days.

"Don't forget to check for leeches, boy," Caleb laughed.

Micah scooped up his wet hat and muttered under his breath as the others enjoyed themselves at his expense. He resumed his place beside the cart.

The water grew deeper and the current stronger. Three more men slipped under by mid-stream. With so many men carrying wet powder, they were all in danger. No one was laughing anymore.

The cart lifted off the stream's bottom, drifted a few inches and touched again. Stretching to keep its mouth above water, the ox strained for the bank. The cart lifted again and began to move downstream, dragging the struggling ox with it. Amos stood and shouted, "We're losing the cart!"

Caleb threw his rifle next to Jean-Marc. "Help me free the ox," he called. Amos jumped into the river. For several minutes, they were dragged downstream, fighting the current, the wet harness, and the straining animal. Finally, they lifted the yoke. The ox waded to the far bank. Freed from its massive engine, the cart gathered speed. Amos and Caleb tried to pull it to the bank.

Inside the cart, Jean-Marc lay on his side, tied and helpless. He cried out for help. *Do they understand me?* He tried to call for help in English but couldn't remember the words.

The others struggled to the bank. They dropped their weapons and ran along the river. Captain Converse shouted unheard directions to his men as he rode along the bank.

"Caleb!" Amos shouted. "Grab the yoke-ropes! Try to pull it to the side!"

"I got 'em, but the cart's pullin' me with it."

Several of the men ran along the bank. They passed the cart and plunged into the water. As the cart rushed toward them Caleb shouted, "Some of you grab the yoke ropes and pull 'er to the bank! The rest o' you push!" Hezekiah wrapped a rope around his massive right arm and pulled with Caleb and Amos. Others pushed against the rushing current.

Jean-Marc's panicked cries for help added to confusion. More men reached the cart. Every man had a different idea about what to do.

"Give me a hand here!"

"Help me get the rope from the cart. We can tie it to a tree."

"Maybe we should push it back to the other si—"

"Lift the front. We'll tip 'er."

They shouted over one another. They accomplished little. The cart floated toward a small waterfall. As the cart neared the fall, the militia men jumped to the side. The cart, with Jean-Marc inside, tipped over the edge.

The fall was small enough that one of the cart's wheels was visible from upstream, but when the cart tipped, Jean-Marc was thrown, screaming for help, into the river and pinned under water. Caleb's first thought was that at least the cart was no longer floating away. Then he remembered. "Amos, he's under. The frog's sank."

Moving so they would miss the cart, they allowed themselves to wash over the fall. Standing in the chest deep, swirling water, Caleb signed toward the far side of the cart and shouted, "I'll look over there."

Amos nodded and plunged under water. Seconds passed. He came up for air and plunged under again. Caleb dove to the far side of the cart. On his fourth dive Amos felt Jean-Marc's foot. He groped his way along the body to the shoulders and stood pulling his head above water.

"Caleb, I've got him!"

Caleb thrashed his way to them. Together, they dragged their prisoner to the bank, pleased that nothing worse had happened. Jean-Marc spit water, choked, and gasped for air.

The men tied a line to the cart and used the ox to drag it to the bank. Micah was the first to notice the problem. "Look to the cart."

Ahab, the rich farmer who owned the cart, cried out, "The axle's broke!"

Another of the men said, "What's to do? Without the cart, the Frencher needs to walk."

This was followed by another explosion of opinions.

"There's eleven of us—"

"I say kill him now—"

"Leave the cart. We'll—"

Ahab shouted, "Easy to say when it's not your cart! They're dear to buy and hard to build!"

Converse called out above everybody, "Listen now! 'Tisn't safe letting the prisoner walk. We need the cart."

"What then?" asked Caleb. "There's no village round abouts."

"'Tis nothing to do but make a new axle." Converse said. "Tie the Frencher to a tree. Micah, keep a close eye on him. The tools were in the cart's bed. We'll have to fish them out."

Micah pushed Jean-Marc to the ground by a large tree, where he sat choking. Ahab and another man went back into the water to find the tool box. After ten minutes of diving they managed to recover most of the tools.

They tipped the cart back onto its end. The pegs holding the wooden wheels to the axle were pounded out, freeing the wheels. Then they freed the axle from the cart.

By this time, Jean-Marc was done choking. He looked around at his captors. *They're all so busy with the cart, they forgot about me. Now's my chance.* He struggled to his feet and took a few halting steps toward the thick brush lining the river banks. *But, tied like this, I wouldn't get far. What would they do when they caught me? If I got away, how far would I get? Where would I go? What would I eat?* He moved back toward the river bank and slid down against a tree to wait.

Ahab located a straight, young tree, sawed it off at the base and dragged it to the cart.

"Push the axle back together." Amos called. "We'll have to line the log against the halves of the old axle to size it." When this was done, the tree was trimmed and sawn to size.

"Bring the wheels," Ahab called out. "We need to check them for fit."

Hezekiah rolled one of the wheels to the new axle and held them together.

"She's too wide for the wheel," Ahab said.

Caleb, the carpenter, chiseled each end of the axle. Time and again he lined the wheels up against it to check for fit. Once the ends were small enough he chiseled each end round so the wheel would roll on it. The others mounted the wheels. Then, using an awl, he drilled four holes through the axle for pegs. Others cut and sized pegs from the unused portion of the tree, secured the wheels to the axle and attached the new axle to the cart.

Captain Converse looked at the repaired cart and then up at the sky. "Well done, men. She's good as new. But the day's over. It's pigeon again tonight."

The tired Englishmen set about gathering wood. Jean-Marc watched with great interest as Caleb knelt to start the fire. He fashioned something like a bird's nest from small twigs and dry grass. In this he placed a small piece of charred cloth. Then he placed a small stack of twigs next to it. Kneeling, he held a piece of flint in his left hand over the nest and struck its edge with his knife. Sparks shot onto the tinder. When a spark landed on the cloth, Caleb scooped up the nest and blew on it. A red spot formed on the cloth. Caleb kept blowing. Then a flame burst forth from the cloth. He dropped the burning twigs and began feeding small sticks to the flame, gradually increasing their size. Soon, the fire cast a small circle of light and heat into the cool June night.

Jean-Marc was amazed. *So that's how it's done! I'll never be without fire again.*

The men sat around the fire and ate. Then they spread their blankets to cover themselves for the night.

Hezekiah untied Jean-Marc and took him a short distance from the fire so that he could relieve himself. Returning to the circle of light, Hezekiah tied him to the tree. He realized that no one thought to bring an extra blanket for the prisoner.

"Your clothes're as wet as ours. Can't let you freeze without a blanket." Saying this, Hezekiah took his blanket, draped it around Jean-Marc's shoulders and tucked it around him.

Jean-Marc said, "*Merci.* Sank you, Hezekiah," and smiled.

This time Hezekiah smiled back. He collected a pile of dead leaves and pine needles to cover himself, then doused the fire, so as to attract no attention from the Abenaki. Captain Converse assigned a man to the first watch. The others went to sleep.

It was an uneventful night. They ate pigeon and jerky for breakfast and were on the trail again not long after dawn. By noon they reached the Cock and Hen Inn. There were hours of daylight left.

From his saddle, Captain Converse called to the fat inn-keep who hurried to greet them.

"Good day, squire. Are you in need of a mid-day meal for yourself and your men?"

"Not sure. We were delayed by a broken axle yesterday, so we're already behind. How far's the next inn?"

"I've no good news for you there. The Black Stallion's a hard day's ride. But I've soft beds and hot food for tired men."

Converse looked down at his men from his saddle, then at the road ahead. "Take your ease, men. We'll stay the night, rather than sleep in the woods again."

"Between the broke axle and stopping early we've already lost a full day's travel," Amos complained.

"That we have." Ahab smiled, "But I'll take the afternoon's rest."

"Are we the first to stop today?" Converse asked the inn-keeper.

"You are."

"Then show me your rooms. I'll pick the ones for my men and the prisoner. We don't want to share rooms with others."

"There's enough of you. 'Twill be no problem. You can have two rooms." The inn-keep led the Captain to his largest room.

"The bed'll do us, but what ho?" Converse pointed to a wrought iron ring bolted to the floor. "What's this?"

"No idea. I bought the inn a year ago. 'Twas there then."

"This room'll serve, inn-keep." Converse pointed at the iron ring. "We'll tie our prisoner to that. He'll sleep lying down this night."

After Converse selected their second room, the inn-keep had his son bring fresh straw and arrange it near the iron ring. Then he threw a bear skin over it, making a comfortable bed.

The inn-keeper's boy set benches and a table in front of the inn so the travelers could sit in the sun. For a mid-day meal, he brought them a large plate covered with roasted venison and hard cheese. To wash it down they drank tankard after tankard of good dark beer.

Even Jean-Marc was given some degree of freedom. His hands and arms were untied allowing him to eat and drink with the militia. Only his left leg was tied to the table.

The men drank and relaxed. Micah said, "Did you hear of the sailor walking near the docks in Boston?"

"I did not," Amos replied.

"He was walking behind a lass he thought to be handsome, so he doubled his pace to overtake her and see her face. But when he got to her front and saw her face, he no longer found her comely. So, he said to her, 'Seeing at you from behind, I did think you to be pleasing to look upon, but now, in your front, I see that you are not.' The girl looked him well in the eye and said, 'I'm sorry to have disappointed you, good sir, but would you do me the kindness of kissing that which first pleased you?'"

The men roared with laughter. They told other jokes, laughing for the first time since the attack.

"Look at these beards," laughed Ahab. "I think I've found Israel's lost tribes! Your wives won't know you."

Caleb laughed, "Your wife won't want to know you when she sees that shirt. It was white, wasn't it?"

"And yours is cleaner?" Hezekiah returned.

Jean-Marc understood much of what was said. With his simple understanding of English, he didn't get the jokes, but he laughed along with the others. They were all enjoying themselves. As the beer flowed and the day wore on, the relaxed men treated him almost as one of their own, now pouring him beer from a pitcher, then passing him some cheese or meat. He smiled.

Can a man in my situation enjoy himself? He drained his tankard, looked about him and realized he was happy.

The men soon realized that no one ever buys beer. It's only rented. Their light afternoon led to frequent trips behind the inn.

Jean-Marc signed to no one in particular that he needed to use the outhouse again.

"Again? He's already gone three times," Ahab complained.

"How many times you go?" another man asked.

"'Tis a different matter. I'm no prisoner who needs tying and untying," Ahab said.

"I say we untie the frog," Hezekiah shouted.

After much loud debate, they decided to free Jean-Marc's leg from the table. A short piece of rope was tied between his ankles as one might hobble a horse. This would prevent him from running. Any time he needed the outhouse two men would go with him. This way each guard would also be able to relieve himself and Jean-Marc would not be left alone.

The men did not even have to move for supper. The inn-keeper brought a large pot of stew to their table with many loaves of bread and much more beer. They ate and drank until dark. Then they went to bed. Captain Converse paid the keeper with the rest of the pigeons and some silver before retiring. The bill was large. The Captain felt it a small price.

In their room, Amos said, "This won't do. We'll all be going back and forth, out back, all night. If we tie the frog, we'll be untying and tying him all night long."

In their present state, no one argued Amos' point. Tying Jean-Marc to the iron ring made little sense. After what passed for deliberation, they decided to leave Jean-Marc's legs hobbled, and to tie his hands.

"He'll just have to wake one o' us or he can wait for one o' us to get up and he can go with 'em."

Converse told Jean-Marc to wake one of the militia if he needed to go behind the inn. Assuming he understood, they all went to bed.

Escape will never be easier. Where would I go? ... Now, I am treated better ... I should not be a prisoner but what is there to do? He fell into a drunken sleep.

The Cock and Hen was crowded when the militia from Wells wobbled from their rooms the next morning. "We'll eat at the table outside again," Converse told the keeper.

The men trickled from their rooms to the outhouse and then to the table. The inn-keeper's son brought each man a bowl of porridge and a tankard of beer. They left late that morning. Jean-Marc, whose hands had been untied to eat, was allowed to ride sitting next to the driver with his legs hobbled.

Despite their late start, the men made good time over the next two days and began feeling that, at least for this journey, all would be well.

On the evening of the seventh day of their journey they approached a burned-out frame where an inn once stood. Thirty-two scalped bodies littered the ground. Some died when the inn burned. The men from Wells flashed back to their burned-out village. Jean-Marc was horrified at the carnage. Several of the men from Wells dropped to their knees and began to vomit.

Hezekiah shouted, "Look to what the Frencher's friends done." He threw a punch at the astonished Jean-Marc.

The punch caught his left cheek, driving him to the ground. He knew better than to fight back against one of the militia. Hobbled, he could not run. The men from Wells attacked Jean-Marc, kicking and stomping on him. He curled into fetal position and screamed in pain.

"Kill the Frencher, like they killed my wife and boy!" one shouted, kicking at him.

"'Tis no Christian's business bringing savages down on other Christians!"

"This papist's no Christian!"

So, it went for over a minute, until the men from Wells gave full vent to their fury. Jean-Marc lay beaten on the ground.

Both his eyes were beaten shut. Blood flowed from his mouth and ears. His right hand had been broken by someone's heel. He was left lying in a pool of blood while the others caught their breath.

Long minutes passed. The Captain spoke first. "We sinned. No Christian should set upon an innocent like that."

"The damned Frencher attacked our village! He killed our wives and children. He's no innocent!"

"'Tis sure he sinned then, but the sin here was ours. He'd naught to do with this raid."

"The same red devils he went with did this. If we'd not taken him, his belt'd carry some o' those scalps."

"That said," Converse persisted, "Christian men ought not attack one hobbled and helpless."

Most of his men thought the beating was God's justice. Others said that it was to their shame. They argued until Jean-Marc began to groan.

"Pick him up. Tie him fast and put him in the cart," the Captain ordered.

Ignoring his pain, they tied him and threw him into the cart. He couldn't understand why they attacked him, but he vowed revenge.

"These men all deserve Christian burials," Converse said. "See if you can find a shovel we can use."

For the second time in three weeks the men began the task of cleaning up after a massacre. They took turns digging while others gathered the bodies for a mass grave. At dark, the men moved away from the dead to a nearby clearing and sat to eat some jerky.

Jean-Marc got no food or water that night. Neither was he untied and taken to relieve himself. He had soiled himself during the beating. As he lay in pain, caked in blood, he did again.

At dawn, the men began to rouse. They ate some jerky and drank from a small stream. Caleb brought Jean-Marc some jerky, but he did not eat. He drank the water he was offered. Other than that, he lay in his dried blood and filth while the men from Wells completed their gruesome tasks. By nightfall, prayers were said and the dead were buried. The men left the grave and returned to the clearing where they slept the night before.

Caleb again brought Jean-Marc some jerky and water. This time he ate. Then Caleb took him to the stream, handed him a cloth and said, "You're covered with blood. You stink. Clean yourself the best that you can. We've no other clothes for you. Do your best. You'll hurt but feel the better for it."

Jean-Marc took the cloth and began wiping away the blood and mud that covered him. He looked at Caleb. *Mon Dieu, does he expect me to thank him? Damn him! Damn all the English. My day will come. When it does, my revenge will be sweet.*

He finished cleaning himself. Caleb took him to the cart and tied him. Hurt as he was, he would go nowhere.

In the morning, the men ate in silence and resumed their journey. Except for the occasional slap, punch, or muttered curse that Jean-Marc received for no apparent reason, the remaining six days of the journey passed without incident.

He stopped trying to speak English. His wounds began to heal. His hatred for his captors, for all Englishmen, grew. On the evening of the sixteenth day after leaving Wells, the exhausted small party walked along the banks of the Charles River into Boston.

Chapter Five
Boston

**"The city is what it is because our
citizens are what they are."**
Plato

The militia followed the North River into Boston. In the distance, they could just see the sails of the ships plying the harbor. Converse turned Belam to face his men. He called out, "I need see Governor Phipps over the military response. The rest of you follow the river to the waterfront. Amos, Caleb, take the frog straight to the harbor and find a seller of indentures. He'll hold him for sale. Most indentures are for seven years." He pointed at Jean-Marc. "This one's a Christian who joined savages against others o' his kind. We'll sell 'im for twenty-one years. That should fetch a pretty penny. I never sold an indenture before. Don't know what's to do. Ask the seller how it works." He turned on to a road leading away from the river then turned back and called, "You others go to the Three Cranes Inn a few blocks from the harbor. Anybody you ask'll know how to get there. Arrange for rooms and supper tonight. We'll all meet there." He turned back to the road and trotted away.

Caleb jumped into the cart with Amos and Jean-Marc. Small farms gave way to a scattering of houses along the dirt road paralleling the river. As they neared the city, this road was intersected by others that led inland. Now houses lined both sides of the roads that were paved with small stones. The men from Wells looked from side to side, awed by the largest city in British America.

A city? I thought to see only wilderness. This is not Paris but it is no wilderness.

Wharves and docks lined the busy waterfront. Ships were loading and unloading. Across the narrow street large warehouses, mercantiles, and taverns lined the harbor and extended on to side-streets leading away from the water. Men, oxen and horses moved heavy carts along crowded streets. Amos asked a man where they would find a seller of indentures.

80

"You'll want to see Samuel Smith. He'll get you the best price. Like as not, he'll be in the Red Lion Inn." The man pointed south. "It's another few blocks along the front."

They reached the Red Lion minutes later. The large white building had a covered porch under a wooden sign showing the rampant Scottish lion. Amos waited in the street with the prisoner. Caleb went inside and called, "Samuel Smith?"

A large grey-haired man raised his hand and shouted, "You've found him. Of what service may I be?"

Caleb crossed the room to him. "We've an indenture to sell."

"We?"

"The militia from Wells."

"I trust you have papers. Man, or woman? English, or German? If German, does he speak and understand English?"

"I have no papers. Captain Converse'll have to speak to that. Indenture's a man, not English or German. We've got a Frencher. Understands English better'n he makes on. Speaks but little. Took'm prisoner after he raided our village with a tribe of heathen savages. Selling 'im as a military prisoner, so the captain says we're to treble the seven-year indenture."

Smith looked up from his seat and shook his head. "A Frencher, taken in a raid with savages is an escape risk ... and a threat ...Speaking little English further lowers his value." The table moved as Smith pushed against it, slowly raising his bulk from the chair. "Where is he?"

Caleb led the seller to the cart.

"Been years since I've seen one this filthy. You say he understands English? Boy, look at me."

Jean-Marc glared straight ahead. Caleb said, "No sense pretending you don't understand. Look at the seller." He slapped Jean-Marc's face. Furious, Jean-Marc spun to glare at Caleb, revealing his face to the merchant.

"He's been beat. Bruises all over his face." Smith pried at Jean-Marc's lips.

He pulled back, shouting, "*Ne me touche pas paysan!*"

Caleb held him while he tried to pull away.

"Young enough. Seems to have all his teeth. You don't often see that."

Jean-Marc struggled while Smith prodded him, feeling his stomach, chest, back, legs, and arms as he would a horse he might buy. "See him wince? Something's wrong with the shoulder." He pointed at Jean-Marc's hand. "See the thickened hand. Probable it's broke." He turned and looked at Caleb, who pushed Jean-Marc down into the cart.

"He's damaged goods that don't even speak English. Can't get you much for 'em. A strapping lad who speaks English can bring ten or eleven pounds. A damaged frog who trucks with savages won't get much. I'll need papers and proof that I can indenture him for twenty-one years. Then we can fix a price and decide if you want to sell him outright or consign him and have me sell him for my fee."

"Captain's with Governor Phipps. He won't want to be interrupted." Caleb said.

"Then speak to him after his meeting. I need a clear title and a known term. I'll not sell free flesh just as he can't make his case to me. If you want, you can leave him with me. I'll store him for you at six pence the day."

"Six pence the day?" Caleb blurted out.

"You're at liberty to keep him with you, but you if want me to hold'em, the cost's six pence a day. There's no dickering on that."

"I don't see as I have much choice, do I?"

"The choice is yours, Goodman, but the price is mine."

Caleb looked at Amos, who shrugged his shoulders. Caleb looked back at Smith. "Seems steep to me, but if it's gotta be."

He and Smith shook on it.

"Stay with him. I'll get one of my boys." Smith turned back toward the inn. He opened the door and called, "Boy!" A youngster hurried from the crowd. "There's a half-penny in it for you if you hurry to my office and come back with Obadiah. Tell him we've got a new boy to keep while they find his papers."

"Yes, Goodman," the boy called over his shoulder as he ran up the street.

Smith made small talk with Caleb and Amos while they waited for his servant. In a few minutes, the boy returned with the biggest man either Caleb or Amos had ever seen. He was dressed in a home-spun white shirt, russet breeches, and white stockings much like theirs, but the sleeves strained around his arms and massive chest. Shoulder length brown hair, pulled straight back, surrounded his pock-marked face. A full head taller than any other man on the crowded street, he carried a thick hickory switch in his hand.

"You sent for me, Goodman Smith?"

Caleb was shocked at the man's deep voice.

"I did, Obadiah. We have a boy to watch over while these men wait for his papers. Take him to the yards and feed him, but don't start any training. It's not clear he speaks English."

"Yes, Goodman."

Jean-Marc's hands were still tied behind his back. His eyes bulged as Obadiah dragged him from the cart. "*Maudit,*" he said under his breath as he found his footing. The big man pointed and pushed him up the street. "Go that way, boy. Do as you're told, and I'll not hurt you."

What does this man want? Don't want him mad at me.

Jean-Marc moved in the direction he was pushed. It took about five minutes to walk the half-mile along the busy waterfront to Smith's office.

A red sign hung over a gray, solid wooden door. White lettering announced, "Samuel Smith. Imports, Exports, Servants." A three-feet by two-feet glass window, with gray shutters, broke the small building's otherwise plain gray façade. Obadiah opened the door, pushed Jean-Marc through a small office and out the back door into a large, enclosed courtyard. Heavy oaken doors lined one side of the yard. Each door had an opening at face level, blocked by iron bars.

Jean-Marc's eyes flashed around the yard. Here and there hands, some white, some black, some men's, some women's, protruded through the bars. Another large man unlocked one of the doors. "Put him in this one. The ones on either side are going tonight."

Obadiah untied Jean-Marc's hands. He pushed him into a tiny, dark cell and slammed the door behind him. Iron keys on an iron ring sounded loud against the door as the lock was thrown. His only light came through the door's small opening. The smell of excrement was oppressive.

Why am I here? What will they do with me?

His eyes adjusted to the darkness. He saw a wooden platform, about six feet by three feet, fastened to the floor beside narrow back wall. There were about two feet of floor space between the bed and the walls to the right and in the front of the cell. Under the platform was a wooden bucket.

This must be what they call a bed. The straw on it's as filthy as the straw on the floor. He went to the door and looked out the opening. *Voices! What are they saying?* He pushed his mouth against the bars and shouted, *"M'etendez-vous? ... "Pourquoi es-tu ici?"*

He heard voices but understood nothing they said. Sitting on the wooden bed, he stared into the darkness and tried to understand what was happening. Hours passed. He lay down and cried. He was cold but had nothing to cover himself. Much later he fell asleep.

*****

Caleb and Amos found their way to the Three Cranes Inn. A wood-shingled roof pitched to the central chimney of the two story, grey clapboard building. They left the ox and cart in the barn with the servant and went into the inn. They ordered tankards of beer and sat by the fire with the others.

Converse got there near dinnertime. Before sitting he asked how much they got for the sale. "The seller won't do business without papers," said Caleb.

"What papers?" Converse asked, sitting down.

"Whatever papers you need to sell an indenture." Caleb took another swallow of his beer.

"Where am I supposed to get these papers?"

"Can't tell you that, Captain. I just know the seller won't do business until we show him the necessary papers."

Converse's lips tightened. His voice was angry. "Isn't that what I sent you to find out?" He looked around the room. "I'll have to do it myself. Dinner's not for another hour." He stood and headed for the door. "I'll go find the high-sheriff and ask him about these papers." He got directions to the high-sheriff's house from the inn-keep.

It took Converse ten minutes to reach the sheriff's house. He knew of Converse and was happy to meet the old Indian fighter. He told Converse that the governor should be able to help him with the papers. The Captain swore under his breath, then thanked the man and left to see the governor again.

At the Governor's Mansion, he explained the reason for his call to an older servant who told the Captain that the Governor was at prayer and could not be disturbed. After prayer, he would eat then go to church for the evening. "If you come back first thing in the morning, I'll ask if Governor Phipps will see you some time tomorrow."

"Of course, he'll see me. I met with him earlier today," Converse said, implying that he was a man of great importance. "Waiting until tomorrow will force my men and me to stay in Boston yet another day."

"That you lack papers of indenture creates no emergency for His Excellency, now does it? I'll not interrupt him from his prayers or his supper. But His Excellency attends the North Church. He often stops for a toddy at the inn next to the church before entering. He may speak with you there."

Converse asked for directions to the North Church. A five-minute walk brought him to the inn where he hoped to meet the governor. He ate supper and waited over a tankard of beer. Three hours later Governor Phipps arrived. The Captain approached the Governor as he was ordering his toddy.

"Converse, will you join us for worship?"

"Sorry to say, I cannot, Your Excellency. This morning I told you we had an indenture to sell. The agent would not take him without papers. I inquired of such papers with the sheriff, and he told me I must see you."

"How is it that you don't have papers for a man you seek to sell?"

"Your Excellency will recall 'tis the Frencher we took when the savages raided our town. We decided to treble his indenture, given that he conspired with the savages."

"You can't just decide these things by yourself. This needs be done by Judge Sewall in the Magistrate Court. To your great fortune the court meets Tuesday next." The governor sounded upset.

Now it was Converse's turn to be upset. He raised his voice. "That's four days. How am I to pay the room and board of my men all that time?"

"Forget not your station, Converse! You should have thought about your needs before you came." His voice turned icy. "I expect you'll pay room and board for your men from the sale of your indenture. Be sure to bring your frog with you to the court. Judge Sewall will want to examine him. Not all who go to court are truthful. The judge will want evidence. Good eve to you, Captain." Governor Phipps removed his hat and coat, making a show of turning his back on the Captain.

Converse was furious. *Did he just dismiss me?* For a moment, he glared at the governor's back. Then he shook his head. *Naught to do but go to the Three Cranes and wait.*

He stomped down the streets of Boston.

I could release the men. Don't relish risking the seventy miles home alone, though.

At the Three Cranes, his men were no more pleased with the delay than the captain.

Caleb put down his tankard and stood. "We're already gone over two weeks. We've crops and animals in need of tending."

"All our homes and barns were damaged. Who's to fix them?" Hezekiah added.

Amos stood, too. "And you'll want to call us up again when the colony goes after the savages. How are we to stay here longer, just to sell the Fren—".

"We should have just killed 'im with the savages!" Caleb added to general nods of agreement.

Converse decided to send eight men home the next day, leaving two men as escorts for the Captain. He promised each of the men now returning would receive three shillings from Jean-Marc's sale. The two who remained with the captain would receive another five pence for the additional time. Lots were cast to determine who would stay. They fell upon Hezekiah and Amos.

*****

The sound of keys woke Jean-Marc at dawn. He was on his feet when Obadiah entered his cell, "Stand back now," and used a hickory stick to push him against the back wall. The man who had unlocked the cell the day before took the bucket from under the bed, emptied it into a barrel on a cart outside the door and threw the bucket back under the bed. Then he put a smaller bucket, filled with water on the floor, and a large loaf of black bread on the bed and stepped out of the cell. Obadiah backed out of the cell and the door slammed shut. Again, there was the sound of keys in the lock. Then nothing.

Jean-Marc ate the bread and drank most of the water. He stood by the door with his hands protruding between the bars. He heard voices he did not understand. He shouted things to people who did not understand him. As the day passed he was able to see men and women taken out of cells and out of the courtyard. He saw others brought in and put in the cells. Those just brought in would stand with their faces pushed against the doors and shout things Jean-Marc did not understand. Then nothing. He sat on the bed and stared.

After dark, he lay on his bed, cursing his father, then his brother, then God. Then he cried. Cold, he fell asleep.

*****

The men who were returning to Wells left Boston at dawn. Captain Converse, Hezekiah and Amos could do nothing but wait. Samuel Smith would not even discuss a price until the proper paperwork was produced, but he was happy to charge an additional six pence for each day that he held and fed Jean-Marc.

Goodman Smith turned a comfortable profit on these six pennies every day. The bread and water that he gave Jean-Marc, once a day, cost less than a penny. At five pennies profit every day, Smith was in no hurry.

*****

Jean-Marc's only human contact came near dawn each morning. Obadiah would open the cell door and say, "Move back." Then, slapping a hickory switch into his hand, he stood between Jean-Marc and the other muscular man who emptied his bucket, leaving him bread and water.

He despaired. *Is this my prison? How long will they keep me here?*

As the days dragged on, his depression deepened. He received no medical attention for his injuries. They would heal on their own, or they would not. Goodman Smith didn't care.

It would have been better if I died in the wilderness.

Using the moon's pale light, Jean-Marc tore at the wood around the iron bars in the door until his fingers bled. Torn fingernails and bleeding fingers were no match for the oak door.

What can I use on the door? He looked around his cell. *The bucket!*

He grabbed the stinking bucket, spilling the waste on the straw covered floor. He tore at the metal straps and rivets that held the bucket together. Fingernails tore and bled, but the straps did not move.

The bed must have nails. He tried to pull the bed up from the floor, but it would not move. He tried to tear it from the wall but it would not move. He felt all over the bed for nails but only found the wooden pegs the craftsman used to hold the bed together.

He was furious. He threw himself against the door, knocking himself backward. Falling to his knees he pounded his fists against the door until they bled. *God, why are you doing this to me?* Then nothing. Cold, he leaned against the door for hours.

After dawn, the door opened. Obadiah said, "They're coming for you," pushed a bucket of clean, cold water through the door. "Clean yourself up for court. Then we'll give you some clean clothes." The door closed and locked again.

Did I understand? For court? That cannot be right. Am I to see the king? What else can court mean?

Jean-Marc stripped and used the water to clean the blood from his hands and the accumulated filth from his body. Obadiah opened the door and handed him a large cloth.

"Dry yourself then put these on."

These are peasant's clothes! I cannot appear in court dressed in these.

"*S'il te plait,* how you say, please, in such *vetements* I must not go."

He must know court requires proper dress.

"Get dressed." The door closed.

Jean-Marc pulled the worn, green, knee-length breeches over the coarse, white shirt then pulled the woolen stockings to his knees. His right big toe stuck through the stockings. He tucked the stockings under his breeches and put on the shoes he wore since leaving Wells. Then he sat on the bed and waited.

When the door opened, Obadiah and the other large man locked irons on his wrists and pushed him out of the cell. Hezekiah and Amos stood in the yard.

"Looks none the worse for wear, but I can smell him from here," Amos said with a chuckle.

Why are they here?

Nothing made sense. He looked around the yard, with no idea what he was looking for. "*Nous allons.*" He paused to think. "We go … to court, no?"

"We go to court, yes," Hezekiah said. He pushed Jean-Marc toward the door that led out of the yard and into the street. The two men led their confused prisoner to the meetinghouse.

*****

Captain Converse was first in line when the Court proceedings began Tuesday. Hezekiah and Amos pushed Jean-Marc to a sitting position against a large oak and stood guard at a distance, to avoid his odor.

The black-robed bailiff entered the gray, unadorned main room of the Town Meeting Hall and faced the rows of benches. He slammed his thick, five-foot long oak staff into the floor and cried in a loud voice, "Oyez! Oyez! Oyez! The Magistrate Court for the Colony of Massachusetts Bay, His Honor, Judge Samuel Sewall presiding, is now in session! God save Good King William. All desiring to be heard by this honorable Court stand to be recognized!"

Everyone hoping to have their case heard that day stood and one by one the bailiff called each forward. He asked the nature of their business, if all parties to the case were present, if there were witnesses to be heard and similar questions. More than one supplicant was sent away, lacking necessary paperwork or evidence, or if one of the litigants were not present. Converse began to worry that his case would not be heard that day, if at all.

After the bailiff spoke with each person asking to be heard by the court, he left the room. An hour passed before he returned. He called out the same court opening. The people stood, and the judge entered the room. He sat behind a large wooden table. Judge Sewall was a small, elderly man. He wore a black robe and an ill-fitting, white woolen wig.

Although he was the first in line that morning, Converse watched as case after case was heard by the court. Morning became afternoon and approached evening before the bailiff called out, "Captain John Converse of the town of Wells!"

Converse jumped to his feet and said, "Here, your Honor."

"Approach the bench, Captain" directed the judge. "It says here that we have an issue concerning indentures."

"We do, your Honor."

"And what would that issue be?"

"As Your Honor well knows, the town of Wells was attacked by a band of savages over a fortnight ago. A Christian man from France traveled with the savages and took part in the attempted sack of our town—"

The judge interrupted, "Is he a Christian from France, or a papist?"

"I believe him to be a papist, Your Honor."

"Then be clear," the judge scolded. "Not all white men are Christians."

"Yes ... your honor."

In Wells people deferred to Converse. He came to Boston to meet with the governor. He considered himself an important man. Now he was, again, being spoken down to. He was not accustomed to being kept waiting or being interrupted. Converse was shaken.

"During the ... um ... the attack our militia assembled. We ... um, repelled the savages. Afterwards we found him, the Frenchman, dressed like a savage lying among the dead and the ... the injured." Converse looked down at his feet and took a deep breath to calm himself. "We took him prisoner and we seek to ... uh, to sell him into servitude to defray the expenses our town will, uh ... will incur as we rebuild from this savage attack. Him being a Christian—"

"Ahem!"

Converse reddened and looked up at the ceiling. He drew another deep breath and looked back at the judge.

"I'm sorry, Your Honor. Him being ... uh, being a white man in league with savages, we, thought trebling the usual seven years of indenture was ... would be fitting."

"I assume you have witnesses who will attest to your account."

Converse thought. *When wasn't my word good enough for anyone?* He said, "I have, your honor. Two yeomen from Wells, members of our milit—"

"Would that not be one and the same, Captain?" interrupted the judge.

"Yes, Your Honor, that it would be. Our yeomen serve in our militia."

"So, I would hope," the judge sighed.

"The two, they sit outside the court, holding the ... the villain."

"Bailiff, bring these men into the Court."

The bailiff left the room, returning with Hezekiah, Amos, and Jean-Marc.

Who is this man? He cannot be the king. Why am I here? What is happening? Do these peasants mock me?

"Yeomen, was this prisoner taken as part of the attack by savages on your town?"

Both men nodded their assent. Hezekiah said, "He was, Your Honor."

"Was he seen taking part in the attack?"

"I don't know direct, Your Honor, but he was found in a savage's clothes lying injured after the attack," Hezekiah said.

"How do you know that this man is French?"

"He jabbers it at us when he wants to be heard."

"I see. And what say you, Frenchman?"

Jean-Marc understood little that was taking place, but he understood that they were talking about him, and this was his opportunity to speak. After his mistreatment on the journey from Wells and his harsh captivity in Boston and now being mocked, he looked at the judge and growled, *"Anglais"* and spat toward the bench.

Before he could say more, the bailiff slammed his staff into the back of Jean-Marc's legs, dropping him to his knees. A strike to his back drove him face forward to the floor. The bailiff shoved a foot on the back of his neck, pinning him down. When he tried to get up, the bailiff pushed his foot harder, forcing Jean-Marc's face to the floor again. He tried to speak, but another push of the bailiff's foot stopped him. Furious tears welled in his eyes.

Judge Sewall stared at Jean-Marc for an extended period before speaking. "Bailiff, remove this man from the room. The Court sees he has all of the manners expected of his nation."

The bailiff, Hezekiah, and Amos pulled Jean-Marc off the floor and dragged him outside.

"Captain, the papers you request are called indentures. An indenture binds the person named in the document to servitude for the term of the indenture. When an indenture is granted, the holder of said indenture has the right to assign this servitude by sale to another. Such an indenture for this man is hereby granted. The traditional term of indenture for indebtedness is seven years. Recognizing the heinous nature of this man's outrages, your requested trebling of his servitude is granted. The bailiff is to prepare these documents upon the conclusion of this hearing. Indenture to take effect as soon as the Court's signature and the seal of this colony are affixed there unto. So let it be written. So let it be done." Judge Sewall hammered the case closed.

*****

The indenture in hand, Converse went to see Goodman Smith, who was not in his office. Smith's clerk suggested he might be at the Red Lion. Converse found him sitting before the inn's fire, enjoying a tankard of beer.

"Good eve, Goodman Smith."

Smith turned from the fire and said, "Good eve, Captain Converse. What news?"

"I have the indenture papers for twenty-one years."

Smith held out his hand. "I'll see it, if you please."

The captain handed Smith the indenture.

Looking at the papers, "Yes. Yes. All is in order. How do you wish to sell, direct to me or on consignment for a fee?"

"I've seen enough of your fees. What'll you pay for him?"

"As I've said, he's not of best quality. Understands but little English, speaks less. French and consorting with savages, he's a threat and an escape risk. His wounds may not heal well. I'll pay six pounds, six shillings and absorb the room and sup he's accumulated."

"You'll pay a fair sight above that. Men pay eleven or twelve pounds to buy a servant for seven years. You'll get him for three times that."

"True sir, but eleven pounds buys a strapping one who speaks the king's own tongue, has no need to heal and's not likely to run."

"Our Dutch king speaks but little English. I'll wager the Frencher knows as much."

Smith laughed. "You have me there, Captain. English is none too familiar to our new king. For more than six pounds six, and remember, I am forgiving your debt to me, you need a servant that speaks the queen's tongue, if not the king's. But, the point's made. He speaks but little English, and I'll need to sell him at some profit for myself."

"Fourteen pounds and you forgive the board."

"For that you can keep him. I'll give eight, not a shilling more."

"I can't go back to Wells with less than ten pounds — "

"Then don't go back. You'll take eight pounds, or you'll pay my fees and leave."

Again, Converse felt slighted. "Then eight it is."

Smith stood. "I'll need your mark as transfer. I have both pen and silver in my office. Please come with me."

They walked the two blocks to Goodman Smith's office where the transfer was completed. Feeling cheated, Captain Converse went back to the Three Cranes for the night. He and his men would leave for Wells in the morning.

Smith took Obadiah and his other man to Jean-Marc's cell. "Release him and stand aside. 'Tis time his training's begun." He looked at Jean-Marc and spoke louder. "Boy, do you understand me?"

Jean-Marc nodded. *"Oui ... je comprends."*

"Good. I've just purchased your indenture. That means you are to be my servant for the next twenty-one years unless I sell you to another. Whether these years pass well or ill is up to you. I'll treat an obedient servant well, but with servants as with children, a spared rod spoils them. You should remember this point. Do you understand?"

What does he say? Jean-Marc nodded again.

"Good, then let's begin."

He handed a long, flexible stick to Obadiah. "Thrash him well with this. Ten strokes will do. Welts but don't slice him. We need him ready to be sold."

The two armed men grabbed Jean-Marc and tied him to an iron ring mounted on the wall opposite the cells. He winced at pain in his shoulder. Obadiah stood next to Jean-Marc and raised the stick.

What did I do? Why are they beating me? He screamed, *"Non, non!* No! *Arretez!* Stop!"

The first strike whipped across his back, buckling his knees. He threw his head back and screamed. The next stroke found the same place, as did the third raising a large welt. The fourth stroke fell and then the fifth. The stick had a whip's sting. The pain was exquisite, but in expert hands it tore no skin.

Tears filled Jean-Marc's eyes. His mouth dried. He shouted and swore at the men. Then they stopped. His head dropped forward between his arms.

Goodman Smith said, "Good. That's well begun. Unbind him. We'll continue in the morning."

Smith's servants untied Jean-Marc, dropped him on the dirty straw in his cell and left.

His back throbbed. He cried in anger and despair. *How have I sunk to this? If God made me a noble in France, why does he make md an animal here? Will I ever be free again? Francois could not wish this on me. If I could somehow get a message to him, surely, he would save me.* Past midnight, sleep came.

Early the next morning the same three men returned to his cell. Goodman Smith spoke, "Good morning, boy. I trust our lesson was well learned. Have you any doubt that I'll have you flogged?" Obadiah slapped a switch into the palm of his hand.

Wide-eyed, Jean-Marc shook his head and said, "Non! Non! No!"

"Good. Then the lesson's well learned. I am also merciful to those who obey me. Feed him well. Clean him up. Provide him with decent clothing and bring him to me. We have a customer."

Goodman Smith left. The other guard left, locking the cell behind him. Obadiah spoke, "Understand me, boy?"

Jean-Marc looked down and nodded.

"Good, then learn well. Goodman Smith's rod is heavy, but he'll treat you fair if you serve him well. We're going to give you water to clean yourself, then clothe and feed you. After you eat, we'll bring you to the Master. He'll have work for you. Do this well and all's well. Do this ill, and you'll be beat again. Understand me?"

He nodded again, which seemed to please the giant.

The other guard returned. He carried a bowl of water for Jean-Marc to clean himself and clean clothing made of coarse, homespun wool. Jean-Marc washed as best he could then put on the white shirt, green breeches, white stockings, and brown coat. All of these were too large for him. They hung on his body.

"You'll fatten into them soon enough," the man said. He left Jean-Marc with Obadiah, who told him not to forget his hat, which was too large, or his shoes, which were too small. Jean-Marc looked like a poor Bostonian. The other returned with a large bowl of porridge, a loaf of bread and a tankard of beer. "Eat all of this, even if you think it's too much. You'll be needing it."

"Sank you." He ate it all.

Then Obadiah said, "You're to go with James and me to Goodman Smith at the Red Lion. You'll not be tied, but know you'll not outrun us. There's no escape. Try to run and I'll have to beat you again, worse than yesterday. Come peaceable and you'll work the day without problem. Understand?"

"*Oui* ... yes," he nodded. Jean-Marc's understanding was partial at best, but he did not want to anger the big man.

The cell was unlocked. Bracketed by the two large men Jean-Marc walked the crowded street to the Red Lion.

Inside, Goodman Smith and another man were sitting behind tankards at a table. Smith spoke, "What's your name, boy?"

Jean-Marc just stared.

"Unless you want another flogging, what is your name, boy?"

He thought he understood. "Jean-Marc Bompeau."

"Well, John, meet Goodman Adams. He's one of our town's master brewers. His apprentice died of the pox last year, and he's not found another. Work well and he'll buy your paper. A better place than his you'll not find. By the time your indenture's up, you'll be a master brewer yourself. Not many who survive indenture do so with a trade." Smith smiled and turned to his servants. "Obadiah, you and James go with Goodman Adams and John. See that he works well or flog him, without coming to see me. If he works well, he may not even return to his cell this night." He turned to face Jean-Marc. "Do you understand, John?"

"*Oui* ... yes, under ... stand."

Goodman Adams led James, Obadiah and Jean-Marc to his brewery. Behind it was a large cart loaded with sacks of grain each weighing close to four stones.

"John," said Goodman Adams, "these sacks are to be carried up that ladder and stacked in the loft. It's a fair morning's work. Be done by mid-day or return to Goodman Smith."

Adams went into the shop. Obadiah stepped in front of Jean-Marc. "Boy, I want to be sure you understand this. You have to move all those bags," he pointed to the bags then to the ladder, "up that ladder and stack them proper or you'll be sent back. If you're sent back, the Master will have me cane you again. Do you understand?"

"*Oui ... Oui*, yes ... *je* understand," Jean-Marc nodded.

"See that you do or you'll get another thrashing."

Obadiah and James sat on a nearby bench. Jean-Marc winced as he lifted the first sack, carried it up the ladder and placed it on the floor of the loft. He wasn't sure exactly what was happening, but he was clear that if he didn't complete this task he would be beaten. Despite his pain, Jean-Marc moved and neatly stacked the sacks well before mid-day. When he finished, Obadiah called Goodman Adams who was pleased.

"Good work, John," he said, handing Jean-Marc a tankard of beer. "You may do well. Drink this and I'll have another task for you. Do that and I think I'll keep you."

Jean-Marc smiled and drank. The other three men joined him. When they finished, Adams led him to a large pile of wood. He pointed at the wood and said, "I need this wood split, and I expect it split by dark. Do you understand me?"

He nodded and said, "Yes," in his thick French accent. He picked up the heavy ax. *I understand more than these fools know. They just gave me a weapon. I'm about to be free.* Then he saw James and Obadiah step away from each other, draw swords, and stand with their weapons at the ready.

So, they've had training. To attack one, I'd have to turn my back to the other. For now, I'll wait. My time to escape will come.

He lifted the heavy splitting ax and brought it down on a piece of oak. It did not split. He hit it again and again. His injured shoulder, hand, and back all hurt. He labored hard but split little more than half the pile as the sun set. He cringed with fear when Goodman Adams returned.

"It's not complete, but it's a game enough effort. I'll feed him and show him to his bed. Obadiah, if you'll stand guard to see that he doesn't run, I think he'll do."

Jean-Marc and Obadiah were brought into the kitchen where a young woman served them large plates of meat and roasted vegetables, thick slices of bread and large tankards of beer. They both ate past full.

Goodman Adams returned to the kitchen and spoke to the girl. "Chastity, show our new boy to his bed in the cellar."

She motioned that Jean-Marc should follow her down a flight of stairs into a musty fieldstone cellar. A small space between the brewing supplies contained a bed with a rag-filled pillow and a thick quilt. The bed was pushed up against the base of the chimney. Heat from the cook fire upstairs radiated from the chimney's stones. He would not be cold tonight.

Chastity said to him, "They say you're French and understand little but hear me if you can. Goodman Adams'll not beat you the way Goodman Smith will. And Goody Adams is a fair woman. A body can do well worse than serving here. Those that try to run always get caught and their beatings for't teaches them to not try again. Here you'll be well fed and bedded. A servant can't hope for much more."

Struggling to understand, Jean-Marc smiled and said, "Sank you." *I have not eaten so well since the day we laughed at the tavern.*

She left, and he fell face first into the bed.

This is the best bed I have had since I left France. He smiled and fell asleep.

*****

Before dawn, he heard sounds in the kitchen. He got out of bed and climbed the stairs. Chastity and another girl were preparing breakfast. The other girl said, "You're the new boy. Make use of yourself and fill the wood bin. There's work to be done."

"Geet wood?"

"Yes. If you want to eat get wood for the fire."

Whole body's stiff from yesterday. Shoulder hurts. What do they expect of me? He gritted his teeth and walked to the wood-pile. Several trips to the wood-pile filled the bin. When he finished, the girls served him a large bowl of porridge with molasses and poured him a tankard of beer. He sat and ate.

I'm better off here than I've been in a long time. I'll bide my time before I escape. First, I need a plan.

Before he finished, Goodman Adams came into the kitchen. He smiled when he saw Jean-Marc. He went to the rear door and called out, "Obadiah, the boy's made it through the night without trying to run. My guess is he'll do. Tell your master he can stay. If there's no problems for a fortnight, I'll keep him."

Chapter Six
Beer

"It was a wise man who invented beer."
Plato

He smiled. This is good, no? Jean-Marc dropped his spoon and watched Goodman Adams. *I cannot go back to that dungeon. I must understand him.*

"Today we work on malting, John."

He talks to me, no? What does he say?

Adams turned to the girls, "Abigail, show him around while I eat. See that he knows the brew-house and kilns. After I'm done eating I need to roast so see that he has a good fire ready for me."

"Yes, Goodman," one of the girls answered.

Adams went into the dining room.

The girl he called Abigail crossed the room and leaned close to Jean-Marc. Her voice was quiet but firm. "You finish double fast. After I serve the family, I'll walk you around. But pay close attention. My chores keep me busy enough. I'll not wait while you finish, and I've not the time to show you things twice. Do you understand me?"

Jean-Marc thought he understood, nodded that he did and hurried to finish his meal.

Abigail placed a large white bowl of porridge on a tray with bread and a pitcher of beer. She carried the tray through a swinging door out of the kitchen. Moments later she returned. "Put your dishes by the wash tub and come with me."

Jean-Marc jumped from his seat to follow.

"The dishes. Get the dishes." She pointed at his bowl and mug. "I'll not pick up after you." Then she pointed to a large tub half filled with water. "Put them in the wash tub over there."

He put his dishes in the tub and hurried to follow the girl out of the house.

She led him into a large, brown-painted building between the house and barn. "This is the brew-house." She opened the door into a

100

large room dominated by kilns. "Here's the malting room. You'll do most of your work in here. Malting'll keep you busy."

"No *comprends,* malting?"

"The Master'll show you that. Pay close attention. Now follow me here." She led him to another room. A firebox, stone chimney, and two large brick ovens formed one wall. Rows of oversized buckets lined the opposite wall. Between them, against a third wall, there were three large racks filled with shallow trays.

"The barley sprouts and the malt's dried and toasted in here. Goodman Adams'll see to that, but 'twill be yours to build the fire and keep the heat right. You know where the wood is. Easiest to bring out some coals from the cook fire and build yours from those. Be sure 'tis ready for the Master."

Jean-Marc turned to get in front of her. He looked concerned. "I have not start fire before."

Abigail put her hands on her hips and looked at the ceiling. "Good Lord preserve us! The Master's bought a simpleton." She looked at Jean-Marc but pointed in the direction of the ovens. Without realizing it, she raised her voice, as if talking louder would make him understand. "By the oven is a box of kindling, small pieces of wood." She pointed.

"Small wood, *oui,*" he nodded.

"Splittin' it from the bigger pieces is your chore. You understand?"

"Make small wood, *oui.*"

"You bring coals from the kitchen fire and put them in here." She pointed to the oven's firebox and picked up a bellows made from wood and leather. "You use this to blow the coals into flame and then, little by little, add bigger wood."

"Coals?"

"Watch me but watch well. I'll not show you again."

He followed the girl to the lean-to where she piled wood on his arms. "Bring that to the brew-house then meet me in the kitchen."

"Kitchen *oui* ... yes." He carried the wood into the brew-house and hurried into the kitchen. The girl used a set of tongs to pull several coals from the fire and dropped them into a small iron pot.

"See that my pot comes back from the shed. I've no need to be chasing after you for the things I need."

"Pot back. *Je comprends, oui.*"

Abigail led him back into the brew-house. Using her apron, she tilted the pot into the firebox, dumped the coals, and put the pot on the floor. She took some wood from the kindling box and piled it on the coals. "You watching?"

"*Oui*, yes, I watch."

She pointed the bellows at the coals and pumped. As if by magic, the coals burst into flames. She pumped a little longer, then picked up some of the smaller pieces of wood and added them to the fire.

"A fire's built slow. Wood's added bit by bit, little pieces then bigger. Understand?"

"*Oui* ... yes, yes."

"'Tis easier to keep a fire than start one, so keep it burning even when's not needed."

"Yes, keep fire."

"The fire mustn't be too hot when Goodman Adams is drying the barley to malt but needs be hotter when he roasts. He'll show you the fire he wants when he's ready for it. Keep adding wood to this. If you run out, go get more."

Jean-Marc nodded.

"You tend to the fire. The Master'll be out soon. I've work to do." She wiped her hands on her apron, then used it as a potholder to pick up the iron pot and hurried back to the kitchen, talking to herself.

Jean-Marc managed to build a large fire by the time Goodman Adams finished his breakfast and joined him.

"Good, you've a fire." He reached a bare arm into the oven, counting to five before pulling it out. "Ovens'll soon be hot enough. First chore you need learn is to soak barley. Come with me."

Adams led Jean-Marc to the malting room where he described the process of soaking barley so it would sprout before being spread on shallow trays to grow. Jean-Marc spent much of the day drawing water and carrying it thirty yards from the well to the brew house, where he poured it into buckets filled with barley. It was hard work on a hot day.

When this was done, he had to stir the barley, pour off the chaff floating in the water and refill the buckets. His injured shoulder throbbed. His hands blistered. At last, he put the water bucket back on the stool beside the well. Wiping the back of his hand across his forehead, he walked to the ovens where Goodman Smith was roasting sprouted barley.

"I done, Master."

"Good. The fire's cooling. Bring in more wood and build it up again. I'll be back to show you how to spread the barley for germination after it's soaked."

Adams left the brew-house and went into the cook kitchen. Jean-Marc walked to the wood pile. With blistered hands, he carried wood into the brew-house and built up the fire. Then he dropped on to a stool and waited for Goodman Adams to return.

"I see a roaring fire and plenty of wood in the box. Nicely done, John. I know you're just learning, so little's done today but I see you're trying."

Did he just say little was done? No, I could not have understood him.

Adams continued. "I can see you'll do much better tomorrow. Follow me."

He walked to a series of wooden racks. Some were filled with trays of germinated barley that was to grow until the sprouts could be roasted to make malt. Adams poured water off of a bucket of barley. He explained each step as he brought a bucket to one of the racks filled with empty trays. He spread the sprouted barley on the tray, covering it with a wet cloth. He put the empty bucket against the far wall.

"Now you do it."

Jean-Marc looked at two rows of buckets filled with water and barley. Adams had taken a bucket from the back row against the wall. Jean-Marc took the next bucket in line.

"Good, John. Each row of bucket's a day's work. The seeds you just set soaking will sit for two days just like these seeds have already. The row in front'll be ready tomorrow. Now empty the bucket onto the tray and cover it with the damp cloths."

He drained the bucket, spread the seeds out on the tray, covered the tray with a cloth and slid it onto the rack Adams had used.

"Well done, John. Now do the rest of them. When you're finished," Adams took a small wooden rake from a hook on the wall, "take this and rake all the other trays to turn the seeds, then wet and replace their cloths." Adams demonstrated as he talked. "Do you understand me?"

"Do that, too. *Je comprends.*"

"Good. Show me." Adams watched as Jean-Marc repeated the process. When he was certain Jean-Marc understood his tasks, he smiled and said, "You finish that." Then he walked to the larger of the ovens and used tongs to pull a broad shallow pan to the oven's edge. The roasting grain smelled sweet and toasty. He turned the grain with a wooden paddle and examined its golden color. "Not yet," he muttered pushing the tray back into the oven. Adams left the brew-house and went back into the cook kitchen.

A few minutes later the girl who showed him the brew-house that morning came out carrying a tray. Jean-Marc looked up from his chores, wiped the sweat from his face and smiled at her.

"The Master ate a while back, and he's come for more. He said nothing of feeding you, but I'll wager you'd eat a bit." She returned his smile as she placed the tray on a small work table. "There's meat, bread and beer for you."

"Sank you." He wiped his face again then wiped his hands on his breeches as he walked to the tray. His sweat-soaked shirt clung to his chest and back. Abigail noticed sweat running down his neck and arms.

"Take your fill fast, before Goodman returns. He'll not be happy, you eating, instead of working during the day."

"I eat fast." He poured and drained a tankard of beer then took some meat.

"You really French?" Abigail sat on the stool.

"I am." He smiled, bit into the meat and wiped his face again.

"I never met a Frencher before. Your talk's strange, but you look like us."

"Angland and France, they be not so far apart, yes? Zee people, zay be same, yes? Only our kings be different, no?"

"No, I mean, yes ... I guess so." She stood, pulled a cloth from the apron strings behind her back, and walked to him. "You're soaked." She wiped his face and neck with the cloth. He reached up and took the cloth then wiped his hands and arms.

He looked into her face and said, "Sank you."

Abigail's face reddened. She reached for her cloth. "You'd best finish quick or the Master'll have both our hides."

"I eat fast."

They sat in silence while Jean-Marc finished the food. When he was done, Abigail straightened the things on the tray. He reached out, touched her wrist and looked into her face.

"Sank you again. How you are called ... Abigail?"

Her face got redder. "Yes."

He watched her hurry away.

Afternoon turned into evening. Goodman Adams dried and roasted malt while Jean-Marc loaded tray after tray with barley, moved bucket after bucket between rooms and carried water from the well again and again. With darkness nearing, Adams sent him into the yard to split wood and went into the house for his supper. Just as the sun disappeared below the horizon, the kitchen door opened.

"John, come join Abigail and me for supper," Chastity called into the yard. Jean-Marc was sure he understood her. He returned the ax to the tool shed, wiped his hands on his breeches and walked into the house.

The kitchen smelled wonderful. Abigail put a bowl of hot biscuits on the table to go with a plate of roasted ox and root vegetables. Chastity poured beer into tankards. She looked up, "Run those hands through some water before you sit at our table. Splash some on your face and body too. You smell worse than you look."

"Haff you leenins I can use to clean myself? Perhaps some perfume?"

"What need would you have for linen? There's a bowl of water by the tub. Splash yourself with that and wipe with the towel. And where would you expect two indentures to get perfume? We're servants just like you. We was sold for our labor. If we could afford perfume we wouldn't been sold, now would we?"

"You are right—"

Abigail cut him off. "Look at your hands. The blisters are bleeding. Let me see to them."

Taking one of his bloody hands in hers, she led him across the room. She waited while he rinsed off and dried. Then she put a bowl under his hands, made a cup with her right hand and poured water over his wounds. She patted his hands dry and wrapped them in clean cloths. His hands, already much larger than hers, looked immense in their bandages. "Come to the table, John." She led him to a chair and filled a plate for him. "I'll cut your food," she said. "Using a knife will hurt with hands like that."

He smiled at the thought of this girl cutting his food for him. *I was just splitting and stacking wood with the same bloody hands and no one cared.* He reached for a biscuit and winced at the pain in his shoulder.

"What's wrong?" Abigail asked. "Did you hurt your arm too?"

"*Mon bras?*" He touched his arm. "My arm, no?"

Both girls nodded.

"My arm? *Je me suis blesse* ... I was hurt when I was made the *prisonnier. You comprends?*"

Chastity nodded and said, "You were hurt when you were a prisoner."

"Yes. Then when the mens from Wells, they beat me because of the *indien* that killed people at the *taverne*."

"They beat you because Indians killed people?" Chastity sounded incredulous.

"It will be fine."

"It'll be fine after I put a poultice on it," Abigail said. "You two eat. I'll make the poultice now."

Jean-Marc and Chastity ate. They talked with each other as best they could while Abigail boiled an onion wrapped in a cloth with

106

mustard seed and pepper. When the onion was soft, she pulled the cloth from the water, squeezed it dry with a towel and brought it to the table. She loosened the laces in the front of Jean-Marc's shirt and placed her hand on his shoulder.

"Is this where it hurts?"

He reached inside his shirt, took her hand and moved it toward his neck. "Here she hurts."

Abigail placed the poultice on that spot. She threaded the cloth under his arm and over his shoulder, tying it in place. "That should help."

He smiled at her gentle touch. It had been so very long since a woman touched him. Abigail smiled at him, then blushed again. She sat on the far side of the table, looked into her plate, and ate without speaking. The warmth from the poultice felt good on his shoulder.

When they finished eating, he asked, "What do I now?"

"You can go to bed!" Chastity sounded frustrated. "Abigail and I have to clean the kitchen, prepare for the morning's meal and bank the fire. Your day's done. Ours has yet another hour."

He got up from the table feeling that Chastity expected him to feel guilty for going to bed after his long hard day. He did not. In his cellar, he took off his shoes, stockings, and breeches, allowing his long shirt-tail to drop to his knees. He lay on top of the quilt that covered his bed and fell into a dreamless sleep.

*****

Jean-Marc's servitude developed into a routine. Every day he got up before dawn and went into the kitchen. Abigail, up an hour before him, would be preparing the morning's meal. He sat at the large wooden table, and Abigail served him an ample breakfast.

She seemed to make a point of sitting beside him, even if only for a few moments every morning. They would sit and talk about little things. Abigail was fascinated when she learned Jean-Marc had been a noble in France. One morning she asked, "What must it be like, from being a noble to being a servant now?"

He folded his hands in front of his mouth and thought. Then he said, "In my country there are three *Sociétés*, the *Oratores*, how you say the *Clergé?*"

"The clergy?"

"*Oui*, yes, those who pray, the *Bellatores*, these are the nobles, those who fight and the *Laboratories*, those who work. We were teached, each man, his place was willed by God. In my family, the men, we were to be *Guerrier*, ah … fighters. The *Laboratories*, these we saw like oxen, beasts of burden."

Abigail looked shocked. "So am I nothing but an–"

"This is my point. Now, I am a *Laboratore*. Has God changed his mind? I think this is not so. I think men, they are put in their *Sociétés* by other men, not by God, and each does what he can. The boy I was in France, he was not so good as the man I am becoming here. In France you would have been no one to me." He stopped. Tears welled in his eyes, "Now…"

She took his hand and started to speak, but Chastity burst into the room. Jean-Marc lowered his eyes and shook his head.

Every day, soon after he came up from his cellar, Chastity came down from the room she and Abigail shared in the attic. Now all conversation would be about Chastity. Somehow, even as a servant, she found a way to make herself the center of attention. Goodman Adams' customers all noticed Chastity, who did nothing to discourage them.

Somewhat older than Abigail, she was slender, taller than most women, just over five feet two inches with light brown hair and eyes.

This Chastity, she is prettier than Abigail. Why do I resent her when she comes down? She is brash, no? Everything changes when she comes in.

Jean-Marc looked from Chastity to Abigail and thought, *This little one, she confuses me. She sits always in the chair beside mine. It can be no accident her hand touches mine and her leg brushes mine so often. Yet she rejects my every advance.*

Abigail seemed a bit younger than Jean-Marc. She was about average height at four feet eleven inches and was quite thin. Her dark hair contrasted with her pale skin and blue eyes. If a customer paid attention to her, Abigail would redden and smile. Then she would excuse herself as soon as she could.

Why do I treasure my time with Abigail? Chastity, any man would notice. This little one, who sees her? But she sees things others do not. She had no need to bring me something to drink my first day here ... or to wrap my hands. About her, there is more than meets the eye, no?

More and more he resented Chastity's loud intrusions into their quiet moments.

*****

Most days, after breakfast, Jean-Marc split wood. The Adams children often played behind the wood pile, while he worked.

This place they play in, it is so small. Why do they not play by the house?

The older girl, perhaps eight, often played dolls with her small sister and brother. The bigger boys ran and wrestled.

I remember such days. I even played with Francois. The memory made him smile. *All was not bad when I was a boy. They were better times.*

Day after day, he would watch the children and smile.

One morning the older boys played sword-fight while the others watched. Jean-Marc laughed at the boys and said, "You must know that is not how to use the *epee*, no?"

The boys stopped their play. The larger boy asked, "What's the *epee*?"

"*Epee... sabre*? How do you say this in Anglish?"

The bigger boy said, "Sword?"

"Ah, *mais oui*, sword. That is not how one must use the sword."

"You know how to use a sword?" The boy sounded impressed.

"I do. Does your *pere*, your papa, not show you to use the sword?"

"No," the boy said. "But he has a big one."

"This, I have seen," Jean-Marc said. "Do you see, the sword, it is just a big *couteau*, oh, how do you say it ... a knife?"

"Yes, but you don't fight with knives."

"Oh, but of course you can fight with the knife. But fighting with the knife, is not so very much like how to fight with the sword."

The boys walked closer to Jean-Marc. The older girl stopped playing dolls with the younger children and listened.

"How are you called," he asked the boys.

The bigger one said, "I'm Daniel."

The smaller one said, "I'm Jonathan."

Jean-Marc smiled. Looking at the smaller boy, he said, "Such a big *nom* for such a little boy, no?"

The boy reddened. "And the others," Jean-Marc said, pointing at the three sitting children.

The older girl stood. "My name's Ruth. This is Esther and Ezra."

"*Enchante*, Ruthy,"

"*Enchante?*"

"*Enchante*, I do not know the Anglish word. How do you say, by meeting you, I am made happy?"

"Do you mean, pleased to meet you?"

"So, I am pleased to meet you, Ruthy."

"Why do you call me Ruthy? My name is Ruth," the girl said, moving closer.

"Do not come too close to where I work. I do not want that you should be hurt," Jean-Marc said as he put another piece of wood on the block and slammed his ax into it. "I must do my work, too." He picked up the split pieces and threw them to a pile of split wood. "Why do I call you Ruthy? Does not Ruthy sound ... uh ... pretty enough, for such a pretty little girl?"

"But my name is Ruth."

"*Mais oui*, but is not Ruthy more pretty? And your brother, how is his *nom*, Jonathan?" Ruth nodded. "Such a *nom* is too big for him. Him I will call Jon-Jon." Jean-Marc turned back to the boys, "So, Jon-Jon, do you like to learn to use the sword in the fight?

The boy came to him, extending his stick to Jean-Marc. "No, you keep your *arme*. I will use, how are you called, boy?" He looked to the larger boy.

That boy stepped closer, extending his stick. "Daniel."

"I will use Dannyboy's *arme*." He too the stick and twirled it in figure-eights. Then he raised it toward Jonathan and said, *"En Garde."* Jonathan copied his actions. "Now, fight with me." The boy drew his stick back, to swing it at Jean-Marc's. Before he could do that, Jean-Marc lunged forward, pushing his stick into the boy's stomach. "The *victoire,* it is mine, no?"

"No fair! You gave me no chance to hit your sword."

"How do you say this is not *juste*? This is how the sword fight is done. I do not want to hit your sword. I want to cut you, no?"

Jonathan looked down, "I suppose."

"Here, Dannyboy," he handed the stick to the other boy. "You try with Jon-Jon. Do not try to hit *epees.* Try to cut him when you fight."

The boys raised their sticks and hit them together, as they did before. Then Daniel swung his stick toward Johnathan's, but pulled it back, missing his brother's stick and slammed it forward, into his stomach. Jean-Marc smiled and cried out, "That you did nice, no? You do not win by hitting *epees.* You win by cutting the other. But, you make another mistake."

"I did?"

"You did. The *epee,* the sword, it is just a big knife. You remember, no? When cutting meat at supper, do you hit the meat with the knife, or do you pull the knife on the meat to cut it?"

"I pull it. 'Tis how meat's sliced."

"What is the man you fight but meat that tries to give you harm. When you hit that man with the ... the sword, you must push the sword on him, but also you must pull the sword to you. That is the way you will cut him. Hit him with the sword and he will say *aie*, but you will no cut him. You must hit him and pull on the sword, if you want to cut him."

He picked up another log to split. The boys resumed their fight. That day, Jean-Marc showed them how thrust, parry, and block a strike with a sword. He also spent more time playing with the boys than Goodman Adams ever had.

"Now, I must carry this wood into the brew house. You must fight with the sword each day. You must learn to do this, so you can defend your *belle* sister, Ruthy. You must never let someone do harm to you sister. That is *une obligation*, I think the word is the same in Anglish, no? It is an obligation of honor for the gentleman to protect his sister."

Jean-Marc tousled the boys' hair, then started tossing wood into a wheel-barrow. The children went back to their play. But every day, the children came to play near him. The boys became skilled at sword fighting with their sticks. Ruth was thrilled by stories about the beautiful women in King Louis' court. In return, the children taught Jean-Marc English.

After several weeks, Daniel hit Jonathan on the hand with his stick. The smaller boy dropped his stick and began to cry. Jean-Marc knelt and hugged him, rubbing his sore hand. He said, "The real sword, it would have the hand-guard, so your hand, it will not be hit. You must not cry my little—"

"Why are you hugging my son," Goodman Adams demanded, walking toward Jean-Marc. The children looked startled and moved away from the men.

"His hand, it was hurt when they played the sword-fight."

"And for this you hug him?"

Jean-Marc stood and lowered his eyes. "I am sorry Goodman, if I should not hug him, I will not."

"You must not!" Adams looked down on the smaller man. "Children are not to be hugged. It spoils them. How will I break their wills if people go about hugging them?"

"You would break your childrens?" Jean-Marc sounded incredulous.

"'Tis a parent's duty. Children are born willful. We have to break their will to make them better people."

"I do not understand. You would break your childrens. Do you not love your childrens?"

"I would break their will. I must make them learn to do as I would have them, not as they would please. Because I love them, I must break them of their willfulness. Children are born sinners. If I break not their wills, they'll be damned."

"It is not my place to question, Goodman," Jean-Marc said, looking down, "But I do not think little Jon-Jon, he will be damned. He is a good little boy."

"And many a good little boy's damned."

"I am sorry. I do not understand, Goodman. Why would God damn a good little boy?"

"God damns most. He grants salvation only to the elect few."

"Did God not make these childrens?"

"Of course, He did."

"Again, Sir, I do not understand. If God, He makes the childrens, would he not make childrens He likes?"

Adams went to speak but stopped. He thought for a moment, then said, "I've seen you play with them. At first it troubled me, but it seems there's little harm to it. So long as your work is done, I'll not stop you playing with them. This hugging bothers me, though. I'll think on that."

He turned and went into the house. He found his wife sitting before the fire, in the parlor. "I've waited to say something on this. The children like John."

"I see no harm there," she said, looking up from her needlework.

"They go by him while he works, and he plays with them."

"He what? He needs to attend to his work, not play with children."

"That he does. His work gets done, but he finds time for the children. I'm not sure 'tis a bad thing."

"I'll not have them spoiled—"

"Nor I, but they are happy by him." He glanced back toward the yard.

"Better unhappy, better beat, than damned." Estelle put the cloth in her lap and moved in the chair, as if trying to find a more comfortable position. "Is he improper?"

"Today, Daniel hit Jonathan's hand with a stick and Jonathan cried."

"Did you beat Daniel?"

"No. There was no intent. 'Twas done in play, but John hugged Jonathan to soothe him."

Her head snapped back. "Did you beat John for that?"

"I did not that either. I know you speak often with your sister, but beatings are needed less than she would have you think. And the boy was soothed. I think he liked the hug."

"You spoil those children, Jeremiah."

"And there's those that tell me I spoil you. Would you have me beat you more?"

"The circumstances are different. My will's been broke. Theirs not."

Adams sat in the wooden chair opposite hers. "Mayhap their's broke enough. I think God may be pleased with that which He made."

Estelle just looked at her husband. She could think of nothing to say.

*****

The children played near Jean-Marc while he worked every day. When his work was done, they came to be with him in the kitchen, while he ate, or while he sat with Abigail and Chastity. The women taught them how to cook or mend. Ruth particularly enjoyed needle-work. Abigail and Chastity began baking special sweets for the children to eat while they visited them in the kitchen. The servants enjoyed the children's company. The children enjoyed the kind attention the servants were happy to give them and their stern parents did not.

Goody Adams was not sure this was good. She often complained to her husband, who ignored her.

*****

Seven months passed. Jean-Marc chopped more wood and drew more water than he would have believed possible. He also learned much. Adams trusted him to soak the barley for malting, although he always roasted and raked the malt himself. Jean-Marc knew how to make the malt mash and boil it to make the liquid, sweet wort. He could identify, collect, and dry the hops that grew wild in the woods around Boston. He knew roughly when and how much hops, or if making ale how much of each spice, to add in order to bitter the wort. Still, hopping or spicing was another task Adams always did himself. Jean-Marc also knew how to measure out and freshen the sour dough that turned the wort into beer or ale. He knew how to cool the brew to stop the yeast. He was becoming a brewer.

But most of all, he learned English. He had to think when he spoke and had a heavy accent, but people now understood him with little effort. And he understood almost everything said to him.

*****

A bitter winter wind blew through the yard. Goodman Adams came into the brew house wearing his heaviest coat, a scarf around his neck and another under his hat covering his ears and tied under his chin. "John, is the barley soaked for malting?"

"It is, Goodman." Even indoors Jean-Marc's coat was buttoned to the neck.

"Good. There's been little enough business with the harbor froze over, but now a captain with a full hold's convinced he can get through the ice. He wants beer for his trip and he takes all ours that's aged enough. We need to soak double our barley, malt what's ready and roast the malt we've got tomorrow or we'll not have beer ready for others when the ice is gone. Tell the girls to have your breakfast two hours before dawn on the morrow. You need to fire the oven so I can begin the roasting at first light. Tomorrow's to be a busy day."

"Yes, Goodman." He made a short bow and pulled on his gloves, scarf, and hat before going to the kitchen where Chastity and Abigail were cleaning up after supper.

The girls often worked together. They had more freedom and with it more responsibility than most other indentures. Goody Adams gave them almost total responsibility for the feeding and clothing of the household. As long as there were no problems, they did as they thought best. Goody Adams had little interest in the kitchen, laundry, or loom, so she ignored them whenever possible. From their discussions with girls in other households, Chastity and Abigail were sure this was to their advantage.

Jean-Marc got along with both girls although he spent little time with them during their busy days. The three ate in the kitchen every morning before the family rose and every night after the family ate dinner.

Entering the kitchen, Jean-Marc said, "The Master says to have my breakfast two hours before the dawn. I must fire the oven so he can roast."

"Oh, that means I need be up an hour before that," moaned Abigail.

"Mayhap not. Let's think on it. If we start it now, you can get up when John does. That saves you an hour's sleep." Chastity was thinking aloud. "Porridge cooks the night. Build up the fire and I'll start some porridge. It'll be ready when John comes up. The beer and bread's already here. You can build up the day's fire whilst John eats." Chastity thought another moment then laughed. "Fact is, do it this way and I can even sleep a bit later, though I'll scarce be able to sleep there alone."

"I'd kill to sleep later," Abigail said, shaking her head. "We always rise afore the family."

"Wonder why that would be, hussy?" Chastity laughed again. "Our lives are hard. Up before light and busy past dark. But others have worse."

Abigail nodded. "Aye, Goodman's a fair man. He beats us hardly more than his family."

"Look at what Goodman Emerson done last month," Chastity said.

"What did he do?"

"Oh, John, 'twas terrible." Abigail was upset. "He beat one of his boys to death." She left the kitchen to bring in wood for the fire.

Chastity picked up the story. "The sheriff arrested Emerson, but the court ruled he had the right. Said his boy was disobedient and slothful. Judge said Emerson was 'justly angered'. I tell you, John, there be others have it worse than us."

"So, it seems," he agreed. He returned to the malting shed and cleaned up for the night. Then he went to bed in his cellar room which he shared with brewing supplies and beer barrels.

Chastity and Abigail finished preparing the porridge, which would cook overnight. Then they filled a large iron pot with hot stones from the fire, and together carried it to the attic. They pushed the pot under their bed.

Their attic was hot in the summer and cold in the winter. Its only heat came from the hot chimney and the pot of stones they brought from the kitchen. In past winters, the girls were able to make do. But this was the coldest winter in living memory. Even with their bed pushed against the chimney, they shivered all night

Chastity went downstairs with the bed-warmer and brought back coals from the fire. She lifted the pile of quilts and ran the bed-warmer under them, then put the warmer on a stone next to the bed. She and Abigail got into bed fully clothed.

"Oh, 'tis cold!" Abigail said.

Chastity snuggled beside her. "Aye, I'd be glad to trade this attic for John's bed in the cellar. 'Tis dark and musty there, but not cold the way it is up here. And in summer 'tis cooler there."

Abigail's teeth were chattering. "Last year 'twasn't so cold."

"Aye," Chastity said. "Goody told me they find someone new froze in the streets near every morning."

"We're able to keep the fire burning night and day, little that it helps. Think about the people without wood enough," Abigail said.

"There's suffering enough to go around. Today Goody told me many a well's froze over. They can't even draw water. That'll try your soul."

"What do they for water?"

"Got to take an ice-bore to the river and make a hole. Goody said the ice is near two feet thick."

"If Goody knows 'tis so cold, why don't she find us a warmer place to sleep?" Abigail asked. "In the morning, I'm asking her agai—"

"Why? We've begged her for somewhere warmer. But she just says there's no room to be had."

The girls shivered through another frigid night. Hours before dawn Abigail climbed out of bed wrapping one of their quilts around her and went downstairs to build up the kitchen fire and finish preparing Jean-Marc's breakfast. Minutes later he came up from his cellar.

"*Sacrebleu!* It is cold here, no?"

"Not so cold as in our attic."

"Can this be? My cellar, she is not so cold."

Abigail wiped a tear from her eye and hunched over the growing fire. "We're cold all day, even in the kitchen unless right by the fire. Then we go upstairs and shiver all night. We can't sleep. We both be sick."

"Have you told the Master?"

"We cried to Goody." Abigail wiped another tear from her cheek.

"You must tell her again."

At that moment, Chastity, also wrapped in a quilt, came down the stairs. "'Tis too cold to stay up there alone!" She blew on her cupped hands and stamped her feet.

"You must go down the stairs to my bed. She is not so cold there."

"I can't go to your bed, John." Chastity sounded amazed at his suggestion.

"Why not? I am no in it, and it is no so cold there."

Without another word, Chastity opened the door to his cellar and ran down the stairs. Abigail stood by the fire trying to warm herself. Jean-Marc wore a coat while he ate a large bowl of steaming porridge and drank a mug of beer. When he finished, he stood and began putting on extra layers of clothing.

"You, too, should go to my bed and warm. The fire, she burns, and the Master will not rise for another hour." He pulled a cap down over his ears, pulled mittens on over his gloves and went out the door.

Abigail thought a moment, threw another log on the fire and ran downstairs to climb into his small bed with Chastity. For the first time in weeks they were both warm.

Abigail knew she should only stay a short while, but she could not drag herself out of the warm bed into the cold kitchen. When she heard Goodman Adams calling to her from the kitchen, she knew she would be in trouble. She climbed from the bed and hurried up the stairs, apologizing as she went.

"So sorry, Goodman. 'Tis just that we are so cold in the attic and John told us he stays warm at night. I had to be warm for at least a little while."

"You belong in the kitchen now, not abed! I should cane you. Chastity does well in the attic."

"Chastity's in John's bed warming, Sir. The attic's so cold. We can't sleep. We're sick, the both of us."

"What?" Angry, Adams stormed into the cellar. "Chastity, get yourself from John's bed. I'll have no such behavior in my house."

"Behavior, Sir? The bed was empty, Sir. We've shivered for weeks."

Adams stopped and looked around. "It is warmer here, even warmer than in my room, with its fireplace."

"Please, Goodman, we meant no harm but we freeze in the attic."

As Abigail told Jean-Marc when he first arrived, Goodman Adams was a fair man. He shook his head. *Guess I can't cane them for trying to get warm. And John wasn't with them.* He looked at his girls. *Cold's taking its toll on them.*

"I'll talk to Goody Adams about the attic later. But now get me my breakfast."

*****

After he roasted the malt, Adams gave Jean-Marc directions and returned to the house. Goody Adams and the children were in the parlor, bundled together before a blazing fire.

"I found Abigail and Chastity in John's bed this morn."

"The hussies! I trust you caned them."

"I did not. John was in the brewery. The girls were cold, and his cellar is warmer than their cold attic."

"Jeremiah, the girls do freeze at night."

119

Adams shook his head. "This winter's hard on all."

"Harder on those in an unheated attic," his wife said.

"They've quilts. Can't they sleep clothed?"

Goody Adams saw her chance. She knew the girls were sick and was afraid they would not survive the winter. They could not afford to buy more girls if these two died. And she had no interest in taking over their duties.

"They do sleep in their clothes and look at their condition. We'll lose them if we don't do something."

Adams shook his head. "They won't run away in this weather."

"No, but they might die."

Goodman Adams had not considered that possibility. He paid little attention to the girls, assuming his wife would see to them. He called into the kitchen, "Abigail, Chastity, come to the parlor."

The girls hurried into the parlor wiping their hands on cloths. "Goodwife, they don't look cold to me."

"They come from the kitchen, husband, where there be a fire. There be none in their attic."

"If their attic's cold, can they not sleep in the kitchen?"

"There be room for one of them not two."

"Master, we freeze at night. There must be some other place we can sleep. Having one of us sleep in the kitchen'll not do. The one alone in the attic, would die for sure," Chastity said.

"Oh Master, we do freeze," Abigail said.

"We'll see to this. Wife, come with me." The three women followed Goodman Adams into and through the kitchen, then up the stairs. In the attic, he said, "Bless me, it is cold. Goodwife, how long have you known of this?"

"The girls came to me over a week ago. I brought it to you."

"Did you? I have no memory of that. It matters not. The girls cannot sleep here. Go back to the kitchen's heat."

The women were glad to leave the cold attic for the relative warmth of the kitchen and huddled by the fire.

Goody Adams spoke, "See Jeremiah, one could sleep on this floor but not two."

"So, I see. Could one sleep in the kitchen and one in the parlor?"

"I'll not have servants sleeping in my parlor." Goody Adams was firm on this point.

"The only other place would be in the cellar with John." The Goodman seemed to be talking to himself. "Men and women share beds at an inn. The young bundle."

Goody Adams interrupted his musings. "That they do, but if they're familiar with each other, the court will at least whip them and make them marry. Then we'd be stuck with their bastard. If they married, we'd not be able to keep them apart and we'd be stuck with all their whelps. And the court could send them to the scaffold. Then you'd lose two servants."

"What then?"

Chastity interrupted, "I know 'tis not my place to speak, but could John sleep in the kitchen?"

The Adams looked at each other. "There you have it, Jeremiah. John can sleep here and the girls below."

"John'll not like it. Even now it's colder here than in his cellar, and there'll be no bed."

"John'll like the roof over his head and meals he gets. There's nothing else to it. John can move the girls' things downstairs."

"There's too much work this day."

"They can't spend another night in that attic."

Goodman put his hands in his pocket and thought. "The girls can set a bed for John on the floor. He can see to the rest on the morrow. I'll go tell him."

"Thank you, Sir," the girls said almost in unison.

Adams put on his coat, hat, and mittens to go to the brew-house. He found Jean-Marc building up the fire so the malting trays would not freeze.

"John." When he looked up, Adams began. "John, the girls' attic has no heat. They can't sleep there in this cold. I've looked for options, but there's none to be had. They'll have to sleep in the cellar. You'll move to the kitchen the rest of the winter."

Jean-Marc straightened. "The girls, they told me they are very cold. In the kitchen, I will not be so cold. It is good."

"The kitchen will be colder than your cellar."

"But not so cold like the girls' attic, yes?"

"You are right, not so cold as their attic and they do need to be warmer. 'Tis well you understand. Tomorrow they'll show you what of their things need go to the cellar. Some of what's in down there'll need be moved to the attic to make room."

"What must be must be. *Est-ce pas?*"

Adams returned to the house leaving Jean-Marc to his chore. He told the women, "It's decided. John understands."

*****

Well before supper, the girls brought their quilts to the cellar. Chastity moved John's things to the side.

Abigail asked, "Shouldn't we ask him where he'd like his things?"

"What matters it? This'll be ours. He'll sleep in the kitchen."

"With what for a bed? With the fire, we can't put down straw."

Chastity shrugged. "We can put extra cloths under the quilt. I didn't notice he lost any sleep while we froze."

"He knew not. When I told him how cold we were, he told us to come down here."

"At no cost to him. You can spend your time worrying on him. I'll not."

*****

The brewery kept Jean-Marc busy through supper. Abigail bundled herself against the cold and brought a plate of hot food out to the cold brewery.

"I thought you'd be hungry."

"I am," he said stamping his feet in the cold before taking the plate from her and putting it on the workbench. Without sitting he began to eat.

"It saddens me you're to be moved from your cellar."

Jean-Marc chewed and swallowed before speaking. "What else is there? You must not freeze."

"You lose your bed."

Again, he waited to swallow before he spoke. "I have lost so much since I left France. This thing, it is so little. Do not be troubled."

"We'll set you a soft bed by the fire."

"This would be nice."

*****

After supper, the girls did their best to prepare a bed for Jean-Marc. Instead of banking the fire they built it up as if preparing to cook. Then they hurried through their other tasks, deciding that some of their work could wait until morning after all. They wore their clothes to bed and sound asleep by the time Jean-Marc finished his work for the day and came in.

So, this is to be my bed.

Exhausted, he climbed beneath the quilt and faced away from the fire to avoid its light.

The girls were warm and slept well for the first time in weeks. As dawn approached, they were even too hot and pushed the quilts away from their shoulders. On the hard floor, Jean-Marc slept little.

At her usual pre-dawn hour Abigail got up. This day Chastity joined her in the kitchen. Jean-Marc was not able to sleep while the girls fixed breakfast.

"You should go down stairs and sleep," Abigail said.

Without speaking, Jean-Marc did.

The girls rushed to prepare a special breakfast of biscuits, molasses, and bacon for the family. They selected four of the best biscuits and an ample pile of the bacon for Jean-Marc. Just over an hour later he smiled when he walked into the kitchen and saw the over-burdened plate the girls set for him. He ate well past full, pushed back, and drained his tankard of beer.

"Such a meal. Of this King Louis himself would boast, no? Thank you, ladies. The Master he says I must move some things to the cellar for you, so I must also move some things from the cellar to make the room. You will please show me what I must move."

The girls agreed that Chastity would show him what to move to the cellar while Abigail did double duty in the kitchen. That the larger bed would move was a given, but Jean-Marc was amazed at all the things the girls deemed necessary for a temporary move: along with the bed and mattress, they wanted extra quilts, chests of clothing, shoes, candle holders and small tables, brushes and combs, even some trinkets. Again, and again he tried to protest that they wanted too much moved.

"You must know my other chores for this day, they will not do themselves. And for everything I move to the cellar, there is another thing I must move from the cellar into the attic."

His protests were to no avail. Chastity's list of things to be moved never changed.

He set about moving things from the cellar into the frigid yard. This made room in the cellar for all the things the girls wanted moved from the attic. Between trips to the cellar he drew water, ladled barley, stoked fires, and moved heavy wooden kegs for filling.

The cellar cleared, he began to move things from the attic.

"Stop. You can't move that downstairs yet. I need to clean down there," Abigail said.

"You make sport of me, no?"

"I make sport of you, no. I'll not sleep down there until it's cleaned."

He was mystified. "You did notice that you will be sleeping down there, yes? This means your eyes, they will be closed."

"Eyes closed or no, I'll not sleep there until it's cleaned."

"The floor, it is dirt."

"The rest is not!"

"Did you perhaps notice that you slept there last night? It is no dirtier now than it was then."

But again, his opinion did not matter. Moving stopped until Abigail spent several hours cleaning the cellar.

Jean-Marc labored throughout the day. Several times, Goodman Adams got angry because some chore still was not done. He didn't finish until long after dark. The girls prepared another special meal for him of roasted pork and baked apples, but he just drank his beer refilled the tankard, drank again and went to bed. This night, he slept.

Jean-Marc woke when the girls came up to fix breakfast.

"You're in our way," Chastity said, pushing a foot into his back. "Go sleep another hour downstairs. We'll call you when it's ready."

Without speaking he headed downstairs. The cellar looked so different. So much was crammed into the small area. Colorful cloths separated the sleeping area from the brewing supplies. There were small tables with candle stands on either side of the bed. It looked like a bedroom, not his cellar. He climbed between the quilts and tried to sleep.

About an hour later Chastity called him to the kitchen. He climbed out of their bed, put on his shoes and went upstairs. He noticed that the girls had prepared porridge for the family to eat. When he sat at the table for his breakfast, Abigail set a heaping plate of roast pork and baked apples before him. He beamed.

She leaned over, said, "Thank you, John," and kissed him on the cheek. Turning bright red, she made a small noise as if she'd shocked herself and hurried back to her chores.

Chastity laughed out loud. "If our wee mouse Abigail kisses you, you've done well. We know you toiled long yesterday. For that we thank you. We've little enough to give but you do have our thanks."

She returned to her tasks, chuckling to herself. *Look what little Abby's done. Haven't seen that in her before.*

*****

For the rest of the winter, every morning Abigail crept into the kitchen while everyone else slept. She tried not to wake Jean-Marc, but always did. He would get up, roll and store his bedding, and sit at the table with a tankard of beer. They would whisper to each other until Chastity burst through the door. Quiet conversation would be over.

Then Jean-Marc began helping Abigail with her chores. He would carry wood and stoke the fire while Abigail fussed over porridge or biscuits. When the chores were done, they would sit together at the table, at first opposite, then next to each other. One day Abigail put her hands on his as he told her about his day ahead. He could not believe the excitement he felt.

Then Chastity came up the stairs and everything was different. Abigail took her hand from his and jumped to her feet. There was work to do.

All three were friends, but nothing was the same after Chastity got up.

*****

One morning the servants discussed how they came into Goodman Adams' service.

"My parents, two brothers and sister all died of the pox," Chastity said kneading dough. "It's a hard way to die and hard for a young one to see. They all suffered. I was but a babe, so I was sent to the poor house. There they worked us harder than Goody Adams ever does. The food was bad and there was little of it. When I turned twelve, they said I was old enough to see after myself and turned me out. Many a day I went without food. Many a night I slept under a bridge."

Jean-Marc sat opposite her at the table. He asked, "Could you find no work?"

"Work I found in a tavern for food and bed, but I was sent away by the keeper's wife. She thought that at thirteen I was after her fat husband. It was the streets for me again. I seen some younger than me hanged for stealing food. So, I knew better than to steal no matter how hungry I got. I knew girls who lived as whores—"

"Oh, Chastity, you couldn't have," Abigail said looking up from the porridge she was stirring.

"No. I often seen them in the morning bad beaten by one o' their men and still not paid for the night. I vowed I'd starve 'fore I would do that for food or for silver. I near starved and I near froze. Then at sixteen, when I should be gettin' married, I heard I could sell myself for seven years to work off fare to America. Servants at least eat regular and have a bed. For these seven years, at least I'd eat daily and have a roof over my head."

Abigail nodded. "'Twas good you were sold here. Not all servants eat regular. We do."

"Could you not serve in Angland?"

Chastity shook her head. "There's indentures in England but more be needed here. When you sell yourself, expect to go to the colonies, Virginia or here. Most be sent to Virginia. I hear thems as go to there have a worse lot than us."

She floured the board again and went on. "The trip from England was torture. T'were over forty other indentures, all but five of them men, stuck in that dark hold, never allowed into the air above."

"Oh, the boat, that was terrible" Abigail agreed.

"That it was. Us women were careful to relieve ourselves in the bilge water. That was foul enough but the men just used any wall."

"Aye, on my boat, too," Abigail said.

"In no time, the hold stunk of sweat and shit. And there we ate, right in our own filth. They gave us nothing to eat but sea biscuits." She picked up the dough she was kneading and slammed it back down. "Nothing like these'll be. And water that was green and full of bugs."

Now she laughed. "I learned to suck the water through my teeth when I drank to keep out the bugs. 'Tis funny now, with all the worms and weevils I was eatin' in the biscuits."

"Some say it was the weevils kept us alive," Abigail said.

"That may be. The biscuits sure couldn't. I was sold to Goodman Adams three years ago, at seventeen, and I've lacked not food nor bed since. This time serving here's been the best o' my life."

"'Tis true," Abigail said. "As masters go, he's a good one. I'd want not another."

"In four more years, I'll be a free woman and I'll not go back to the streets."

"What will you do? You'll have no money. That old, without money or family, what man would have you? 'Twould be different were you a rich widow," Abigail said. She swung the arm supporting the kettle, moving the bubbling porridge back over the fire.

"I'll have me a man to marry so soon as I'm free. I've got my eyes on some lonely widowers. Between the pox and birthing, there's sure to be more. I could make a rich old man happy. Then could I be a happy widow myself. I've four years left in this house. Do what I must, I'll not be poor again and neither will I stay some other woman's servant."

"But Chastity, we serve Goodman Adams not Goody," Abigail said.

"Do we? When did you last do a brewer's chore? Does Goody make bread or sit at a loom?"

"She does not."

"But that's my story for you, John. Abby'll have to tell you hers."

Abigail came to the table and sat down. "My father was a rich wool merchant in London's Steelyard, trading with the Hanseatic League cities. Then he lost all. He said changing times caused his losses. Mum said it was his gambling on dog fights."

Chastity stopped arranging balls of dough on a flat pan and said, "Two things I know. Biscuits rise in the oven and gamblers lose their money. He pissed that money away."

Abigail reddened. "By one or the other, mayhap both, my father lost all and was bound for debtor's prison until his debts would be paid. Who pays off a debt while in prison? Men go to debtor's prisons to die. 'Tis punishment for their debt. And their children starve as punishment for being born to such a man. My father decided he'd not go to prison, so he sold me for three pounds and my two brothers for four pounds each. This kept him from prison but bound us for seven years."

"How sells your father you?" Jean-Marc was incredulous.

"He went to a friend who trades in indentures, and we were sold. I was twelve. I've seen neither parent nor brother since. Now I'm sixteen with three years of service left. I've worked off over half of my time but don't know what I'll do when it's up. I'll not have money and nineteen's too old for a poor girl to marry. Who wants a penniless old maid? A rich widow or girl from a rich family'd be different. Mayhap Goodman Adams will let me stay in his service. I'd work for little more than food and bed. But what of you, John?"

Jean-Marc shared his story with them, much to their disbelief.

"So, you know the King of France?" Chastity laughed, as she put his breakfast on the table.

"*Mais oui.* I have seen him many times." He paused to bite into one of the steaming biscuits. "I do not belief he would know me but he knew my father and knows my mother and brother."

Still laughing, Chastity mocked a curtsey and said, "Should we bow before your grace?"

"You should show some respect to one who speaks the truth."

The three laughed together.

The wind is ill that brings no good. From this cold winter, I have real friends. Had I friends before? Jean-Marc thought as he ate.

In the kitchen, around the table, the three formed a close bond. Chastity had no interest in another servant. Her sights were set on someone old, fat and rich. The relationship between Abigail and Jean-Marc grew into something deeper.

He spent as much time with Abigail as he could. He thrilled at her touch. Just seeing her lifted his mood. He loved the way her face brightened when she noticed him watching her. He loved that she went out of her way to see or to touch him. For the first time he could remember, he found joy making someone else happy.

With Abigail, all is different. But her service will be over long before mine. Will she leave then? Could I live without her? I will not.

Jean-Marc and Abigail realized that they were not their own, yet somehow this wasn't important. They were happy.

*****

When the winter passed, Jean-Marc was sad to move the girls' things back into their attic.

"What are you doing," Abigail asked.

"Goodman, he told me to move your bed back to the attic."

"Not until I clean up there you won't."

"This again? How did the empty attic get dirty?" He lowered the bed frame on the cellar steps.

"You're just a man," Abigail said walking toward him. "You can't even see dirt."

"But I can see you," he said reaching out to grab her around the waist.

The bed frame slid down the stairs knocking over the barrels and kegs below. Both looked down the stairs and laughed.

"Now we've both cleaning to do," Abigail laughed, poking him in the ribs and running up the stairs.

"Your eyes, they will still be closed," he shouted to her, laughing as he walked down the stairs.

*****

Although sleeping in the cellar again, he continued to get up when Abigail did. Their time together was precious to them both. Without realizing it they began talking about a future together, having no idea how they could make it happen.

He dedicated himself to learning the brewer's trade.

With a trade, I could give Abigail a good life. But she will be free. I still owe twenty more years of service...No! That long, I will not serve. Somehow, this will change. I will find a way to free myself by the time Abigail is free. Do not know how it will happen...but it will happen.

In the meantime, he paid close attention to Goodman Adams. He asked about everything. He learned he could add honey or maple syrup to the wort, producing a stronger, sweeter beer. He also learned that he could produce a similar effect using molasses which cost less. He learned that he could use grains other than barley to make the wort and produce vastly different beers.

When I am free, I will be the best and richest brewer in Boston. And I will be with Abigail.

Chapter Seven
The Pox

**"No man dared to count his children as his own
until they had had the disease."**
Comte de la Condamine

Goodman Adams shook his head and read the Governor's proclamation, nailed to the church door, aloud:

Whereas the Anger of Almighty God has again fallen upon this Colony, and His Hand has delivered unto it a second great Affliction of the Pox, brought by the Sins and Wickedness of His People, and considering the manifold Sins, Perversity and Wickedness prevailing in our midst, one must wonder at God's Grace, Patience and Mercy which reduce these Rebukes. We cannot but fear something yet lacks in our Supplications.

Therefore, it is commanded that Thursday next, January 10 in the Year of Our Lord 1692, be appointed a Day of Humiliation, Repentance and Prayer with Fasting throughout this Colony. Thereon all Servile Labor is strictly forbidden whilst all Taverns, Inns and Publick Houses shall be closed and shuttered, except to Way-farers, thereby all Iniquity that stirs God's Righteous Anger and Indignation against this Land may be expunged, that He would shew us that which we do not know and what we have done amiss, that we may do so no more, thereby turning away His Righteous and Holy Wrath.

His Excellency
Sir William Phipps, Governor

Adams sighed, "The pox is again amongst us."

"It passed our family two years ago. It may do so again," Goody Adams said.

131

He took off his glasses and put them in his vest pocket. "Would that I had your confidence, Estelle. I fear most for our children. The pox last killed over a thousand here, most children."

His wife tried to sound hopeful, "It can't be so bad again. All in Boston attend church."

Adams turned and began walking home. "Aye, they do. Those that don't are fined or put in the stocks." He sighed again. "But you know most have not saving grace. All go to church, but they're not all permitted to join." He walked in silence, seeming to think, before continuing. "More than half in town are not saved. How will God not smite us?"

Estelle struggled to keep up with the pace he was setting, "Jeremiah, slow down. I can't keep up." He looked back at her and walked slower. She tried to walk faster. "Think about where the pox has struck," she said. "I'm told the first to die was a girl who lived in the hovels by the docks and then her family."

"And their neighbors all fled. I fear they've taken the pox with them." He stood still while his wife caught up. "Mayhap you'll be right. God's hand may be light."

*****

Chastity greeted them at the front door. "Your sister be here to see you, Goody. She waits in the parlor."

"Thank you, Chastity." The girl helped Goody Adams out of her coat and took both their coats to the closet.

The tall, heavy women shared a quilt while a fire blazed in the hearth. They had the same blue eyes and greying blonde hair. Estelle's sister brought the latest news. "I heard there's over a hundred dead already. Some were even refused graves in the churchyard."

"I pray you heard wrong, Martha. That would be cruel."

"The pox is cruel. Goodman Hawthorn's sick. His house is not twenty rods from mine."

"I'll pray for him and his ... And I'll pray the pox doesn't find its way to your door."

"I fear it'll find every door. Have you seen the roads leaving town? Even in this cold, they're filled with wagons and carts."

Estelle shook her head and stared into the fire. "Those the pox misses may freeze. Mayhap the day of repentance will lift God's hand."

"Pray that it does." Martha decided to change the subject. "How are your children in this cold?"

Abigail and Chastity stood, wide-eyed on the other side of the parlor's door.

Abigail whispered, "Oh, Chastity, it can't be back, can it?"

"We both know the pox comes every few years. Pray this house is passed over again."

*****

On Thursday, people thronged to their unheated churches before dawn. Goodman Adams led his family and servants to their church. He stood at his seat, five rows from the front of the unadorned church, behind the gentlemen, with the other tradesmen and merchants who were church-members. Today, none of them talked or nodded hello. In the cold, the men stuffed their gloved hands in their pockets and stamped their feet to stay warm but avoided each other's eyes.

Goody Adams and their children sat seven rows farther back, behind the freemen and gentlewomen, with the wives of other prosperous, church-member, merchants. She bundled the children into a quilt, on the pew, but like the other adults, she stood in front of her seat and moved to stay warm.

Jean-Marc stood among the male servants, behind all church members and other free people, but before the female servants. He looked around nervously.

What will they do? 'Tis too cold to keep us here long.

Chastity, Abigail sat, huddled near the back with the other female servants. "Would that Goody let us bring a quilt too," Abigail complained.

Chastity nodded, "Aye, the day'll be long. Mayhap this'll work. I'm already sorry."

The few negroes, slave or free, sat in the balcony above the rear of the church. People below could hear them shuffling about.

Front and center in the church, the Reverend Mister London climbed into the pulpit. The large, blue eye-ball painted on the pulpit's front gave the impression of God staring at the people. Most of the congregation sat when he started speaking.

"My message today is from the twenty-eighth chapter of the book of Deuteronomy, beginning in the fifty-eighth verse:

If thou will not observe to do all the words of this law that are written in this book ... THE LORD will make thy plagues wonderful ... even great plagues and of long continuance, and sore sicknesses ... Moreover, He will bring upon thee all the diseases of Egypt, which thou wast afraid of; and they shall cleave unto thee. Also, every sickness and every plague which was not written in this book of the law, them will the LORD bring upon thee, until thou be destroyed. And ye shall be left few in number ... because thou wouldst not obey the voice of the LORD thy God.

"God's word is clear. You have brought this pox upon yourself through your manifold sins and wickedness. God, in His great mercy, stayed His hand until this time, but now you drink of the full cup of His fearful vengeance."

London thundered his sermon for over two hours, seeming to not notice the cold.

Most of the people in the pews sat in stunned silence. Some cried in fear and sorrow. Most women stared straight ahead, afraid to meet the eyes of another. Most men looked around. Then came the repentance. Goodman Gerry stood first.

"I stand before God ... and before my, my neighbors." He fought back sobs as he tried to speak. The servant women in the back and the blacks in the balcony strained to hear him. "I stand ... to confess my sins and to beg forgiveness, for I have brought the pox upon our colony." He twisted his hat in his hands. Tears streamed down his face as he tried to speak. "I have coveted that which others have ... have and I have not." Here he paused for a long moment. "In my heart ... I have lusted after women who are not my wife."

Four rows farther back, his wife's face reddened. She locked her eyes on the great eye-ball.

He broke into sobs, dropped his hat, and leaned forward on the back of the pew before him for support. People sitting more than four rows away couldn't hear him. "I once blasphemed and took our Lord's name in vain." His knees buckled. He fell forward onto them, sobbing. Goodman Adams thought he said, "I am not worthy of forgiveness. Please forgive me." No one could be sure.

Jean-Marc looked about to see how others reacted to the confession.

These are the sins he thinks brought the pox? He wanted things others had? Wanted another woman? Who has not? Public confessions should be for real sins, no?

He looked at Gerry then around again. Everyone else seemed to take the confession seriously. Awed silence broken only by Goodman Gerry's sobs filled the church. Long moments passed.

Then, Goodwife Alden stood. Her whole body shook. "I beg your forgiveness ... I spread malicious ... untrue lies about, about my husband's sister. God forgive me. I have no love for her." She collapsed into her seat.

Jean-Marc pulled his coat tighter and looked around the crowded church.

She doesn't love her husband's sister? Who does? He shoved his hands into his armpits and shuffled his feet to warm them. *It's cold. If we're to stay here until someone confesses a sin that brought the pox, someone who committed a real sin needs say something.*

Confession followed confession. The congregation shivered. First a few, then many, trembled with fear as they stood to confess their sins. Each begged for God's and their neighbors' forgiveness. Others shuffled their feet and pulled their coats up around their necks.

Esther's teeth chattered. She tried to snuggle against Goody Adams. "I'm cold, Mama."

Goody whispered, "Sit straight. 'Tis good that you be cold. It helps repentance." She pushed Esther away. Daniel pulled his little sister to him. He put his arm around her and whispered, "Pull your feet up under the quilt and bundle in against me. If we hold hands, we'll both feel better." Without speaking, Jonathan moved closer to Daniel.

People repented and cried for hours. Jean-Marc sat and shivered. As the confessions droned on, Jean-Marc began to think. *If these are the sins that brought the pox, what have I done? This man cursed his father. Is that a sin? How many times did I curse my father ... my mother and Francois? No ... that cannot be sin, look at what they did to me. I was right to curse them.*

More time passed. Men and women shook and cried as they confessed to greed, to anger, and to placing themselves before others.

Could these, in truth, be sins that brought the pox? This is the second fever I've seen since leaving France. Is this my doing? ... Did I bring the fever to the ship? No. This cannot be. He clapped his gloved hands together and rubbed them on his thighs. *These are no sins. A sin would be something like killing someone ...* He thought of the innkeeper in Le Harve. *No, this cannot be. He knew not his place.* He looked about the crowded church and for a while forgot he was cold.

The repentance continued.

Hours later, exhausted, they left the church and walked home to cold houses where the fires in the hearths had burned out long ago. Cold fingers fumbled with flint and steel to start fires. Then people who ate and drank nothing that day fell, exhausted, into comfortless beds.

The next morning, over thirty more people showed signs of the pox.

A week later, Goodman Adams woke with a fever. Fearing the worst, his family and servants tried to be hopeful. Chastity took charge in his room. "I've had cow pox. I can't get this. Be gone, the lot of you. I'll see to the master. You see to yourselves."

Everyone else cleared the room. Chastity brought in a bowl of water and cloth to wipe her master's head, cooling his fever.

Two of the Adams' children, Esther and Ezra cried as they tried to peek into their parents' room. Abigail crouched and pulled them both into her arms. "Papa will be fine." She tried to sound confident.

Little Esther tried not to cry, "Promise?"

"I promise. Would Chastity let anyone hurt your Papa?" She stood and led the children toward their rooms, "Say a prayer for Papa, then play with your dolls."

Abigail herded the frightened children into Esther's room, closed the door and went for her coat. As she left, she could hear them crying. *I should stay with them ... But there's nothing I can do.* She put on her coat and went to the brewery. Opening the door, she cried out, "John, Goodman has the pox!"

He put the large wooden paddle back in the bucket of barley and water and crossed the room. Putting his arm around her shoulders and drawing her to himself, he said, "Are you sure?"

"He's on fire! Why else would he be feverish?"

"Many things cause a fever."

"John!" Her voice was angry. When she looked up at him he could see tears filled her eyes.

"I only say it could be another fever."

"Chastity's lived through it. She says it's the pox."

"What can I do?"

"Nothing ... Hold me."

He held her close and said nothing. Almost a minute passed. "This is childish," she said stepping back. "There'll be work to do. The children need seeing to. They be scared."

"You'll need help. What can I do?"

"You need make beer, don't you?"

"No. I make beer because Goodman tells me to. With this cold, we don't sell any."

"I don't know, John," She stepped toward him and buried her face into his chest. "I ..." her voice trailed away.

He pushed her away from his chest and with his arm around her shoulder, walked toward the house with her. "There'll be more to do than you and Chastity are able. I'll come and see how I can help."

Together, they walked to the kitchen. *Please God. Did I bring the pox on this house? Spare Abigail ... spare the children. If this be my doing, take me but spare them.*

Goody Adams was pacing in the kitchen when they walked in. She spun to look at Jean-Marc. "I'll not trust my husband's life to that hussy." She seldom took directions from anyone, much less from a servant girl, "Hurry, John, go to the church and bring Mister London. He's the best physician in Boston." Without waiting for his response, she returned to Jeremiah's side.

"Yes, Goody," He ran to the church, where he found the reverend walking from the graveyard.

"Mister London, Goody Adams sent me to bring you to our house. The Goodman, he is sick."

The Reverend Mister London had survived a previous outbreak of the pox. It left him scarred but with the knowledge he would not be infected again. As he put it, "He, upon whom God has once visited the pox and has found pure, need not fear this scourge again." Secure with this knowledge, the reverend followed Jean-Marc to the home of the wealthiest brewer in Boston.

Upon entering Goodman Adams' room, the doctor ordered Chastity out. He examined the patient then came into the parlor where Goody Adams sat fretting. Jean-Marc and Chastity stood outside the door and listened. Abigail was in the children's room, trying to comfort them.

"'Tis good you sent for me before 'twas critical. Mayhap we can sweat his fever out. Have your girls boil a large pot of water filled with cloths and keep it boiling." The doctor handed Goody Adams four small glass cups. "Have them boil these as well. If covering Jeremiah with the hot cloths doesn't sweat out the humors, I may need blister him. There's not a moment to lose."

Jean-Marc and Chastity hurried into the kitchen, hoping Goody Adams would not catch them listening. Goody called, "Chastity."

In the kitchen, she turned and went back into the hallway. "Yes, Goody?"

"Boil a big pot of water. Fill it with cloths." She handed Chastity the glass cups. "Put these in it, too, in case the doctor needs to blister—"

"Goody," Chastity interrupted, "We shouldn't be boiling water. The Master needs cool cloths to sooth him and break his fever."

Goody Adams slapped Chastity's face. "Know you more than the doctor? Do as you're told, girl, or I'll have you flogged."

Without another word, Chastity turned on her heel and went into the kitchen. She pointed to a large cast iron kettle. "John, we need that filled with water."

He grabbed the bucket and went to the well. Chastity built up the fire. After three trips to the well, Jean-Marc helped Chastity lift the kettle filled with water, cloths, and the glass cups on to the hook and rotate it over the fire.

No watched pot ever boiled slower than this. Goody Adams scolded Chastity again and again for taking too long to bring the hot cloths.

Once the water boiled, Chastity scooped out the cloths with a wooden paddle. She placed them in a wooden bowl and brought them to Mister London. He picked up individual pieces of cloth with a set of tongs and spread them out over Goodman's Adams' exposed skin. The semi-conscious patient cried out as each scalding hot cloth was placed on him. His wife left the room in tears.

London covered Adams' chest, stomach, arms, and legs, then turned to Chastity and ordered, "Quick now, bring me more. As these cool they'll work less and need reheating."

Chastity thought, *Only a fool would cover someone burning with fever with hot cloths. If the fever don't kill him, the reverend will.*

Chastity did as she was told, noting each time the cloths were changed Goodman Adams had more blisters than before. This pleased London. He went into the parlor and told Goody, "We make progress. The blisters draw infection from his body. We may avert the worst. If his fever breaks in the next several hours he may live."

She looked up with reddened eyes. She tried to speak but only managed to stammer out, "Thank you."

He returned to the bedside and continued his rotation of the cloths, pleased when blisters broke and oozed.

Abigail brought the children into the kitchen to feed them. Daniel and Jonathan sat on either side of Jean-Marc. Daniel looked up to him, "Will Papa be better, John?"

"I think so, Dannyboy. Mama has brought a very good doctor to care for him. Have you said your prayers for your Papa?"

"We have. Abigail told us all to pray and we prayed all day," Jonathan said, sounding excited.

Jean-Marc tousled both boys' hair. "That's a good boy, Jon-Jon. You must all pray for Papa."

Ezra sat opposite them, with Ruth and Esther. Little Esther was too young to understand what was happening, but Ruth said, "We prayed, too, John, even Esther kneels by us, with her hands folded."

Abigail placed a bowl of stew in front of Ruth. "And you must keep praying. That's how Papa will get better."

Jean-Marc and Abigail managed to get the frightened children to eat most of their stew before putting them to bed. Abigail kissed each child goodnight and reminded them all to pray. Then she and Jean-Marc joined Chastity in the kitchen for their supper.

"He's going to kill him, you know," Chastity said, staring into her stew.

"How can you know that," Abigail asked.

"I had cow pox as a girl. Because I won't get it, when there's a pox, I'm sent to help. The rich send for a doctor who sweats or bleeds them 'til they die."

"But most die from the pox, no?"

"They need not, John. Those too poor to pay a doctor see to their own. When the sick throw off their quilts and complain they're hot, we pour cool water on their cloths to comfort them. Like as not, they get better. This man heats him all the more."

Abigail's eyes widened. "Do you say you know more than Mr. London—"

"The man's a simpleton. The Master knows he's too hot. He keeps trying to throw off his quilts and pull off the cloths. Every time he gets a cloth off, London puts a new boiling hot one on. The Master's nothing but blisters."

"This is good, no? It takes out the bad humors, no?"

"Think that if you want. I say he's killing him."

*****

When the fever did not break after several hours, Mister London went back into the parlor. Chastity was leaving the room just as he walked in. Goody Adams sat on a straight-backed, wooden chair. An untouched bowl of stew was on the table next to her. The fireplace cast the only light. She looked up.

"The fever's not broken, and I must leave a while. We need cup and purge him."

She twisted the handkerchief in her hands. "Do what you must, Mister London, but please look in on my sons." Her voice quivered. Moments passed before she went on. "Chastity tells me Ezra and Daniel be feverish."

London called Chastity. "Your mistress tells me two of the boys are feverish. Have you seen what I've done?"

"I have, sir."

"Get the other girl now and show her what to do. Between the two of you, you must keep water boiling, cover the three of them with the hot cloths and keep changing them." His voice was urgent. "You'll need help to keep the boys from cooling. I'll purge your master to rid him of the humors. Bring a bowl and bed pan for the evacuation. Now, see to it, girl."

Chastity roused Abigail and Jean-Marc from their beds. In the kitchen, she said, "Ezra and Daniel've got it now. London wants to sweat them too and he's going to purge the Master. Abby, I'll need your help."

Abigail looked confused. "If the sweating's no good for them, why are we helping?"

"So we don't get flogged. I love those little ones, but if we don't do as we're told, Goody'll have us flogged and they'll sweat them anyway."

"But you should tell her," Abigail protested.

"I did. She hit me, and said she'd have me flogged. They be hers. If she wants to kill them, nothing we can do'll stop her and I'll not be flogged over it."

Jean-Marc looked up from the chair while pulling on his shoe, "You should tell them this—"

"Did you hear me? I did tell her. It got me hit. If you're lookin' to be flogged, you tell'er."

He stared at her. He could think of nothing to say.

"Abby, he's going to purge the Master. We'll need another bed pan and a bowl of wet cloths to clean him. And bring an empty bucket. John, you keep plenty of water boiling. London'll want plenty of hot cloths to kill the rest of them with."

She used a set of tongs to take the blistering cups out of the kettle and covered them with more boiling hot cloths. Muttering to herself, she took them into her Master's bedroom. Jean-Marc and Abigail set about their tasks.

In the Adams' bedroom, Mr. London took the tongs and removed one of the glass cups from the bowl. He placed the cup, open end down, on Goodman Adams' forehead. This immediately raised a large blister. London held the cup in place with a dry cloth. Adams made a feeble attempt to push it off. When the cup cooled, Mr. London returned it to the bowl and repeated this process with another.

"We'll need more than these. Take the cool ones and heat them again."

Chastity did as she was told.

Again, and again London placed the scalding cups on Goodman Adams' face, raising blisters that formed and broke with the heat.

He then called for a cup of hot water. He stirred in a powder. "This'll purge his bowels and stomach. He'll need constant attention to be kept clean. If he soils himself, be sure to clean him with a cloth. We want the humors we bring out to stay out."

He went into the parlor, where Estelle sat staring at a portrait of her husband. The twisted handkerchief in her hands had torn hours earlier. London said, "We've cupped and purged him. If this doesn't work by morning, we'll have to bleed them all. There's still the chance of preventing the pox. See your girls stay attentive. If your husband or the boys cool, there'll be no stopping it. I need go. There's likely others come down with fever. We need to prevent the pox in them, too, and I need some rest. You pray repentance for your family. I'll return in the morning. We'll know more then."

She tried to stand. "Thank you, Mister London."

He looked at her red, swollen eyes and said, "You need rest. This day's been hard on you."

"I will." Now she managed to stand and held out her hand. "Thank you, Mister London. My whole family thanks you."

"Pray that my efforts have helped. See that your girls don't let them cool."

*****

Abigail followed Chastity's directions, helping her tend the sick. Jean-Marc kept the water boiling and plenty of cloths hot. Goody Adams came into her bedroom. She sat on the only chair, stared at her husband, and complained not enough was being done.

Then Goodman Adams, still flat on his back, vomited. He choked on the vomit, spitting it out onto his face, the hot cloths and bed. Chastity turned him to his side and placed a bowl under his mouth as he vomited again. She called to Abigail, "Bring the chamber pot. His bowels are sure to let go now, too."

Abigail brought the pot with little time to spare.

"Chastity," Abigail called. "He's got the bloody flux."

"Probably not. Mister London purged him. The blood's from the purging."

His soiled bed and the cloths needed to be changed. Chastity called into the kitchen, "John, start another pot of water. We'll need to clean these things and there's sure to be more. You'll have to take care of that. Our hands be full with the sick."

Jean-Marc thought, *If this is killing them, why are we doing it? Why is Abigail in with them? Chastity had cow pox. Abigail did not. We should take the children who are not fevered and leave.*

Chastity turned to Goody Adams. "We'll need your help. We can empty the bowls and pots, but we can't take care of your

143

husband, the children, change their things and clean him at the same time."

Estelle grabbed clean cloths and began to clean the filth from her husband. "He's on fire."

"That's what happens when your wrap him in boiling cloths all night. Abigail, hand me the bucket. We can empty the pots into it then dump it in the outhouse."

Jean-Marc opened the door and called in, "Chastity, listen. The girls, they are crying."

Chastity ran to their room. Esther was burning with fever. "John, we can't tend to them all over the house. You bring the boys to the Master's room. I'll bring little Esther. We'll put as many as we can in the bed. We can put bedding on the floor for the others."

Jean-Marc brought Daniel, placing him in bed with his father, trying to avoid as much filth as he could. As he went for Ezra, he thought of Father Montcalm and the servants below deck on the ship. *So much has changed.* He stopped, looked up and said a silent prayer. *Lord, heal these little ones. Heal them all. Protect my Abigail.* He scooped the boy into his arms and carried him into the room.

The servants worked with Goody Adams through the night. They were all exhausted when the reverend returned.

"The fever's not passed. The purging was not enough. We've little time to prevent the pox. Girl, throw a poker in the fire and bring me a bowl. They must all be bled. Boy, come here." Jean-Marc came to the bed. "I need you to hold their arms still whilst I bleed them."

Goody Adams gave a small cry and left the room.

He took the bleeding lance from his bag. It looked like a tiny, steel hatchet. Mister London dipped it in hot water and wiped it on the leg of his breeches. "You can't let them move away from my lance or away from the bowl. The humors be their blood."

He showed Jean-Marc how to hold his master's arm. Abigail brought a large bowl. He showed her where to hold it, then he cut into the Goodman's arm. Ill as he was, Adams tried to pull his arm free. Blood came out in spurts. Jean-Marc struggled to hold the arm still, so the blood would fall into the bowl.

After he bled out enough to fill a large tankard, the doctor called to Chastity, "Bring me the hot poker." He used the glowing rod to seal the wound, filling the room with the smell of burnt flesh. The poker was returned to the fire.

London bled Esther next. The lance looked immense against her tiny arm. She screamed and struggled against Jean-Marc's grip. Tears formed in his eyes and splashed on her thin arm as blood spurted out.

This man is a butcher. Why does Goody let him do this to her childrens? Jean-Marc gritted his teeth and looked at the wall, while London finished torturing Esther. After the poker sealed her wound, London said, "We'll do him next," as he moved on to Daniel. Jean-Marc could not look. He locked his eyes on a crack in wall's plaster. *This man, I should kill. He enjoys hurting helpless people.*

London shouted, "Have a care, boy! You're letting the blood run on the bed. We don't want the humors getting back in them."

Jean-Marc whipped his head around and moved Daniel's small arm over the bowl. London did not notice the hatred in Jean-Marc's eyes.

When the bleeding was completed, the reverend told Jean-Marc, "Get rid of this boy." He went to the parlor, where Goody Adams sat on a wooden chair, and said, "I fear the worst. Am I right, you have three other children?"

"Two, Ruth and Jonathan." Her voice trembled. Tears ran down her face.

"Can you move them elsewhere?"

"I have ... a sister. She's blocks away. We could send them there."

"Good. Have your boy take them there, away from the pox that visits this house."

Goody Adams broke down. She put her hands over her face and cried. Chastity took over. She hurried into the children's rooms and helped them pack a few necessities. "John, bring them to their aunt's house. Do you know where it is?"

"No. Where—"

"Have the children show you. They'll know."

Ruth and Jonathan cried while they dressed to go out in the cold. Jonathan looked at Jean-Marc. "Will Papa die?"

Jean-Marc knelt and hugged the children. "We'll not let that happen, my little ones." His eyes filled with tears again.

"How will you stop it?" Ruth asked.

Would that I knew little Ruthy, would that I knew.

He helped them with their coats and picked up their bags. "You will have to show me where Aunty Martha lives."

Ruth looked up, "Button your coat John or you'll get sick."

"I will, little one." He led them out the door and buttoned his coat as they walked through the frigid morning air. They were all shivering when they finished the fifteen-minute walk to their aunt's house.

Martha opened the door. Her family could not afford servants. She often complained to her husband that Estelle and Jeremiah's servants made them slothful.

Jean-Marc said, "Goody Adams sent me to bring the childrens here, away from the pox."

"What, you be not satisfied watching my sister's family die? Now you bring them here to sicken mine?"

"Would you have me take them back to that house?"

"They be here now. I'll not send them away."

He knelt and rubbed his hands on their heads and said, "Ruthy, Jon-Jon, you must be good for Aunty Martha." He hugged them both and stood.

Martha snapped, "No one gave you leave to be familiar with me. I'm Goodwife Smythe to you."

Jean-Marc stood, his hands on the children's shoulders. "I am sorry, Goodwife Smythe."

"And who gave you leave to hug those children?"

"Goodman Adams knows that we hug the childrens. He does not mind."

"My sister's husband spares the rod with all in his household, to their detriment. Had I my way, you'd all be under a sterner hand. No ill could come from that. Now be on your way. We let out the heat."

The children cowered behind Jean-Marc's legs. He looked at Goody Smythe, then turned and hugged the children again. "Be brave my little ones."

"Stop hugging those children! I told my sister about you spoiling them. Their parents'll never break their wills if you keep hugging them."

Jean-Marc stood and glared at her then turned back to the children. He put his hands on their shoulders. "You must go in now. I'll come back for you soon." *Not soon enough, I'll wager.*

Martha pulled the crying children into the house and shut the door.

"What do they call such women here? Biddies? That dried up old biddy should not concern herself that I hug Goodman's children. Let her be content ruining her own children's lives ... She lives in this shack and judges my master? I have seen her likes before. Such as she should learn their place.

*****

Jean-Marc returned to the Adams home. Abigail came to hug him as he took off his coat in the kitchen. "It's good you're back. We need help."

"I should have brought Ruthy and Jon-Jon back with me. I do not like that woman. I think she does not like her sister's wealth and so is unkind to our childrens."

"Still, 'tis good they're there. We've all we can manage here, without worrying about them."

Jean-Marc took her in his arms. "You are tired. How long is it since you have slept?"

"No longer than you." She put her head on his shoulder and cried. "John, I'm afraid."

"We are all afraid." He stroked her head with his right hand, "We are all afraid."

*****

The ill did not get better. The care-givers got sick. Goody Adams was soon in bed beside her husband. Jean-Marc and Abigail became feverish. Chastity sent them to the cellar.

"With all I have to do upstairs, there's little I can do for you," Chastity said as she tucked them into their bed. "But's good you're servants. They'll not waste their money having Mister London see you. He's killing them upstairs." She looked upward and wiped the back of her hand against her forehead. She was exhausted. "Try to stay cool. Drink plenty. I'll bring porridge so you won't starve." She trudged up the stairs to the kitchen.

"She may feel worse than we do," Jean-Marc said with a wry smile.

Abigail groaned and tried to reposition herself in bed." She's labored long. We have too. I'd be glad to take her place. She'd not take mine."

They did their best to care for each other.

That night, Abigail, drenched in sweat, sat up. Every bone and muscle hurt. She reached to the table for the mug and drank some beer. It hurt to swallow. She put her hand against the base of her throat and grimaced as she drank again. *Look at John ... He's soaked too. He needs to drink.*

She tried to rouse him, but he would not wake. "John, you need drink." He only groaned and thrashed against the covers, already pushed down to his waist. She put the mug back on the table. *If he hurts like I do, the sleep's best.* She pulled the blankets over his shoulders and laid back, pulling the covers over her shoulders too.

The fever made both delirious, but in their delirium, they kicked off their quilts and somehow managed to undress. When Chastity brought them hot bowls of porridge, they were both lying flat on their backs, wearing nothing but their knee-length shirts. The cool cellar air helped ease their fevers.

Chastity shook Jean-Marc's shoulder. "John, John, wake up, you need to eat something." He only groaned and tried to turn away from her. Chastity walked around the bed to Abigail and shook her. "Abby, can you eat something?" One of Abigail's arms rose in an attempt to push Chastity's arm away.

They both be soaked. 'Tis good they're uncovered, but they're too hot.

She went back to the kitchen and returned with a bowl of cool water and some rags. She put damp cloths on both their foreheads. Several times, she took off the cloths, wet and replaced them.

Seems to be helping.

She shook Jean-Marc again. He opened his eyes and said something that Chastity could not understand. "John, you need to drink something." She wet his lips with warm beer. Without appearing to wake, he licked at his lips. Chastity continued this for several minutes before he opened his eyes and took a small sip of the beer, then dropped his head back to his pillow, as if exhausted.

At least it's something.

She walked around the bed and wet Abigail's lips. She licked at them but did not wake.

Sleep's best.

Chastity reached for their quilts, to cover them, but thought better of it. She pulled the quilt from their legs and folded it at the base of the bed. *If they wake cold, they'll find it there. Cooling's best for them.* She took the cloths from their heads, dropped them in the bowl and went upstairs. *If we can keep Mr. London away from them, they might live.*

*****

After two days, they felt less feverish. They were still very sick, but they were awake. Jean-Marc, managing a small smile, told Abigail, "I feel so sick. I fear I'll not die." Abigail tried to smile.

Their relief was short lived. That afternoon Abigail curled into a fetal position. With her left hand, she reached for the small of her back and groaned. "Oh, John, my back hurts so much."

He rolled onto his side behind her and rubbed her back. "Does this help?" She said nothing, so he stopped.

"Don't stop! It helped."

He rubbed Abigail's back until they both fell asleep.

Chastity brought them more porridge and some tea. Seeing them asleep, she took the porridge back upstairs, leaving the pot of tea by their bed in case they woke thirsty.

Jean-Marc woke around midnight. "Abigail," he groaned. "My back, she hurts. Can you rub it?"

She closed her eyes in a grimace. "I can't ... I hurt everywhere. 'Tis like all my skin hurts."

He reached out for her, touching her arm. She pulled it away from his touch.

In the dim light, he could see her lying on her back. Her legs were spread apart, arms away from her side. He tried to cover her with a quilt.

"Leave me," she groaned, "Take the quilt off my legs!"

His back had throbbed when he pulled the quilt over her. The pain was worse as he struggled to pull it off. He curled up with his back toward her. *Never have I felt such pain.*

Early that morning, the pain spread into Jean-Marc's legs and shoulders. He turned onto his back and groaned. They lay beside each other, covered in a painful rash, each crying out if touched by the other.

Near dawn, Chastity checked on them again. She placed a candle on the table beside their bed and opened the teapot. It was untouched. Pouring some of the cold tea into a cup, she sat next to Abigail, and held a spoonful of tea to her lips. They parted. The tea soaked into her parched tongue. *That's my girl. Perchance the tea'll soothe those sores.* Spoon by spoon Chastity managed to get Abigail to take the whole cup. Then she refilled it and spoon-fed tea to Jean-Marc.

She dragged herself up the stairs to the kitchen, ladled porridge into two bowls and brought them to the cellar. Chastity held a spoon of porridge to Abigail's lips. Moving it as if she was feeding a baby, she got Abigail to eat most of the porridge. *This'll help. She needs the strength.* She walked around the bed and fed Jean-Marc the same way. *There's a good boy.* Chastity smiled. She left large tankards of beer on small tables on each side of the bed, hoping they would drink. Resisting the urge to cover them, she went upstairs.

Assisting Mister London while also caring for Abigail and Jean-Marc left Chastity exhausted. She threw more wood on the cook fire and sat down. Her head sank to the table, and she fell asleep.

Hours later, she woke. Her face, arms, and back hurt. Shaking her head, she struggled to her feet and went back into the cellar. The candle was burned out, but enough daylight came down the stairs for her to see. Abigail and Jean-Marc were both asleep. She saw the beer tankards were both empty and smiled. She went to get them more beer.

Then Chastity went into the parlor where she found Mister London asleep on the broad, dark wooden bench, softened only by a dark blue seat cushion. The room was cold. Only embers glowed in the fireplace. She went into the kitchen for wood to build up the fire. In doing so, she woke the reverend.

He sat up, stretched and yawned. "How fare they in the cellar?"

"Still ill, sir, but they may have turned a corner. They've eaten a bit and drunk some."

"'Tis better news than I've had. Servants seem made of sterner stuff." He stood and stretched again. "What is there to eat?"

"I've some porridge hot."

"Good, I'll take it in the kitchen."

Chastity led him into the kitchen. She brought him a large bowl of porridge and a tankard of beer.

"You need eat too, else you'll get sick."

"I had cow pox, sir. I'll not get this."

"But from exhaustion you might. I've seen you eat nothing in days. Sit and eat. You're no help to me sick."

Chastity got a bowl of porridge and some beer for herself and sat.

"How does the family?"

"Not well, I fear. I've blistered, purged, and bled them again and again, but the pox still spread." He shook his head and took another spoon of porridge. "No matter how much or how often I bleed them, they only grow worse." He took another swallow of beer and stared into the blazing fire. "Now they're so weak they can't even drink the purgatives. I fear they may all be lost."

Are you so simple? Chastity shook her head and said nothing. London took it to mean she felt sorry for him, because after all his hard work, he was losing his patients.

He finished his breakfast, stood, and stretched. "We can't give up though. I'll bleed them all again. We both should pray." He walked from the room without waiting for any comment from Chastity.

If God heard my prayers, you'd leave those poor people alone. She got up and brought him clean basins for the blood and linens to clean the patients. Then she put on her coat and went for firewood.

When she had a chance, Chastity went back to the cellar to check on Abigail and Jean-Marc. Time and again she found the tankards empty. *Good, they're drinking.* Unfortunately, they were also soiling the bed. Despite their discomfort, she replaced their bed clothes and changed them.

*****

That afternoon Goodman Adams died, soon followed by Esther.

"Come here, girl," Mr. London called. Chastity hurried into the sick room. "We can't leave the dead here. You'll have to go to the docks and fetch some of the black slaves who work there. No freeman will come, and I doubt they'd send a white servant. Tell them to bring a cart and take the bodies to the cemetery for burial. The pastors there'll be doing funerals."

Chastity bundled against the cold and walked to the docks. There she found Goodman Standin who ran a small carting company.

He took off his glasses, wiped them on his coat, and inspected them by holding them up to the flame in the fireplace. "'Twill be a while afore they come. There be dead all over the city. The ground frozen the way it is, they can't even dig graves. Tell Mister London I'll send Rufus and Caesar with the cart as soon as I can." He motioned out the window. "Goodman Franklin's just across the way. His blacks are as busy with the dead as mine are. I'll tell him about the Adams. If his boys are back before mine, he'll send them. These are hard times. We'll help as we can."

Chastity returned home, told Mister London the news, and went into the cellar to check on Abigail and Jean-Marc. Abigail was sitting up, against a pillow. A few hours later Jean-Marc improved too. That night, when Chastity brought them food, they each ate full bowls of stew and drained two tankards of beer.

"'Tis good to see you moving," she told them.

"'Tis good to be able," he said, reaching for a bowl. He looked at his hands and laughed. "So, this be the dreaded pox, huh?"

"Don't worry about those little spots. The pocks are yet to come. Try not to break them. 'Twill be hard, and some'll break anyway, but when they break they hurt, and they leave terrible scars. You're through the worst, but you slept through most of that."

Abigail laughed and said, "You make it sound so terrible."

"Oh, it will be," Chastity said, heading up the stairs without smiling.

A few hours later, Abigail felt a sore spot on her forehead. "John, what's this?"

He leaned close to her, then kissed her sore spot. "It seems you have your first pock. I fear there will be more."

Abigail's eyes filled. "John, you've seen how people look after the pox. This will be joined by thousands. If I live, the marks will scar me so, you won't even want to look at me."

He kissed the pock again. "'Tis sad you think so little of me. I love you and I will love you pox or no, scars or no. If you die, I will die too."

Abigail buried her face against his chest and cried, now for joy.

Over the next week, the pox spread from Abigail's face to her neck, and arms then covered her body. She rolled to look at Jean-Marc and said, "The pox in my mouth and throat are choking me." Speaking made several of the pox pop. When they broke, she gagged on the bitter pus.

She refused to swallow it. Instead, she leaned over the side of the bed and let it drain from her mouth into a basin Chastity left there. Jean-Marc winced as he rolled toward her. He rubbed her shoulder to comfort her.

"Stop!" she shouted. Several pox broke under his light touch. The shoulder of her shirt soaked with blood and pus. The pox in her throat constricted her breathing. She could just manage to swallow beer. She could not eat.

At least they're not in my mouth. Without even noticing, he began to rub the painful pox in his groin. *Ow! I have to stop that.* Pox on his legs and groin broke, leaving raw skin to rub against raw skin, causing him to rub the area more.

Any movement hurt. Any movement caused pox to break, soaking their shirts. The raw skin bled. Their suffering was made worse by vomiting and diarrhea. Their retching caused more pox to burst. Cleaning themselves after diarrhea caused broken pocks to bleed.

The next day, the vomiting and diarrhea passed. They were weak but no longer in pain. They slept hours in each other's arms.

Another two days and the pocks began to scab over. Together they laughed at how ugly they were, covered from head to toe with scabs.

"John, I love you, but it's good your mother can't see you. That is a face not even a mother could love."

"Look at who talks. From such a face, dogs and childrens would run."

Then they would laugh together. They were still weak but they felt sure they were going to live. Over the next week, their scabs fell off. They began to move around and take care of each other.

Several days earlier, Mister London declared the family's crisis was over and left. They soon began to improve, confirming the learned doctor's wisdom. Chastity went into the attic for the first time in days and slept. She did not hear Goody Adams calling to her for something to drink.

*****

Chastity was still in bed when someone knocked at the door. Goody Adams struggled from bed, pulled on her robe and with effort went to answer. She was surprised to see Mister London.

"May I come in?"

"Of course." She led him to the parlor and sat in the closest chair.

"How fare you and Daniel?"

"Weak, but we improve." Speaking was difficult. "Daniel's bad scarred and still cannot open his eyes."

"He may yet improve. I shall pray for both of you." London looked exhausted. He'd slept little since the pox struck.

"It was good of you to look in on us."

"In truth, I come with sad tidings from your sister's home." He seemed sorrowful but looked straight into her face. This frightened her. "I know no way to soften this. The pox has taken Martha and four of her children." He paused and looked away for a moment.

Martha ... and her children?

She put her hand to her face and began to cry. After losing Jeremiah and Esther and all she and Daniel suffered, she wasn't sure how much more she could bear.

"As well as your precious son, Jonathan," London went on.

She knew he said more but did not hear him. She wailed, "Jonathan too? And Martha? Why, God, why?"

Mister London moved his chair next to hers, put his hand on her arm and sat without speaking. She cried a long while before she was able to speak again. "You said nothing of Ruth."

"I have better tidings about Ruth. She has been brought to Goodman Braddock's home where his goodwife cares for her. I expect her to recover. When circumstances settle here you can send your girl for her. She is eager to come home."

Goodwife Adams had always heard that at times of great loss, the mind becomes numb. Her mind never numbed. She just felt great pain, suffering, and loss.

*****

Goody Adams sent Chastity to fetch Ruth that day. The family began their recovery together. All were scarred by the pox. Only Daniel was badly scarred. He did not recover his sight.

In the cellar, Abigail and Jean-Marc suffered, but less than those in the house above. They both recovered. Their scars were visible, but not disfiguring.

And they were in love.

Chapter Eight
The Merchant

"A Merchant's desire is not glory, but gain."
Samuel Johnson

With time the household, as the city, recovered. Ruth and Ezra returned to their schools. Most days, Daniel, now blind, sat in his room until the other children came home. Goody Adams resumed not presiding over her home. She had girls for that. Despite the pain the family went on.

By July, life was developing into a new normal. Abigail regained strength and took back her share of the household duties. Jean-Marc started brewing again. He ruined more than one batch of beer in the process.

Still speaking with a thick French accent, he told Goody Adams, "Do not worry that I am so slow. After the pox, the ships, they do not come here anyway. With no ships, no one buys the beer. This works well. We have not beer to sell."

Goody Adams laughed for the first time since the pox but thought, *'Tis fine to make sport, but how long will Jeremiah's money last? What does a brewer do without beer or ships to sell her beer to? The inns in town all brew their own. Would that there was a way I could sell beer to them- if I had beer to sell.*

*****

People thought Goody Adams was a rich widow. She received seven marriage proposals within a month of her return to health but refused them all. In a city accustomed to seeing impropriety everywhere, several of the rejected suitors complained to Mister London that an unmarried woman should not live in a house with a male servant. Her pastor spoke with her about the situation after Sabbath worship.

She was polite, but firm, "There is nothing improper in my home. Jeremiah provided for our needs. My family wants for nothing. We need no man to provide for us." However, the conversation upset Estelle.

The next morning, she sat in her parlor with a cup of tea but could not swallow. She put down her cup, walked to the window and looked out at the light rain falling on hot cobblestones.

What need have I for a husband? Those who ask me have more interest in getting into my money than into my bed ... 'Tis comedy there. Money's my one concern ... Ships are returning and I know nothing of brewing. Without Jeremiah can the brewery support us? ... Mayhap I should sell an indenture ... but Abigail has what, two years left? Chastity three? Neither'd bring much. Only John has real time left, but without him, who would run the brewery? He goes out there every day. What does he do? I need a brewer, not a husband. She went back to her chair, sat, and began to cry.

*****

The next week, Jean-Marc gathered the women in the kitchen. "You must wait here. When I am ready, you must come to the dining room." He was excited about something. The women sat in the kitchen and waited.

Goody Adams asked, "Know either of you what this is about?"

Abigail and Chastity were mumbling their confusion, when a call came from the next room. "Goody, Abigail, Chastity! All is ready. Come to the dining room."

His voice reminded the older woman of a little boy eager to show his parents some new accomplishment.

"I'm ready! Come, come, you must try these."

The brewery sold almost nothing since the pox, but Jean-Marc still made beer every day. After many missteps, he proved to himself that he could brew quality beer. Now he intended to prove it to Goody Adams.

"Sit, sit. Here you are." He held the large, oaken, ladder-back chair for Estelle to sit. Then he sat Chastity and Abigail on matching chairs around the table.

There was a small pewter cup filled with beer at each chair. "You must try these and tell me what yous think." He stood grinning, hands on his hips, as the women tried his beer.

Goody took a small sip, smiled then sipped again. Her eyes lit up. "John, you shock me. This beer is good! No woman could brew such beer for her family." Abigail and Chastity nodded their agreement.

"It tastes so much like the master's," Chastity said.

Abigail just smiled. When she thought Goody was not looking, she reached out and squeezed Jean-Marc's hand. He put his other hand on hers, squeezed, and smiled.

Goody Adams filled her mouth and seemed to chew the beer. "You've done it. If you can make such a beer every time, with the ships returning, we're ready."

"Thank you, Goody, but you must know Goodman Adams, he teached me that each beer, it is a little different. He said, 'Know when you change your makings you change your beer.' He made me to pay attention to the things we use to make our beer. So, I can make different beers when need be."

Goody Adams looked perplexed. Abigail and Chastity, the cooks, nodded.

"Goodman said when the beer is for a ship to be long at sea, the brewer, he puts maple syrup, honey or molasses in the wort. This makes the beer stronger. This beer, it will last longer. She no, how you say, spoils."

"As when we speed sour dough with sugar," Chastity said.

"With no spoiled beer, that pleases the customers, *n'est-ce pas*? And then some things we use to make the beer we find easily in spring but not so much in the fall. Other things we find in fall."

"'Tis why we bake with berries in the summer. There be none the rest of the year." Chastity nodded her understanding.

"So, the beers and ales we make, they taste a little different in those times. A spring brew it will be different from a winter brew, no?"

"I knew beer tasted not always the same, but I never thought of it in that way, John." Abigail seemed surprised.

"When I worked alone, I wondered over this. No ships came. No one came to buy the beers, so I thought to see if I could make good beers that are different from each other, like the wines in France are different from each other."

All three women looked confused.

"In France, there were wines I liked more than others because of the different taste, no? But even this, it would change. Some wines, they were good with one food, and not so much with another. With different food, you must drink different wine. There are wines, they taste better without the food or after the meal. Some peoples even liked wines that I liked not at all."

As he was saying this he went into the pantry and returned with a cart on which there were three pitchers. "So, I think that people, they will like different beers, too, no?"

"Isn't beer just beer? There's good beer and bad beer, but beer is beer, isn't it?" Goody Adams asked.

"I maked the beer you just had the way Goodman Adams, he teached me."

"And it is good, John." Goody nodded.

"But also, I tried putting different things in the beers. I keeped the notes of how I maked each beer so I can make the same beer again, if I like. Many beers I did not like, but these I did. Tell me what yous think." If possible, his smile grew broader as he filled their cups with a bright yellow brew. "Try this one. I think women and the childrens will like this beer more."

The women sampled the new beer.

Abigail agreed. "Oh, I like this one better. It tastes so fresh."

"This beer is truly good, John," Goody Adams told him. "I think some people will come to buy this just for its taste. Well done."

Still smiling, he took each woman's cup and dumped the beer from it into a bowl. He poured a deep golden beer into cups for the women to sample.

"I like this one better," Chastity said, looking into the mug. "It's not so bitter."

"For this beer, I use less barley and more wheat. And I add just the little bit of honey, but few hops. In France," he told them, "wines, they are named for the grapes peoples make them with, *n'est-ce pas?* I do the same. This, I call honey wheat beer. The first, lighter beer, for this I used not barley but rice. But there is more." He emptied the women's cups again and poured a beer as black as coffee into the women's mugs.

This time Abigail spoke first. "John, this beer's heavy, but tastes creamy."

"'Tis nutty, not bitter at all," Chastity added.

"For this beer, I put oats into the wort. The beer, it is heavier and darker. This I call the oat beer. Now I have learned. I can make the oat beer anytime I wish, or the honey wheat or the rice beer. I think peoples who like these beers will come buy from us because others can no make such beers."

Goody Adams was pleased.

This is good. If I please her she'll not interfere with my brewing. Jean-Marc had developed strong opinions about beer. *No matter what Goodman Adams said, maple syrup or molasses must not be used in honey's stead ... If I cannot gather the type hops I need, I will buy them. For the ingredient I need, supply or time of year, matters not ... With bad ingredients, I cannot make good beer. I will use what tastes best, not garbage, just to save some money. This way, I will make the best beers, not the cheapest. People will pay more money for better beer. Of this I am sure.*

Fearing she would not understand, he did not tell Goody Adams.

*****

As weeks passed, more ships came to Boston. That meant the agents who supplied the ships returned to the brew house to order beer for their voyages. Goody Adams met with them, just as her husband did before. When they learned of Goodman Adams' death the suppliers often turned, as if to go.

Goody Adams would stop them. "We remain in business still. We still brew and sell the best beer in Boston. We can fill your order with the same quality beer."

However, when a customer asked about price or delivery, she had no idea what to say. She would try to hide her confusion, and call

Jean-Marc into the conversation. To her surprise, he had learned more than how to make beer from Goodman Adams. He understood pricing and delivery schedules. And he added a new wrinkle.

"Which beer you would like?"

"Which beer? I want beer. The same beer I've bought here for fifteen years."

"This beer we sell, at the fair price. But we sell other beers too, yes? Beers with the different taste."

"Other beers?"

"Do wheat, barley, or oat breads taste the same?"

"Of course not. Each has its own taste."

Jean-Marc would explain, "The beer, it too, is like that. I brew beers with all these grains. Just the way wheat bread it is different from the oat bread, the wheat beer it is different from the oat beer. Some beers, they taste one way, others another. Barley, it costs less to buy. So, barley beer can be bought cheaper. The choice, it is yours." Then he led the buyers into the brew house and gave them samples. At first the buyers were confused by these choices. But they soon came to prefer one type of beer over another. When they returned to order for their next voyage they would reorder the beer they preferred.

Season after season, word of these options spread among ship owners and among the sailors. Buyers, who had purchased from other brewers for years, gradually began to come to Jean-Marc, to supply their ships. After a few voyages, the sailors recognized the different beers Jean-Marc produced and learned their names. On shore, they began asking for that type of beer in the local inns, only to be told that each inn sold only the beer or ale it produced.

*****

Jean-Marc found himself turning customers away. *I sell nigh on to as much beer as we did before the pox. But then there were two of us. Had I help, I could make more.*

Without consulting Goody Adams, he started hiring teamsters make his deliveries. With more time, he could brew more beer. In the busy spring and summer seasons, he could sell yet more beer, if he could find a way to make it.

One morning, after refusing his second order of the day, he walked into the house. He found Goody Adams reading her Bible, in the parlor. "Goody, can you spare a moment?"

She looked up from her reading, took off her spectacles and nodded.

He took a deep breath before going on. "Goody, we sell near as much as the Master did before the pox, but he had my help. This morning, I sent away two buyers—"

She slammed her Bible shut and pointed her spectacles at him. "You did what?" Her voice was angry.

"I am sorry, Goody, but I had to send away two buyers—"

"Why would you do that?" she demanded.

"Because they wanted to buy beer we do not have. We sell all the beer I am able to make. Could I make more, we would sell that, too, but I cannot make more working alone. I already hire teamsters to make deliveries."

"Who gave you leave to do that?"

"I've long bought supplies in your name. I did the same for this. By paying teamsters to make our deliveries, the brewery earns more money. By me running the brewery alone we lose sales."

Goody pursed her lips, put her Bible on the table and motioned that he should sit. He pulled a small wooden chair from across the room and sat opposite her.

"We sell more than enough to meet all the family's needs, but we could sell more. With help to move grain, haul water, and split wood, my time would be spent brewing beer, as the Master's was."

She nodded. "You need help clear enough. I know all that you do. But Jeremiah always handled the brewery without me. I don't know as I can do what you ask. How would I hire a man or buy an indenture?"

"I could speak to Samuel Smith for you, Goody, though I think he'd insist you sign the papers."

She stood and walked across the room. For almost a minute she stared out a window. Then she looked at him, "Can we afford another indenture?"

"I see all that comes in. You've enough silver now and with another indenture, you'd earn more."

She turned back to the window. "I suppose it must be. Will you see to it for me, John?"

"I will. Thank you, Goody." He got up and left the room.

An unspoken agreement had just been reached. Jean-Marc ran the household for his owner. As long as there was always enough for her needs and desires, she wanted no information about the business or the house. What she wanted was no inconvenience.

That afternoon, Jean-Marc walked to the Red Lion Inn. Samuel Smith sat before the fire, with a tankard of beer and a plate of cheese. As Jean-Marc approached him, Smith looked up. "You're the boy I sold to Goodman Adams."

"'I am. Goodman Adams was lost in the pox."

"I'd heard. I also heard you now run the brewery for his widow. Seems you were a fortuitous purchase."

"Goody treats her servants well. In return, we serve her well."

"Strange she hasn't married. People talk, you know."

"I am certain this is true, Goodman. But without Goodman Adams, there's more to do than I'm able. I'm here to purchase another boy for her."

"A servant buying a servant? And scripture says there's nothing new under the sun. How do you buy an indenture?"

"I only represent Goody Adams. She buys the servant."

"How am I to know that?"

"When we agree, you can have Obadiah bring the papers to Goody Adams. She can sign when he brings the boy. Have you a sturdy boy?"

"I do. Young Justin arrived from England a fortnight ago. He's already trained."

"You mean you beat him 'til he fears you."

"We have made him obedient. Would you want him otherwise?"

"How old is he?"

"I believe fifteen. His seven years are just begun. Would you see him?"

"I would."

Together, they walked to Smith's office. "Obadiah," Smith called as they walked through the office and into the yard behind it.

"Yes, Master." Jean-Marc remembered the big man's deep voice and muscled body.

"You remember the boy Goodman Adams bought before the pox?"

Obadiah looked at Jean-Marc for a moment. "I do." Turning to Jean-Marc he said, "Why come you back here?"

"His master died in the pox. It seems his mistress has sent him to buy young Justin from us. Bring him out."

"Yes, Master." Obadiah unlocked the nearest cell. "Come out boy. Meet, uh, what do they call him?"

Smith turned to Jean-Marc. "I remember not your name. How are you called?"

"My name is Jean-Marc Bompeau, but Goody Adams calls me John."

"Justin, this is Master John. He represents Goody Adams, who wants for a husband to manage her affairs," Smith said.

Justin was smaller than most but looked well-fed and healthy.

"Can he work?"

Smith looked at Justin, "Tell him boy, can you work, or would you like additional instruction?"

The boy flinched. "I can work," he looked at Jean-Marc. "Buy my papers, Master John, and you'll not regret it."

"If we buy your papers, boy, neither will you regret it. Servants are not beat in our house."

Smith looked surprised. "A novel approach. Twelve pounds will take him. You remember Obadiah will go with you to see he doesn't run."

"At twelve pounds, you'll keep him. If he works well, Goody will buy him for six."

"You insult me, John. The price for a servant's gone up since the pox. Take him or leave him."

"Then I'll leave him." The boy looked as if he'd just been hit. "You forget, Goodman Smith, I work with the shippers. I know I can get a boy off a ship for five pounds eight, but I'd as soon have one today as wait. To have the boy now, and for your efforts, I'll go six."

"You act as though the money was yours. Six and eight. I'll take it in tobacco or rum."

"I'll pay six in silver or I'll walk now."

"Goodman Adams was an easier man to deal with than you. Where get you that much silver?"

"Send Obadiah with the papers for Goody to sign. When we agree to keep the boy, I'll give him the silver."

"How will a woman sign a contract?"

"She has no husband. Would you have me sign?"

"How could a servant sign?"

"What matters it to you? Send Obadiah and the boy, with the papers. So long as he returns with silver, you're paid."

"And you think I'd trust Obadiah with that much silver?"

"So, come yourself. At six pounds sterling, Goody will take the boy. At six and one, you'll keep him."

"Obadiah put the boy away." Smith's voice was angry. "No servant speaks to me in such a manner."

Jean-Marc turned to leave. Obadiah pushed the boy back to his cell. The boy cried out, "Please, Sir, take me. I'll be a true servant." The cell's door slammed shut as Jean-Marc was about to leave the yard.

"Stay," Smith called out. "Six pounds it is, but sterling, not tobacco, when he arrives."

Jean-Marc returned to the yard. "Six pounds sterling, when he proves himself."

"Done." Smith was unsure what to do next. Jean-Marc held out his hand. Smith looked at the hand, into his face and at the hand again, then shook it. "You're a hard man to trade with."

"When you sold me, you promised I'd be a loyal servant. Your word was good," Jean-Marc said, shaking Smith's hand and looking him in the eye.

*****

In this way, Jean-Marc purchased, Justin, and a year later he purchased another boy, Joshua. They reported directly to Jean-Marc and despite the fact they would be freemen before him, they called him "Master John", as Smith told Justin to.

He also bought an ox, cart, and a black slave, Moses, an experienced teamster, to reduce their hauling expenses. Moses, too, called Jean-Marc "Master John".

The brewery had to expand to accommodate the increase in business. Goody Adams allowed Jean-Marc to approve the plans and hire the tradesmen who built the addition. He was pleased with their work and used the same tradesmen to build an extension on to the house.

Goody Adams refused to allow Jean-Marc and Abigail to marry and she would not permit them to share a bed if they were not. A new room was built for Chastity and Abigail. Rachel, a new girl, purchased to assist them, now slept in their old space in the attic. Jean-Marc had his own comfortable room in the servants' quarters. Justin and Joshua shared the cellar. A room was built in the brewery for Moses.

A small servants' parlor was built in the rear of the house, but the other servants soon learned this room was to provide quiet time for Jean-Marc and Abigail. Every night, when their duties were done, they sat together on the green, silk-covered sofa and looked into the fire.

"It seems we'll never be free," Abigail said.

"You're free now."

"You know my meaning." She snuggled closer to his side and pulled the quilt to her neck.

Rachel brought their tea. "Will there be anything else, Master John?"

"No, Rachel. You can go to bed. We'll see to the dishes."

"Thank you, sir," she nodded to them both, "Abigail." She smiled and left the room.

Abigail got up to pour their tea. "I want a family. I want to be with you."

"As do I. Thus far, Goody is steadfast. If we're together and have a child, we'll both be flogged and you probably indentured again to pay the cost of raising the child."

"I'm all but an indenture now."

"Would you raise your child as an indenture?"

"No."

"There's the rub. Few have what we have," he waved his hand around the comfortable little room, "but many have what we cannot." He took the white china cup and saucer she passed him. "I've asked about a salary, so I can buy my papers, but she refuses."

"Why would she pay a servant? She won't pay me, and I be free." She snuggled back against his side and sipped her tea.

"Aye, she's mean with her money." he sipped tea. "I'll not serve her the sixteen years she thinks I owe."

"What will you do?"

"I know not. Running would be a hardship I'd not put on you. I've been in the wilderness. I've no interest to go there again, or to take you there. And I'll not go without you."

"So, what do we do?"

He finished his tea, put the cup and saucer atop the maple table and put his arms around her.

"Stop, you'll spill my tea." She sat up and finished the tea and snuggled back against him.

"Something will come for us," he said, "Of this I'm sure."

They sat and stared at the fire until they both fell asleep. Sometime later, Jean-Marc woke. He slid his shoulder away from hers and slipped a pillow under Abigail's head. He pulled the quilt over her, kissed her forehead and went to his room.

Something will come for us, he thought as he climbed into his bed.

*****

Some days later, on her way to the butcher's, Abigail overheard two elderly women talking.

"My hands be so crippled with arthritis, I can scarce sew. My husband wants for shirts and I for a dress."

The second woman nodded, "And my eyes have become so bad, I'm not able either. My son's wife tries to help, but with seven of her own, she's able to do little."

Abigail approached them, "Excuse me, Goodwives. I did not mean to listen, but did I hear you say sewing was a trial for you?"

The smaller of the two women turned to face her. "You did. See the worn coat I'm forced to wear. My husband will not let me buy our things from the tailor or the store."

"Would he let you buy the cloth?" Abigail asked.

"That much I can do. It's been long since he made me spin my own cloth."

"Should you provide the cloth, I could come fit you, then sew your clothing for you. I'd want two shillings to make a coat. I could make a blouse, apron or breeches for one."

"Two shilling's a man's wage for't day."

"To make a fine coat takes longer. I'd need payment in coin, not kind."

The second woman said, "Two shillings and in coin? We'll wear these rags."

"Then wear them you will, Mum. I'll take one and six and do shirts at eight pence."

A deal was struck. With Rachel in the house, Jean-Marc had lightened the load on Chastity and Abigail. Without telling Goody, Abigail used her time to become a seamstress. She was soon sewing clothing for three older women. In good weeks, she earned over four shillings, hiding her coins in a sock, in one of her drawers.

When I've earned enough, I'll buy John from Goody and we'll leave this place.

Often, she sewed with Jean-Marc sitting in the same room. He never knew and she did not tell him.

*****

Jean-Marc's activities created a good deal of confusion in the community. His customers, suppliers, and in time even Mr. London, the family's pastor, came to believe he was a freeman. He bought and sold everything needed for the brewing operations. He bought the slave and new servants, including the new house girl.

How was he not a free man?

Suppliers allowed him to sign his name as promise of future payment. Many people thought him wealthy. He dressed the part. He saw to it that Abigail and Chastity were better dressed too. Goody Adams paid little to no attention to any of this. There was always more than enough to buy anything she wanted, and she was otherwise unconcerned. For Estelle Adams, life was good.

This created discord in the community. Most people believed a woman should be married. Several women spread filthy rumors about Estelle and Jean-Marc, although she was almost twenty years older than he.

The gossip reached Mister London, who did not believe it. But even rumors of impropriety in his parish upset him. Several times, he raised the issue with Goody Adams as she left church after Sabbath worship. These conversations were heard by others. Each time they had this conversation, sensing an opportunity, several men would propose to Estelle during the next week. She refused them all.

Mister London was unaccustomed to being ignored. After their third such conversation did not result in a marriage, Mister London decided he must teach about marriage in his Sabbath sermon. That week, he reminded the faithful that it was God's plan, "That women are to marry and bear children, if they may be, and that men are to marry, then provide for and protect their families."

Estelle Adams was furious.

The next afternoon, a younger man in a threadbare suit knocked at her door. Rachel greeted him, "May I help you, Sir?"

"You may. My name is John Moore. I wish to see your mistress."

"I will see if she is available. Will you wait a moment?"

Moore was upset to be kept waiting on the porch, like a common peddler, but he forced a smile and said, "I am at her disposal."

Rachel closed the door and went to the parlor, where Estelle was reading, "Goody, there be another man, this one called John Moore, at the door. Will you see him?"

"John Moore? I scarce know the man. As I recall, Jeremiah once loaned him money that was never repaid. This is Mister London's doing. I suppose I must see him. Show him in but take not his hat or offer him anything."

Rachel brought him into the parlor. Goody remained seated and held out her hand. "Goodman Moore. I remember you well, from your dealings with my husband. What brings you to my humble home?"

Moore flinched, but crossed the room and took her hand. "Widow Adams, it is a fine day. I thought to visit you. Mayhap you would fancy a walk along the harbor."

"I would not, but I thank you for your thought."

Moore realized he was about to be sent away. "I have heard you want for a husband. It would please me to be your provider and protector."

My provider? Look at his suit. He cannot even provide himself with a respectable suit of clothing. "I thank you, Goodman Moore, for your concern, but I was once married to a man I did love. God chose to take my husband from me, but not before Jeremiah was able to see to the needs of his family. I thank you for coming." She stood. "Rachel, will you see our guest to the door?"

"But what of protecting?"

"My trust is in the Lord. He protects us."

Rachel opened the door. "Goodman, I'll see you to the door."

"You could learn to love another."

"I think not but thank you for your concern." Estelle turned her back, walked to another chair and sat.

Rachel said, "Follow me, please, sir."

Moore started to say something, but Estelle picked up her Bible and started reading. He went out of the room with Rachel, who closed the door behind them.

*****

Ezra and Ruth attended school. Ezra went to the grammar school in the North Church. Ruth went to the dame school that met in Hannah Broadbent's kitchen. Being blind, Daniel had received no teaching since the pox. Jean-Marc refused to accept this situation. On his own, he hired a tutor for Daniel. Goody Adams considered this a waste of her money.

"Who told you to hire a tutor for Daniel? You waste my money. The boy is blind."

"As I do with much in your home, I filled a need for your family. The brewery earns far more than you spend. The tutor costs you little."

"What do you expect Daniel to learn?"

"I expect him to learn much. Your son is blind, Goody, he is not dead. With a mother as wealthy as you, there is no need for him to be unlettered."

"Have I that much?"

"Goody, you have more than you know. You are one of the wealthiest women in Boston."

Daniel's tutor met with him in the servant's parlor every day while the other children were at school.

*****

One evening, after the servant's supper, Ezra followed Ruth into Jean-Marc's office in the brewery.

Ruth was angry. "John, 'tis unfair."

"What would that be, Ruthy?"

Ezra said, "She's cross, for I study history and philosophy and she learns to sew."

"'Tis true, Ruthy?"

"'Tis. I hate sewing. Be not servants for that?"

"Not all women are so fortunate as your mother, to afford servants."

"Do you take his side?"

"Ezra, come here." Ezra stood next to Jean-Marc, who put his arm around the boy. "Why thinks your sister that you have a side against her?"

"I said girls are to keep the house, whilst boys are to work. 'Tis God's plan."

"I see. But your mother keeps not the house."

"She works not."

Jean-Marc smiled. "Her work is not plain to you. Do I work?"

"Of course. You run the brewery and the other servants."

"I do so at your mother's direction. Her work is to see that I have what I need to do my work and to see that my work is done. She allowed me to buy Rachel, Joshua, Justin, and Moses. She approved the changes in the house and brewery."

"You didn't just do those things?" Ruth asked.

Jean-Marc put an arm around Ruth too. "I do little without your mother's approval, Ruthy. So, you see," he looked at Ezra, "your mother works. It is important that women can do these things. What do you read in school?"

Ruth said, "We both read the Bible. He gets to read the *Book of Martyrs,* too."

"And you would like to read this?"

"That and his other histories. And he learns Greek and Hebrew."

"How does this work? You both are able to read the Bible in English. I need to read English to do my job, but I find it hard. Will you teach me to read and write English? If you do that, I will teach you to read and write in French and Greek."

"You read Greek?" the children said, almost in unison.

"I do. My tutor insisted that I learn many things. Tomorrow, I will go to the bookseller and have him buy a copy of *The Iliad,* in Greek and *Agathonphile,* in French. It will be long before we get those. The seller will have to order them from Europe for us. I will also buy a copy of *The Book of Martyrs* from him. Together, we can read the Bible and *Book of Martyrs* in English and the other books, in Greek and French. Dannyboy can come too. I am sure his tutor does not teach him French. Then we will all learn."

"Can Abigail come too?" Ezra asked.

"Ah, my little one, did you not just say women were to care for the house and need not letters?"

Ezra looked at his feet, "Yes."

"I am afraid our Abigail agrees with you. I have often tried to teach her letters, but she has no wish to learn them."

The next day, Jean-Marc went to the bookseller and ordered the books. He sat with the Adams children every night and read.

*****

A change came when Josiah Woodley, an innkeeper called at the house's front door.

"Good day to you, Goodman," Rachel greeted him.

"Good day. I need to speak with your master."

"Would you see Goody Adams or Master John?"

"You dare call your master by his given name?" Woodley sounded indignant.

"Master John's a servant, sir," Rachel explained. "But he's the master of the house for Goody Adams."

This confused the innkeeper. "Who do I see to buy beer?"

"That would be Master John. Please come in. I'll fetch him. Who shall I say calls?"

"Josiah Woodley, proprietor of the Crown and Scepter Inn."

Rachel led him into the sky-blue parlor. She could still smell the fresh paint. "Please be seated. I'll see if the master can meet with you." He sat on the new, dark blue, silk couch and noticed it matched the drapes. The room was appointed with pewter lampstands and candle holders with glass bulbs. The carved, dark wooden end tables were topped with white marble.

In a few minutes, Rachel returned with Jean-Marc, who greeted Woodley with a smile and an extended hand.

"Good day to you, Goodman."

Woodley stood, unsure if he should shake a servant's hand. He decided to shake the hand but did not smile. He considered Jean-Marc over-dressed for a servant.

"Good day. I come to inquire about buying beer for my inn. I need see your mistress."

"I speak for Goody Adams' business interests. It will please me to assist you." Jean-Marc turned and called, "Rachel." She returned to the parlor. "Prepare a sample selection for Goodman Woodley."

"Yes, Sir."

Hearing a servant called sir made Woodley cringe.

Jean-Marc led him from the house to the sampling area in his office. "The shippers who buy our beer order large quantities. I would assume that you would be interested in a small order, perhaps a variety of our beers."

"I sell more than most," Woodley did not like hearing his purchase referred to as small. "The seamen ask me if I can serve your beers in my inn. By doing so, I may be able to help us both."

"And we would appreciate your patronage. Come into my office."

The white walls were stenciled with a recurring theme of green willow trees, to signify long life, and yellow pineapples, to signify hospitality. Against the wall was a large oak desk with an inkwell, several quills and a penknife. It was covered with papers and invoices. In the middle of the room there was a small table and three comfortable wooden chairs. Jean-Marc seated the innkeeper.

"The girl will be here with some samples of our beers in a moment."

In less time than the innkeeper expected, Rachel came with samples of all of the beers. While Rachel prepared the beer samples, Jean-Marc prepared a plate of sliced cheese and black bread.

"Please try them all." He motioned to the small mugs, smiling. "I've learned you should start with the lighter beers. After tasting the darker beers, the lighter ones'll not taste right."

Still unsure of the situation, Woodley sampled each beer, while helping himself to plenty of the bread and cheese.

"These are very good, boy. But I need to know what they cost and how they'll be delivered. I need to speak to your mistress on these matters."

"There is no need for that. I can explain our pricing and delivery."

The innkeeper was shocked that a servant felt free to discuss such matters, but he was given a very low price. He raised an eyebrow. "I scarce can make beer myself at these prices. How can your mistress sell so cheap?"

Jean-Marc nodded. "We make a good deal of beer and purchase our supplies in large quantities. This allows us to buy at a low price. This allows you to save."

"All of these beers are better than I make. If your mistress can sell me these beers at these prices, I can sell better beer for the same price I charge now." This made the innkeeper smile. "This will free me for other things. But what of delivery?"

Jean-Marc also smiled and nodded again. "Most of our orders are for twenty or more barrels of a single type of beer, but of late ship owners have been ordering one or two barrels of another type. To fill these orders, I maintain a standing supply of all of our beers. You would be ordering a barrel or two at a time. I can always fill such orders from my stock on the day they're received."

"You'll not sell me stale beer!" Woodley sounded indignant, as if he had just been insulted.

"I would never sell stale beer to anyone." Jean-Marc's face became serious. "I run the largest brewery in Boston, serving more ships than the next three breweries combined. No beer ever stays long in my warehouse. With my reputation, I can ill afford to sell stale beer. Each of these beers you just sampled came from my standing inventory. Which tasted stale to you?"

Woodley was shocked that a servant spoke as if the brewery was his own. It took him a moment to respond. "They all taste fresh."

"As they ever will. If I deliver bad beer, I'll give you your money back."

"But you're a servant, boy." Woodley's voice was gruff. "How make you such a promise?"

This again? My business earns more than any of them and the fools can't even see it. Jean-Marc only nodded. "I understand your concern. Goody Adams' responsibilities to her family take most of her time. Without a husband, she has given me full responsibility over her brewery. I run the brewery under her authority, but seldom under her direction. Any prices I give or promises I make, Goody Adams will guarantee. If you like, you can ask her." His tone betrayed irritation.

The innkeeper thought the price and service promised were too good to pass on. "Your promises sound good, boy, but what's the worth of a servant's word? I need speak with your mistress."

"Very well, Goodman." Jean-Marc still smiled, but the smile and voice were cold. "If you will follow me back into the house, I'll see if Goody Adams can meet with you."

On the way to the parlor he called to Rachel. "See if Goody Adams is able to meet with Goodman Woodley." The tone of his voice startled Rachel. He sounded angry. Jean-Marc seldom sounded angry.

In the parlor, he indicated that Woodley should sit. Jean-Marc sat in a chair opposite him. Woodley was shocked that a servant sat in his presence without permission. The men waited in silence for several minutes until Goody Adams arrived.

Both men stood. Doing his best to hide his anger, Jean-Marc said, "I'm sorry to bother you, Goody, but Goodman Woodley wishes to place a small order with us." Unintentionally, he emphasized small. "He wishes your assurances that the prices I gave him and the promises I made are correct."

Not offering her hand to Woodley or sitting, Goody Adams said, "John speaks for me in all matters of business. Any price or promise he gives is correct." She turned as if to go.

Woodley delayed her. "Perhaps if I spoke to your husband or your son."

"My husband was taken in the pox and my sons are children. Fortunately, God has blessed me with John, who more than capably sees to my interests." She turned to Jean-Marc. "Do you need anything else, John?"

"No. Thank you, Goody. As always, you've been most helpful."

Woodley was shocked. He looked at Jean-Marc. "It all seems to be as you have said. That being the case I'll take a barrel each of your oat, honey wheat, and rice beers. When can they be delivered?"

"Our cart is making a delivery at the wharves just now. It should be back within the hour. I can send him to you when he returns. Will you be ready to pay for it, with hard money, when it is delivered?"

"You can deliver them today?" Woodley was incredulous.

"We can, if you are able to pay today."

"I can."

"Then we can."

Woodley was uncomfortable shaking Jean-Marc's hand to seal the deal but he shook it.

*****

The Crown and Scepter became the brewery's first local customer. This worked well for that inn. Its business increased as customers came for the new varieties of beer. Then other innkeepers felt compelled to follow The Crown and Scepter's example, or they would lose even more business to it.

In time, first this small brewer, then that one, stopped brewing as more and more business came to Jean-Marc. Goody Adams withdrew more and more from the business that enriched her family. People saw Jean-Marc less as a servant and more as a successful merchant.

Abigail was nineteen and a free woman, but she chose not to leave without Jean-Marc, who still owed Goody Adams sixteen years of service. She continued to work for Goody Adams in exchange for food, board, and clothing, all of which improved under Jean-Marc's direction.

Chastity had one more year of service left. She had already decided that one of Jean-Marc's customers, Goodman Isaiah Poole, a wealthy widower of sixty-one years would be her husband when she was free. Goodman Poole had yet to be informed of Chastity's decision, but neither Abigail nor Jean-Marc doubted this would happen.

All would be well, if the free people of Boston could accept an unmarried woman, but they either could or would not. The gossip became worse. Pressure grew on Mister London to do something to protect the city's morality. A neighbor tried to have Estelle arrested for fornication, but with only gossip and no witnesses, Judge Sewall refused to hear the case.

On a regular basis, Mister London reminded her of God's plan for men and women to be married. She pretended to listen but was determined not to remarry. London was not pleased with her effrontery.

Chapter Nine
Social Conventions

**"Marriage is like putting your hand into a bag of
snakes, in hope of pulling out an eel."**
Leonardo da Vinci

Goody Adams fumed. *Do they think me deaf? ... I'll have no part
of another marriage.* She brought her cup to her lips but did not
drink. She couldn't swallow. *I hear them ... Jeremiah was over
tolerant o' me. But even he beat me a' times. I saw how my sister's
man beat her. What's to say a new man'd be not like him? Jeremiah
was enough. I'll not have some man beat me the way Elihu did
Martha.* She forced herself to swallow some tea, got up from the
table and walked to the window.

A small boy played with a white puppy in the street. A fish
monger pushed his cart past, wailing his song. "Liiiiive-o, fissssh-o,
one a penny, two a penny, fish alive-o. Liiiiive-o ..."

*I need no husband to support us. I proved that. So long as I have
John we do fine. And he's mine for sixteen years yet .... I'll be dead
before I need another man.*

Rich widows made more attractive wives than did penniless
virgins. Goody Adams received three proposals at Jeremiah's
funeral. Single men still bothered her, especially after church.
Widows usually remarried within a month of their husband's death,
certainly within two. As months became years her behavior became a
scandal.

So, I'm the talk of the town. She walked back to the table, sat and
tried to drink her tea. *They're naught but covetous men, more eager
to get into my purse than my bed, and a gaggle of dried up old
biddies who'd mind my business. Mr. London ought know better than
listen to such trash.*

Almost every day a single man reminded the clergy of their
responsibility to protect the colony's morals. How could it be God's
will for a woman to remain unmarried? Widows need protection. It
was a poor example for a Christian community. In sermons Mister

London often pointed out that God intended for all adults to be married.

Sunday, he thundered from the pulpit, pausing after each question, to give the congregation time to think. "Scripture instructs women to submit to their husbands, but how can a woman so submit if she have not a husband? How can a woman be loved by her husband, as Christ loved His Church, if she have not a husband? How can people call a woman by that title of respect, Goodwife, if she be no one's wife? How rejects a Christian woman God's intention? This she does at the risk of her soul!"

Goody Adams sat, looking straight ahead, as if oblivious that the teaching was about her. But this sermon felt different from the others Mr. London had preached. It felt ominous.

Monday morning, she was distraught.

*****

Church leaders decided that they could no longer tolerate her effrontery. They requested a meeting with Governor Phipps to address the growing crisis.

They met in the governor's large office, lined with expensive books in glass-fronted cabinets. After prayer Governor Phipps asked, "Has Goody Adams received proposals?"

"She has and many at that. She's refused them all," Mister London said.

Phipps nodded and stroked his chin. "Has she been taught, from Scripture, of her error?

"She has, in private and from the pulpit."

Phipps straightened and raised his eyebrows. "From the pulpit? And she doesn't repent of her error?

"She repents not." London leaned forward. "During the pox, I wondered why a family of God's elect was so hard struck. I have reflected and prayed much about this."

"And has God favored you with a reply?"

"I believe He has, Excellency. Think of the recent events in Salem. Who but a witch rejects God's Word?" London pounded his index finger on the Governor's oversized desk to make his point. "And now, who but a witch prospers by such disobedience?"

"Say you she's a witch?"

"I know not. But I believe God wills us to question the woman's behavior."

Phipps turned and looked at the other man in the room. "What think you, Mister Mather? I value your opinion."

Cotton Mather was the son of Increase Mather and grandson of John Cotton, both giants of the Faith. Among the most respected men in the colony, his investigation into witchcraft in Salem a few years earlier made him one of the world's leading authorities on familiarity with Satan. He stood and walked to the window.

"Excellency, I know the woman not, but her obstinacy troubles me. I cannot dismiss witchcraft as an explanation for her defiance of God's will."

"Go with Mister London. Meet with her. See that you give her the opportunity to repent." Phipps was quiet, his voice tense. "If she does not, convene a Court of Oyer and Terminer to ascertain her guilt or innocence. If she be a witch she'll hang."

The clergy excused themselves and went straight to Goody Adams' home. Rachel opened the door.

"We need see your mistress on a matter of great import."

"A moment please, good sirs. I'll see if Goody Adams is available." Rachel bid them to wait in the foyer. Men of their stature were unused to ever being told to wait, much less to wait in a foyer. They were not pleased.

Estelle was reading in the parlor.

"Goody, Mister London wishes to see you. He has another reverend with him!"

This feels wrong. I remember not a time when even one reverend, much less two, came to my door uninvited. She stood and said, "I'll go to the kitchen. Wait a minute. Then show them to the parlor. I'll be there in a few minutes." She went into the kitchen to calm herself before meeting with the powerful men

Rachel waited before she returned to the foyer and led them into the parlor.

Estelle waited another few minutes before she joined them. "Good eve, gentlemen. Seldom has my home been so graced. Please be seated."

The men said they preferred to stand. She decided to stand as well.

"I must ask. Why has my home been so honored?"

London spoke first. "Goody, know you Reverend Mather?"

"I do." *What brings such a man to my home?*

"Are you aware of his recent efforts to protect God's people in Salem?"

"I am, but I don't understand why men of such eminence have time to visit my poor home."

"That may be the core of the problem, Goodwife Adams, that you call this your home. Surely you have heard my frequent teachings that a woman ought be married."

"I heard you. I did not agree with you." Her voice trembled as she spoke. She understood pressure had been brought on London. *I feared he'd be forced to do more than just preach, but to bring Mister Mather? God knows I've no need for another husband.*

At this point, Mister Mather joined the discussion. "Goodwife, do you claim to understand Scripture better than Mister London?"

"I do not." She tried to sound confident.

"Then do you claim," Mather lowered his voice and stared into her eyes, "after being taught that it is God's will for women such as yourself to marry, that it is your right to ignore His Holy Word?"

"I claim no right to ignore God's Word," her voice quivered.

"If you claim no greater learning or understanding of Scripture than Mister London and you claim no right to ignore God's Word, how do you claim the right to refuse marriage?"

She could feel his eyes on her. The lump in her throat all but choked her as she prepared to answer. This discussion was dangerous. "Mister Mather, I was married and I was content to be married, but my husband was taken from me ... by God." Her dry tongue stuck to her teeth as she spoke. "I cannot explain why God did this. Other men have asked me to marry them. But I see no need. I am able to provide for my family. My wealth has grown since my husband was taken." *What are they planning? Will they cast me from the church? Is my salvation at risk? Would they cast out the children, too?*

"We wonder about your growing wealth, Goodwife. When wealth grows, in opposition to the will of God, we have to question if that new wealth comes from familiarity with Satan."

Goody staggered backward as if struck. "Do you accuse me of witchcraft!?" She reached behind her for the arm of a chair and sat.

"That would explain prosperity outside the will of God." Mather's voice was calm.

"I've done no wrong!"

"You claim the right to ignore God's Word." His voice remained calm.

"I do not! I claim only the right to remain unmarried." She did not realize that she was shouting.

Mather's voice rose to match hers. "You claim the right to remain unmarried in violation of God's will for you and yet you prosper from it. How explain you this?"

"I've had no familiarity with Satan!" Goody's mind raced ahead. *In Salem, how many hanged? Was it ten, a dozen?* She remembered hearing the complaints that witches should be burned and not hanged. *Are they here to arrest me?*

"How are we to know you are not in covenant with Satan?" Mather's stepped closer to her, his voice menacing.

"I'll say The Lord's Prayer!" Her face was pale. Her voice quivered. "Our Father, who art in Heaven, hallowed be thy Name. Thy kingdom come. Thy will be done, on Earth as it is in Heav … Heaven—"

London shouted, "See, she stammers. She cannot say His prayer. There's proof she's a witch! Convene the court. Exodus twenty-two commands that we suffer not a witch to live!"

Goody Adams dropped from the chair to her knees, crying. "I beg you, kind sirs. I am no witch. It was my nerves. I only stammered from nerves … Now I see my sin of willfulness and repent. I'll marry … and be a good Christian woman. Don't burn me." She lay on the floor sobbing with fear. *What made me think I could flout the Church?* Losing her wealth and freedom to a man who would beat her and her children now seemed of little import. *They'll burn me! I've lost my soul. I'm going to go to Hell.* She felt that she was looking straight into Hell's gates.

Mather pursued the opening. He shouted, "Goodwife, you say you now see your sin and repent of willfulness?"

Sobbing, without looking up, "I do!"

He stood over her, bending at the waist to bring his face closer to hers. "And in this repentance, do you reject Satan and all his nefarious ways?"

"I do!"

"And will you prove this repentance by resuming your proper station in life as a good wife?"

"I will!"

"When will you marry?"

"So soon as a man will have me!"

"What man?"

She looked up. Tears ran down her face. She managed to say in a barely audible voice, "I don't know, merciful sirs. I've had many offers of marriage. In my sinfulness, I rejected them all. I'll go to one of those who asked and accept his offer ... If he'll have me."

Mather glowered as he said, "Do that. But know this, Goodwife; another intentional sin would prove your rejection of God and your acceptance of the Evil One. The God who hates all sin will not again forgive you of willful sin. Your eternal soul and your earthly life hang in the balance, Goodwife Adams." His voice was quiet but threatening.

Through her tears, she somehow managed to say, "I know that, kind sirs. I repent my willfulness. I had no intention to sin and will not ... sin so again."

Mather turned to London. His quiet voice still threatened, "By your good services, Mister London, have we saved this woman from her familiarity with Satan. I believe your suspicions were correct, but her repentance has saved her. It is to you, as her pastor, to see that she remains in God's good graces. If she marries not within the month we'll call the court and submit her own damning confession.

She'll hang. See that I am kept informed of this case. It is only by such vigilance that we keep our people safe from Satan's stain."

Goody Adams sobbed at the feet of the Reverends London and Mather while they concluded their discussion and took their leave.

She struggled to her feet, trembling, thanking them for their mercy.

*****

Her mind raced. *This is perilous ground. Am I to bring a strange man into my bed because some other man commands it?* She paced the room, stopping in front of the matched portraits of her husband and herself. *I never liked these paintings. They look nothing like us.* She said aloud, "Oh, Jeremiah, I know I must marry. But I've lived so long without a husband." *God gave me a mind. I need no husband to protect me. We've been fine.* She resumed pacing, then stopped and looked out a window at the darkening streets. *Will a new man understand? Will he appreciate that I make him rich?* She wiped at her tears. *For years, I've lived without a man. Now I'm to obey one I don't even know. I'll have no love for him.* She reached both hands to her face to wipe her tears again but held them there and cried. *He'll beat me, like Elihu beat my sister. He'll beat the children and no one will question him. By what right can they make me do this? I'm no witch!*

She took her hands from her face and put them on her hips. Then she turned from the window and looked at the ceiling. *Mayhap Goodman Moore ... Would he be thankful for wealth and a family? Would he have a light hand?*

John Moore was one of her more insistent suitors. He had known little success as a merchant. His small house in one of the poorest sections of Boston would fit inside Goody Adams' home several times. He was at least ten years younger. Marrying her would make him a wealthy man.

Walking to the fire, she slammed both hands into the mantle and screamed in frustration. She leaned her weight into the mantle, crying through closed eyes. *If I marry someone with money, he won't appreciate all that I bring.* She stood straight, opened her eyes, and wiped at tears with both hands. *A poor man wouldn't take my wealth for granted.*

Her hands went back to her hips. She began pacing again. *On the day we marry everything I own will be his. My children's inheritance will be his. It has to be Moore! Goodman Smythe has children from his first wife. He'd favor his over mine. Can't have that. Goodman Williams is no good man. He'd beat me, and the children, just to show he can. Jeremiah, why did you die?*

She stopped and stared into the ceiling again. *It has to be Moore. He never married. Has no children ... He doesn't seem mean. I'd make him a rich man. He'll appreciate that. He'll be good to us.* Moore seemed the least bad choice. Barely above a whisper, she said aloud, "He's been too poor to marry. The children's inheritance would be safe."

She called out, "Rachel!"

The servant hurried from the kitchen.

Goody Adams struggled to compose herself, "Go to the house of John Moore on King's Street and be quick about it. Tell him I need see him at once."

Rachel left at once.

Estelle went back to pacing. Then she thought of the brewery. *John's become one of the finest brewers in New England. In no way could Moore understand the business better than John Will he let things to go as they do now? That'd be best. Or will he have to show he's the master of his servants? ... Why will they be his servants? Damnation! They're mine! Not his! Nothing good will come from a new man in my house!*

She went to her room, poured water from a pitcher into a bowl, and splashed it on her face. Lifting a soft, white towel she patted her face and eyes dry, trying to collect herself. Looking into her mirror, she brushed her hair, then went to her wardrobe and selected her best shawl.

Returning to the parlor, she called, "Chastity, fill a crystal flask with Madera and bring it into the parlor with two glasses."

Chastity hastened to bring the wine. The whole household knew what was happening.

Rachel returned to the house. "Goodman Moore said he has matters he must attend to but will do so and be here soon, Goody."

"Good! Tend to the fire. Then go help Chastity. Help her find something we can serve with the wine."

"Yes, Mum."

An hour later when Goodman Moore arrived it was clear that the matters to which he had to attend included changing into his best suit of clothing. Still, his brown suit was threadbare. Entering the room, he removed his hat, smiled, and bowed.

"Good eve, Goodwife. It pleases me that you sent word for me to come."

Struggling to appear calm, she said, "Good eve, Goodman Moore. I trust you are well?" *Does he hear my voice tremble?*

"I am, Goody, the more so since I received your invitation."

"Will you sit and join me in a glass of wine?" She gestured to the couch.

He sat, saying, "Nothing would please me more, Goodwife. May I call you by your Christian name?" She sat beside him. He smiled.

"You may call me Estelle."

"And you, Estelle, may call me John." He reached for her hand. She stood. Although she could reach the wine while sitting she walked to the far side of the table to pour.

"Thank you, John," she said as she poured. "I've always enjoyed your company."

Moore considered standing too. Instead he moved to the edge of his seat. "And I yours, Estelle."

"And I have decided, John, that it is not good ... for a woman to be without a ... a husband to protect her and her children."

"You have decided well." Goodman Moore struggled to hide his excitement. He was sure he knew what Estelle was about to say.

"John, should I accept your proposal, would you be that protector, who would see to my best interests ... and those of my family?"

Trying to look relaxed, Moore sipped his wine, "Nothing would bring me more joy than to assume my natural role, as protector of this family. God had not seen fit to bless me with such duty before.

To be given ... given the honor of becoming your protector would be a blessing, a blessing indeed." He stood.

Estelle stepped backward and swallowed her whole glass of wine in one gulp. Then she leaned toward him.

"John, there are men that are hard masters of their family. My late husband was a kind and gentle man. Of what order man are you, John Moore?"

Placing his glass on the table, he stepped toward her. "I have oft asked for your hand, Estelle. If you honored me with it, I would be a gentle husband ... and a kind father."

Estelle poured and swallowed another glass of wine. Trembling, she said, "John Moore, I accept your proposal of marriage on your word that you will be such a gentle husband and kind father." *My life is no longer mine.*

Chapter Ten
In His Master's House

The die is cast.
Gaius Julius Caesar

Mister London beamed when he saw Goody Adams enter his study with Goodman Moore. He rose and held out his hand. "Of what service may I be to you?"

Estelle reddened. *As if you know not.*

John spoke. He smiled. "Mister London we intend to wed. We would like you to announce our contract so we can marry soon."

"It will give me joy to announce your agreement. I will publish the banns of matrimony this day. That will require the use of a crier. The fee's tuppence."

John looked at Estelle who opened her purse and removed two coins. She handed them to John who handed them to the pastor. The contract must be announced three times before you marry. The crier is once. I'll announce your agreement at lecture on Wednesday. We can do the engagement ceremony this Sabbath. As bride, 'tis yours to choose the verse on which you would have me to preach."

Estelle shook her head. "I'm sure you know best, Mr. London."

"Most brides want the perfect verse read and consider long on it."

"I'm sure you'll choose better than I would."

"Then I'll preach from Genesis Two. Among the animals, God found no suitable help-mate for Adam so he made Eve from Adam's rib. They were one flesh."

Moore beamed. "Excellent passage. I look forward to your sermon."

Estelle nodded her head and dabbed at the corner of her eye.

London stood. "Any magistrate can marry you. Goodman Styles worships with us. Would you have me speak with him?"

"Styles is as good as another," John said.

"Then I'll arrange for him to do so. His fee is four pence."

John looked at Estelle. She did not notice. After a few seconds, he said, "Estelle." She looked startled, then nodded and again reached into her purse this time removing four coins. She handed them to her future husband who handed them to the pastor. They spoke for a few minutes about their plans, inviting Mister London to their house to help them celebrate their marriage, then left.

Once on the street John said, "Estelle, it embarrassed me to have you pay for these services."

"I don't mind, John."

"But I do. Give me the money in your purse so when additional fees are found I can pay, as is proper for a husband."

So, it starts. "But John, how are you paying if you just take my money from your purse?"

"In a few days, the money will be mine. Until then no woman should wish to see her husband, or husband-to-be, stand as a beggar before his woman."

His woman! She gritted her teeth. With a tight-lipped smile, she handed him her purse. "To be sure, this woman would not wish to see her lord stand as a beggar before her." *Is it possible he's so dense he doesn't hear my sarcasm?*

*****

The remaining days before the wedding flew by. Chastity took full charge of the arrangements for the gathering to follow. The girls' excitement grew by the minute. Jean-Marc was quiet and grew tense as the day neared. He feared the changes the marriage would bring to the lives of the seven servants, soon to be servants in the household of Goodman Moore.

On Sunday Goody Adams led her children and servants on the short walk from their home to The North Church. Goodman Moore waited at the door, beaming. They entered the church. Each sat in their assigned seat, according to rank. Goody Adams and her children sat nearer the front than the middle. Goodman Moore sat just in front of the servants.

My seat'll soon change. Moore smiled.

The servants sat in the rear, John was closer to the front than the girls who sat close together in the middle of the other servants.

The large church's wooden walls were painted white inside and out. There was little adornment. No cross hung; there were no statues or stained-glass windows. The front of the church was dominated by a large, rather plain pulpit. Its only ornamentation was a large, blue eye painted on its front, as if to emphasize to the congregation that God was watching them. In his two-hour-long sermon Mister London stressed that in the Garden of Eden God showed it was His will for men and women to be joined as one. He also stressed the need, and the blessings, of submitting to God's will.

After the sermon, he climbed down from the pulpit and walked into the center aisle between the pews. "It gives me great pleasure to make the third announcement of the engagement contract between Estelle Adams and John Moore."

He paused, expecting Estelle to stand and turn full circle, as expectant brides did at their engagement announcement. She did not. Goodman Moore's face reddened. The muscles in his jaw tightened. He stared straight ahead. After an awkward pause, Mister London continued, "If any knows just cause why these two should not be joined as man and wife let him speak now." He waited. "Hearing no protest, this being the Sabbath, Goodman Styles will join them at their home on the morrow."

*****

Goodman Moore left his now empty house just before noon. The walk to Goody Adams' home took about ten minutes. Rachel answered the door and escorted him into the parlor. Estelle was sitting in her bedroom when he arrived.

"Goodman Moore's here, Goody."

"See him into the parlor. I'll be out soon."

"Yes, Mum."

Estelle stared into the distance without moving.

Chastity, Abigail, and Rachel had worked hard baking cakes, puddings, and breads for the gathering, to go with roast venison and beans. In addition to the variety of fine beers Jean-Marc provided, they planned to serve a rum punch and wine.

Moore fidgeted in the parlor, alone for an hour, waiting for his bride.

A knock brought Rachel to the front door. "Good day."

"Good day. I'm Thomas Styles. I believe I'm expected."

"You are indeed, Goodman. Come in. I'll call everyone to the parlor." She hurried around the house telling the family and servants that Goodman Styles had arrived.

Goodman Styles was already standing. Moore stood when Estelle entered. Her children gathered against the wall. The servants crowded into the room near the doorway to the kitchen.

Goodman Styles began. "John Moore, is it your intention to be husband to Estelle Adams?"

"It is." His voice was loud and strong.

"And Estelle Adams, is it your intention to be John Moore's wife?"

"It is," she said in a voice so low no one but Styles and Moore heard her.

"Good. I'll enter this marriage into the public records on the morrow." He shook their hands and left.

Abigail looked at Jean-Marc. She whispered, "This is wrong. When I was a girl in England weddings were beautiful."

"None in France would think this to be a wedding," he said shaking his head.

"I'll have me more ceremony than that when I marry me to Isaiah Poole," Chastity said under her breath.

The joining took less than a minute. In that time, Estelle Adams, a wealthy business owner with six servants, one slave and her own home became Goodwife Moore, the wife of a wealthy merchant. She lived in her husband's house.

Mister London came to the small party that followed, as did the surviving members of Goody Moore's sister's family and some neighbors. It seemed that most who came were friends of Goodman Moore. They could be identified by their worn clothing and the gusto with which they attacked the food and drink. The gathering lasted about an hour before the guests began to filter out of the house.

The servant girls set about cleaning. Goody Moore's children, Ruth, Ezra and Daniel, who stood to the side of the parlor throughout the joining and the party, excused themselves. Each retired to his or her own room. Jean-Marc was with the male servants in the brew house where there was malting to attend to.

Goodman Moore looked about his fine home, smiled and said, "Wife, the day's yet young. Shall we walk along the bay and stop at the Crown and Scepter?"

Struggling to smile, Goody Moore said, "Yes, let's."

The rest of the household went about their usual routine.

*****

After supper Goody Moore looked out a window on to the darkened street beyond. Her husband came in from the kitchen. "Wife, we've had a fine day."

Wiping a tear from her cheek she said, "Yes, John, we did".

John crossed the room. Standing behind her, he wrapped his arms around her waist. She felt her body tighten. He said, "'Tis time we retired and tried out our bed."

Goody Moore thought of sharing Jeremiah's bed with another man. Another tear rolled down her cheek. She said, "Yes John, I suppose it is." Turning, she took his hand. Together they walked to their bedroom.

*****

Breakfast, the next morning, consisted of fresh baked bread, cold sliced venison, and a large pitcher of beer. Goodman Moore was first of the family to sit at the table. He helped himself to large servings of venison and bread. "'Tis another fine meal," he said to no one in particular as he poured his beer. His wife soon joined him.

"Good morning, Goody Moore." Her husband was smiling. He rested his elbows on the table, interlaced his fingers and watched her.

"Do you intend to stare at me while I eat?"

"It gladdens me to be able to look upon my wife over a meal."

"There's little enough to see." Estelle reddened. She reached for a thick slice of brown bread and buttered it without looking up. When she did glance up he was still watching her, smiling. She poured some beer into a mug and tried to drink but could not. She put down the mug and looked out the window at a gray sky.

"What will you do today?" John asked.

"I hadn't thought about it. Perhaps I'll go to the market with Chastity." She never went to the market with her servants but wanted an excuse to be away from the house without her husband.

"What do we need?"

"Just things, some buttons, fancy things. Nothing to interest a man."

"But your interests are my interests."

Good God, no. Please God, don't let him come with me. "I'm sure there are important things you need attend to, much more important than watching me buy buttons."

Moore smiled and tried to lighten things with a little joke. "Maybe I need go to see you don't waste my money."

She felt her face redden more. Her whole body stiffened. *Your money! You have no money you little beggar!* Forcing a smile, she said, "John, I've run a frugal house these years alone. Having a husband will not change that in me."

She toyed with her food and only sipped her beer. Her new husband tried to have a conversation with her but found it one-sided.

Long minutes passed before Estelle's children came to the table. Ezra, the youngest came first, then Ruth, leading Daniel who was left blind by the pox. There was an unmistakable look of disappointment on their faces to find their step-father still in the kitchen.

"Have you not a business to run, Sir?" Ruth asked.

"I do, but I would get to know my family better."

"There's little to learn, Sir. Ezra and I go to our school. Daniel can't see, so he can't read. He'll sit in his room until his tutor comes, then wait for us to return. When we get home, I read to him from the Bible."

"That's kind of you."

"Ma makes me." She reached for a slice of bread, buttered it and handed it to Daniel, then took a slice for herself.

"Daniel, sitting in your room cannot excite you. What else do you do?"

"I'm blind. What would you have me do?"

Moore was shocked to be spoken to this way by the children. He considered cuffing Daniel but thought better of it. Ezra ate his bread, oblivious to the tension.

Ruth stood. "We rose late. We'll be late to school and be beat. Come on Ezra. You can finish that while we walk." Over his protests, she led Ezra away from the table and out the door.

Estelle had been silent through this. "Daniel, do you need help?"

"Only back to my room," he said.

She stood and led Daniel back to his room but did not return to the kitchen. Moore looked around the empty table then at Rachel, the only other person in the room.

"I have business to attend to and must see to the sale of my other house. I'll be gone much of the day. See that my wife knows this. Also, tell John that I would like a tour of the brewery when I return." He swallowed the remainder of his beer, grabbed another thick slice of bread and left the kitchen.

Rachel sighed with relief.

*****

Toward dark, Goodman Moore returned and went to the brewery. He called to Jean-Marc, who stood. He told Joshua to finish cooling the wort. "Good eve, Goodman Moore. How may I serve you?"

"Show me our operations, John. I've heard naught but good regarding your labors."

This begins well. Jean-Marc thought.

He gave his master a tour of the brewery complex and a quick description of the business. Moore asked sensible questions and was given thorough answers. All seemed well. Moore thanked him and went to the house in time for supper.

The girls prepared another special meal with roast goose and ox for the couple's first supper together. Goodman Moore presided over a quiet table laden with a feast. Several times he initiated conversation with one of the children, receiving the briefest of responses. Goody Moore tried to lighten the mood but it would not ease.

She was glad when they were done. *Such things take time. I'll ask the children to try harder.*

*****

As days and weeks passed tensions eased. Moore's relations with the children settled into a kind of truce. They were not pleased with a new man in their father's house and their mother's bed but were not defiant. Moore contented himself with his new wife and new wealth. He believed the proper disciplining of the children to be his duty but managed to defer to his wife.

He searched for a place to assert his mastery over his home and business. He started spending time in the brewery. This displeased Jean-Marc. Moore made frequent, useless suggestions. If he inserted himself into a discussion with a customer he created problems, making promises that could not be kept or insisting that some minor request was impossible. Jean-Marc spent much of his time repairing damage done to his relationships with customers.

When Moore discovered Jean-Marc was later going to customers and telling them the brewery would not be able to fill their requests after all, he became furious. "This is my brewery. You are not to speak to customers! At all! Ever! Any promise I make is to be kept. Do you understand me?" This was not a question. "I'll not accept your incompetence and your failures any longer."

As customer relations deteriorated Moore began to cut prices in order to keep their business. When the brewery began losing money, he blamed Jean-Marc.

In the house, Moore began to find fault with meals. He often declared them ill-prepared. Breakfast seemed to be a particular problem. Boston tradition was for breakfasts to be left-over meat from the previous night's meal, perhaps with some porridge and bread, often not even fresh bread. This was not good enough for John Moore.

Chastity took the brunt of this criticism but remained silent. She started rising earlier to make a meat pie or hash. She prepared special sweet biscuits or rolls. Moore called porridge "pauper's food," so it disappeared from their table.

One morning in late summer the girls overslept. There was not enough time to prepare the expected breakfast. Abigail built up the fire to heat the oven. Chastity hurried to prepare biscuits. There was no time to make a meat pie or hash. She told Rachel to slice the left-over ham and to place it on a plate with slices of cheese, hoping the cheese would make it acceptable.

When he saw the meal, Moore called Chastity from the kitchen. His voice was taut but controlled. "Last night's supper may have once done for breakfast but in my house, we'll have a proper morning meal. I'll not tolerate such sloth again."

"Husband, slicing yester-eve's meat for the morning's meal is common. The breakfast is fine."

"And I'll not have my wife contradict me before my servants. Do you understand me woman?"

She looked away and said, "I do, John."

Daniel spoke up, "Don't you talk that way to my mother."

"My wife's children will not so speak to me." Moore shouted. "Or interfere with how I run my house." He stood and leaned toward the boy. "If you wish to stay under my roof you'll keep a civil tongue in your mouth. 'Tis plain the rod's been too long spared here."

"This is my father's house not yours!"

Moore slapped Daniel across the face. "Speak out of turn again boy and I'll cane you."

"Don't ever hit my son!"

"I'll not be disrespected in my own home, woman!" He turned and slapped his wife. "I see no cane in this room but trust me by the time I return tonight I'll have my cane with me. I will be respected and I will be obeyed in my house." He turned and stormed out.

Goody Moore sat crying. Her children crowded around her. "If he touches you again, Mother, I'll—"

"You'll what, Daniel? You'll strike your mother's husband?" She held her hands to her face and sobbed. "How will a blind boy

198

fight a man? And if you did hit him, he'd give you to the constable to be flogged. This is his house. Best we learn to live by his rules." She called to the kitchen. "Rachel!" The girl stared at the floor as she came through the swinging door. Goody Moore's voice trembled with anger. "Tell the other girls my husband will have meat pie or hash with his morning bread. Fail not." She stood and shouted. "Do you hear me?"

Rachel curtsied "Yes, Goody. I'll see to it." She turned for the safety of the kitchen but Goody stopped her.

"And at supper see he is asked his preference for other meals."

"Yes, Goody." Rachel curtsied again and went into the kitchen. Chastity and Abigail were already buzzing about the incident. In minutes, the men in the brew house knew what happened.

Jean-Marc told Abigail, "You stay clear of him. I'll lay him low the day he sets hand on you."

"John, you know you'd be flogged if you ever struck your master. You might even be hanged."

"Be that as it may, I'll kill the man who strikes you."

His voice sent a chill down Abigail's back.

He turned and walked back to his work.

Toward noon, Goodman Moore, still angry about the morning's events, entered the malting house. "John, you spend in this brewery like the money was yours. Your waste costs us more by the day. I've long made my own beer with far fewer goods than I here see. Why do we use all these supplies?"

Jean-Marc turned to face him. "First Goodman, we brew beer and ale for hundreds of customers not one small household." His tone shocked Moore, who took a step backward. "We make many different beers. For each, we need different ingredients. Some use wheat in with the barley, some oats. Some get molasses in the wort, some honey. By now you should know this. You claim to run this business."

Moore was intimidated. He tried to lower the tension. "Is not such variety expensive?"

Jean-Marc tried calm himself. "It is. Different makings produce different beers and we have a good selection."

"It must be that we could do with less. You use honey." He pointed at a large ironware pot. "Why use honey? You must know molasses to be cheaper?"

"If I use molasses instead of honey the beer'll not be as good. Good beer needs good makings."

"And wasteful spending will ruin a business. We cannot afford such waste in the future. You lose us money daily. When you use these up, buy supplies that are not so dear. We'll brew one good beer made with barley and malt and we'll earn the more for our efforts."

"Begging your pardon, Sir, but our customers expect fine beers. Make a cheap brew and you'll lose us business."

"You mean I'll lose business, don't you?" Moore was trying to take back control. "Remember this business is mine, not yours. You're a servant who would do well to learn his place. I may lose some trade but I'll recover my loss by not wasting money on supplies in the first place."

"That sounds well, Sir, but I know my customers. They'll go elsewhere."

"And where will MY customers go? Most other brew houses have closed."

"They closed because their product equaled not ours."

"And now they've closed there's naught to fear from them is there? Do as I say, boy."

"I'll discuss this with Goody Adams—"

"Trouble Goodwife Moore with my business and I'll cane you, boy." He turned on his heel and walked out of the brew house. Jean-Marc fumed. The servant boys stared. No one ever spoke to Master John in that way.

"Get about your business. The brew house is Goodman Moore's. He'll do with it as he sees fit." They looked down and tried to seem busy. They worried what would happen next.

The change was rapid. Moore decided to take the brewery and household in hand. As the varieties of ingredients were used up he would not permit them to be replaced. The new ingredients he did buy were the cheapest available. This forced Jean-Marc to limit the variety of beers he produced. Quality suffered. Customers found other suppliers. Goodman Moore blamed Jean-Marc's incompetence for the loss of sales.

Jean-Marc chafed under Moore's interference. He chafed even more at being treated like a servant. He was used to living almost as a free man and a wealthy one at that. Now he had to ask permission to go anywhere. He was no longer permitted to buy anything for the brewery or for himself. He saw the great wealth he created being spent by someone else. The business he built was being destroyed.

Moore complained Jean-Marc forgot he was a servant. He told anyone who would listen that he intended to remind Jean-Marc what an indenture's life was like.

It seemed Goody could only make him angry. He beat her often. Daniel left the house to live with his uncle. Even being blind, he hoped to find an apprenticeship. Ezra and Ruth stayed away from the house whenever possible.

They struggled to sell cheap beer. Household expenses soared. Moore wanted expensive meals. There was talk of selling the new boys. The servants gossiped among themselves about the pauper who lived like a prince.

At last, Rachel lost control and spoke for everyone. "You lived in a hovel before you married Goody. You never ate so well. You should be thankful for what you've got."

Moore was furious. "I've seen how you've wasted my wife's money. Servants with their own rooms! All the girls could have slept in the attic and the boys in the cellar. The servants' rooms are as big as the house. You all abused my wife's generosity. I'll not tolerate such a waste."

Moore caned Rachel.

The girls in the kitchen stayed out of Goodman Moore's way whenever possible. His anger was unpredictable and often violent. Jean-Marc began carrying a mallet in his belt. He said he used it to seal casks but he had never carried a mallet before. Privately, he decided he would not permit Goodman Moore to lay a hand on either Abigail or himself.

*****

The inevitable event came some five months after the wedding. Goodman Moore caned Goody for some offense, real or imagined. She struggled to get away, knocking over chairs and slamming the dining room table into a wall, smashing lathe and knocking broken plaster to the floor. Plaster dust filled the air.

Abigail could take it no more. "Goodman," she cried, "There were no beatings in this house for years before you came. How can you call yourself good when you beat your wife so?"

Moore spun. He shouted, "I'll not be questioned in my house!"

He brought the cane down on Abigail's back, striking her again and again. She crumbled to the ground, sobbing amid overturned chairs and broken plaster.

He shouted, "Wife, see to your household. Now you see why you needed a husband. Had you run your house properly before we married I'd not have to deal with such insolence now. I'm going to the Crown and Scepter. See that this is cleaned ere I return." He stormed from the room, leaving two weeping women lying on the floor.

Chastity ran for Jean-Marc.

He entered the room, saw Abigail and Goody Moore on the floor bleeding through their smocks and crying. With tears in his eyes he stooped to comfort Abigail. Helping her to her feet he made a solemn vow. "This man has crossed the line. I told you that on the day he struck you I would lay him low. This I promise, he will not live to raise his hand to another woman."

Abigail cried, "You can't! You can't! You'll be hanged."

"Then hanged I'll be. This night, he dies."

Goody Moore dragged herself to her feet. Leaning against the table she said, "John, there's nothing to be done. The law is with him."

"Then the law be damned."

He turned to Abigail, "Pack some things, but see you pack light."

Goody Moore heard this. "You still be my servant. If you run, I'll have the sheriff on you!"

The house was in turmoil. Jean-Marc ignored everyone but Abigail. He took her by the shoulders and looked into her face. There could be no mistake. "Be ready to leave at dark."

He went to his room and threw some things in a pack for himself. After years of running the brewery he knew where the money was kept. He took the key, opened the chest and filled a large purse with silver. Without another word, he left.

While Jean-Marc did this, Chastity went into the kitchen for a bowl of water so she could tend the women's wounds. "Rachel, go into Goody's closet and fetch a robe for her." Rachel ran from the room while Chastity helped Goody Moore remove her blouse. Her back was covered with raw, red welts. Several of them were split open and bleeding. Chastity wet a cloth and gently dabbed it on the wounds while Goody winced in pain. Rachel returned with a thick grey robe.

"Hold this in front of her while I see to her back," Chastity directed Rachel. She finished cleaning the wounds then wrapped clean cloth around Goody's back, chest, and over her shoulders to stop the bleeding and cover her wounds.

Abigail picked up a chair and sat. "'Twas wrong that he hit us. He doesn't own me. He'd no right to hit me," she said to no one in particular.

To everyone's shock, Goody Moore defended him. "Keep a civil tongue in your mouth girl. 'Tis a man's right to correct his family and servants."

Abigail spun to face her. She was incredulous. "And you defend him? You can let him beat you if you want but I belong not to him. You forget. 'Tis mine to leave when I choose."

"Then leave, hussy. You're no longer welcome here. But John's mine. If your man tries to go with you I'll set the sheriff on him." The hatred in Goody Moore's voice shook her servants.

Abigail struggled to her feet. For the first time, she shouted at Goody Moore. "I'll leave as soon as John gets back but have a care for your husband. Mayhap he can beat you as he sees fit but my John'll not tolerate him beating me. He'll lay your man low!"

"Will he now? In this colony, the sheriff'll hang the servant who lays hand on his master."

"But I can see he does nothing to the man who beats women." Despite the pain in her back Abigail stormed from the room knocking over the chair she had just picked up.

Chastity and Rachel were dumbstruck by the exchange. Goody Moore just stared at the door. Almost a minute passed before Chastity said, "Rachel, clean this mess. Goody, let me help you on with your robe."

*****

The house was in chaos throughout the day. The children stayed in their rooms. The male servants went to the brew house and pretended to work. It was almost dark when John Moore returned home. His wife told him of Jean-Marc's threat and that Abigail was leaving.

"I'll thrash them both!" Moore shouted. "I'll not be disrespected in my own home.

This only increased the disorder. While people in the parlor shouted at each other, Jean-Marc rode a large black stallion into the brew house yard. He held the lead for a smaller brown horse in his right hand. Dismounting, he handed the horses' leads to Joshua. "Hold these for me. I'll be back in a few minutes."

Joshua took the leads. "Yes, Master John."

The house was still in an uproar when he walked into the parlor. John Moore ran straight at him cane held high, knocking furniture out of his way. "Lay me low, will you?"

With two hands Moore swung the cane to crush his servant's skull. Like a skilled swordsman, Jean-Marc side-stepped the blow and pulled the mallet from his belt. Moore brought the cane back up from the floor aiming at his face. Jean-Marc deflected the blow with the mallet and ducked under the cane as it passed wildly over his head. Then he stepped forward and smashed his mallet into his master's nose. The man dropped to the floor. Jean-Marc pounced on him, straddling his chest. Again, and again he pounded the mallet into Moore's bloody face. Moore reached up to block the blows but

Jean-Marc hammered through his hands, breaking fingers and wrists. Finally, Moore's arms fell to the ground. Jean-Marc kept pounding the mallet into Moore's face. There was a gurgling noise as he struggled for breath. The hammer still slammed into the bloody face. At last, the gurgling stopped, then the twitching. Covered with blood, Jean-Marc stood and exhaled.

He turned to the Widow Moore who was cringing against the wall. "This monster will trouble you no more." Then to Abigail, "We go now. Get your things and come with me."

Chapter Eleven
Flight

"Fear cannot be without hope, nor hope without fear"
Baruch Spinoza

The room was silent. Shock paralyzed everyone, except Jean-Marc. He grabbed Abigail's arm. "Come with me." He dragged her to her room. "Where's your bag?"

Moving and speaking in slow motion she said, "Here it is."

He grabbed the bag with one hand, her hand with the other and hurried into the yard.

No moon. That's good.

Joshua held their horses.

"Get on the brown horse," Jean-Marc directed.

"John, I don't know how to ride," her speech was no faster.

"Put your foot in the stirrup, lift your skirt and throw your leg over the saddle."

"I can't lift my skirt. Joshua's here."

"If I don't leave I'll die. If you would be with me, you must lift your skirt. Put your foot here. I'll help you up."

In slow motion, Abigail raised her leg and put her foot into the stirrup. She raised her skirt and Jean-Marc boosted her into the small horse's saddle. He took her horse's lead from Joshua and jumped on his stallion.

Joshua said something that Jean-Marc did not hear.

Even as a small boy, Jean-Marc raced large, powerful horses. Abigail had no similar experience. At a trot, he led her horse out of the yard. She tried to hold on. As they rode off cries of "Help!" and "Murder!" came from the house.

Leaning forward he urged the horses into a canter. "Hold tight. We have to go faster." *The constable'll be there soon and he'll raise the militia. We've a start but we'll not outrun them. Don't have much time.*

Earlier that day he put a plan into operation. He knew they would die if he ran for the wilderness. They rode north. He hoped the constable would assume he was making for New France. There he would be safe from English law. About two miles north of the city he met a man he knew from an inn he had sold beer for years. The man stood by a straw filled ox-cart with solid sides and an open back.

"Good to see you made it." The man called as they approached.

Jean-Marc leapt from his horse, threw their bags into the cart and pulled Abigail out of the saddle. "Thank you, Malachi. I owe you my life."

Malachi handed him a bundle of clothing and mounted his horse. "The silver and these horses'll be payment enough. Go with God." He dug his heels into the stallion. Both horses headed north at a gallop.

"Get into the cart. I'll cover you."

She half-climbed as he pushed her into the cart and covered her with straw.

Please God have them take the bait!

Malachi was to ride north, hard, for several hours then turn west and trot toward Deerfield where he had business.

They have to follow him.

For his efforts, Malachi was paid fifteen shillings and got to keep the horses, which he would sell.

Jean-Marc hurried to change into the soiled farm clothes Malachi handed him and pushed his bloody clothing beneath the straw. Mounting the cart, he steered it toward Boston. About half an hour later the militia neared them at a gallop.

One of the men cried out, "You see a man and woman riding this way in a hurry?"

Beneath the straw Abigail held her breath. She was sure they would hear her heart pounding.

"Saw two riding north, hard," Jean-Marc replied, without looking up.

"Obliged!" the man shouted. They spurred their horses to the north.

When she heard the militia ride into the distance Abigail sat up.

"Get back down. No one can see a couple traveling tonight. You must stay hidden." She slid back under the straw.

Jean-Marc drove the cart to Boston's water-front. Reaching the wharf, he steered the cart to a small coastal freighter scheduled to sail on the morning tide.

The ship's master greeted him. "You did it, my friend." Jean-Marc helped Abigail out of the cart. The captain called out, "Eli, take this cart to the stable on King's Street. They expect it."

"Aye, sir!" The young man left his task, hurried down the gangplank, and led the ox and cart away.

"Come with me. You can spend the night in my cabin. I'll be busy all night anyway."

In the captain's cabin Abigail sat on the bed, which moved on its pivot under her weight. "Move over and lie down or it'll tip and we'll both fall." Jean-Marc lay next to Abigail and took her in his arms.

"I'm afraid, John." She sobbed, burying her face in his chest.

"We're safe now." He held her tight and stroked her hair while she cried herself to sleep. He checked to be sure he could grab the knife in his belt. *I'll be damned if I let them put me back in chains. If we're found I'm a dead man. I'll take as many as I can with me.*

He did not sleep that night. In the dark, he stared at the closed door and held Abigail. Just after dawn he heard the sounds of a ship putting out to sea. *I heard these same sounds in Le Harve, so very long ago.*

The sun was well up when there was a knock at door. "Jean-Marc, I'm coming in."

"Come." This woke Abigail.

"We're well out to sea. You're safe. Join me in my dining room for breakfast. The first meal of a cruise is always the best."

"So, I've heard. Give us a moment."

Captain Wentworth left the cabin closing the door behind him. Jean-Marc got out of bed and helped Abigail from it.

She looked around the dim, tiny cabin. It was a man's room, dingy white walls, cluttered and without decoration. "I see no a mirror."

"Me either."

"I have to clean up, brush my hair, make myself presentable."

They had so very little with them. After she fussed about her face and hair for a few minutes he took her arm and pulled her to him. "You're beautiful. Come, Oliver's waiting for us."

The captain's dining cabin was adjacent to his sleeping quarters. Abigail entered and looked around. *Another man's room. The same drab walls. No decorations.* The room was filled by an unfinished table and chairs. *The plates and flatware don't even match. Goody would be furious.*

Wentworth was young to have command of such a ship. His sun-darkened skin emphasized his blue eyes. He wore his dark hair short. He was clean shaven. His clothing was stylish by Massachusetts standards. His breeches were blue rather than the more common green, brown or gray. His white shirt overlapped in front like a robe without button or tie. The sleeves billowed.

He bid them to sit. "After our meal, we'll move your things to the passenger cabin in the forecastle. You'll be safe there. The men know nothing about you."

A cabin boy brought cold mutton, black bread and beer. The captain thanked him and said, "Eat and enjoy. The pity's our beer is not as good as yours."

Jean-Marc laughed. "Our beer is not as good as ours since Moore involved himself."

"The trip down the coast and up river to Philadelphia'll take a few days. You'll have no duties. The ship's not made for comfort but you've the full run of it. Enjoy yourselves."

After eating they moved their few things into the passenger cabin. Abigail sat on the bed. There was no other furniture in the cabin. Jean-Marc leaned against the dirty wall. A tear rolled down her face. "John, why is he helping us?"

He shoved his hands into the pockets of the work breeches Malachi gave him. "First, he helps us for money. I gave him a pound to deliver us safe to Philadelphia. Then, Oliver Wentworth's a good man. I trust him."

"You trust him with our lives?" Abigail lowered her chin to her chest. Only her eyes looked up. Her voice sounded tiny.

"I have. He'll not expose us." Jean-Marc tried to sound more confident than he felt.

She raised her face bringing her clasped hands to her mouth. "But if he knows where we've gone won't the crew know, too?"

"That's why we must disappear."

"Disappear?"

He pulled his hands from his pockets and gestured with them. "I cannot be Jean-Marc Bompeau." He turned his hands inward, touching his fingers to his chest. "You," now his open hands extended toward her, "cannot be Abigail Hyde."

This did not comfort her. "Who are we to be?"

"Abigail, do you love me?" He stepped over to her, taking her hands.

The contact comforted her. The corners of her mouth turned up into a small smile. "Of course, I do."

"Then we'll travel as man and wife but not with my name." He brought her hands to his face and kissed them. "Is there a surname you'd prefer?"

She shook her head. "I always thought I'd be Goody Bompeau someday."

Releasing her hands, he said, "Jean-Marc Bompeau must be dead if we hope to make good our escape. We could use our master's name and be John and Abigail Adams or John and Abigail Moore but with those names, I'd expect to be found out."

Abigail's hands went back to her mouth, but her voice became stronger as she began to understand the plan. "What of my surname, Hyde. We could be John and Abigail Hyde."

"Does Goody Moore know your surname?"

"She does."

"Then Hyde doesn't work."

"The pastor who so bothered Goody to get married was Mister London. We could be the Londons or what about Paris?"

Jean-Marc frowned and shook his head. "There's no good reminding people I'm French. We could spell it with two esses, P-A-R-I-S-S."

"Spell it how you want. You know I neither read nor write." Abigail still held her hands in front of her face but now she looked more thoughtful than frightened. "Chastity came from Kent. What about Goody and Goodman Kent?"

"Kent, it is," Jean-Marc smiled.

Abigail smiled too. She stood and looked into his face. "Goody Kent needs a kiss."

He took her in his arms, "Then she shall have it." He leaned to kiss her. Then he saw she was crying and wiped a tear from her face. "Why are you crying?"

"Oh John, it makes no sense at all. I'm so afraid for us, but I'm so happy, too. Hold me and tell me all will be well."

He held her tight and told her everything would be fine, as if he believed it. They cried. They kissed. This day, they realized they were husband and wife.

Sometime later Jean-Marc left their cabin. He went to Captain Wentworth. "Have you a moment?"

"I do."

He looked around to be sure no one else would hear. "If we are to disappear Jean-Marc Bompeau must be no more. We are Goodman and Goody John Kent."

Wentworth smiled. "And that's how my crew will know you, but if you would disappear further down your rabbit-hole, you won't be Goodman and Goody. In Philadelphia, they call each other Brother and Friend, but like as not they'll call you Mister and Missus Kent."

"Then Mister and Missus Kent we shall be."

"How do you intend to disappear in Philadelphia? 'Tis a big town but's like Boston. People know each other's business."

John shook his head. "The less you know the better, friend."

The captain chuckled. "Oh, you'll fit right in with Philadelphia, Friend Kent."

John had no idea why Oliver laughed but he smiled and returned to Abigail. Together they enjoyed their quiet time on the ship until they reached Philadelphia. Abigail would always remember these as the best days of her life.

*****

It was mid-morning when they landed in Philadelphia. John shook Oliver's hand. "If all goes well, my friend, we'll never see each other again. It would be good if we were never on your ship."

"I wish you well, John Kent. Take care of your woman." They smiled and shook hands then parted ways.

Abigail and John wanted to get as far from the river as they could that night. They took a street that went straight west away from the river. At the edge of the city they came to The Golden Hind Inn. Entering the public room Abigail sat by a pleasant fire. John went to the next room and found the innkeeper, "My wife and I want supper and a room for the night."

"That'll be tuppence each, Friend."

John was surprised by the high price but forced a smile. "Then tuppence each it will be. Can we put our bags in the room now?"

"Others will share thy room, Friend. To keep thy things safe, thee could leave them with me until thee retire."

"That will do." John handed the keeper four pennies and their small bags.

"Go sit by thy wife and warm thyselves by the fire. I'll bring bread and beer to refresh thee." The innkeeper smiled as if they really were his friends. John thanked him and went back into the almost empty public room. Large wooden tables and benches filled the unpainted room.

Abigail saw that he looked troubled, "What is it, John?"

He shook his head, "We can't stay here long. Their speech is different."

"What do you mean different?"

"Listen and you'll see. You and I'll not disappear into Philadelphia."

The innkeeper brought them two large tankards of beer and a loaf of dark bread. "Call if thee need more, Friend. Otherwise I'll leave thee alone."

After he left Abigail tried to cover her laughter with her hands. "I see your meaning." Her hands fell from her mouth to her breast. Now she looked concerned. "What will we do? Do we get on another ship and leave again?"

"Then there'd be another crew to know of us. And by our speech, all will know us to be strangers to Philadelphia. We need to disappear." John took a swallow of beer and stared into space. *Can't believe what I'm about to say.* "What if we buy the necessaries and go into the backcountry? We could disappear there. In spring two other people would come out. Then, if we just keep going east, we couldn't miss the river, could we? If we crossed the river we could be different people, in a different colony. Would that not work?" He looked at Abigail, starting to talk faster, getting excited, "We could travel along the river until we find a town in need of a brewer." John was thinking out loud but liked what he was saying. "We have silver to buy what we need, and still have enough to start a small brewery in the spring, when we settle into our new home, in another colony. But ... we'll have to endure the winter."

Abigail's eyes widened as he spoke. "Endure the winter! In the backcountry? How do you suppose we'd do this? We know nothing of living there. 'Tis a wilderness. What will we eat? Where will we live? We'll freeze! What about savages?" The words tumbled out of her mouth not leaving time for John to answer her questions.

She paused for a breath. John saw his opportunity and tried to squeeze in some answers.

"Just now, I know not how to answer all your questions." He tried to show a confidence he did not feel. Before he could go on she interrupted him again.

"Do you hear yourself? You've no idea what be out there. No idea how we'd live, or what we'd eat—"

John cut her off. His voice was an angry whisper. "Be quiet! 'Twould be better you told not the whole town we're in hiding." He held his hands up trying to quiet her.

"But—"

Still in his angry whisper, "If you'd have us caught, keep going. Or you could quiet and we can talk."

Abigail took a deep breath and nodded. "Good that we're alone in the room." She tried to smile.

"Oliver told me the winters here aren't so cold as Boston's. How if we bought food and clothes to take with us? Might we do well?"

She interrupted, trying to keep her voice down. "But won't the savages kill us?"

John made a small down and up motion with his hands to quiet her. "Oliver said the Delaware here are friends with Christians." He looked around. "This may be our one chance. If we're found I'm a dead man. You'd be whipped, branded, and sold again."

This frightened Abigail into silence. After a long minute, she whispered, "So, how can we do this?"

"As yet, I know not. Let's see what we can learn." He stood, looked around and called the innkeeper.

"Can I help you, Friend?" He was smiling.

John returned the smile. "Our hope is to build a farm in the backcountry, but we be not sure of our needs. Who can advise us? Be there a trustworthy merchant for our supplies?"

The innkeeper frowned and shook his head. "Thee be out of season. People leave for the frontier in spring, not in fall."

"What if I brought food enough for the winter? Could I not build my house before the cold, spend the winter and then be ready to plant in spring?" He tried hard to sound confident. "I would think that a better plan."

"If that be thy plan, Friend, thee'll find most of thy needs at a fair price in William Fuller's mercantile two blocks east. 'Tis not how I'd go about it, but it may work for thee."

"Thank you. We'll go see Fuller now. Save our places at the table and in our bed. We should be back before dark."

"I'll save them for thee."

A five-minute walk brought them to William Fuller's store. Stacks of cloth bags filled with beans and grain divided the floor into aisles. Fuller sat behind a wooden counter in front of a wall covered with small wooden drawers filled with merchandise. He looked up from his ledger and smiled. "Good day, Friend. How may I help thee?"

"We're set to leave for the wilderness to build us a farm. We need supplies to get us through winter." *I hope I sound more confident than I feel.*

"Why go now, Friend? As you say, winter's almost on us."

"My hope is to clear land and build a cabin before snow. Then when the snow melts to be ready for planting. Seems more sensible than going in spring and need to clear land and build a house before getting crops in."

"How do thee plan to carry all thy needs?"

"We'll want an ox and cart."

"That thee'll find at the livery, another block east." Fuller sounded dubious. "Have thee coin for thy needs?"

"We do."

Fuller smiled. "Then tell me thy needs and I'll get them together while thee go for thy cart. Thee'll want flour. How much?"

Abigail said, "At least twelve stone. And another six stone of beans."

Fuller nodded. "I'll have to send my boy to the miller for that much flour but I'll have it this day."

"There'll be meat in the forest," John said, "but I'll want a hunting piece."

"That thee'll find at the gunsmith by the river."

"Do I get my powder and shot here or at the smithies'?"

"That thee buy here."

"Good. Then I'll want eight or nine stone of each."

"A cask of powder weighs two stone, of shot weighs four."

"I'll take four of powder and two of shot, bird and ball."

Abigail put her hand on John's shoulder. "And we'll want for more clothing."

The merchant nodded. "I have some breeches, shirts, vests, bodices, and petticoats. I can sell thee what I have. Most make their own. I suggest bear robes for the cold. I've some I took in trade. Will thee want two?"

"I'll take four." John turned to Abigail. "Can you finish here while I go for the ox and cart and see the gunsmith?

Abigail forced a smile and nodded.

"Which way to the livery again?"

"Another block east. Thee'll smell it before thee see it."

John left Abigail to complete their list of needs at the mercantile while he went to the livery, bought an ox and cart, then on to the gunsmith, where he bought a rifle and a fowling piece. Returning to Fuller's mercantile he paid for their supplies and watched as Fuller and his apprentice loaded the cart.

They returned to The Golden Hind just in time to store the ox and cart in the barn and sit for supper. There were more people at the table than there was stew to go around but there was plenty of bread and beer. That night they shared a bed with another man and two women. No one slept well.

After a morning meal much like their supper they bought a cask of beer, a smoked ham, and two large loaves of bread to eat while they traveled. Taking a road headed almost due west, they left Philadelphia.

Abigail noticed the bright colors of autumn and shuddered. *No joy in the colors this year ... We've left everything and everyone. Just us two now.* She smiled at that. *We belong to none ... but ourselves.* She tried to convince herself things would work out. *John will protect me ... We had to run. John was right to lay Moore low. Moore attacked him first.*

Then the girl who lived her entire life in cities looked around a countryside of unending trees and fields and shuddered again. *He knows no more about the wilds than I do. Where will we live? What about the cold? What will we do for meat?*

She leaned into John wrapping her arms around his right arm and hugged it, burying her face in his shoulder. She kissed his arm looked up at him and smiled. "Tell me all will be well."

Turning his attention away from steering the ox he smiled at her. "It will." He put a hand on hers and squeezed to reassure her.

His thoughts raced too. *What was I thinking? I'm wanted for murder ... and I bring her into it. Had to run ... Moore deserved to die. That was right. But Abigail? ... How'll I care for her? I can't even care for myself out here.*

He looked at her again, forcing another smile. His jaw muscles flexed. He clenched his teeth. His jaw began to ache.

Riding past small farm after small farm little seemed to change. They spoke little, each lost in thoughts they were afraid to share. As darkness approached they found a secluded place near a small stream where they could water and feed their ox then eat themselves.

"Looks to be a good place to stop."

She nodded her agreement. "There's some wood and leaves to use for kindling. I can start a fire while you see to the ox."

"And I'll collect some wood."

John cared for the ox and returned with an armload of dead wood. She sliced some ham and bread. They ate in silence. Everything was different now. They spent a cold night under the cart wrapped in their bear skins.

The second day the scenery began to change. Their thoughts did not. The farms were farther apart. They were, perhaps, larger. The buildings looked more like cabins and sheds than they looked like the substantial farmhouses and barns they saw closer to the city. Neither found this comforting.

The road narrowed to a trail just wide enough for the cart. John thought that they would not have to go much farther west. That night there were many secluded spots to choose from. They only needed to find a stream. Again, they slept under the cart wrapped in their bear skins. Abigail wept. John ground his teeth until his jaw ached.

At mid-morning the next day a smaller side trail broke off to the north.

"Take it?"

"Probably should." Abigail began to hum. *Like I'm humming past a graveyard.*

They took this trail for several hours before coming to a small clearing by a river.

"You think it'll run all winter?"

"Should," he nodded.

It was decided. They would spend the winter here. John unyoked the ox. Abigail began unloading the cart while John gathered wood for a fire. As she started the fire he took the ax from the cart.

"The trees won't chop themselves," he smiled, "We need logs for our cabin."

"Be careful, John. I know you split wood aplenty for Goodman Adams but did you ever chop a tree down?"

"I'll soon learn." He walked to a large oak at the edge of the clearing, hefted his ax and slammed it into the tree. The ax chipped the bark and rebounded away from the tree. Shifting his feet, he pulled the ax back again and slammed it into the wood. A small wedge, mostly bark, fell to the ground. John had expected his ax would drive far into the tree as it did when he split wood at the brewery. Instead his powerful blows only dented and chipped the wood. Blisters formed on his hands then broke and bled as he chopped the great trunk. He labored until Abigail called him for supper. He'd chopped a wedge about a quarter through the tree.

He brushed his sore hands together as he walked over and sat on a large rock. Abigail brought him a plate with several thick slices of the ham they brought from Philadelphia and two large, hot biscuits.

"Look at your hands." a tear formed in her eye.

"Not the first time you've seen them bloody from swinging an ax." he forced a smile.

Abigail laughed. While he ate, she tore some cloth into strips. Brushing dirt and grass away from his bleeding blisters, she wrapped the cloths around his hands. They burned against his torn skin. He tried not to wince.

After supper Abigail saw to the ox and John climbed under the cart. She joined him, then kissed his bloody hands. "You can't chop that tree tomorrow."

"I have to, there's none here to help us."

"Look at your hands. How do you expect to do that?"

"As best I can." He rolled over and fell asleep.

At dawn John returned to the tree. His hands bled. The cloths Abigail wrapped around them ground into his raw skin. He decided that they made his hands hurt worse so he pulled them off. He tried to cushion his hands with leaves. They throbbed, but he kept chopping.

Late in the day, he slammed his ax into the tree. A cracking sound came from inside its trunk.

Abigail looked up from preparing supper.

John reset his feet, slid the ax through burning hands and hammered the tree again. They heard more cracks. He wiped his forehead with the back of this arm and powered the ax into the tree. This time the tree moved.

Abigail stood and took a step toward him. "Be careful."

He swung his ax again and again. Long splinters of wood sprang out from the trunk above and below the jagged wedge hacked from the tree. John pulled the ax back and swung. The ax bit into the stressed wood. Cracking sounds became louder, more frequent. The tree moved again. He drove his ax into the breaking trunk, pulled it free and hit the tree again. More splinters broke loose.

Abigail's hands went to her mouth.

He reset his feet and smashed his ax into the tree twice more. The tree rotated and began to fall. John stepped back and smiled. Abigail stepped to his side, looked up at him then back to the falling tree. It shuddered, then fell, tearing huge branches from other trees as it crashed to the forest floor and extended across the river. Abigail squealed with delight.

John shook his head, "Now I need get it to the bank."

"How'll you do that?"

"The ox but got to clear the limbs first."

John climbed on the fallen tree. Dozens of small branches came off with a single blow. Abigail went to the river and dragged the fallen limbs she could move to the near bank. She stripped off their leaves and mixed them in with grass she'd collected for the ox. The limbs she could carry, she stacked for fire wood. Her hands too became cut and sore.

The larger branches were like trees themselves. John left those for last. Then he got the wood-framed saw from their cart to cut them off. This took the rest of that day and most of the next. At last the tree looked more like a log. When it was limbed as far as he thought would be useful, he tied his rope over a branch and around the trunk. Returning to the clearing, he yoked the ox and attached the rope to the yoke.

"Get on now!" he shouted and slapped the ox on its rump. The animal started forward, taking up the rope's slack. The rope became taut, the animal grunted and strained, but neither the ox nor the tree moved.

"Whoa, now." John stopped the ox and untied the rope. "Tree's too heavy for 'em."

"What will you do?"

"Tie the rope farther out on the tree and try a different angle." He moved the rope another ten feet toward the tree's top. This time, he led the ox along the stream's bank.

"Get on now!" The ox again took up the slack, but the tree didn't move. John slapped the ox and shouted, "Go now, pull!" The animal strained. John thought he saw the tree move. *Pull harder!*

He whipped the ox with a stick. It bellowed, straining against the rope. Its hooves dug into the ground. The sandy clay gave way under one of the animal's feet. It fell forward, struggled to its feet, and pulled again. The ground tore loose.

John whipped the animal and shouted, "Pull you *salaud!*"

The animal strained and bellowed. Its feet dug deeper into the churned ground. John beat it until the stick broke off in his hand.

Abigail shouted, "Stop! Stop, John. 'Tis too heavy. You'll kill him." She pulled the broken stick from his hand. "Beating the ox lightens not the tree."

He tore the stick back. "And leaving the tree where it is builds you no cabin!" He thrashed with what was left of the stick across the animal's rump. It strained left then right trying to break free.

"John, the ox can't move it."

"Go tend to your cooking and leave me be. It has to."

Furious, Abigail went back to the fire. She grabbed a piece of wood and pounded it into the ground.

John kept whipping the ox, "Pull you *salaud*! Pull!" The terrified animal's hooves dug deeper into the ground.

Abigail threw the piece of wood into the fire and screamed, "I said stop!"

"I worked days on it. What else is there?" He dropped to his knees.

She knelt, putting her arms around his shoulders, "You did. And now we've firewood, but you'll not move the tree by beating the ox."

He looked into his bloody hands and sobbed.

"None could work harder than you have. The tree be just too heavy. We both know oak to be heavy. What of a softer, lighter wood, cedar or pine?" She put her head against his and held him.

Minutes passed. He raised his head and whispered, "I know ... you've the right of it." He looked into his hands, then around their clearing. "The cedars be tall and straight ... Had I thought, I'd a' chopped one o' them." A tear rolled down his cheek.

She leaned in, putting her face to his. "Tomorrow be another day. I'll see to the ox. You go by the fire. Supper'll be soon." She kissed his forehead and stood. Then she unyoked the frightened animal. It stumbled into the dense brush at the edge of the clearing and cowered. Abigail waited for it to stop shaking before she tied it to a tree.

John climbed to his feet. Wiping tears from his eyes and sweat from his face, he walked to the fire, sat, and stared.

When she came to the fire, Abigail touched his head, but said nothing. Making biscuits, she prayed, *Dear Lord, give him strength. None have worked harder.* Tears welled in her eyes. *How'll he make a cabin before the snows?*

They ate in silence, then John climbed under the wagon and fell asleep.

Abigail sat beside the fire, staring into the night sky. Hours later cold drove her under the wagon and her bearskins.

The next morning, she woke to the sound of an ax hitting wood. Climbing from under the wagon, she saw John had chopped a deep wedge from the trunk of a large cedar tree. "You started early."

John smiled. "Winter's soon. We need a cabin."

Near noon, the cedar fell, close to where he planned the cabin. Abigail worked, pulling branches from the clearing while John limbed the tree. When they finished, she said, "We've neither eaten today. I'll fix supper."

"Good. I hunger."

He paced the tree and decided the useable portion of the trunk was about forty feet long. *Can't build a forty-foot-long cabin, but twenty'll do.* "Time to stop. Tomorrow I'll chop the log in half and start the cabin."

After another wordless supper, the exhausted couple climbed under their cart and slept.

In the morning, Abigail said, "John, the nights be cold already and we've but one tree down. How'll we have a cabin by snowfall?"

He looked at the huge log on the ground. "Knew I how to split a log we'd need fewer trees, but I know not how. I'll have to get better and get stronger as I work. Today I'll chop the log and notch it. 'Tis a start."

Abigail tried to look confident for him. *If I lose faith in him, all's lost. What else can I do? Dear Lord, give him strength.* She forced a weak smile.

By mid-morning the log was chopped in half. Together they rolled the logs to where they planned to build the cabin. He chopped a notch near the end of each log. Using branches for leverage they managed to lift the smaller log onto the larger one. The notches fit but weren't deep enough. The higher log tilted at an angle away from the ground. They lifted it out of place and John deepened both notches. They replaced the log but the notches were still too shallow. They did this twice more before the upper log settled into the notch and onto the ground.

"'Tis a start. 'Twill get easier as we learn." He walked to another tree.

"'Tis good the cabin's started, John, but the ham's gone. You need to hunt."

He smiled. "A cabin's no good if we starve 'fore 'tis finished. I'll go see what hides in this forest."

Glad for time away from the ax, he walked along the river carrying his rifle and fowling piece. A mile upstream, he saw two fat geese pecking at insects along the shore. He put down his rifle, raised his fowling piece, aimed, and fired. Both geese took wing, but the larger one only flapped its wings twice before falling back to the ground. John wrung its neck to be sure it was dead and carried it to their clearing.

Abigail smiled when she saw him. The smile broadened when she saw the goose. "We'll have us a fine roast goose for dinner tonight." She cleaned the bird and put it in her cast iron pot. Then she buried the pot in hot coals.

John started chopping the next tree. Before dark it fell into the clearing. He limbed the tree's underside, creating a space beneath its trunk. He called to Abigail, "Help me cover this with as much moss and leaves as we can. 'Twill be warmer under here."

Dear Lord, he wants me to sleep in a tree. Why not a cave?

They worked covering the tree with moss and leaves until Abigail stopped to finish their supper. John leaned the limbs he'd cut from the tree's underside against the downed trunk to secure the debris they'd piled on it.

As dark approached Abigail called him to eat. They agreed they never ate a finer meal. She put the leftover goose back in the pot and stored it in the cart. Placing two bear skins on the ground under their tree they climbed in and covered themselves with their other two skins. That night they were warm.

John chopped and notched two more trees the next day. He looked at the twenty-foot square of logs on the ground. *How am I to do this? These logs'll just roll off the others. I've no spikes or nails.* He stared at the logs. *Need I flatten their sides and stack them? That would take days. I've no chance to finish before snow!*

"Abigail, come see this." He explained the problem.

"Can't you tie them on?" Her voice cracked.

John thought, *Is that frustration or fear I hear?* "I see not how. We might have to stay under the tree."

She spun to face him, hands on her hips, and shouted, "You jest! How long do you expect me to live under a tree? 'Tis scarce room to sit up!"

He dropped his ax and shouted back, "Until I can think of something else."

She stepped closer. "Would you thought of something else 'fore you brought me here."

"We'd of been found in Philadelphia."

"We could have stayed in Boston, had you not killed Moore."

"I killed him to save you–"

"You'll not blame me! You killed him in your pride, not to save me. Now you've brought us here to die."

"I ought've left you there for Moore to beat, like he did the others."

"In a warm house with food aplenty."

John picked up his ax and threw it across the clearing, "Then go back. Tell them I took you by force." He followed the ax, picked it up and disappeared into the forest.

Abigail dropped to her knees and cried. "Damn him."

John walked a few hundred yards up stream before throwing the ax again. He punched a tree until his fist bled. Then he swore, sat against the tree and swore again. Tears welled in his eyes. *I ought've left her there to be beat.* He stared at nothing and swore.

Long minutes passed. Abigail looked at the spot where John walked into the woods. *Will he come back?*

She didn't fix anything to eat that night. At dark, she climbed under the tree. Crying, she pulled a bearskin to her face. *Smell of John.* She pulled it around herself, lay back and cried herself to sleep.

In the woods, John stared into the dark. *Should have left Boston without her.* He shivered and swore. Hours later he fell asleep.

In the dim light before dawn, John woke, cold and wet from dew. Still angry, he climbed to his feet. *What does she want of me?* He stamped his feet to warm himself. *Can't leave her alone.* He picked up his ax and headed back to their clearing.

Abigail was sitting by the fire, wrapped in a bearskin, when he walked in. She wiped a tear from her face and watched as he neared toward her. "Are you hungry?"

"No."

"You couldn't have eaten."

"I didn't."

"Then let me fix you something."

"No. Sit. I should not have brought you. Moore needed dying. I should have left alone."

"I wanted to go with you."

"Had you a choice?"

"Had I one, I would have gone."

John sat and put his arm around her. They both cried. Then Abigail got up and began fixing breakfast. John picked up his ax and walked to the square of longs on the ground.

*****

He labored the next two days shaping the logs. *This takes longer than I feared.* He sat on the log he was chopping. *And, the goose is most gone.* He looked at his calloused hands and clenched his teeth. *Tomorrow, I must hunt.* He looked at the square of logs. *And the cabin's naught but logs on the ground ... Need to think of something.*

Abigail watched him while she made supper. She prayed, *So much needs doing. How can he? Good Lord, please protect us. Give him strength? Show him a way.*

Neither spoke much as they ate. They couldn't think of what to say. Abigail cleaned up after the meal. John worked shaping the logs until dark. Then they climbed beneath their tree and fell into restless sleep.

After breakfast, he left the clearing with his rifle and his fowling piece. Several hours later he saw two bucks grazing in clearing. He put down the fowling piece and aimed his rifle. His shot startled both deer. One fell, got back to its feet and ran into the forest. John would have to follow it through the woods until it died.

Tracking the deer was no problem. The blood trail was easy to follow but the animal ran an erratic path, turning often. He wondered how he'd find his way back to Abigail. After noon, he stepped through some brush and found the dying deer. It looked him in the eye as he ended its misery.

He knew the buck had to be gutted or the meat would spoil. *I managed to gut that moose with a cutlass. Saw servants gut the animals I shot hundreds of times.* He pulled the knife from his belt. *I can do this .... Servants did it easy.* By the time the deer was gutted he was covered with blood and gore.

He lifted the buck's front legs to his shoulder and leaned forward to pick up his weapons. Struggling to straighten, he headed back to the clearing, dragging his deer along the blood-marked trail. John weighed a hundred and thirty or thirty-five pounds. He struggled with the buck's hundred pounds plus his two guns. *Should I leave the guns and come back for them? Can't do that. What if I can't find them again?*

He often stopped to rest. Once, while he sat trying to regain his breath, he thought he saw something move in the woods to his right. He spun to look but saw nothing. *Is someone here? We've seen no one for days ... Must just be fancy.*

He pulled the knife from his belt and got to his feet. After several minutes of looking, he found a broken twig, then noticed blood on it and laughed. *I've become quite the frontiersman. I can find twigs a wounded deer broke running through the forest.*

He looked around again, just to be certain. *Have to move ... Been gone too long.*

He sheathed his knife and picked up his guns. It was getting late. He pulled the buck's forelegs to his shoulders and tried to increase his pace. The sun lowered in the sky.

Be dark soon. Will I find the clearing? I can just follow the river ... Abigail'll be worried, in the dark, alone. She'll think me hurt. Should I leave the deer and go to her? He shook his head. *If I do that wolves'll come in the night and eat my buck.*

He heard a voice come from the forest, in a language he did not understand. Dropping the buck, he raised his rifle, which was not actually loaded, and pointed it in the direction of the voice. "Hold!" he shouted, "Who's there?"

Leaves parted. A native walked out of the forest. His open hands, held out at shoulder height, showed he wasn't holding a weapon. The muscular man was taller than John. The sides of his head looked shaved. Black hair running down the center of his head stood about four inches high. In crude, accented English he said, "You not talk Unami. I talk little white tongue."

He's been following me. "Who are you? What do you want?" John's voice betrayed his fear.

"I Tamaqua." The big man's voice was calm. His face showed no emotion. John kept his rifle aimed at him. With slow, deliberate motions, the Indian reached into a purse tied to the belt supporting his loin-cloth. He pulled out two rawhide strips. "You need help. I help."

He tied the dead animal's front legs together just above the hooves then did the same to the back legs. Standing, he held his hands in front of him again, nodded at John, and drew the tomahawk from his belt. He held out the other hand again and walked to a small tree. Using the tomahawk, he cut it, and stripped the leaves and branches to about ten feet, then cut off the rest. He stood and put the tomahawk back in this belt. Sliding the pole between the animal's legs, he lifted one end and said, "You lift there."

Should I? He could have killed me before I saw him. He didn't. Dare I trust him? Papisse Conewa helped me ... Not sure that ended so well though.

"Why?"

The stone faced native repeated, "You need help. I help you carry deer."

John stooped under the pole, took a gun in each hand and stood, lifting the deer. Keeping the pole on his shoulder, the native took a step.

"No, I need go this way," John pointed to the trail of blood the deer left.

The big man turned to face him. "Why?"

"'Tis how I came."

"Want follow trail or get to woman?"

John dropped the deer and fowling piece, raising his unloaded rifle, "How know you of my woman?" This came out in a rush, like an accusation.

The big man looked at the rifle, then at John. "Many men have woman. We see you chop tree with her."

"We? Who else be with you?"

"I Tamaqua of Lenni Lenape. Lenni Lenape see you."

Did this savage just say a whole tribe's been watching us? How are we still alive? The Delaware are said to be peaceful, but what of these Lenny somethings?

"You want see woman go this way." Tamaqua pointed into the forest almost at ninety-degree angle from the deer's trail.

Should I follow? I need help. If he wanted to kill me, he'd not have warned me, would he? Holding the rifle in one hand, John kept it pointed at the native, as he crouched for his fowling piece.

"How you shoot me with empty gun?" The big man smiled and pointed to the rifle. "Hammer not cocked, no powder in pan."

John's eyes fell on the uncocked hammer. His face reddened.

The Lenape chuckled. "Pick up other gun. You want see woman, follow me."

John felt for the knife in his belt. *At least this way I can watch him.* He crouched to pick up the other gun, then lifted the staff between the deer's legs.

The Indian started walking. Carrying two heavy guns, John struggled to match his pace. They walked in silence. In less than half an hour they entered the clearing.

Abigail saw a savage walk into the clearing. She jumped up and stood behind the cart. John called to her, "'Tis safe, Abigail. This is Tommykay. He helped me carry this fine buck back to you.

"I not Tommykay. I Tamaqua." They set down their load. Tamaqua said to Abigail, "You skin." Turning to John he pointed to the beginnings of their cabin. "Why you use big trees?"

"I'm building a cabin."

"Why use big trees?"

"I just said I'm building a cabin."

Tamaqua shook his head. "Why not use small trees?"

"Small trees won't stack on each other and if they did they'd fall under the weight of snow." *Isn't this obvious?*

"Small trees not fall. I come tomorrow, show." Tamaqua turned and walked out of the clearing, disappearing into the forest.

Abigail was silent during this exchange. When Tamaqua left, she whispered, "John, you brought a savage to our clearing!"

"He seems harmless enough," John said still looking at the spot where he left the clearing. "He helped me carry the deer. Seems there be a whole tribe of them, called Lenny somethings, that know of us. I heard the Delaware were peaceful. All I know of these is they know how to carry deer."

"A whole tribe knows we're here?" she shouted.

"He said they've watched us for days. Methinks we've less to fear knowing they're there than when we knew not."

Unconvinced, she said, "Mayhap."

Abigail built up the fire while John skinned the deer. She cut some meat from the animal and threw it in her pot, "At least we've meat to go with our biscuits and beans."

While she cooked, he threw his rope over a branch and tied an end of it to the buck's antlers. She helped him raise the animal high above the ground to protect the meat from animals. It was dark and getting cold when they finished eating. They climbed into their niche under the tree and tried to convince each other they actually were safe surrounded by Indians. Neither slept well.

Abigail was preparing their morning meal; John was chopping another tree when Tamaqua returned. A woman followed him. Like Abigail she was small but with dark skin and jet-black hair pulled straight back, then tied together, extending past her shoulders and down her back. She wore a deerskin smock decorated with red and white beads and beaded deerskin shoes.

"This is my woman, Wisawtayas. She show your woman to dry meat and make buckskin."

John and Abigail stared, trying to think of something to say.

Wisawtayas nodded at John and signed that Abigail should follow her. She looked around the clearing and saw the deer skin where John left it draped over some bushes. Speaking in the native language, she folded the skin and walked to the river, where she pushed the skin underwater and pinned it down with a large rock.

Tamaqua told John, "Wisawtayas say leave skin in water for three days."

"Why?"

"Two days not enough."

The woman walked from the river toward the hanging deer. With a tomahawk, she began cutting small trees and stripping them of leaves and branches. Pausing, she looked up said something and signed to Abigail to join her.

Abigail looked at John. He shrugged and said, "The man helped me. We ought not anger them. Do as she signs."

She glared at him.

The man said, "They dry meat today. We make wikiup."

"Wikiup?"

"You call cabin. You get ax."

Should I do this? John was as uncomfortable as Abigail, but he got his ax.

"We cut small trees like women."

Why would I need trees like those? They be too thin to make a cabin ... I'll never finish the cabin on my own anyway. What's to lose? He knew how to carry the buck, and how to get back here. Mayhap I should see what he knows.

On the other side of the clearing Abigail was furious. *Now two savages be here. How many'll come tomorrow?* She looked at the woman's tomahawk and knife. *He's right we'd best not anger them.* She picked up her cleaver and followed the woman's lead. *At least I've my cleaver, should she try scalp me.*

Together the women cut and stripped small trees. When they gathered a large bundle of what were now long sticks, Wisawtayas took out a knife and began peeling off long strips of bark. Again, she signed Abigail should copy her.

Why are we doing this? She looked across the clearing. *John and that Tommykay are doing the same thing.*

Soon they had a large pile of bark strips. When all the sticks were stripped, Wisawtayas used bark strips to tie two sticks together, near their ends. Then she lashed another stick to the end of one of those already connected. Again, she signed Abigail to do the same. Working together they fashioned a low, broad frame in just over an hour.

Wisawtayas signed Abigail should follow and walked to the hanging deer. Together they lowered it. The native took her knife cut a long, thin strip of meat and laid it across the frame. Again, she said something. Abigail did not understand her words but was sure the woman wanted her to cut strips of meat and lay them on the frame.

I see what she's doing. This'll dry the meat.

Meanwhile, John and Tamaqua also cut and stripped a large pile of small trees. The Indian took two sticks and lashed them together. "You do same."

John tried to lash two sticks together but broke the bark several times.

"Not pull so hard. Make tight, not break."

He tried again. After several false starts the sticks were tied.

"Good. Now do more."

The big native had several sticks connected by now. The men worked together in silence. When each man's length of sticks was several times a man's height Tamaqua took the end of John's sticks and attached it to his. He handed John one end of the sticks and brought the other end to it. He lashed the ends together and said, "Put on ground."

The sticks formed an irregular oblong shape. The big man adjusted the shape and pegged it to the ground using crotched branches from the trees they'd cut.

"Now tie more sticks."

John looked across the clearing to the women laying meat on the frame they'd made. *The woman had a plan. There must be one here.*

Together they made long lengths of sticks, then Tamaqua formed them into arches which he tied to the frame on the ground. The arches swayed in the breeze.

John thought. *Why are we doing this? Are they distracting us so others can kill us? How many are there?* He said, "If this is to be a cabin, 'twill never hold snow's weight."

"Watch."

After attaching the arches to the frame, they lashed other sticks to the sides of the arches. The sticks began to form a framework. They stopped moving in the light wind.

Abigail looked across the clearing, *Could that work? They live here. They must have a house? 'Tis this how they made theirs?*

Tamaqua used his tomahawk to cut sections of bark from the trunk of one of the trees John had already chopped down. He took it to the river, pushed the bark under water and put a rock on it.

"You cut bark like me. Put it in water."

The men worked together stripping the bark from all the trees John had hoped to use for their cabin. Then they cut bark from other large trees in the area, putting all the pieces of bark in the water to soak. An hour later Tamaqua pulled the first piece of bark from the water and flattened it on the ground. Then he placed it against the base of their framework. He used sticks to wedge the bark against the frame. Pulling another piece of bark from the water he said, "You do, too."

John watched and tried to copy his teacher.

Soon they had a row of overlapping bark sheets around the framework, leaving a space near one end. Row after row of bark was placed around the frame, like shingles, first covering the lodge's sides, then its roof. They left a gap in the roof for smoke to escape.

John was shocked. *This may work.*

More sticks were tied together. The men lashed these to the outside of the wikiup, locking the shingles in place.

They just finished lashing the last lengths of sticks over the bark sections on the roof of the sturdy, dome-shaped lodge they had built in a single day when Wisawtayas called to Tamaqua, in the Unami language, "Husband, I have to leave to prepare our meal."

Tamaqua took John into the lodge and pointed. "Still be cold. Hang bear skins to cover door and hole in roof. We go now. In morning, do not eat. I show you to hunt. Your woman dry meat. You have much to eat in winter."

Tamaqua turned and walked into the forest. Wisawtayas followed. She asked, "Husband, how do white people live in their villages?"

"I do not know, but we must show them how to hunt game and store food or they will starve, unless they freeze first."

"The Great Spirit must protect them. He watches over all idiots."

Tamaqua just shrugged. They walked in silence to their village.

In the clearing, John said, "You should have seen him make this cabin."

"I did, and she taught me how they dry meat. They know things we know naught of."

Abigail prepared their supper, while John moved their things from under their tree into the wikiup. He laid out bear skins for them to sleep on, covered by another.

That night they slept in their new home. Wind rushed through the open doorway, through the gaps between the bark shingles and out through the smoke hole in the roof. Despite being wrapped in bear skins they were cold, far colder than they had been in their tree shelter. As soon as he saw a ray of sunlight in the clearing John left the wikiup to stand in the warm light. Abigail joined him.

"Last night was too cold. Should we move back under the tree?" he asked.

"The tree won't keep out much rain. I think this cabin will. The man told you to hang a bear skin over the doorway. In the winter, Goody had us hang quilts on the walls to keep out the cold. I can't make so many quilts, but could you hunt bears enough to hang their skins on the walls like quilts?"

"I could try. The hole in the roof's to let smoke out. We ought build a fire inside, too."

They were just finishing their morning meal when Tamaqua walked into the clearing.

"Why eating? I said not eat. Hunter who not hungry not pay attention."

John laughed. "I can pay attention without being hungry."

"You not ready for hunt. Smell like man. Need sweat bath but have no sweat- lodge. You go rub with sweet fern."

The Indian led him to a cluster of ferns by the river. John consented to strip and rub fern leaves all over his body. As he dressed the sweet, pungent aroma upset his stomach.

"Now animals smell ferns not you. Get gun. We go shoot deer."

John went into the wikiup to get his guns.

"Put back bird gun."

"What if we see birds to shoot?"

"Not hunt birds. Hunt deer."

John shrugged. *Thinks he that he can decide what animals we see?* He put the fowling piece back in the lodge, bringing his rifle, powder. and shot.

When they entered the forest, Tamaqua stopped to pick up his rifle, powder horn, and bag of shot. He set off at a brisk trot.

John followed, calling out, "Won't we find more deer if we sneak up on them?"

"Come."

John struggled to keep up for about half an hour before they came to a large clearing. "Sit." Tamaqua loaded his rifle and sat in tall grass at the edge of the clearing.

John sat next to him, gasping for breath. "Shouldn't we ... walk, looking for deer?"

"Deer come us."

"Why would deer come to us?"

"Deer always come. Quiet."

Tamaqua sat motionless, only speaking when he said to John, "Not move!" or "Quiet!" After sitting this way for several hours, which felt like several days to John, a group of four does wandered into the upwind side of the clearing, grazing on low shrubs.

Tamaqua raised his rifle, aimed, and whispered, "I shoot first. You shoot right after. You shoot nearest."

John raised his rifle and aimed. Tamaqua fired, striking the deer farthest from them. The others reacted to the wounded deer, running away from it, toward the hunters. John fired, hitting one of the panicked deer in the throat as they ran toward him. His deer ran another hundred yards before it fell dead. Tamaqua's deer ran in the opposite direction before falling. When the men reached Tamaqua's deer, it lay on its side panting. He knelt beside it and put his mouth to the dying animal's ear. Then he looked skyward, raised his hands and sang a short song in his native language. He pulled the knife from his belt and slit the animal's throat.

"What was that about?"

"I thank Sister Deer. Tell her we happy she here for us. That you need her body for meat. Then I give thanks to The Great Spirit for all He provides."

"Why did you do that?"

"Why did you not?"

Tamaqua showed him how to gut a deer with a minimum of effort. "You go. Gut your deer. Come back."

John went to his deer and gutted the animal the way Tamaqua showed him. When he finished, he went back to Tamaqua. The Lenape was threading a pole between the deer's legs. Together they carried it to John's deer. Tamaqua tied the second deer's feet and showed John how to arrange two deer on one pole. They were heavy but with the pole the men could handle their weight. They carried the deer to the clearing without resting.

In the clearing, Tamaqua pointed at Abigail, "You skin, dry meat." Then he pointed at the wikiup. "Why door not covered?"

"We only have four bear skins. We used them to sleep in," John said.

"You need more skins. Tomorrow go down river to big pool. This time year it not deep. Bears go catch fish. You shoot bears. Woman skin them and dry meat. You be warm and have meat for winter." Tamaqua turned and left the clearing.

Abigail looked at the deer the men left at her feet. "Two John? How am I to skin two deer?"

"My wager'd be one at a time." John smiled. "'Tis not our worst problem. I'll skin one." As they worked John said, "He amazes me. You can't imagine how this man knows the forest. He knows where deer go. He just sits and waits for deer to come. Now he says if I go down river I'll find bear fishing."

"I heard. Do bears fish? Do you think he's right?"

"He knew where there'd be deer."

When the deer were skinned Abigail folded the skins, took them to the river and pinned them under rocks. Then she made some biscuits to go with the roast venison. Before dark John covered the doorway with a bear skin and brought in dry leaves for them to sleep on. She built a fire in their wikiup to keep them warm. They covered themselves with their remaining bear skins and slept.

After their morning meal John picked up both his guns and said, "He's been right so far. I'll go down river and see if bears fish there."

"Bears be dangerous. Be careful."

When John reached the pool, he saw a bear sitting on the bank, eating. Two more were standing in the large, shallow pool swatting at fish. John crept forward. He lowered to one knee placed his fowling piece on the ground and raised his rifle. Aiming at the bear sitting on the bank, he fired striking the animal in the chest. The bear roared and reared up. It ran at John who grabbed his fowling piece and shot again hitting it in the face. The wounded animal stumbled backward and charged again. John turned and ran. Then he heard a gunshot come from the forest. The bear fell again. Tamaqua ran out of the shadows carrying a spear. As the bear struggled to get up Tamaqua thrust his spear into its throat, pulled it out and plunged it in again. The bear's roaring stopped. Its body stopped moving. The big man knelt over it and leaned toward its ear, then faced the sky, held out his arms and sang.

John stood at a respectful distance until he finished singing. "You saved my life."

"Now you know how kill bears. You need skins to cover door and smoke hole, meat for winter. Next time bring ax to kill bear."

"With an ax? 'Tis that not dangerous?"

"Not dangerous you. Dangerous bear."

"Shouldn't I shoot it again, like you did?"

"You have extra rifle?"

"No."

"Bring ax."

"Couldn't I shoot the bear and run from it until it dies, like trailing a wounded deer?"

Tamaqua chuckled. "That be dangerous you. Bear run faster. Climb tree faster too."

While they talked, Tamaqua gutted the bear. He then tied the bear's legs together. He cut a small tree and ran it between the bear's legs. "You lift." They carried the bear back to the clearing where Tamaqua said to Abigail, "You skin and dry." Then to John, "Put down bird gun. Take ax. You need more bears." Without much thought, John put his fowling piece in the wikiup, picked up his ax and followed the Lenape.

There were four bears at the pool. One was gorging itself on the entrails of the bear the men had killed. Two were sitting on the bank eating fish. One was wading in the water. Tamaqua whispered, "I shoot closest bear. You shoot far one." Both men took aim. Tamaqua shot first. Both bears bellowed and charged.

Tamaqua pressed the back of his spear into the soft earth. When the charging bear closed on him, he lifted the tip of the spear. The animal impaled itself and fell. He leaned to the dying bear's ear, looked to the sky and sang, then finished the bear with his knife.

John saw none of this. The other bear charged straight for him. Dropping his rifle, he raised his ax over his head. His eyes locked on the charging beast. Without realizing it he took step after step backward, stumbling once, without falling. He looked down, saw the rock that tripped him and looked up to find the bear almost upon him. With the skill of a swordsman he brought the ax down on the bear's head splitting its skull. It fell dead at his feet. He knelt beside the bear and bowed his head.

"See. Dangerous bear." The big man was smiling.

Each man gutted his bear. "Is this how you always kill bears?"

"No. I use arrows. Shoot bear three times, sometimes four."

"Why didn't you use arrows today?"

"I show you how kill bear. You know how shoot arrow?"

"No. I've never touched a bow."

"So, bring rifle and ax."

Tamaqua gutted the bears then cut two saplings. He laid them side by side and lashed them together at one end. "You do same," he told John, handing him a rawhide strip. When John finished,

Tamaqua rolled one of the bears onto his trees. He separated the trees at their unlashed ends, stepped between them and lifted, bringing the bear off the ground. John followed Tamaqua's lead. Using the trees as litters, they dragged the bears to the clearing.

*****

Wisawtayas came to the clearing several times over the next few weeks. One day she showed Abigail how to tan a deer's hide using urine and the animal's brain. Another she showed her how to make fishing net and how to line pits to store food for later use. Other than that, they saw little of Tamaqua or Wisawtayas.

After harvesting five or six bears John began thinking of himself as a skilled bear slayer. Confident of the kill, he no longer backed away when wounded bears charged him. This time, as he swung his ax at the wounded animal's head, it lunged at his arm. The ax dug deep into the bear's shoulder. It bellowed again and with its dying act raked its claws down John's front, tearing through his coat and into his chest.

Struggling to his feet, John staggered back to the cabin, covered with blood.

Abigail screamed, "Oh, dear God, you're hurt!"

She ran to him as he stumbled toward her. She helped him into their lodge and tore off his clothing. There were four deep gashes across his chest. She grabbed the bucket and ran to the stream for water. Ice was beginning to form along its banks. She cleaned his wounds with the cold water and wrapped them with cloth. John cursed himself for missing the bear's head. Then he cursed himself again for leaving the rifle, ax, and bear at the pool.

In time, he bled through the bandages. Abigail decided not to disturb the wound. She put dry grass on the bloody bandages and wrapped over the grass with clean cloth. John refused to eat and drank little. Hours later, he fell asleep.

Late that day, Tamaqua came into the clearing dragging the bear, John's gun, and ax on a litter. Abigail heard the noise made by the dragging poles and hurried outside. When she saw Tamaqua, she started to cry.

"John hurt?"

"Yes! He was mauled by a bear." She wiped a tear from her cheek.

"Let me look." Tamaqua said walking into the wikiup.

"He's asleep. We should leave him," she whispered.

Tamaqua knelt by John and felt his forehead. "He hot. Lost much blood. Not good."

"I know. My hope's that he'll sleep and the fever'll break by morning."

"I get help." Tamaqua stood and walked out. Abigail followed him. He left the clearing, saying nothing else.

It was dark when Abigail again heard something. She went to the entry, moved aside the bear skin to look outside. In the darkness, she could just see Tamaqua, Wisawtayas and a second man. Now that it was cold, both men wore deerskin shirts and leggings along with their loinclothes. The older man's head was not shaved. He wore his gray hair pulled straight back, as Wisawataya wore hers. Abigail stepped back and held the skin indicating that they should enter.

"This Tamanend, medicine man."

The old man knelt by John and felt his head. Then he began removing John's bandages. Abigail began to speak, but Tamaqua motioned she should be quiet. She held her tongue.

After inspecting the wounds, Tamanend said, in the Unami language, "His wounds are bad, but he should live. You pray for his recovery. I will put incense in the fire to get the attention of the Great Spirit. Then I will make a poultice to draw the poison from his wounds."

Wisawtayas began quiet singing, flexing and straightening her knees in rhythm. Tamaqua translated for Tamanend. "John hurt bad but should get better. Tamanend will put on medicine. We pray." He started singing, gently bouncing at his knees as Wisawtayas did. Abigail thought praying was a good idea. She knelt beside John, lowered her head and begged for healing.

Tamanend put a rock on the fire's coals. Next, he pulled a deer skin bag from a satchel he wore and removed some powder. He threw the powder into the fire, filling the lodge with a fragrant smoke. He drew an eagle feather from his satchel and waved it in the smoke rising from the fire, directing the smoke toward John. Kneeling by the fire, he almost whispered a quiet song. After singing for fifteen to twenty minutes, Tamanend filled a gourd with water. Using two knives he took the rock off the coals. He dropped it into the gourd causing a loud hissing sound. After a few minutes Tamanend took the rock from the water. He removed another bag from his satchel. From this he sprinkled a powder into the water, stirring it into a paste. When he was satisfied with the paste's consistency he poured it out onto John's chest and rubbed it into his wounds. Though unconscious, John pulled away from the medicine man's hands. Tamanend removed a bag of dried leaves from his satchel, spread them over the wounds, and replaced the bandages Abigail used.

"He will sleep now for many hours. He will wake when his fever breaks. You two stay with the whites and continue praying. I expect the Great Spirit to bless this man as he always blesses us. I will return to our village. If this man's fever has not broken or if he is still asleep by sundown tomorrow, come get me. This man's life depends on your prayers." Tamanend stood and walked out.

Again, Tamaqua translated for Abigail, adding, "Prayer most important. You pray. We pray, too. Don't stop."

Abigail thanked him, knelt by her man and prayed. Tamaqua and Wisawtayas sang just above a whisper as they bobbed. Hours later, Abigail slid to her side and fell asleep while praying. When she woke Tamaqua and Wisawtayas were still singing their prayers to the Great Spirit.

I wonder if we pray to the same God. She said another prayer then went out of the lodge, built up a cook fire and fixed a breakfast for all of them.

The Indians would not eat. "We must pray." They prayed all day, refusing food or drink. Often Abigail joined them. Again, she fell asleep while praying. This time she was wakened by John groaning. He was waking up.

Abigail sat up and cried, "John? Can you hear me? John, how are you?"

He opened his eyes and tried to smile at her. He turned toward the Indians and asked, "Why be they here?"

"Tamaqua found the bear with your rifle and ax. He saw the blood and knew you were hurt. He brought a medicine man from his village. They've prayed for you all night."

John struggled to raise himself on an elbow and managed to say, "Thank you."

Hearing this, Tamaqua said something in Unami and both the Indians sang louder, their bobbing more forceful. Abigail brought John some water and some bread to eat. He sipped the water and ate some of the bread. Then he lay back and said, "I'm so tired."

"Then sleep."

"It'd be easier were the room quieter." John smiled and closed his eyes.

When it was clear that he was again asleep, the Indians stopped their prayer. "Great Spirit saved John. You thank Him. We go to our lodge. Be sure you thank Great Spirit. Then eat, sleep."

Wisawtayas made a sign toward her breast, toward John, then toward the sky. She looked up, touched her breast again and making a bowing motion turned and left the wikiup. Tamaqua followed her out of the clearing.

John and Abigail slept through the night. Near dawn, John tried to roll over in his sleep. The pain jolted him awake. It would be days before he could move without pain.

Most of the time he huddled under a bearskin beside the fire and tried to stay warm. Every movement hurt.

The bearskins Abigail hung to keep out the cold only covered about half of their wikiup's walls. Gaps between the bark shingles forming the shelter's sides let in light. They also let in cold winds. John knew he needed more skins.

A week later, he starting trying to help Abigail with her many tasks. In another five days, he went hunting.

Hunting and skinning bears consumed John's time. Days grew shorter. Nights grew colder. Little by little Abigail lined the walls of their little cabin.

*****

The river was broad and shallow near their clearing. When Abigail fetched water, she had to either step into the river to reach water deep enough to fill her bucket, or crouch at the edge and use her ladle to fill the bucket. Ladling the water took too long. To save time, she took off her shoes and stockings, lifted her skirt and waded into the water.

Then she had to carry the heavy bucket up the bank to their clearing. The muddy ground was slippery. She often fell, spilling the water and covering herself with mud. Most days she labored to haul three buckets of water into their camp. Her neck and shoulders throbbed in pain from the work of dragging the heavy bucket up the bank and into the clearing. She also led the ox to the river at least three times a day. The animal struggled climbing down the steep slippery bank and even more climbing back up.

As winter neared, the mud froze. She slipped on the ice more often than she did on the mud. The ox slipped and slid on the way to the river. It struggled even more climbing back up the steep, slippery bank. Several times she had to pull the animal's harness to coax it back up the slippery bank. After a freezing rain, even with her coaxing, the ox couldn't climb the slick bank. John tied a rope to the animal's horns and they both pulled to help the ox up the bank. She stopped bringing it to the water after that. That meant she had to bring water to the ox, which drank four full buckets a day.

Her shoulders hurt all the time. Many nights she couldn't fall asleep. If she did fall asleep the pain would wake her and she would stare at the roof praying for relief.

The days grew shorter, the water grew colder. Ice extended almost a foot from the river bank. Abigail couldn't force herself to wade into the freezing water. She began breaking through the ice with her foot, then leaning over the hole to ladle water into the bucket. Fetching water took hours every day, but still she had to tend to the fire, cook, and clean.

Abigail shivered as she slipped down the bank. *More water. All the cursed animal does is eat and drink.* She stamped her foot through the ice, getting freezing water into her shoe. *Damn!*

Crouching over the hole she leaned one hand on the ice and scooped ladle after ladle full of water into the bucket with the other. The ice gave way under her hand. She fell forward, breaking face first through the ice and into the frigid river.

Her head went under. Freezing water filled her coat. Abigail thrashed to stand, slipping and falling again. She was soaked to the skin by the time she found firm footing. Leaving the bucket, she slipped her way up the bank to the wikiup.

Damn, I let the fire burn down.

Shivering, she got an armload of wood and threw it on the fire, then went for another. Her clothing stiffened as it began to freeze. The fire was no more than a bed of coals.

Got to get out of these.

Abigail shook as she stripped off her soaked, freezing clothing. The bear skin she pulled on felt almost as cold. Kneeling next to the fire, she leaned in and blew on the coals.

She threw another bear skin on the ground beside the growing fire, lay on top of it and covered herself with two more. Unable to stop shaking, she curled up as close to the fire as she dared.

Hours passed before John returned, dragging a bear. "Abigail? Where are you?"

"Here, John, inside."

"Something's amiss. "He rushed into the wikiup. "What's done?"

"Oh, John, I freeze."

Her skin was white, her lips and eyelids blue. She shook under the bearskins. "What happened."

"I fell into the river."

"You're freezing. And the fire's near out."

"Stoked it once. Too cold to move now."

John built up the fire and bought in more wood. Then he stripped and climbed under the bear skins with Abigail. "You're near froze."

She wrapped herself around his body, sweaty from the exertion of dragging the bear to their clearing. He shivered and held her. Almost an hour later, she stopped shaking.

John climbed out of the skins and dressed. He stoked the fire again, then put some dried venison in their pot and looked around for water. "Of course." He went to the river, stomped through the ice and filled the bucket. Slipping several times as he climbed the bank, he went inside, poured water in the pot and put it on the coals. Then he pulled off his cold, wet shoe and stocking and sat with his foot next to the fire until the water boiled.

He scooped a cup from the pot and woke Abigail. "Here, drink this. 'Twill warm you."

Abigail sat up, drawing the skins close around her and took the cup. Strands of still damp hair hung around her face. She sipped the steaming broth and smiled. "Thank you." She took another sip. A shiver shook her body. "The broth's good."

"The broth's hot. How did this happen?"

Abigail told John how difficult fetching water was, how much they used and how she fell in.

"I ought've known. I carried water for years. 'Tis too heavy for you."

"John, women fetch water. 'Tis what we do. None like it."

"But they draw it from a well, and carry it to the house, not up a slippery bank. I'll do that now."

He tied his rope over the fire and hung her wet clothing to dry. Abigail finished her broth, then fell asleep. John finished the broth, ate some jerky, then undressed and slid next to her again. *She's still cold.*

Fetching water became his job. *Thought myself done with this when Goody bought more indentures.* When the river froze over for a week, he had to chop a hole through the ice every day. *Spring'll not come too soon.*

*****

Hordes of dried venison and bear meat were wrapped in skins and stored in the lodge or buried outside. The trees John had cut to build his log cabin became fire wood, some of which they stored in their cabin, for drying, but he had to cut more.

Abigail stopped cooking outside. The skins on the door and walls kept the cold out. They also kept out fresh air. Without moving air, the small hole in the wikiup's roof allowed too little smoke to escape. Their cabin was warm but filled with smoke from burning green wood. Their eyes reddened and burned. Both developed a shallow, persistent cough.

John worked in the cold carrying water and splitting wood every day. Abigail fed the ox and prepared their meals. They spent the long winter nights huddled by the fire. As much as possible, they stayed in the lodge and talked about their lives, now, before they met, and best of all, their plans for the future.

They did not see the Lenape that winter, although John was sure Tamaqua kept watch over them. On occasion, he would see moccasin prints in the snow outside the clearing. He wondered how his friends were faring.

In the spring, they intended to cross the Delaware and settle into a town in West Jersey. John realized he would miss the Indians who watched over them. *We'd both have died but for Tamaqua, Wisawtayas and their medicine man. Don't expect I'll meet their likes again.*

By the time the snow began to melt Abigail ran out of flour and beans. Their diet of dried bear, venison and fish bored them but filled their bellies.

Leaves burst from the trees. The mud dried on the foot trails. It was time to head east.

Chapter Twelve
A New Home

**"How often things occur by mere chance
which we dared not even hope for."**
Terence

The afternoon before they left for West Jersey, they took down the bear skins that lined their wikiup. "You near died for these. 'Twould be wrong to leave them."

John rubbed his chest. "For certain, they were hard won. We can use them for barter."

After she packed the bearskins in the cart, Abigail got on her knees, and pulled a hemp sack from under their low sleeping platform. "I saved these for our return. We can't wear the clothes we wore all winter."

He looked at his stained and patched linsey-woolsey shirt and breeches, then nodded his agreement. He chuckled at his appearance. *If my family saw me now... I wonder how they fair.*

Abigail disturbed his reverie by handing him a light tan, tow-linen shirt, a pair of black linen breeches and almost white stockings. "Take those off. I'll burn them."

His mind went back to Papisse Conewa, who burned the clothing he had worn on the ship. Then he thought of the women in Wells, who burned the clothing Papisse had just given him. He chuckled again. "Enough of my clothing's been burned in this country. I wager I'll need these again as we settle. I can't wear my best to labor in."

"More's the shame this is our best. I'll make us better when we're settled." She pulled out her new clothes, holding an off-white, mid-calf length shift, blue gown that extended just past her waist and light petticoat in front of her. All were made from inexpensive tow linen. She turned her shoulders and hips, as if modeling her wardrobe. "Will I be presentable for you, sir?" She giggled.

"Mayhap I should keep so beautiful a wife on the frontier, away from other men." He put his arms around her waist and pulled her to him.

"Wait. I've more to show. I bought pretty things, too. Would you not see them?"

"I'd rather see less."

*****

Abigail looked around as they packed to leave their clearing, "Strange to say, I feel blue to leave."

John dropped a pot and his ax in the cart, "And I. Makes little sense."

She walked to him and leaned her head on his shoulder. "This was our first home."

He leaned his face against her head. "'Twas. Pray God our next be better."

They finished packing just before dark and slept in their wikiup one last time. Then after a breakfast of dried bear meat they yoked the ox and headed south along the trail that brought them there last summer.

"We ought to say goodbye to Tamaqua and Wisawtayas. Like as not they saved our lives," Abigail said.

"Like as not?" John laughed. "We'd have froze before I built us a cabin." He laughed again. "At least it would've kept us from starving." He looked from the trail ahead to Abigail. "You be right. We ought to say goodbye, but where'd we find them? I've no idea where their village be."

"'Twas their intention," she said, shaking her head. "Oft as they came to us, they never spoke of their village or took us there. 'Tis as they wanted. We ought respect that."

John laughed again. "Have we a choice?"

Abigail changed the subject. "Moves the ox slower than he did last year?"

"Mayhap. Winter was hard on him, too," He looked at his wife. The dark circles under her eyes aged her thin face. "We're all the worse for wear."

Before noon, they reached the trail that they took west a few months earlier.

Keep heading this way and we'll in Philadelphia again in three days. Were we so close? John thought. *Scarce seems possible.*

They followed the trail until dark. After a cold supper, they climbed under their cart and wrapped themselves in bear skins. That night they were cold. They missed their wikiup.

The next day the road began to widen. They saw signs of farms and fields. That afternoon they reached a broad trail headed north. Last fall it was of no interest to them. Now they took it, hoping to avoid Philadelphia. They thought they were on the edge of white civilization, paralleling the Delaware River.

While they rode, John said, "We need new names again, and a new story."

"We could be the Smiths."

"Or the Joneses."

Abigail turned on the seat to face him and said, "We had a customer, Goodman Hawthorn. I liked his name."

John nodded. "Hawthorn's a good name. What about Deer or Doe?"

"John Deer, Abigail Deer, John Doe," she frowned and shook her head, "They sound too plain. What of Abigail Brown, John Brown?"

He laughed. "You thought John Doe and Deer sounded plain, and you would use Brown? Why not Smith?"

"You're a brewer. What of Abigail and John Brewer?"

"Because I'm a brewer, best not."

"You're not a cooper, or a sawyer. Do they strike you?"

He turned to look at her. "What are we doing now?"

"I don't know. Are we arguing?"

"I think not, but we are riding. Aren't we riders?"

"Riders, John and Abigail Rider." She paused and looked away then said, "It rings well. Sitting on this cart, Rider makes sense."

"So, we're decided, Missus Rider?"

"We are, Mister Rider." She hugged his arm and rode a while with her head on his shoulder.

They decided they couldn't claim they quit farming the frontier and still explain their purse filled with silver. There was little hard money in the colonies. Backcountry farmers who gave up would have none.

John said, "I left France to make my fortune trading in furs. We've skins enough to say we trapped."

"What trapper takes his wife?" she asked, her tone was dismissive.

"None." John nodded, then shook his head.

"We could say we sold our farm."

"How?" It was John's turn to sound dismissive. "Land be free."

"How if we say we sold a brewery in another colony to try farming and learned we're no farmers?"

"That part's true enough."

"When farming didn't work ... we thought to leave while we'd silver left."

"Where'd we come from?"

She looked at him, "Massachusetts—"

He turned to face her, "I see no good coming from that."

"What of Mary's land? 'Tis in the other direction."

He nodded. "The shippers talked of Lord Baltimore's city in Mary's land"

"So, we got our silver when we sold the brewery in Baltimore?"

"We did." He smiled. "Selling 'twas a mistake. We seek a new place to start another. May be our best story."

It was decided, the Riders, former brewers and farmers, traveled another two days north along the Delaware, before taking another trail east. For two days the trail broadened, before it came to a ferry crossing.

"How much to cross?" John asked.

"Ha' penny each. Penny for the ox and cart," the sunburned ferryman looked at the ox with a frown and said, "Short of feed where you come from?"

"The ox, like us, near starved in the backcountry. 'Tis why we've left." John reached into his purse. "We're hoping to settle in Jersey. What towns be near?"

The ferryman took off his worn hat and wiped his face with a huge, calloused hand. "Near's mostly farms. An inn here and there.

There's Elizabeth and New Ark of the Covenant over in East Jersey. Above them's York City, all a fair ride. Burlington City's West Jersey's capital. Might be three day's ride, a little north of Philadelphia, on this side o' the river. Settled by Quakers, even before Philadelphia, but just now startin' ta grow."

A small but growing town near the largest port in the colonies interested John. "Three days south, you say."

"Three, maybe four."

"And the road there?"

"The river trail's straight enough to it."

John handed him two pennies and led their ox cart onto the ferry. The ferryman stood on his wide, flat craft and pulled on a thick rope, between trees on either side of the river, until they arrived in West Jersey. John led the ox up the dirt path from the river.

"Feed your animal." the ferryman called as John turned the cart south.

Abigail looked over and shoulder and said, "Seems he didn't believe your tale."

John looked back, too, and grumbled, "Then we've trouble. 'Tis the only truth we can tell."

It was already late and an inn was just to the south. They decided on a hot meal with fresh meat, bread, and beer.

Their supper did not disappoint them. They had run out of flour weeks before. The thick slices of black bread, with sour butter reminded them of what they missed. After months of drinking nothing but water, beer tasted good. The stew was thick with meat, potatoes, and onions. They were happy to get back to civilization until they went to their room. After months of solitude they shared a bed with two snoring, gassy men. Neither of them slept.

After a breakfast of porridge, bread, and beer, they were up and out early the next morning. The day passed without incident. They stopped in another inn for supper that night but decided not to sleep there. They headed south again until they found a secluded spot, just off the trail. Sleeping cold, under the cart, was better than sharing another bed with strangers.

After another day on the trail, and another night under the cart, mid-morning brought them to Burlington's inn, where they discovered there were no brewers in town. Every household, including the inn, made its own beer. A ferry crossed the river to Philadelphia. John believed he would be able to sell his beer in America's busiest port.

When asked, the innkeeper told them one of the town's original settlers had recently died, and the town's solicitor was trying to sell the man's house. Over a venison stew, John asked Abigail, "What think you? Should we stay?"

"Are you asking if I'd like us to have a home of our own? I never dreamed to have my own house. 'Twould be a blessing for all three of us."

"Three?!"

"I've waited for a good time to tell you ... This may be the time. I'm with child." Abigail's voice sounded like a little girl's.

A smile exploded over John's face. He threw his arms around his wife and held her close. "Appears we need to see that solicitor today. Our family's in need of a home."

Abigail smiled, but straightened and pulled back. Public embraces were inappropriate. John leaned closer and whispered that he loved her. Then he hugged her again.

They finished their meal and asked directions to the solicitor's office. Leaving their ox and cart at the inn, they walked through a thriving small town. John knocked at the door.

"Good day, Friend. Name's Josiah Peck. How may I be of service to thee?"

"My wife and I are told you've a house to sell."

"That I do. William Merton recently died, leaving a respectable house by the river. His heirs have asked me to handle its sale. Would thee see it?"

"We would."

A short walk brought them to the Merton house. Larger than most, it had central chimney and white clapboard siding. The house was in good repair, with two large rooms. "The family wishes to sell the furnishings with it."

There were four chairs, painted black, with floral stencils and a broad, wooden table in the kitchen well supplied with cast iron pots, pans, and utensils. Green vines were stenciled along the top of bright yellow walls. The front room had a large bed, two cushioned chairs, covered with green silk and a small black table. The dark green silk wall covering made this room dimmer than the kitchen. Both rooms had white linen curtains over real glass windows. There were even two brass lamps, with glass globes. Abigail smiled and said, "John, everything's beautiful."

The out building was large enough for a brewery. He would be able to start brewing as soon as he bought the necessary kettles and found a mason to build a malting oven. There was sure to be a cooper, either in Burlington or across the river in Philadelphia, to provide buckets and casks. For a home in the village and on the river, the lot was large.

John asked, "Be there others for sale?"

"Available houses in town proper be rare. Town's growing. Newcomers tend to build farther from the river where there's land to clear and farm."

John and Abigail went out and stood looking across the river. He asked, "Would you have it?"

"'Tis finer than I hoped for. Can we afford it?"

"Wait here, while I go find out." He found Peck sitting in the kitchen. "How much do they ask for this house?"

"What have thee to barter?"

John smiled and said, "I've silver."

"Silver! That be rare enough. With payment in silver, I'd be authorized to sell as cheap as ten pounds."

"Would you take nine?"

"Nine and five would do it."

John held out his hand. "Nine and five suits us well. When can we move in?"

Peck smiled as he shook John's hand, "When will thee have the silver?"

"Today."

"Then I can give thee the deed today. Thee can sleep in thy house tonight."

John did not want the lawyer to know how much cash he was carrying. He said, "I need go for my silver. My wife and I will meet you at your office in an hour."

When John told Abigail of the agreement, she squealed with delight. "I never imagined to have such a home. 'Twill be a blessing to raise our family here."

"That's certain. And we've yet silver enough to start our brewery. Let's walk a while so Peck thinks we had to go somewhere for the silver."

After a short walk, John noticed they were alone. He scooped her into his arms and spun her. "Abigail Rider, you be the most beautiful woman in this colony."

She laughed. "Easy said by one who knows none other."

"I know the one I need to and she be beautiful."

"She'll soon be fat."

"The most beautiful fat woman in the colony." They kissed. Abigail wept tears of joy.

*****

When John handed Peck nine pounds and five shillings in silver coins, Peck said, "We see little enough hard cash in this colony. 'Twas hard to believe thee had such wealth. I'll write a bill of sale and give thee thy key. Thee've bought a fine home."

John had lived in finer, to be sure, in France. After his additions, Goody Moore's home was finer. But that night, as Abigail slept in their bed, her head on his shoulder, he felt that they had the grandest home in the world.

Chapter Thirteen
The Riders

"Remember that what you have now was once among the things you only hoped for."

Epicurus

Building a malting oven and buying the kettles, kegs, and supplies to start their business took most of their remaining silver. After buying some cloth, necessities, flour, and beans, they were almost penniless.

John understood how to build a brewery's business, but starting one took time, and money. He bought barley from a local farmer and using hops he gathered from the surrounding forests began to brew beer. When the beer finished aging, he took samples of it to Philadelphia's waterfront every day. Now and again, he received an order. He was confident more would follow.

There was not enough money to buy food, but brewing the little beer needed to fill his few orders left him time to hunt. Rabbits and fowl were plentiful. He found a clearing in the forest where deer grazed. He sat in the high grass, downwind from the clearing. Often, he came home dragging a deer on a litter he built.

Their lot was too small to farm, but Abigail started a kitchen garden to grow beans, potatoes, onions, and carrots. At the suggestion of a neighbor, she planted some Indian corn, although she had no idea what she would do with it if it grew. John said he could use some to make beer.

Until Abigail's garden started producing, they lived on rabbit, fowl, or venison with beans, bread, and excellent beer. Their diet was simple, but they never did without.

By summer, Abigail's garden produced all the fresh beans they wanted. She began drying some for winter use and for seeds. Other crops soon followed. They were amazed at the quantity of Indian corn they harvested. They discovered they liked it roasted, still in the husks. The neighbor who had encouraged Abigail to plant corn showed her how to dry it for winter use, and to grind the seeds into meal.

John's brewing business was growing. It could not support them yet, but soon would. Life was good. The leaves were turning and John turned his attention to laying in a supply of firewood and dried venison for the winter.

They could hardly believe their good fortune.

*****

John dragged a litter home through the fading sunlight of an October afternoon. He heard a voice come from the forest shadows. "My brother hunts well." He turned and saw Tamaqua emerge from the trees.

A smile lit John's face. "Tamaqua! We wanted to say our farewells, but we knew not where your village was."

"Lenape not want whites in village. Whites not good for village."

This surprised John, but he went on. "'Tis good to see you, friend. We'd have not survived the winter without your help. How are you? How is Wisawtayas?"

"She caught Dutch fever, died," Tamaqua said, without visible emotion.

John's smile disappeared. "Oh, Tamaqua, I am sorry. I've not heard of Dutch fever. What is it?"

"Lenape not get fever before Dutch come, long ago. When Dutch come, they bring fever. Many Lenape die." Tamaqua seemed to look past John. "Tamanend said too many Lenape get sick. Not enough left to pray for them. Long ago my people covered this land, like sand at ocean's edge. Now we are few. But we still get fever. Many in my village died. We moved to this side of river. Leave fever on other."

"Your loss grieves me. How are you, my friend?" John put his hand on Tamaqua's shoulder.

"Tamaqua is Lenape warrior. Crying not bring her back."

"Still, I sorrow for you. Have you any children?"

"A son."

"I'm glad of that. How old is he? What's his name?"

"He has only three winters. He has not earned name yet."

John dropped his hand from Tamaqua's shoulder, shoving it into the waistband of his breeches, behind his back. "If he hasn't earned a name, what do you call him?"

"I call him son. Others call him boy."

John tried to imagine a world where children were not named at birth. *How*, he wondered, *would a child earn a name?* "Then it is my hope that he will soon earn a fine name and make his father proud." John paused, wondering if he should go on. "We have news too, good news. We now have a house in the village and Abigail is with child. The baby comes late next month."

"You make my ears glad."

"Will you come see Abigail? She will be saddened about Wisawtayas, but pleased to see you."

Tamaqua pointed to town. "I will not go in the white village." His voice was stern. "White village not good for Lenape. Whites cheat us. They want trade us beer and firewater for pelts. We not need beer. Not need firewater. Lenape need guns and knife to hunt. Firewater, beer, make men crazy. I stay in forest." Tamaqua gestured toward the forest around them, then looked at John. "Whites not need beer, firewater either. It make them crazy. You not give Abigail beer. Not good for her or baby."

"I'm afraid the beer is a good deal better for a woman with child than water is." John chuckled. "I'll tell Abigail I've seen you. She'll be sorry to hear of Wisawtayas, and that you'll not visit."

"After baby comes, listen at night. I come then."

"How will you know where we live or when the baby comes?"

"How did I know you hunt here?" Tamaqua turned and disappeared into the forest.

John shook his head, picked up the end of his litter, and headed home. Abigail was glad John saw Tamaqua and sorry Wisawtayas was dead. She had never heard of Dutch fever either.

She smiled when John told her Tamaqua thought she should not drink beer while she was pregnant. "The Lenape be people of the forest. They know nothing of beer. 'Twould be unfair of us to expect them to understand." John nodded his agreement.

After supper, they sat in front of a glowing fire and reminisced. "I scarce believe how our lives have changed, John, in so little a time. When we worked for Goodman Adams, I dared not imagine a time when we would own a home or a business. And now I carry our child." She looked at John and smiled, then reached for his hand.

"Things have changed." His face was serious. "I said nothing then, but there were times in the forest I doubted we'd live the winter."

She nodded. "They were fearsome times. Now we're truly blessed." She stood, and banked the fire. "The day's been long. I'm going to bed."

John slid his feet from his moccasins. "Two'll be warmer."

Before sleep came, Abigail held John's hand to her stomach. "Can you feel the baby's kick?"

"I can. 'Tis a good kick from a strong baby." He bent his face to Abigail's stomach and said, "How are you, my child? Know this, yours be the finest mother in the world, and your father the most fortunate." He kissed her stomach. Then he straightened and kissed her lips. That night they named their child. A boy would be William. Abigail thought they were naming their son after England's new king. John knew they were naming him after the French duke who conquered England in 1066. If they had a girl, she would be Mary, Abigail thought for King William's wife. John knew they were naming her for the Blessed Virgin. They slept in each other's arms.

*****

John's business grew. As Abigail's time neared, he spent more time on Philadelphia's docks, meeting with shippers and their agents. Several days after he saw Tamaqua, while walking along the waterfront, he heard, "Jean-Marc, how fare you?"

John spun to see Oliver Wentworth. "I'm sorry sir, you mistake me for another." His words were more confident than his voice.

"I mistake you for none," Wentworth whispered. "You be safe with me, but not so with others. Why be you on the waterfront?"

Wentworth looked around them. "Every shipper and seaman from Boston knows you. You must know you're wanted for murder. There's a ten-pound reward for your capture. Keep coming here and someone's sure to collect it."

"And where am I to go?" John whispered. "Brewing's all I know and brewers sell to ships."

"That may be, but you be not safe here. I'm going back on board. When I return, it would be good if you were gone. Stay away from the docks, my friend, or your rabbit hole will never be deep enough."

Oliver turned and walked up the gangplank of his ship. John turned and walked straight away from the river. His mind raced. *What do I do now? Oliver's right. How lucky was I that a friend saw me and not someone who'd report me for ten pounds? I can't come back here.* John realized he was running, drawing attention to himself. *'Tis the last thing I need.* He forced himself to slow to what he thought was a casual walk. He walked much too fast. *If I can't go to the waterfront, how can I sell my beer? The shippers are just beginning to buy from me. The inns don't see any need to buy my beer. They make their own and think it good enough.*

He went into an unfamiliar inn, sat before the fire and ordered beer. He stared into the glowing coals. *I was a fool to think I could escape so easily. Damn! Now Abigail's in the middle of all this too! And then there's the baby.* Tears welled in his eyes. He sat back and stared away from the fire. The lump in his throat felt so large, he didn't think he could swallow. Lifting his beer, he took a sip. It was bitter, with a skunky smell. *How can they sell such piss? I could sell them good beer for little more than it costs them to make this swill.*

When the innkeeper came into the room again, John said, "Your beer could be better, keeper. I could sell you a better beer for little more than your costs to brew this."

"If thee like not my beer, do me the kindness of not drinking it! I make my beer for free. How'll thee match that price?"

"Your barley be not free, neither your time."

"And my beer's worth the price thee paid. If thee like it not, feel free to leave."

Seems good beer at a fair price matters not, if people'll pay for piss. For the first time in a long time, he felt trapped. *How'll I provide for Abigail and the baby? What happens to them should I be caught? What can I do? Do we move back into the wilderness and live like savages again?*

John had to think. He managed to finish his beer and order another. The innkeeper smiled but did not comment. Midway through the second tankard of bad beer, he had an idea. *There be shipping agents all along the waterfront. They sell and arrange shipments for others every day. If they buy things from England for their clients, why can't one sell my beer in Philadelphia?* Warming to the thought, he took a large swallow of beer and made a face. *Oh, this is bad ... If I do hire an agent, he'll not work for free. How much would it cost to hire one?* He reached for his tankard to take another drink but changed his mind. *Even hiring someone to sell my beer won't keep me out of Philadelphia.* He shook his head and ran his hands over his face. *The beer still must be delivered ... I'll need a teamster, or an indenture to deliver it. There's a farce. Where'd I get money for an indenture? Hiring a teamster to move my beer and an agent to sell it'll add to my cost. Higher prices mean fewer sales ... Can we do with less? We've little enough now ... Sales are growing, but they'll slow again if I raise prices.* He couldn't stay seated. He got up and paced the room. *What if the agent's dishonest? He could cheat me of whatever's left? None of this seems good, but I see no other way ... Have to try ... Business just starts to grow. This could ruin all, but more's to lose by not trying.*

John called, "Keeper, know you an honest business agent?"

The keeper came into the room, laughing. "Friend, I doubt an honest business agent exists, but thee'll find William Bartlett to be as honest a man as the trade attracts."

"Where will I find this William Bartlett?"

"Right where you'd expect an agent to have his office, at the wharves. His office be next to the customhouse."

John thanked him. Leaving half a tankard of beer on the table, he hurried to William Bartlett's office. Bartlett's stomach stuck out beneath his vest. Over his round face, he wore the plain black hat of a Quaker. Gray hair fell to his shoulders.

"Friend Bartlett?"

"I am, Friend. Who be thee?" Bartlett stood behind his desk to shake John's hand, then sat again.

"John Rider, a brewer from West Jersey."

"What brings a brewer from Jersey to my office?"

"I brew finer beer than any to be found here and sell it at a lower price. I'd sell to the shippers but haven't the time to make and sell my beer. I need an agent to handle sales, collect fees, and send my earnings to me in Jersey. Would such an arrangement interest you?"

"It could. How am I to know the quality of thy beer?" Bartlett motioned for John to sit on the chair opposite his desk.

"I brew several. I'll send samples to you, for your tasting and to encourage sales. The beer'll sell better once they've tried it."

"How know I thee can deliver the beer I sell? I cannot have my good name damaged by an unreliable supplier."

"I've already customers to vouch for both my beer and my service. Until now, I brewed, sold and delivered all my beer. But now I sell more than I can manage this way. The beer I must brew myself. But another could sell my beer, and a teamster deliver it."

"Send me samples and I'll consider thy offer, but I work not for free. I'll want fifteen per hundred of all my sales."

"I'll wager I could find many an agent to handle my trade at less than fifteen per hundred. You've been well recommended. I'll shake your hand at ten per hundred."

Bartlett stood and held out his hand. "Thee'll never starve with that business sense. If thy beer is good, we have an agreement."

"Then we have an agreement." John smiled as he stood and shook Bartlett's hand. "I'll send a teamster tomorrow with two kegs of my beer for you to try and to use for samples. He'll give you a list of where he's delivering. I'll see that he delivers. You can collect the payments and keep your full share of the sale price, though I sold it. Tonight, I'll reckon my new costs and include the sale price on the list of deliveries." My *profits just fell ten per hundred. What costs a teamster?*

Riding the ferry back, he stared at the river then spun to look at his ox. *I'll not need the ox or cart! Mayhap the teamster'll buy them ... Mayhap he'll take them in trade for a month's or two's deliveries.*

Samuel Slade was the only teamster in Burlington. "I'll make thy deliveries every day but the Sabbath."

"I need daily, Friend Slade. Ships sail daily." *There's the rub. Could go back and hire a teamster across the river. Best not risk that.* "If you'll make my deliveries until the Sabbath, I'll use that time to seek other arrangements. What price?"

"Tuppence a keg and three each way to cover the ferry for the ox, cart and me."

John forced a smile, *Three kegs'll run a shilling ... Hard to make a living with that price.* "Silver's scarce, what barter'll you take?"

"I'll take corn, a penny a bushel."

"Most will give two."

"Then hire most. I'll take corn a penny a bushel. A half-pound sweetscent tobacco or pound of oronoco'll buy a cart-load a day, until Sabbath."

"I've the tobacco. I'll pay with sweetscent when you pick up tomorrow. I'll need you early."

"I'll leave the barn at dawn."

They shook on their agreement. Frustrated, John headed home. *Mayhap I should look at this different. I have a cart and ox. What I need's a driver. Most men be farmers ... They'll not leave their farms in spring or fall. The smithy can't leave his forge. Miller's too busy. The inn-keep can't leave the inn. What of his son? He's young. Can he deliver beer? I wonder if there be anyone at the inn in need of work.*

Hoping against hope, he went to the inn. Outside the door, John saw a tinker's hand cart and smiled. *There's many a hungry tinker. Would one deliver for bed and board, and a chance to learn brewing?*

A tinker's craft was to repair broken things that were hard to replace. Pots were expensive. After years of use, a pot would develop a hole. A tinker would fix this by filling the hole with lead. Almost anyone could melt lead into a hole. Tinkers just did it better. But

261

because almost anyone could plug a hole with lead, tinkers worked cheap. Journeyman tinkers had hard lives.

John opened the door and walked in.

"I'll bring you beer and bread when I see your pennies." The keeper was arguing with the tinker, who was hungry, but had no pennies.

"You must have something in need of repair. I'll repair something in exchange for beer and bread. For stew with some meat, I will repair several things. The bargain's your keeper."

"Then be off with you. I've nothing needs repair, and I'll not feed beggars."

"Stay, tinker." John said, although he had little money. "I'll buy your stew and beer, in exchange for a task."

"Look. This man knows a bargain. Be sure there's meat in my stew, and the loaf is large, keeper." The tinker sat at a table and smiled. His lean frame showed he had missed many meals.

John reached into his slender purse and handed the innkeeper coins he could not afford to spend. "Bring a beer for me, too." He sat next to the tinker.

"What have you in need of tinkering?"

"Nothing, but I have an ox and cart in need of a driver. The village teamster'll not deliver on the Sabbath. I need someone to deliver my beer to Philadelphia every day. The Sabbath is a day. Eat today, make my deliveries in Philadelphia tomorrow and we're even. But I have deliveries to be made every day. My hope is to soon have more. I can cancel the teamster. Work for me for bed and board, and you'll never be hungry. Stay only so long as you want. I'll require no set term of labor."

The tinker bridled. "I'm a journeyman. Why should I work for food without pay?"

"Because you've missed many a meal and I just heard you begging to work for food. I'll give you work. You'll be well fed, and I'll have my driver." He looked at the tinker for a moment, as if waiting for an answer, then raised a hand to his head and went on. "What ho! You're a tinker, and tinkers can build things. Together we can build you a room on my house. You'll be done sleeping under your cart. As my trade grows, my need for a teamster will grow, and my funds will increase. When I can afford it, I'll add four shillings a month to the bed and board. It may even be that you'll learn a brewer's trade. Brewers eat better than tinkers."

The innkeeper brought a tray with a large bowl of meaty stew, loaf of bread and two tankards of beer. Eating as only a famished man can, without looking up, the tinker said, "Name's Amos Quincy. I'll be your teamster. May we grow rich together."

"John Rider." He held out his hand to shake, but Quincy did not look up from eating.

John's mind raced. *Much has changed since this morning ... If I just show up with this tinker to live with us, Abigail'll demand an explanation. One I can't give with the tinker there.* There was no place in their house for a private conversation. *For certain, she'll not hold her tongue just because I say we'll talk later.* "There're errands I need run. Stay here and eat while I complete them. Keeper," he called across the room. "See that my friend has plenty to eat and drink. I'll settle costs when I return." John drained his beer and got up from the table.

Amos smiled through a mouthful of stew. "Keeper, I'll need another beer here," he said, as he lifted his tankard and drained it.

John hurried up the path to their house. Abigail, heavy with child, was working in her garden. She looked up at John and smiled.

Oh, she is beautiful.

He helped her to her feet.

"Oliver Wentworth bade me a good day on the docks this morning."

"Seeing a friend again after so long is a good thing," she said, brushing her hands on her apron.

"Not always. Oliver reminded me that if he recognized me, others could as well. Boston has put up ten pounds for my capture."

She gasped for breath. Her hands shot to her mouth.

"For years, I was on Boston's docks every day. Anyone sailing out of Boston knows me." He reached for her hand, but she pulled it away. "Oliver didn't want the silver. Others will. My life, and probably your freedom, rest on our ability to remain hidden. Today, I was recognized without harm. Tomorrow could cost my life."

She returned her hands to her face. Through tears she sobbed, "Oh John, we can't go to the forest again. I'm no Lenape. My child can't be born in that wikiup. We've—"

John put his fingers to her mouth. "Hush. Our child will not be born in the woods. I've a plan. It'll cost us dear, but I think it will work. We'll have less, but we'll be free. I hired an agent to sell my beers at a cost of ten per hundred. We can't raise our cost that much without losing sales. Little though we have, we'll have to do with less."

Using a hand, still dirty from the garden, Abigail wiped tears from her face, leaving a brown smudge. "But we'll still have each other," she sobbed, "and I know the trade will grow."

"There's more. I can't go to the docks to make deliveries. We need someone to deliver for us."

"We've so little now, John. How'll we pay a teamster?"

"The teamster's not our problem. He won't deliver on the Sabbath and we must. I met a tinker in town. He's agreed to deliver for us in return for bed and board."

"Where? He can't share our bed!" Abigail didn't realize she was shouting.

"Hush. You're telling the whole town. He'll sleep in the kitchen until we build him a room."

"We can't afford to build a room!"

"Know you another solution?"

Through her tears, Abigail said, "No."

"I'll talk to the sawyer. Mayhap he'll trade us wood for beer. A tinker knows building. We'll build a small room for him on the front room's wall. Our bigger problem is that I've seen him eat. The man wants for food."

Smearing more mud on her face, Abigail wiped away another tear. "He'll not want for food. You've seen to that. I'll cook plenty."

John put his arms around her ample waist. Abigail said, "Seems something beside a tinker's come between us." She tried to smile.

John wiped at the mud on her face. "Go see yourself in the looking glass. You'll want to clean up before I bring him home." He kissed her. "This I promise; things will get better. Look where we've come."

Smearing more mud on her face, she said, "I know. Just a year ago, we had naught but each other. Now we've a house, a business, and it appears we near have an indenture. Most, we've got each other and soon a babe. We're blessed."

John returned to the inn to find the tinker well through his third bowl of stew and fourth tankard of ale. The bill was more than John could afford, but he paid it with a smile.

If this is to work, none can suspect the hiring an agent and a live-in teamster are anything other than proof of our prosperity.

By the time John returned home with Amos, Abigail's face was clean. She was gracious greeting their new servant who, as she once did, worked for bed and bread. "You are welcome in our home, Amos. John tells me you already ate. I fixed a bed for you in our kitchen. It will serve until we make other arrangements."

"Good eve, Ma'am. 'Tis my good fortune to be here with a full stomach and a roof over my head."

That night, Amos slept, well fed and warm by the kitchen fire.

The next day, the sawyer agreed to provide John with enough wood to add a small room to their house in trade for a year's supply of beer. Amos pointed out that his room would have no heat without a chimney. John winced. Adding a room for Amos would be more complicated than expected. Sending Amos on his delivery, John left to see the stonemason. They were able to reach an agreement similar to the one John had made with the sawyer. For a year's supply of John's best beer, the mason agreed he would build a chimney for the new room in two weeks' time.

By the time the chimney was done, the sawyer delivered the wood.

A tinker was a good fellow to have around when building a room. He knew about building and fixing things. John did not. While keeping up with their brewing business, they completed a fine room in another two weeks.

Amos now had a more or less permanent place to live. Having a house with two chimneys and three rooms, one for a servant, made John look prosperous. He and Abigail were well on their way to becoming part of the respectable class in Burlington.

They could scarce believe their good fortune.

Chapter Fourteen
Together

**"True love is like ghosts, which everyone talks
about and few have seen."
Francois de La Rochefoucauld**

Sometime after midnight on November 22, 1697, Abigail roused John from his sleep. "John, 'tis time. Fetch Sarah Gibby and Elsie Longstreet. Do you remember where they live?"

"I do. Sarah's is the red house by the river and Elsie's next to the blacksmith."

Abigail laughed. "You'll find Elsie there all right, but old man Jones, in the red house by the river, will not be pleased when you wake him asking for his neighbor who lives in the white house next door."

John nodded as he hurried into his breeches and shoes. "Should I get Amos to stay with you while I'm gone?"

"What could he do? Let him sleep. Before long, you'll both be sent from the house. Set the birthing chair by the fire and be on your way. We've both a long day ahead."

John finished dressing and carried a chair with a "Y" shaped seat from their bedroom into the kitchen, placing it before the fire. He hurried out the door, past the smithies and up the path to the unpainted Longstreet house. He pounded on the door, "Elsie, George, open up. 'Tis Abigail's time."

It took a short while for George Longstreet, candle in hand, to open the door. "What's this? Why're thee bothering us at this hour?"

"Sorry, Friend, but my Abigail sent me for Elsie. Her time's come."

Before George could reply, Elsie pushed past him. "George, Abigail's birthing. I'll be with her 'til she and the baby be safe. See to thyself. John, have ye fetched Sarah yet?"

"I've not. You were closer."

"Go get Sarah. She'll get Sadie. Hurry thyself! This be no time to dawdle."

Elsie rushed past him, hurrying toward his house. He followed her down the path, turning right, where she turned left. He ran to the white house and pounded on the door. After a delay, the door opened. Edward Gibbs was snarling about being awakened when Sarah pushed past him. "John, tell Elsie I've got the birthing bread. I'll get Sadie York. She'll have the beer. We'll soon be there."

"You bring beer to my house? What be wrong with mine?"

"Men know nothing of birthing. The beer and bread'll speed Abigail's labor. Hurry now and tell Elsie we be on our way, then decide where thee and thy man will go. Thee cannot stay in thy house." Sarah carried a small satchel as she hurried down the path.

"Should we go to the inn?"

"There's a man's thought. Then ye'd be across town and drunk when thy son's born."

Amos was in the front yard when John arrived home, out of breath from his run.

"John, we've been thrown from the house."

"So, I gather. I've a message for Elsie. Wait here. My guess is I'll be right back."

The kitchen fire was blazing. Elsie was stuffing blankets, rags, and rugs around every window or doorsill. Abigail paced the kitchen floor which was now covered with straw. "Sarah said she and Sadie'll soon be here and to tell you they have the bread and beer."

"Good, now thee have to leave, but I must know where to find thee."

"I don't know. I've not thought on where to go."

"The baby seems in no hurry. Go to the inn. Spend the night and break your fast there, then go to my house and tell George I said thee are to stay there. When the baby comes, I'll know where thee be. Now off with thee."

John left as Sarah and Sadie arrived. They placed a loaf of bread and a small cask of beer on the table.

"Welcome ladies. Sadie can thee finish blocking the drafts? The water for the licorice root tea's ready. Sarah, fetch the chamber pot from the other room. After this tea, Abigail'll need it."

Elsie poured boiling water over licorice root and handed Abigail the mug, "Here dear, this'll purge thy bowels. Drink it as quick as thee can."

Abigail reached for the mug, but stopped, put both hands on her stomach, bent at the waist and grimaced. She made a noise, as if she stubbed her toe and stood still.

Elsie said, "Good. Thy body's beginning to push the baby out. Ye'll have more and they'll grow stronger."

Sarah returned with the chamber pot and placed it on the straw, under the birthing chair. Abigail's contraction subsided. She exhaled and inhaled a few times. Elsie handed her the tea.

Grimacing, Abigail said, "'Tis bitter."

"That it is but force thyself to drink it. Thee need to purge thy bowels."

Sadie finished blocking any potential drafts, then joined them. "This be thy time, Abigail. All but barren women know what thee'll go through. We be here to help, but this is thy trial. So, we've suffered since Eve. So, we always will."

Abigail smiled. "The tea's worse than the pain."

"That will change," Elsie said, taking the mug. "Thee'll want another mug of tea, so thee're purged before hard labor." She prepared another mug of tea.

Sadie said, "Dearie, thee're new to Burlington. Where'd thee live before?"

Abigail groaned. *Oh no. Will I need lie through my labor? I'll not keep my story straight.* "John apprenticed brewing in York City. We decided to move to West Jersey, where land be cheap, and mayhap there'd be fewer brewers."

"Surprised thee didn't go to Philadelphia. A brewer'd find more trade there."

Sarah said, "Hush now, Sadie. Leave the child alone. Her lot's heavy enough this night." She sat by the table. "Child, walk when thee can. 'Twill speed thy babe. Sit when thee must. The babe will come when it be ready."

Sadie and Elsie sat, too. The heavy-set, gray-haired women told Abigail the history of women in Burlington. Labor became a bonding experience, as the older women shared ancient wisdom and new gossip with her. This seemed to help. Adding a link to an endless chain, one generation of women passed their customs and knowledge to another.

"I feel such a bother, bringing you from your beds."

Sarah said, "Don't even think about that, child. We've all had our turn. When a babe's coming, a woman needs the help of others."

"Thy time will come to help the younger. This be how you learn," Elsie added.

Abigail looked startled. "Where's the chamber pot?"

"Good, the tea's working. The pot be under the birthing chair."

Contractions came and went. They grew in frequency and intensity. The women talked and encouraged Abigail to eat the bread and drink the beer to speed delivery. They took turns helping Abigail pace the small room. By mid-morning, the contractions were much closer. Abigail neared exhaustion. Elsie gave her a cup of mother-wort tea. "This'll strengthen the contractions and speed thy labor."

Several hours later, Elsie said, "'Tis time. Sit on the birthing chair." Elsie sat in front of her. She reached under Abigail's skirt and placed a hand on each of her thighs. Abigail cried out in pain as they sat this way through a number of contractions.

"I feel thy babe's head pushing through. Push now, push."

Abigail's face contorted. She screamed as she fought exhaustion and pushed.

"'Tis a good start, child. When thee need to again, push with all thy might."

Sarah wiped Abigail's face with a damp cloth. "Suck the cloth, child, to dampen thy mouth."

Abigail's face contorted. She screamed again. Lifting her shoulders, she forced them downward. She took a deep breath and pushed, holding this position for fifteen to twenty seconds, threw her head back, took another breath and pushed again. This went on for three or four minutes. When the contraction passed, she slumped forward, resting her head on Elsie's shoulder.

Sadie brought her some birthing beer. "Take a sip. Thee need the strength."

Sarah again wiped Abigail's face. This pattern continued for several more contractions, then Elsie said, "There's the shoulders. Another push, and we'll have thy babe."

Abigail looked up at the ceiling, took a deep breath, gritted her teeth and pushed down with all her strength. Elsie smiled and sat back. She brought Abigail's baby out from under her skirt. "Child, thy daughter's as beautiful as a spring morn."

A smile lit Abigail's sweat-drenched face. Sarah cut the cord. Elsie wrapped the baby in a blanket Sadie held open for her and handed the baby to Abigail. She unbuttoned her frock and held the baby to her breast, but she did not suck.

"Don't let that trouble thee, child. Many a babe's born too tired to suck. She'll come along."

After a few minutes, Abigail delivered the afterbirth into another chamber pot. Sadie helped Abigail to bed with her baby. Sarah said, "Elsie, go and fetch John from thy house. Sadie and I'll clean up here."

Elsie walked over to Abigail and kissed her forehead. "Rest, child. Thee're needful of it. Thy babe is beautiful. I'll return later to check on thee."

Sarah told Sadie, "I'll stay with her now. Thee should go see to thy house. Decide with Elsie which of thee'll come back later."

Sweeping the soiled straw from the floor, Sadie said, "I will, once I've cleaned this mess." She collected the straw, threw it in the kitchen fire and headed home.

"Thee're still bleeding," Sarah said, handing her some cloth. "Hold this there to stop it."

Abigail took the cloth and placed it between her legs. She held her baby against her breast and waited for her to suck. She did not.

John passed Sadie as he ran up the path to his house. "How be Abigail?"

"Tired. Her night was long."

"And our daughter?"

"As pretty a babe as thee'll ever see. Go to her John, but gently. Her night was hard. She's needful of rest."

John reached the front door, opened it a crack and stuck his head in. "How be Abigail?"

Sarah said, "Come in. Ask her thyself."

Abigail's eyes were closed. John sat on the bed next to his family. He leaned in and kissed Abigail's forehead. She opened her eyes and smiled. Then he kissed his daughter. Looking at the wisps of dark hair on her tiny head he said, "She's the image of her mother." He smiled and kissed her again. "Hello, Mary. I be your father. I've waited long to meet you."

"Did you see, John? Her eyes are blue," Abigail tucked the blanket around Mary's chin, then reached up and ran her hand over John's unshaven cheek and smiled. She pulled Mary closer to her breast, but Mary did not suck.

*****

"By now, thy bleeding should have stopped." Sadie muttered, replacing the bloody rags.

Abigail suppressed the urge to cry. She managed to say, "By now Mary should suck stronger, too. She be three days old. She needs my milk."

"'Tis true. She sucks, wets, nor cries enough. If she sucks not soon, thy milk'll not come in."

"John wants to send to Philadelphia, for a doctor."

"Mayhap for the babe, but not for thee. Child bed fever's no business for men. They know little of it and care less."

"John says we must try."

"And would thy husband have another man look at thee there? Would thee let another man touch thee there?"

Elsie came through the door. "What news?"

"Foul indeed. She still bleeds. She needs sleep but can't and the baby be too weak."

"Amos says John's gone to Philadelphia, for a doctor." Elsie said.

"A doctor may see the babe, but he'll not see Abigail."

"Truly said. A tea of lavender may help her sleep. I'll see to it."

Abigail drank the tea, and finally slept. Sadie placed Mary at Abigail's breast, hoping the child would nurse. She did a little, from time to time, it seemed more for comfort than for milk. Sadie left for home, leaving Elsie to care for Abigail.

Several hours later, John entered with Dr. Carter. As Sadie predicted, he would not examine Abigail. "The women know all there is to know about child bed fever and her bleeding. They'll see to that. Let me see the babe."

John went into the room and lifted Mary, trying not to wake Abigail. Dr. Carter laid her on the table. He opened her blankets and felt her abdomen. She barely moved to his touch. "Bring the candle here. She's too thin, no doubt. Thee said she sucks little?"

"I think she sucks not enough." John leaned forward with both hands on the table. Tears welled up in his eyes, watching his motionless daughter. "The women say she should suck longer and stronger." He straightened and looked at the ceiling. Tears ran down his cheeks. He choked out, "I know naught of babes. The women say she should suck more. That I know."

Dr. Carter brought the candle closer to Mary. "Her color's not good. A baby should be pink. She's yellow." He shook his head and looked at John. "The build-up of foul humors in her blood poisons her. 'Tis rare to see such poisoning of the blood in one so small." The doctor turned back to Mary and put his little finger in her mouth. "Put thy finger in her mouth." John did. "See. 'Tis dry. A babe's mouth ought be wet, like thine." He bent over Mary and smelled her breath. "There's foulness to her breath from the poison. Was she born so?"

"She was born beautiful," John said, choking back tears, "but she never really sucked ... and she weakens. She was pink ... but, as you said, she's turned yellow."

"And your wife still bleeds?"

"She does."

The doctor stood and looked into John's face. "Your wife bleeds from womb blood poisoning. 'Tis rare, but a mother's blood can mix with the babe's at birth, passing bad blood to it. These three days, the foul humors have grown in thy child. I hate to bleed one so small, but we must rid her of those humors." He paused, looked down at Mary, then back at John, shaking his head. "Often as not, we can take not enough, but we can try."

John put his hands to his face and cried. "Do what's best." He brought his hands down and looked at the doctor, "But save my child."

Dr. Carter opened his bag and removed a blood lancet and cup. He told John to hold Mary while he bled her. The lancet looked huge next to Mary's tiny legs. Carter sliced Mary's left heel. John looked away. He and Mary both cried. A few drops of blood fell into the cup. "Lift her over the cup." John lifted Mary into an erect position, and the doctor kneaded her leg toward her foot. Both cried louder, waking Abigail.

"Where's my baby? Who has Mary?"

John tried to answer, but his voice broke.

"She's with a doctor." Elsie told her.

The doctor called to Abigail over the crying. "Thy babe's with us in the kitchen. I'm Dr. Carter. We be trying to let her of foul humors. Her cries be a good sign. Pray we be not too late."

"Bring her to me! Bring me my babe!"

Elsie put her hands on Abigail's shoulders, "Stay, mother. There be naught there you should see." Abigail pushed at Elsie's hands, then laid back, crying.

John tried to calm her, while holding Mary as the doctor milked blood from the baby's heel. All he could make was a choking sound. The doctor managed to drain a few ounces of blood from Mary. She stopped crying. John exhaled. Tears ran down his cheek.

The doctor wiped Mary's blood from his lancet and began packing his bag. "Pray that helps. Hold a cloth to her foot, but the bleeding should stop of its own. Pray she sleeps. 'Tis best for her now. We know not how dense the humors were. Should she start to suck and wet as expected, we may be done. I'll return on the morrow. With prayer, she may be better. If not, my druthers are not to bleed one this small twice. We may need to blister her."

John regained enough composure to thank the doctor, who took Mary from John's arms, wrapped her in her blankets, and handed her to back to her father. "Bring her to your wife and comfort them. Tomorrow, we may be able to offer more than hope to a frightened mother." The doctor tipped his hat and left.

John carried the still child to Abigail, nuzzling her close against her mother. She pulled Mary to her breast, but Mary did not suck. She looked at her sick child and cried until they both slept.

*****

John spent as much time as he could with Abigail and their baby. She reminded them that if he did not work, none of them would eat. Fighting to hold back tears, he went to the brewery where he managed to go about his business. Amos made the deliveries. None of this mattered to John. He finished his tasks for the day then he and Amos ate the stew Elsie made for their supper and went to sleep.

Mary slept with her mother in Abigail and John's bed. Sarah Gibbs slept in a bed, made up on the floor, next to them. John slept by the kitchen fire, where Amos used to sleep. Sometime after John fell asleep, he had no idea how much after, he woke to hear the front door of his house open. He jumped to his feet. Three Indians walked through the door. Just rousing from sleep, his kitchen only lit by the fire's embers, he did not recognize Tamaqua.

"Stay! Who be you?"

"Not worry. You safe."

John recognized Tamaqua's voice. "Why come you here?"

"I come to see baby. Abigail sick. Baby sick. I bring Tamanend to make both well."

Tamanend and a strange woman came into John's view. Tamanend spoke. Tamaqua translated. "Bring them here."

For the first time in days, John felt hope. He went into his bedroom, wondering how to explain the situation to Sarah. He shook his wife, also waking Mary and Sarah. "Abigail, Tamaqua's here with Tamanend. They think they can help."

Abigail remembered how Tamanend healed John. She prayed for another miracle.

Sarah sat up. "Did thee bring another doctor?" She seemed both sleepy and irritated.

"I did not. Lenape friends have come to see us. They brought their medicine man. He once saved my life. Pray he'll save my wife and daughter."

Abigail struggled from bed and carried Mary into the kitchen. John helped her sit. The fire was already stirred into flames. The pungent smell of incense filled the room.

Amos opened the door from his room, screamed "Indians!" and jumped back inside.

John said, "Have no care Amos. These be friends. Come greet them, or stay in your room, as pleases you."

Sarah and Amos each peered through the doors of their respective rooms.

Tamanend spoke to Tamaqua, "Ask if our friend's woman is still bleeding."

"Does Abigail still bleed?"

"She does," John replied.

Tamaqua translated the conversation.

"What they have done for her."

John said, "Sarah may best answer that. Sarah?"

She edged from the bedroom into the kitchen. "She lies in. Rags soak up the blood. We give her tea so she'll sleep."

After Tamaqua translated Tamanend said, "That much is good. Ask if the rags are put inside or held against her."

"In truth, both."

After the translation, Tamanend said, "That is good, but putting rags into a bleeding woman can make her worse." He reached into his bag, brought out a small deerskin bag filled with powder and handed it to Tamaqua. "Tell them to sprinkle this powder on the rags they put inside her. This will stop her from getting worse. She should soon improve."

Tamanend waited for the translation, then spoke again, "Also tell them to make a tea for her from this." He handed a bag to Sarah. "This tea will help her sleep and will kill the evil spirits inside her that make her sick."

Sarah looked unconvinced.

John said, "Please do it, Sarah. Tamanend's medicines work miracles. They saved my life." Filled with doubt, she set about to boil water.

"Now, let me see the sick child."

John reached to take Mary from Abigail's arms. For a moment, she clung to her baby before relaxing her grip. He handed her to the medicine man, who placed her on the table and called for a candle. When he had light, he unwrapped Mary and examined her.

"How did this baby get a cut on her foot?"

John looked down, "The doctor ... bled bad humors from her."

After the translation, Tamanend shouted, "What savage would drain blood from a sick child? He may have killed her. When did this happen?"

Abigail glared at John and whispered. "This afternoon."

Tamanend said, "It may have done little harm. This child was sick before today. She needs to eat. Have the woman rub some honey on her nipple. See if that makes the baby suck. Have her sit here. We all must pray the Great Spirit will heal her. Now, there is little we can do."

Tamaqua turned to Abigail. "Bleeding baby not good, but she already very sick. She needs to suck. Put honey on nipple. Then put baby to breast. See if she suck. All now pray."

John took a jar of honey from the shelf and handed it to Abigail. She turned away from the men and smeared some on her nipple. Tamanend handed Mary to John, who handed her to his wife. She drew Mary to her breast. Mary began to suck. Abigail cried, "She sucks! Not hard, but she sucks!"

Sarah poured water over the powder to make the tea. "Do I give her this now?"

Tamaqua asked Tamanend and was told she should.

Abigail sipped the tea and smiled at her baby. John wiped a tear from his cheek.

"The baby is very sick. Only the Great Spirit can save her. We all must pray and not stop. With more prayer, she may live. Whatever happens, we will know before sunrise."

"Baby very sick. Only Great Spirit can save her. Pray now." Tamaqua motioned to Amos, who was still peering into the room from behind his door. "You pray. All must pray. Do not stop."

John and Sarah dropped to their knees and began praying. Tamaqua and the Lenape woman bounced, flexing and straightening their knees, and chanted, each something different in the Unami language. Tamanend put more wood on the fire and added several different incenses to it, then he prayed as Tamaqua and the woman did. Tamaqua looked at Amos and shouted, "You stupid? You pray now! Not watch others! You pray! Pray now!"

Amos knelt and prayed for Abigail and Mary. After praying for almost an hour, Amos began to get up. Tamanend saw this and shouted, "Tell the lazy Whiteman if he wants this baby to live, he will pray. This child could die."

Tamaqua stopped praying long enough to say, "I not know why whites not dance when pray, but on knees or dancing, you pray now! Not make me hurt you!"

Amos again dropped to his knees and prayed, now including prayers for himself. They prayed for hours. Several times, Tamanend added different incenses to the fire. Finally, he stood in the middle of the room.

"Tell the whites to stop. The Great Spirit told me he has taken this baby's pure spirit. She has gone to the Lands of Plenty where she will never want for food. Tell her parents not to grieve for her. She is with the Great Spirit." Tamanend wiped a tear from his cheek, turned and left the house. The woman followed him without speaking.

"Tamanend say stop. Says Great Spirit takes baby. She not suffer. Not cry. John and Abigail not be sad. Baby not suffer with Great Spirit." Tamaqua looked at John and Abigail. "My spirit cries with your spirits. Your pain is my pain. Some day you have another baby. Then your joy be my joy." He turned and left the house.

John burst into tears.

Abigail shouted, "They may be wrong! Keep praying!" She looked at the baby at her breast and realized Mary was not breathing. Abigail held Mary tighter and cried. John dropped to his knees beside them, put his hand on his dead child and cried too. They stayed this way for a long time. Amos got up and walked into his room. Tears fill his eyes.

Sarah felt a need to make herself useful. She brewed another cup of the tea from the powder Tamanend gave her. When Abigail quieted, Sarah handed her the cup.

"Try to drink some." She then put the other powder on clean rags. "We need to change your rags."

John went outside.

Sarah helped Abigail change her rags and tucked her into bed. Abigail slept.

The first hints of light showed in the east. John hit a tree with the back of his ax again and again and again.

The doctor came back that morning. John's red eyes told the doctor all he needed to know. He expressed his condolences and left.

Mid-morning, Sadie came to relieve Sarah, and was told the news. She went into the bedroom to express her condolences to Abigail and John. Then she sent John from the room, so she could change Abigail's rags. She was no longer bleeding.

Sadie and Sarah washed Mary, dressed her in a white gown and laid her in her cradle.

That afternoon, John supported Abigail as they walked together to the new English Church that had just started holding services in Burlington. Abigail was raised in the English Church and said she would be more comfortable worshipping there than with the Friends. They arranged to have Mary baptized and buried in the new churchyard. Her's would be the yard's first grave.

Then they walked to the stone-mason and arranged for a stone to be placed on Mary's grave.

The stone would read:

Mary Rider

Age four days

Beloved of John and Abigail

After making these arrangements, they walked home.

Chapter Fifteen
Grief

"The Lord gave and the Lord hath taken away."
1692 Anglican Book of Common Prayer

John sat on the wooden chair, staring across the dark kitchen at the cradle he'd worked on for weeks. Now it held Mary's lifeless body. "Father Farnsworth says people oft wait over a week to bury." He looked at his hands. "Gives time for news to reach family and them to travel ... Why would we wait? We're alone ... None mourn Mary but us."

Abigail cried harder. For the past two days, she'd done little else. He stood and walked to her. Crouching next to her chair, he tried to take her in his arms, but she pushed him away.

John straightened. Tears welled in his eyes. "We left Boston, just us. We lived in the forest, just us." He reached to stroke her hair, but she shied from his touch. "And now, here ... 'tis just us. We need only stay together to come out the other side."

Abigail looked away. She started to say something but was interrupted by a knock at the door. She looked around the disheveled room, wiped tears from her eyes and managed to say, "Who'd that be?"

John ran his forearm across his face and opened the door to find Elsie and George Longstreet. George, a big man, in the plain clothing of a Quaker, white shirt and stockings, black breeches and shoes, filled the doorway. He removed his hat, holding it with two hands at his waist. "Good day, Friend Rider."

Naught's good about it.

"Elsie and I come to express our sorrow over thy loss. A child's loss be never easy. Losing your first be harder."

What do I say now? Really, Elsie's here to see Abigail. "Thank you. Call me John. Come in."

Abigail looked up and panicked. *He asked them in! Get out! I'm not dressed. The house isn't fit.* She ran her hands across face and ran through her uncombed hair. She brushed at her dress.

Elsie put a basket on the cluttered table and went to Abigail. "I thought you'd want for something to eat. I brought some stew." Abigail tried to say something, but instead threw her arms around Elsie's neck. They cried together.

After Elsie and George's visit, John was not surprised when Sarah Gibby and Sadie York came with their husbands. Both brought food. He was surprised when others came. Many, people he hardly knew. In couples or in small groups it seemed all of Burlington came to share John and Abigail's grief. Most brought food. A large man John thought he'd seen in town stood at the door, welcoming people into their home.

Abigail sat in a plain, gray housedress, on a straight-back, wooden chair in front of the kitchen fire. The red and yellow embers warmed her. It felt good. Then she felt guilty about feeling good. John, in his rough-spun, off-white work shirt and black breeches, stood beside her. He put his hand on her shoulder, but she shrugged it off. People came to them, took their hands, and said something meant to be comforting.

"The Lord works in mysterious ways."

John replied, "That He does." Neither statement made sense to him.

Another said, "Just know she's in a better place."

I don't know that. How do you know that? John said, "Thank you," and shook the man's hand. *Do these people make this day better or worse?*

Abigail was sure. *Get out! All of you. Get out and leave us alone!* Without a word, she got up and walked into their bedroom, closed the door and threw herself, face-first, on the bed.

John had no idea what to do. *I can't just go with her and leave all these people standing here.* So, he stayed where he was and continued shaking hands. His eyes kept drifting to his daughter. The lump in his throat kept growing.

"Know that she isn't suffering anymore."

Tell me why my baby suffered at all. Why wasn't she born healthy, like others? Why did my baby die? He managed to say, "Thank you," and shook some stranger's hand.

Sarah Gibby went into the bedroom, closing the door behind her. She closed the shutters on the glass window. Then she sat on the bed next to Abigail and held her hand, saying nothing. Abigail found this comforting.

Amos, who had often stayed away since Mary died, returned. He tried to make himself useful. As people came in, he took the food they brought and found a place for it on the table. Then he ushered them to John, explaining that Abigail was resting. As soon as possible, he encouraged them to leave.

They endured an endless day.

*****

John and Abigail were up before dawn. Neither bothered to build up the fire. Sitting in the cold dark, Abigail said, "You need to make beer today."

"What difference does it make?"

"You've orders to fill. If you don't fill them, you'll lose customers you labored hard to win."

"Orders be damned! Let them go unfilled."

"You know we promised silver we don't have for Mary's stone. We'll have other needs. You have to work, else we'll lose what little we have."

In the dark, Abigail could not see the tears brimming in John's eyes. He left for the brewery. When the door closed behind him, Abigail buried her face in her lap and cried bitter tears.

Amos opened the door from his room. "Sorry, Abigail. I didn't hear you. Should I leave?"

She lifted her face from her lap and stood up, wiping her hands across her face. "No, no. You'll need breakfast and John'll need you in the brewery." She began to fuss over the mounds of food, brought the previous day.

Amos grabbed a small loaf of black bread and said, "I can eat this. I'll have some beer out back." He thought about trying to say something to ease Abigail's pain, but couldn't think of anything. He walked out the door into the gray early morning light.

As difficult as it was for John to drag himself to the brewery, in many ways it was good for him. It forced him to think about something else. Moving his body and directing Amos on his morning's deliveries forced the minutes to pass. *Abigail's right. We need the money.*

Abigail tried to find something to do. No matter what she started, her eyes were drawn to the cradle holding her dead baby, and she broke down again. For her, the minutes did not pass.

At dusk, John and Amos took shovels to the new church yard and dug Mary's grave. The funeral was the next day.

*****

Friday, November 29th dawned clear and cold. Amos was up first. Abigail got up, stirred the fire and changed Mary's dress. She wanted her to be in something pretty. In the dark early morning, she dressed her baby and cried. John came into the kitchen a short time later.

There was more food than they could eat, but they weren't hungry. None of them knew what to say, so they didn't speak. John stood behind his wife and put his hand on her shoulder. She grunted and turned away. Both were crying. John walked out to the brewery and tended to the beer. Amos had already loaded the wagon and was leaving to make the first deliveries.

"I'll deliver these and be back in time."

*****

Mid-morning, they all dressed in their best clothing. John and Amos had built a small pine box to hold Mary's body. John brought the box into the kitchen and placed it on the table, without saying a word. Abigail lined the box with a blanket, and laid Mary in it. They all cried again when John put the lid on the box and nailed it shut. Saying nothing, he picked up the box, raised it to his right shoulder and walked out the door. Abigail and Amos followed.

They walked the half mile to the church in silence. As they neared the churchyard, still cluttered with construction debris, they realized this would be no small service. John had thought Amos might choose to come, but he wouldn't force him. He thought Sadie,

Sarah, and Elsie might come and bring their husbands. Except for the priest, he expected no one else.

Approaching the small, still unpainted church, they realized that most of Burlington had come for Mary's funeral. At the churchyard, townspeople grouped around the small hole John and Amos had dug the day before. Two chairs, for John and Abigail, were next to the grave.

Father Farnsworth met them at the entrance to the churchyard, reading from the English Book of Common Prayer, "I am the resurrection and the life saith the Lord; he that believeth in me, though he were dead, yet shall he live: and whosoever liveth and believeth in me shall never die. I know that my redeemer liveth and that He shall stand at the latter day upon the Earth. And though after my skin, worms destroy this body yet, in my flesh, I shall see God, whom I shall see for myself and my eyes shall behold and not another. We brought nothing into this world, and it is certain that we can carry nothing out. The Lord gave and the Lord hath taken away, blessed be the name of the Lord."

Abigail's legs gave out. With a loud wail, she collapsed. Several women rushed to her. A large, young man reached for Mary's casket. His deep voice was gentle. "I'll carry her for you. See to your wife."

John looked from the man, to Abigail, then back at the man but did not move. He seemed frozen. The man whispered, "Please let me help." There were tears in his eyes.

Two strange women helped Abigail to her feet. They brushed dead leaves and debris from her dress. Abigail thought they said something.

John released the casket. The stranger lifted it to his shoulder and turned to face the church. He stood, without moving, as if on guard.

Amos put his hand on John's shoulder. "Your wife needs you."

John nodded, stepped to his wife, slid his arm around her waist and more carried than led her to one of the chairs at the grave side. Tears rolled down his face.

The priest droned through two psalms and a reading from an epistle. Abigail sat, staring at the tiny box and cried. John stared at the same box. He locked his teeth together. He could smell the small pile of dirt next to the grave. The muscles in his jaw clenched. He took Abigail's hand and squeezed so hard he left a bruise. Abigail did not react.

The priest read, "Man that is born of a woman hath but a short time to live."

Two well-dressed men slid ropes under the box and lowered it into the ground.

Abigail shrieked, as if someone hit her. At home, she promised herself that she would be brave during the service. It was a promise she could not keep.

The priest read, "Forasmuch as it hath pleased Almighty God of His great mercy to take unto Himself the soul of our dear sister, here departed, we therefore commit her body to the ground; earth to earth, ashes to ashes, dust to dust; in the sure and certain hope of the resurrection to eternal life through our Lord Jesus Christ".

The men began to shovel dirt over the box that held her baby.

Abigail's strength gave way. She collapsed from the chair and wailed. John knelt beside her, doing his best to comfort her. In truth, he needed someone to comfort him. Together they cried and were not ashamed.

Then the funeral was over.

In small groups, people John did not know tried to say something comforting. They all knew their words would not help. It didn't matter. They had to try. Many of them had lost a child. Perhaps as much to comfort themselves as to comfort the grieving parents, one after another stopped to say the same comfortless things that were said a few days before. Elsie offered to come back to the house with them, but Abigail said she really just wanted to be alone. Elsie left.

Once home, Abigail went into their bedroom, threw herself on the bed and cried herself to sleep. John took Mary's cradle out to the workshop and covered it with a cloth. Amos picked at the huge pile of food on the table and told John that he had to make the rest of his deliveries. John nodded. He went to the brewery to prepare beer for tomorrow.

Several hours later, Abigail came out of her room. She screamed when she saw the cradle was missing. John heard her and rushed in from the brewery. He tried to hold her, but she looked away from him. She just kept repeating, "She's gone. Her cradle's gone. She's gone."

Throughout the day, Abigail and John sat alone, seldom talking. They ate or drank little. Now and again, he went to the brewery, as much to get out of the house as to do anything productive. In the late afternoon, Abigail stood up and went to bed. At dark, John went into their room.

Abigail shouted, "Get out! If you'd not brought that doctor Mary'd be fine! Leave me alone."

John had no answer. He backed into the kitchen and sat. *She's right. I saw the doctor kill the Adams. I ought've known better.* He stared out the window and cursed. Hours later he arranged a bed for himself by the fire in the kitchen. He climbed in and stared at the dying fire.

Amos' deliveries should have only taken a few hours. John heard him come in after midnight. He went into his room and went to bed.

*****

John and Amos were both up and about their tasks by dawn. Abigail was awake but stayed in bed until mid-morning. There was no need to fix anything to eat. There were still piles of food the townsfolk brought. It was beginning to spoil in the kitchen. Abigail ate some and sorted through the rest, throwing much of it away.

John and Amos came in for lunch and returned to the brewery. While they worked, Amos said, "John if I get an early enough start, there's plenty of daylight left when my deliveries are done. Will you teach me brewing, like I was your apprentice?"

John looked up from stirring the toasted barley. "I'd be glad of the help." Neither man said anything else that day.

Abigail sat in the kitchen and stared out one of the few glass windows in Burlington. When the men returned to the house, she was in bed.

The men sat before the fire. Then Amos got up for bed. John fixed his bed before the fire. He slept very little. He cried a lot.

*****

Abigail sat staring into the fire. A knock on the door drew her attention. She stood, brushed at her clothing and ran her fingers through her hair before she went to the door. The stonecutter, holding his hat with both hands said, "I've placed the stone on your daughter's grave."

She sucked for air before managing to say, "Thank you."

"'Tis never easy to ask, but do you know when you'll be able to pay?"

Abigail looked over the big man's shoulder and managed to say, "I'll have to ask my husband. Soon, I'm certain."

He thanked her and left. Abigail walked to the brewery. "John?"

"Abigail," he smiled, "It's been long since you've come here."

"The stone cutter came to say he's placed Mary's stone. He wants to be paid."

"I'll pay him as I can. We should go see the stone." He took off his apron and grabbed his hat.

"I need to make myself presentable."

Abigail went into their room, changed and brushed her hair. They walked side by side to the churchyard, for the first time since Mary's funeral.

They stared at the stone for a long time without speaking. Then Abigail said, "You'll want lunch." She turned and left for home. John hurried to walk next to her, but she did not look at him, or speak.

At home, she looked at the remnants of food people had brought before Mary's funeral and said, "There's still that. You can make do." Then she went into their room and closed the door.

A pattern was set. When the food townsfolk brought was gone, whether eaten or thrown out, Abigail started cooking again. She resumed the myriad other tasks performed by women. She ate and drank almost nothing. She was in bed before the men came in for supper. John and Amos talked until Amos went to bed. John slept on the kitchen floor.

*****

One cold winter night, John lay looking into the fire's dying embers. The door opened from the bedroom. He turned to look at Abigail. In the dark, he could hardly see her. *She's become so thin.* It seemed she'd aged years. She stood in the door and whispered, "John, are you awake?"

"I am."

"Come, be with me. I don't want to be alone."

John climbed out of his covers and walked to Abigail. She put her head on his shoulder and cried. For the first time in weeks, he put his arms around her and cried with her. After some minutes, she turned, took his hand and led him to their bed. He climbed in beside her. She buried her face in his shirt and cried. He wrapped his arms around his frail wife and cried with her. Neither spoke. They both fell asleep. They slept better than they had in weeks.

When John awoke that morning, Abigail was already awake, but still in his arms. She was smiling. John smiled too.

*****

A corner was turned. Abigail began to eat and drink. She spoke and laughed. She ate with the men. As long as no one mentioned Mary, or that terrible time, the household seemed to return to normal. But the slightest reference to Mary or her death sent Abigail into her room, sometimes for days. The men learned to keep a careful tongue.

In some strange way, Mary's passing introduced John and Abigail to Burlington's social life. Abigail was invited to quilting bees. They began attending church. They were making friends.

John's business grew. By spring, he'd paid the stone cutter and Amos got a small salary.

Amos approached him with a suggestion. "If you had an indenture, he could deliver the beer and I could work full time, in the brewery. You have need of the help."

"That I do, but I have no money to buy an indenture. Where would—"

"If I worked full time with you, how long before I knew brewing full well?"

"Three years, maybe four."

"Then, I'll stay on without salary if you hire an indenture and treat me as an apprentice."

"You learn brewing now."

"But there is so much I don't know. Would I not learn faster?"

"You would."

"Then we'd both benefit. Could you manage this if I worked only for my food and bed?"

"Where would he sleep?"

"Two could sleep in my room."

"Why would you do this Amos? I don't underst—"

"I get no younger. I can't stay as I am forever. Someday I'd like a wife."

John tried to say something, but Amos held up his hand and went on. "Let me finish. I'm a tinker by trade, and I've learned tinkers starve. I see no time when, as a tinker, I could marry or if I did, how I'd feed a family. If I were a brewer, I could move to another city, Baltimore or York City, start my own brewery and earn enough to support a family."

"Let me talk to Abigail and with my agent in Philadelphia. Mayhap we could do this."

In this way, Hans Mueller came into the Rider household, as an indentured servant.

The impact in the community was predictable and immediate. People believed John and Abigail had to be rich. They paid for their house, one of the few houses in town with real glass windows, with silver. They soon added a new room. Their business looked to be successful. They seemed to own two indentured servants. Many would be surprised if they learned how little John and Abigail had.

They were new to the community, but the community itself was new. It just seemed natural that John and Abigail were brought into the top echelon of Burlington's society.

John was asked to sit on the English church's board of vestry. Governor Hamilton attended this church when he stayed in

Burlington, West Jersey's capital. They were soon on a first name basis with each other. Abigail was invited to tea with the priest's wife, as was Mrs. Hamilton, of whom Abigail was very fond.

There was also something mysterious about the Riders. Sarah Gibb told friends about Tamaqua's visit the night Mary died. Her friends repeated the story, which grew with each retelling. And there was the blanket. An Indian blanket appeared on Mary's grave during the night before the first snow fell. In a colony where all lived at peace with the Lenape, John and Abigail seemed to have a special relationship with them. This could only be a good thing.

Months turned into years and reality approached the image. John's business grew. He expanded his oven and brewing buildings. He and Abigail considered the purchase of another indenture. They now had a small purse filled with silver that they kept hidden in a niche in their fireplace.

As the year 1700 approached, Abigail found herself to be with child. They thought they would never be happy again, but somehow, they were.

Chapter Sixteen
A Leader in the Community

"The cautious seldom err."
Confucius

Six inches taller than any other man in Burlington, but no heavier, clothes hung on Henry Gaunt. As head of the Board of Justices and Chosen Freeholders, he called a meeting of all freeholders to order. Only freeholders, landowning men, were permitted to attend or able to vote. Standing under the big elm tree on the green he opened the meeting.

"Who among us is not filled with terror at the sound of the fire bell in the night?" Henry made a point to look the others in the eye. "At that sound, all else is forgot. Thy only thought's to stop the fire, to save thy family, thy homes and thy town." Saying this, he pointed his long index finger from man to man. "Then, naught else matters. People rush, filling buckets pell-mell, to save the town. Many a building's destroyed; many a town's lost to fire."

The important men in the semi-circle around Henry looked at one another, and nodded agreement. Henry went on, his pointing hand sweeping the crowd. "Ask thyself why John Robin's barn was lost last year."

A well-dressed, muscular man called out, "We rallied to the bell, but the barn was a good mile from the river. The only water was from his well. No number of men can draw water from a well fast enough to stop a fire."

How far's thy house and barn from the water, Will? Further than John Robin's I'll wager." Will Tudor, a member of the Anglican Church and the Board of Freeholders, frequently opposed Henry on town issues.

"'Twas nothing to be done—"

"So, we thought!" Henry pointed again. "Though we sit on the river, there's parts of town with no water but a well. Thee're right, Will, none get water from a well quick enough to fill buckets and fight a fire."

Will nodded. "Then we agree. There's nothing to be done."

"Sorry Friend. There was nothing we could do for John Robin's barn, but there are things we can do now. What if we built goodly troughs throughout the town? Then, in a fire, there'd be a supply of water for use by the bucket line everywhere."

One of the men raised a hand and stepped forward. "And who's to build these troughs?"

"Thank you Sam. Happens, I've thought on this. We need a fire brigade, made of all able- bodied men in town. We assign each man to a crew. Each crew builds its own trough and keeps it full. The troughs could be used to water draught animals too—"

"Where's the time for this to come from?"

Nods of agreement followed little conversations through the small group of men.

Henry smiled, held up his hand for quiet and spoke louder. "In most of His Majesty's colonies, all men serve in a militia. Praise God, we've no need for one. We're most blessed of all His Majesty's colonies." Heads nodded again. The small conversations grew louder. Henry raised his voice. "None threaten us. New York stands between us and the French to the north. Pennsylvania does the same in the west. Delaware, Maryland and Virginia, all His Majesty's, stand to the south. Pirates trouble East Jersey." Henry pointed in each direction as he spoke. "They don't bother us." Circling his hand over his head, he went on. "The Delaware, Lenape, call them as you will, live among us in peace. Friends, we need no militia to fight men but could use one fight fire. It's a constant threat. We use it for cooking, for light, and for heat. Fire's everywhere. Too often, it's out of control. We all know of houses, barns, and whole towns that burned."

Small groups started talking among themselves. It took Henry several minutes to restore order. When he did, the debate was brief. The Freeholders decided every able-bodied man in Burlington was required to join a fire brigade. The Board of Justices and Chosen Freeholders would divide the men into crews. Each crew was to build its own trough, ten large wooden buckets and a ladder, to be kept at the ready near each trough. The same men would be assigned to keep the trough full and to see to the care and maintenance of the ladder and buckets.

Over the next month, the Board assigned men to crews with ten or twelve of their neighbors. Each crew was led by a chief, who was a Freeholder. As a Freeholder in his section, John was made chief of his crew.

On the last day of every month, unless it fell on the Sabbath, the men gathered by crews on the green. Then they went to their troughs to practice fighting the fire they prayed would never come. They practiced which men would carry the ladder, how they would organize the passing of buckets, and who would wet down neighboring buildings to prevent the fire from spreading.

After the tiring drills, the men retired to the inn for hot rum punch in cold weather or beer in warm. The drills and the time after them became the most important opportunities men had to establish bonds and form friendships.

On a hot summer day, John brought a cask of his beer to the drill. "This saves us the walk to the inn!" John shouted, opening the cask, when the work was done. For a few hours, he was the most popular man in Burlington, at the expense of Peter Hutchinson, the inn keeper.

"Peter, why's your beer not like this?"

"Don't you know? Peter sells ox piss, not beer."

"Ox piss or no, this be better."

Soon Peter was forced to buy his beer from John. He was not happy.

*****

Not all public issues are so easily resolved.

The Board of Justices and Chosen Freeholders met in Henry's store after he closed for the day. Sitting on the counters or standing between piles of cloth sacks filled with grain or beans, among the cluttered wares of a mercantile, they argued.

"How can we refuse to send delegates?" Henry was confused and angry. He seldom raised his voice but did now. "Friend Penn's a proprietor. Dare we ignore his call?"

"Hamilton was removed and Basse named governor by the King-in-Council. By what right do the proprietors discharge him to bring Hamilton back?" Will Tudor shouted back.

"We all know Andrew Hamilton governed well," Henry said, trying to control his voice. The men around the room nodded. "Were he not born in Scotland, they'd never of replaced him."

"But they did. The Navigation Act required it," Will said. "And In his place, King William appointed Jeremiah Basse. He's our legal governor."

"Problem's he never governed so well as he stole. He's lost control o' both Jerseys." Henry threw his hands up.

"But the proprietors have not the right to replace him."

"Think thee Basse's governed justly, or well?" Henry started to stand but thought better of it and sat back down.

"If the proprietors want their man back, let them go to the King." Squinting into the light of the setting sun, coming through the store's small glass window, Will worked to lower his voice. "I know you Friends have great respect for Penn, but your William's not King William."

"He never claimed he was—"

"Yet he presumes to replace the King's governor with his own!"

"Basse was recalled by all the proprietors, not just Penn!" They were both shouting again.

The other members stood silently while the argument continued. Finally, Thomas Budd, the oldest and most respected of the Anglican faction spoke. This put a stop to the back and forth.

"Your disputing gains us nothing." Budd, one of the first English settlers in West Jersey, was bent by age. Though his weak voice cracked, his mind was sharp as ever. He seldom spoke during meetings, but when he did his opinions carried great weight. "Word is Penn only wants to hear our grievances and give us his opinions. Does a proprietor not deserve that much respect?"

"He thinks this conference'll calm things because none'll dare challenge him." Tudor knew to tread lightly disputing Tom Budd.

"You'd challenge him, wouldn't you Will?" Leaning into his cane with both hands, Budd hobbled toward him. When they were face to face, Budd said, "Why don't you and Henry go? I trust you to represent us." The old man made Tudor feel uncomfortable and look foolish.

"I'm needed at home. Someone else can go."

Realizing he'd carried the day, Budd smiled. "Just coming here was challenge enough. The trip to Amboy's too much for me. Henry, you'll go?"

"I will."

"The second ought not be another Quaker." Budd looked around the room. One after another, the members of the Anglican faction of the Board explained why they couldn't go.

Will Tudor spoke again. "If no member of the Board will go, we'd need someone respected by the town. Who'd that be?"

Now Henry did stand up. "What if we asked John Rider?"

"He's not even English." Tudor said, shaking his head.

Old Thomas, who still stood inches from Will, turned to face him again. "He's not, but he goes to the Anglican Church. He's not been here long, but in his time here, he's built a business. He does more for the town than most. He's respected."

Tudor knew he'd lost. Burlington would send its two representatives to Penn's conference. He made one last attempt to block it. "I doubt he'd go. Rider's busy. He does most of the work in his brewery himself. Leaving for the conference'd cost him dearly."

Budd hobbled about to face Henry. "Will you take me home in your cart?"

"I will."

"On the way, we can stop at John Rider's." Budd turned to face Tudor again and smiled. "I'm told I can be persuasive."

*****

"How's it wise to go to this conference?" Concern creased Abigail's face. "Why draw attention? It asks for trouble."

"Refusing might bring more questions than we can answer." He pushed away his half-finished meal. "I know none in East Jersey. Who would I meet from before?"

"That be the question. Who would you meet?" Abigail was angry. She got up from the table and began cleaning up from supper. "Perth Amboy's a port. Sailors know you. 'Tis why you stopped going to Philadelphia."

"'Tis, but with only two men from Amboy, the conference should be—"

"You'll eat or sleep at the conference. You'll eat and sleep at an inn, where there'll be sailors. You can't—"

"What if I stay at the best inn Amboy offers? Most of the delegates are to be men of means. They would stay there by choice. You'll not see sailors in such a place."

"There needs only one." The fear in her voice was palpable.

*****

Henry kicked dirt over the coals of their cook-fire. "We've still a day's ride to Amboy. I knew we should have sailed."

"Sailing down the Delaware and up the coast to Amboy is no short trip," John said, smiling.

"Sitting on a boat's a sight easier than riding a horse for three days."

John laughed as he tied a pack behind his saddle, "Neither of us've been on a horse in years. Think of it as fun."

Mounting, Henry said, "I'm thinking of my sore rump. The cost to hire these horses would've bought our tickets to sail there."

And I'm thinking of my neck. There'll be no sailors on this road. John pulled himself into the saddle cursing the years he had gone without riding. "Lazy, a complainer, and a miser. This becomes you not, Henry." He laughed again, kicking his horse into an easy trot.

*****

After a supper of roast venison, roast goose, ham, and fresh-caught trout, John put his feet up, leaned back into his cushioned chair and enjoyed his third tankard of a fine dark beer. "Hutchinson never served such a meal." He looked around the room at brocaded furniture, brass chandeliers, and stenciled, painted walls.

"Hutchinson never charged five pence a night."

"Smile Henry, we share our room with no others, the meal was fine. We meet delegates from other towns. Seems five pence well spent."

The long summer day faded into a hot, mosquito-filled night. The common room filled with angry delegates. One argued Hamilton abused his position when he was governor before, the colonists just didn't notice, until Basse's misrule drew their attention. Another argued Hamilton favored the Quakers in West Jersey and cheated East Jersey's Puritans.

"'Tis good half be Quakers," John whispered to Henry, "Else they'd come to blows."

"The heat's half the problem. They drink to cool off, and filled with drink, they argue and get hot. Then they drink more, to cool off."

"Seems a fine place to be a brewer," John laughed, slapping another mosquito. "Needs no fortune teller to see the conference'll not go well."

"Hamilton's a fine man, but he can't run the colonies alone. Some must work with him."

John smiled at Henry. "I'll drink to that." He drained his tankard and headed for the broad stairway to their room. "If we're not drained dry by the mosquitos, we'll have a long day tomorrow. I'm to bed."

Henry stayed behind to hear the other's arguments. He also drank another three beers, which he regretted each time his bladder interrupted his sleep. He woke with a dry mouth and headache.

*****

The conference was called at the birch tree a few rods from the Governor's House on Perth Amboy's town common. William Penn stood on the large grey rock speakers used during such meetings. His plain Quaker clothing somehow looked expensive. People, straining to hear, stood on porches of the expensive houses surrounding the green.

"Andrew Hamilton has earned thy support!" Penn shouted to be heard over the large crowd. "He knows us and sees to the needs of our colonies—"

Someone shouted, "If he's for us, why's Perth Amboy not yet a free port?"

"We work on that, Friend. Thus far, the King-in-Council's refused."

Hamilton stepped on the rock and whispered something into Penn's ear. Penn nodded and stepped down. Hamilton looked in the direction of the complaint and began, "Friend—"

He was cut off. "You're no Quaker and I'm not your friend. You favored the Quakers over your own kind before. Why should we submit to you again?"

Hamilton raised his hand to speak, but another man shouted, "Has the King approved your appointment?"

Penn climbed back on the rock and stood next to Hamilton. "His Majesty has not, but we work with the Ministry to gain His approval."

Someone else shouted, "Without royal approval, he's no governor!"

Penn again raised his hand for quiet and tried to explain the intricacies of colonial politics. The assembly's strong opposition surprised John. He knew Hamilton to be a good man. He looked around the crowd of angry faces and saw William Miller, a shipper he'd sold beer in Boston.

He turned his back. *Don't think he's seen me yet.* He leaned toward Henry and whispered, "I'm not well. I'm going to the inn to rest. Any can see naught'll be accomplished here. After resting, I think I'm bound for—"

Henry looked shocked. "We represent the town. You can't just ride away. You owe—"

"I owe nothing. We gave our time and paid our own expenses. 'Tis clear there'll be no resolution. I'm not well. I go to the inn to rest. Then I leave for home—"

"You look fine to me—"

"Good that you find me pleasing. If Abigail ever tires of me, I'll come to you. You're well and you speak better than me anyway. I'll see you back home." John turned and made his way through the contentious crowd. Henry called after him but was ignored.

"Hamilton's always been fair—" shouted one man.

Another shouted, "To you—"

A third cried out, "Without King William's writ, he's no governor. Why are we wasting our—"

Trying to not draw any attention to himself, John worked his way through the small crowd. He hurried to the inn.

"Keeper, what d' I owe you? I've an unexpected need to leave. Have my horse saddled."

"I've already started meals for you, and unless I put another in your room—"

"Yes, fine. What do I owe?"

"I'll need a shilling. At that I'm losing—"

John dropped a silver shilling on the counter. *'Tis highway robbery, but I've no time or interest in his lies.* He bounded up the stairs, threw his pack together and hurried back down.

"For three pence more, we can fix you a fine meal for the—"

"Is my horse ready?"

"The boy's in the stable, saddling him now."

Without acknowledging the inn-keep, John went to the stable. The boy was just putting the bit in the horse's mouth. John threw the blanket on its back and grabbed the saddle.

"See here, sir, Master Owen'll have my hide if you have to saddle your own—"

John threw the saddle on his horse and began cinching it. "Who's to tell him? Hand me my pack. I'm needed at home."

John finished saddling his horse, pulled his pack from the boy's hands, tied it behind the saddle and threw himself on the horse. Without another word, he kicked the horse into a trot and headed out the stable's door. In his haste, he gave no thought to either food or water. After several hours of hard riding, John and the sweat-covered horse both leaned forward and drank from the same stream. The horse found plenty of grass growing on the stream's bank. John would have to wait to eat at an inn.

Pushing the horse as hard as he could, John trotted into Burlington late in the afternoon two days later. When he told Abigail why he was home early, she tried not to say, "I told you so." She did not succeed. She lectured him long into the night.

Chapter Seventeen
A New Life

"That which we call a rose, by any other name would smell as sweet."
Shakespeare

A pleasant winter passed into spring and spring into summer for the Rider household. Abigail felt well throughout her pregnancy. Sadie had passed away, but Sarah and Elsie did their best to allay Abigail's fears that she would give birth to another frail child.

John's business continued its growth. With hard cash in short supply, his business agent often traded beer in exchange for a quantity of tobacco, molasses, or rum. He would then trade it for another commodity and often that for another, which he often exported to England. Money for any individual sale could be long in coming. But Bartlett was a shrewd businessman. He managed to turn a comfortable profit on each exchange. In this way, even after Bartlett's ten percent fee for each transfer, John's money grew. He enjoyed a steady and comfortable flow of income both from the sale of his beer, and Bartlett's many trades that followed. The purse of silver hidden in the fireplace was no longer small.

Amos was becoming a competent brewer. John now paid him and he was saving to start his own brewery in another city.

Hans, the indenture, was learning English, made his deliveries on time and was helpful in the brewery. He understood the arrangement between John and Amos and hoped John would someday be as generous to him.

The major controversy Abigail and John faced was a name for the baby. John suggested name after name for a girl, Rene, Celeste, Genevieve, but Abigail always returned to her grandmother's name, Hermione. One night that fall, Abigail rested her head on John's shoulder as they lay in bed. Yet again, she was explaining the virtues of naming their daughter Hermione. He rolled his eyes.

"I cannot name my daughter Hermione. I'm sure your grandmother was a wonderful woman, but she had a terrible name. I'll accept any other name, just not Hermione."

At once she said, "Elizabeth!"

"What? You'd name my daughter after that shrew of an English queen?"

"It's not Hermione."

"A trap! I fell into a trap! You planned this all along."

Abigail snuggled in against him, burying her face against his chest. After a moment, she turned her face up to his and smiled. He laughed, leaned down over her now prodigious belly and slapped her bottom.

"I can't believe my daughter will be named after that cow!"

She snuggled against him again. John laughed. They both fell asleep.

Choosing a boy's name proved no easier. Especially after Elizabeth, John insisted on naming his son Louis. One evening, as they finished supper, Abigail said, "You know, no one will say his name the way you do, Loo-EE. Everyone will call him Loo-iss."

"Loo-iss! It sounds like a snake! Why would anyone call a boy Loo-iss?"

"Because we're English, John. Everyone, the boy himself, will pronounce it Loo-iss. It's a battle you'll not win."

She suggested name after name, Elijah, Hezekiah, Hosea, Ezekiel. John rolled his eyes more with each name she suggested. Then she said, "What of Benjamin?"

"At last!" he cried. "A reasonable sounding name. We can name our son Benjamin."

Abigail smiled. "Then we agree. I always liked my grandfather's name."

"What? You did this to me again?" He chased her around the table. She went right, then left, until he caught her. She fell into his arms, and they both laughed.

*****

In late June, a stranger entered Burlington's mercantile. Henry was on the ladder, rearranging yard goods on the top shelf. He turned his head when he heard the door open.

The stranger looked up and said, "Would you be Henry Gaunt?"

"I would. How may I help thee?" As he climbed down the ladder the stranger handed him a piece of paper.

"You hold a letter of introduction and warrant. It explains my charge better than I can."

Henry read:

> Be it known to all presented these credentials that Isaiah Putnam, constable of this colony, is by this warrant empowered to secure the arrest and return to this colony of one Jean-Marc Bompeau, also known as John Bompeau, an escaped indenture. Bompeau is sought for the wanton murder of his master, one John Moore, before numerous witnesses.
>
> Bompeau is believed to travel in the company of one Abigail Hyde, a former indenture and possible accomplice. Bompeau is believed to be plying the brewer's trade in Philadelphia or the surrounding counties.
>
> All persons reading this warrant are requested to render such services as are necessary to secure the capture and transfer to this colony of said Jean-Marc Bompeau.
>
> William Stoughton
>
> Acting Governor

Province of Massachusetts Bay

Henry turned ashen. His mind raced. *This must be John and Abigail ... I've worked with John for years. He be no killer, nor Abigail one's accomplice. If John killed this John Moore, he deserved dying ... How can I even think that? I'm a Friend. What could justify killing?*

He handed the letter back to Putnam. "I've read thy letter. I know of no John or Jean-Marc Bompeau in Burlington."

"Be you sure of that? I've sworn testimony from a ship captain that he saw Bompeau at a conference in Perth Amboy. And I've the sworn word of a sailor who testifies to knowing that Bompeau sells beer in Philadelphia, like he did in Boston. In Philadelphia, I was told of a brewer from West Jersey who sends beer daily across the Delaware. If I watched the ferry, and followed a teamster returning from the delivery of beer would he lead me to Bompeau? With my warrant, I've no need to cooperate with local magistrates, but my preference — "

Henry took a small step forward, leaned toward Putnam and held up his hand. His voice was angry. "Hold thy tongue, man. A Massachusetts warrant 'tis good in Massachusetts. This be not Massachusetts. Attempt the arrest of a Jersey man without a Jersey warrant, and it would please our magistrates to put you in irons."

Putnam shook his warrant at Henry. "Surely, you deny not the rights of Massachusetts—"

"To execute warrants in this colony, I do. 'Tis my duty, as head of the Board of Freeholders to investigate crime and I will do so. But thee've no power to arrest here."

"And how get I a Jersey warrant?"

"From me, but only after my investigation. Or you could see Governor Hamilton. At the moment, he's in Perth Amboy."

"Perth Amboy's three days travel each way. A warned fugitive'd get a good start in—"

The red-faced men were nose to nose. "A warned fugitive could what? Help me understand thee, Friend. Thee know me not at all. Yet thee come to my colony and my store, state thy intention to make an illegal arrest, and then imply I'd help a murderer avoid justice—"

Putnam took a step backward and raised both palms in front of his chest. "I meant no slight."

Henry leaned in again. "Slight was meant. And slight was taken. Thy meanings were clear. State thy intention. Will thee await my investigation, or seek the governor's warrant?"

Hoping to lower the tension, Putnam stepped back again and said, "I await your investigation, sir. Would you like my assistance?"

Reaching for the warrant again, Henry said, "The investigation should take not long. Wait at the inn. If my investigation leaves thee unhappy, thee still have recourse to Governor Hamilton."

Putnam held his tongue but was not happy. He didn't like letting Henry take the warrant. He didn't trust Henry but decided there was little to be gained making him an enemy. He forced a smile, bowed, and said, "I am at your service, sir. I'll be at the inn, should you need me." Putnam turned and left, making a conscious decision to not look back.

Henry waited until he was sure Putnam was gone, then went to the brewery. John heard him coming and looked up, "Henry. What glad tidings bring you here in the middle of the day?"

"This!" Henry handed John the warrant.

John sat back against a workbench. He seemed to shrink as he read. He looked at his feet and said, "Abigail knew nothing. She only left with me."

"So ye don't deny it?"

John looked up, "How can I? This Putnam would know me on sight—"

"Why John?"

"The man beat his wife and children without mercy. I made a vow that the day he beat Abigail or me would be his last. That morning, he took a club to Abigail. When he tried to use it on me, I took it from him, and beat him with his own club. His death was well earned." John looked back at his feet.

Henry put his hands behind his back, inside his breeches waistband, and looked up at nothing in particular. "John, ye be a good and kind man." He brought his eyes down and looked at him. "Thee must know an unjust man needs prayer, not beating. Violence solves noth—"

"He never beat another woman or child. I call that solved." John's voice quivered in anger, but his eyes stayed down.

"Violence begets only violence. It serves no good purpose."

"What will you do?" John looked up and held out the warrant.

Henry took it and looked to the left. "I can stall him a day or more. That will give thee a start."

"Am I to leave Abigail with the baby soon due? She cannot run and I'll not leave her."

"Thee will have to leave her, or thee will hang. What's to gain staying?"

"I know Andrew Hamilton to be a good and fair man." John stood and looked at Henry. "He knows me to be no threat. I'll make my case to him, as best I can. He may see the same justice I see." He took off his apron. "Amos! Take over here. I've business with Henry."

Henry followed him into the house. Abigail looked up from her bread trough and smiled, wiping her hands on her apron. "Henry! Good to see you." Then she looked at her husband, "John, what's the matter? You look a ghost."

He could not look at his wife. Tears ran down his cheeks. He took her in his arms and pulled her close. He felt the swell of her stomach, heavy with child. Now, Abigail was frightened. She pushed herself free. "John! What is it? You frighten me!"

John loosened his arms. He looked into her face, now rounded by the last month of her pregnancy. "Abigail, I've been found—"

"How?" she cried as if in physical pain. "It was in Amboy, wasn't it?" He nodded. She pounded her fists on his chest. "I told you not to go. I told you. I told you." She dropped to her knees. John tried to raise her to her feet, but she would not rise.

Henry stood back, trying to make himself invisible. He thought he should go outside, but somehow, didn't move. John knelt beside Abigail and tried to calm her. After some minutes, Abigail looked up at him. Words rushed out of her mouth. "You have to run. Go! Now! I'll be well. We've money hid. When you're safe, let me know. I'll come to you with the baby. Run to France. You'll be safe there—"

"No ships leave these ports for France. I'd be caught long ere I reached Quebec. If I ran would they come for you? What of our ba—"

"Run for Virginia. They'll not know you."

John took Abigail by both shoulders and looked into her face. Tears ran down his cheeks. He tried to sound calm, "I know Andrew Hamilton to be a fair man. Let me plead my case before him.

Mayhap he'll see I was defending you. At all cases, I'll see he knows you had no part."

Abigail turned and seemed to see Henry for the first time. "Henry, tell your friend. He'll be no husband or father from a scaffold!"

"I've tried. He doesn't lis—"

John stood, drawing Abigail to her feet. "I'll risk not you nor our baby. I've lost one. I'll not lose another—"

"But we can lose you? How are we to do without you— "

"You'll be without me if I run." John tried to take Abigail in his arms, but she pushed him away. She sobbed and fell again to her knees. John reached both hands to help her up. She slapped them away.

"Go then! Get out! If you mean go, go! Why are you waiting? Leave me alone! Get—"

John turned and walked out the door. He managed to say, "Let's go" to Henry, who followed without speaking, glad to be out of the room.

They almost reached the small log stockade that served as Burlington's jail when Henry broke the silence. "Putnam will want a warrant from me this night to take thee on the morrow."

"Then I'm a dead man. My one hope is in Governor Hamilton." John stopped and turned to Henry. "We have to delay this. How can—"

"Thee must plead dire circumstances. I'll refuse Putnam his warrant and hold thee for a hearing with the governor. The choice will be his. A letter will take three days to—"

"To reach him, and he'll take a week or more before coming to court here. That gives us time."

"We'll get letters of support. Father Farnsworth'll testify to thy character. I'll find others."

"Putnam will cry foul."

"How can he complain, if thee be in the stockade?"

The plan was hatched. Together John and Henry went to the Anglican priest. He led them into his small office, and asked them to sit on the straight-backed, wooded chairs. Henry spoke first. Together they explained the situation, often interrupting each other.

After several minutes, Father Farnsworth held up his hand and spoke. "I think I understand. John, I've known you always to be a good Christian man. That murder is sin cannot be argued. But our Lord is a Lord of forgiveness. Do you repent your sin?"

"Repent murdering, I do. Repent murdering this man, I do not. He was a foul and abusive sinner. The world is better without him."

"Be careful here, John. Do you repent of your sin?"

"I do repent of the sin of murder."

Making a cross in the air, the priest said, "My son, your sins are forgiven. In your repentance, you are returned to a state of grace with your Heavenly Father. I can inform the bishop that a member of our church, in good standing, repentant of his sins has asked for and received God's mercy. While in this state of grace, he requests church sanctuary. I would not expect a reply from England by the time of your hearing with Governor Hamilton, but he can be apprised of your application for sanctuary."

Henry stood and paced in the tiny room. "I'll need jail thee, but while we wait, I'll look to the freeholders for action. I can't believe they'll not come to thy aid."

John felt hopeful for the first time. They agreed Abigail should not be alone, but that neither Henry's nor Father Farnsworth's wives should be the ones to stay with her. Henry said he would send word to Sarah Gibb. He was sure she would stay with Abigail for the time being.

The way to the stockade took Henry and John past the store. Henry called to his boy to fetch Sarah Gibb and bring her to the stockade. Henry's wife would mind the store while he was gone.

*****

The cell was small with barred windows, but there were shutters against the cold and rain. There was a rope cot, with a stuffed mattress, against the wall. A chamber pot was under the cot. A small table, against the wall, could be used to eat from. A candle was just past arm's reach, past the cell's bars in the keeper's office. The cell would not be dark at night. The heavy chain wrapped around the iron bars was secured by a large padlock.

John stepped into the cell, and Henry locked him inside as Sarah Gibb arrived. He and John repeated their explanation of events.

"Murder? How could thee, John?" Sarah was shaken.

John walked to the cot and sat. Looking up he said, "Was I to watch as this man beat Abigail?"

"It was Abigail's to turn her cheek, to be struck again, and thine to pray for her safety."

John rubbed his face with the palms of both hands. "I fear Sarah, that my faith is weaker than yours. I could not; I would not allow that man to beat my Abigail."

"Many a sin is veiled in good intention, but I'll not judge. Thee are right; Abigail cannot be alone. I'll get my things and stay with her until all is settled."

*****

Putnam was sitting in the shade of the large elm next to the inn. He stood when he saw Henry coming. "Goodman Gaunt, I didn't expect to see you so soon."

"Friend, thy information was accurate. We've a brewer in town, living as John Rider, who admits he is the man thee seek. He's my prisoner, in the stockade."

Putnam smiled, held out a hand and walked towards Henry. "Splendid! I'll go to Philadelphia to make arrangements for our passage to Boston. I'll see he gets a fair trial before he's hanged."

Henry ignored Putnam's out stretched hand. "Hear my words. He is my prisoner—"

"And as soon as I arrange passage, he'll be mine."

"Not so fast, Friend. The prisoner claims the circumstances were dire. He's appealed to Governor Hamilton. I've forwarded his request to the governor—"

Putnam shouted, "Dire circumstances? What circumstances justify one servant murdering his master and running off with another? Do you justify servile insurrection?" His hands dropped to his sides and formed into fists.

"The man says his master oft beat his wife, his children and other servants. He says he stepped in to stop a young woman's being—"

"A man's right to beat his wife, children and servants is well established. None can argue that—"

"I'll argue anyone's right to strike another—"

"And people wonder why we bar Quakers from our colony! What now? Will you let a murderer go free because the man he murdered acted as a man ought, in his own home?"

Henry took a short step back and eyed Putnam. He lowered his voice and spoke with a cold anger. "None have been set free. But in this colony, we hold that no man may lay hand on another, even on his wife or servants. We countenance none of the brutality you do in Boston." Putnam tried to interrupt, but Henry held up his hand and kept talking. "The prisoner's fate is with the governor now. If this displeases thee, it is thy right to return to Massachusetts and complain to thy governor. Or, thee can await Governor Hamilton's ruling."

"I will await this hearing, and I'll see your governor knows of the wanton nature of this murderer. Know this well, allow one servant to attack his master and you invite all servants to attack their masters. You strike at the very heart of society." Putnam glowered at Henry. His voice quaked with anger. "And, as God is my judge, I will write Governor Stoughton of this outrage."

Henry turned to go, "Do as thee will. Thy unseemly anger will not dictate Jersey law. This Jean-Marc Bompeau will have his day in court"

Chapter Eighteen
The Hearing

"Everything we see is a perspective, not truth."
Marcus Aurelius

Additional chairs were crowded into the small, drab office for the overflow crowd. "All rise!"

"Gentlemen, sit. I remind all that this is no trial, but a hearing." Governor Hamilton moderated his voice and looked around the room. He needed to set the proper tone for this contentious hearing. "We are not assembled to determine guilt. It is my understanding that there is but little disagreement as to the occurrences. Our task is to determine if the facts justify the issuance of a warrant to deport a resident of West Jersey to the Massachusetts Bay Colony. Mr. Putnam, I'll hear you first."

Putnam, holding his hat with both hands, got up from a chair in the second row. "Yes, Your Excellency."

"I am familiar with the particulars of the case. Without giving a prosecutor's argument, tell me why I should issue a writ to support your warrant."

"As Your Excellency knows, this John Bompeau did wantonly kil—"

"As I said, Mr. Putnam, I know the particulars of this case. Mr. Bompeau would argue that his action was justified by his defense of a helpless girl, herself under attack."

"Thank you, Excellency. I will be brief. Under the law and well-established practice of the Massachusetts Bay Colony, a man may discipline his wife, minor children, or servants with a switch no wider than his thumb. That such discipline is necessary for a Godly family and colony cannot be argued. That—"

Several Quakers shot to their feet. One shouted, "I'll argue that, Puritan." A loud murmur went through the crowd.

Governor Hamilton pounded his gavel three times. He leaned forward, placing both his forearms on his desk. His blue eyes narrowed and his voice became stern. "Tread lightly, Mr. Putnam.

311

Many a Friend in this colony will argue as to the need for violence to enforce God's Law, whether within the family or within the colony. This may be the core of our dispute this day. Please finish your statement without judging if another may dispute it." He pounded his gavel again, and sat back, crossing his arms over his chest.

"Yes, Y-Your Excellency." Putnam's face reddened with anger. He did not like Hamilton's apparent prejudices. He looked at the floor and then the ceiling to calm himself before again addressing the Governor. "As I have stated, well established law ... law and practice in Massachusetts allows, I mean, expects a husband ... a husband, father. and master to administer the rod, in the furtherance of ... of a Godly and just society. When Goodman Moore, with love, took the rod to discipline Abigail Hyde, he—"

"Is it true, Mr. Putnam," Hamilton again leaned forward, "that Hyde was not indentured to Mr. Moore, but had fulfilled her indenture to Mrs. Moore's late husband? That she was continuing to serve in the family's employ, as a free woman?"

Putnam dropped his hat, made a fist with his left hand, and kneaded it with his right. "That is true, Excellency, but ... but she continued to live under Goodman Moore's roof, and serve his family. Free woman or no, she ... she continued to be under his guidance and um, responsibility."

"Do you know why Mr. Moore saw it necessary to cane young Mistress Hyde that day?" Hamilton sounded skeptical.

"It was for insolence, Your Excellency. She did insolently speak to Goodman Moore and was therefore rightfull—"

The gavel sounded again. Hamilton sat up straight. His voice became commanding. "Thank you, Mr. Putnam. You may be seated." He turned to face Jean-Marc. "My temptation is to call you Mr. Rider, but I learn I should address you as Monsieur Bompeau. Please stand. I would hear your account of the circumstances."

Jean-Marc stood under his true name for the first time in years. His leg and hand irons clanked as he moved. Hamilton's questioning of Putnam sounded hopeful to Jean-Marc. Still, he was nervous. His eyes found Abigail, who tried to smile at him. "Thank you, Your Excellency. I was born Jean-Marc Bompeau, fourth son of the Comte de Artois. When my father was killed in battle, my brother inherited his title and wealth. Being left penniless, I made for Acadia, as a trader. The ship was hit by plague, and then wrecked, leaving but two survivors. Shipwrecked in that wilderness of Massachusetts known as Maine, I was taken prisoner by Indians, who brought me, against my will, to raid an English village. After the attack, the English tried to question me, but I understood little they asked. Because they believed I had taken part in the raid, I was made a prisoner and wrongfully sold into servitude, for twenty-one years."

"Why say you wrongfully?"

"A court approved the sale in the belief that I consorted with Indians to attack Christians. They mis–"

Hamilton interrupted. "Has that indenture been fully served?"

Jean-Marc seemed surprised by the question. His voice wavered as he responded. "It has ... um, it has not, your honor. When I ran, I still owed a number of years."

"Do you know how many?"

"I believe I had served ... had served five years, Your Excellency."

"Thank you. Go on."

"As I said, I was sold for an indenture to Goodman Adams, to whom I was a faithful servant. When he died of the pox, I continued to serve his wife. I enriched the family business, built an extension onto the house and expanded the brewery, for my master's widow. When she was compelled to marry—"

Hamilton sat straight up again. "Compelled?"

"Yes Excellency, clergy threatened to try her for a witch if she did not marry."

"Indeed. Putnam, do you know of this?" Hamilton sounded amazed.

Putnam stood, feeling that Hamilton was placing him more on trial than Jean-Marc. "I do not, Your Excellency."

"Thank you. Witchcraft, eh? A strange belief indeed. Monsieur Bompeau, continue."

"Yes, Excellency. When Goody Adams married John Moore, he was found to be a disputatious and hard man. In his ignorance, he interfered with the brewery to its detriment—"

Hamilton hammered the gavel. His stern voice surprised Jean-Marc. "Monsieur, do not judge those who are not here to defend themselves."

Jean-Marc reddened. "Yes, Excellency. This new husband often and without cause beat—"

The gavel slammed into the desk. "Again, Monsieur, do not make such judgments. You may," Hamilton paused, "and I may deem the beatings Mr. Moore administered to be without cause, but they would appear to have been within the laws and customs of that colony. Please go on."

Jean-Marc looked down, and then up, trying to calm himself before speaking. "Yes, Excellency. I, um, I ... When he struck my wife ..."

"Were you then married?"

Jean-Marc's stammer grew worse. "We, I mean, um, no, we were not, Your Excellency."

"Thank you. Please continue."

"Yes, Your ... Your Excellency. When he struck the woman, now my wife, I defended her. As chance had it, the man's life was lost in my defense of the poor girl."

Hamilton said, "I see." He furrowed his brow and looked at some papers. He dipped his quill into the ink well and wrote something. He brought the quill up to his right temple and seemed lost in thought. Everyone sat in silence. Feet shuffled. Chairs moved. After several minutes, Hamilton spoke. "So, as I understand it, you still owe, perhaps sixteen years of servitude to the Moore family, do you not?"

"So ... so, it would seem ... Your Excellency, but ... but if sent back, it would not be as a ... as a servant, but to the gallows."

"Would the family not be deserving of the unserved years for which they paid, and from which you have deprived them?"

Jean-Marc whispered, "It would ... it would appear... I believe they would."

Putnam grinned. He wondered if this governor less biased than he thought.

"Perhaps I would be able to repa—"

Again, the gavel sounded. "Thank you, Monsieur. You may be seated."

Henry, Father Farnsworth, and many others rose to testify in Jean-Marc's favor. Each testified that Jean-Marc was an upright man who was no risk and of real value to the colony. Each testified that he would not have resorted to violence without extreme cause.

"I believe I understand the circumstances. Is there anyone else I should hear?" Hamilton looked across the room.

Abigail stood, "Your Excellency, of the many who spoke today, other than my husband, only I was there. I can tell you—" The gavel sounded.

"Mrs. Bompeau, women have no standing before the Court—"

"But you've asked what happened, I can tell—" The gavel sounded again.

"Thank you, Mrs. Bompeau, but your guardian has spoken in both of your behalves."

"Would you not know the truth?"

"I believe I now know it. There's naught you can add. Now, please be seated."

Abigail looked around for support. Father Farnsworth stood and whispered to her, "He'll not hear you and this helps not. Let me take you home."

Hamilton waited until they left. "I thank all of you. I have heard much testimony and have much to ponder. I adjourn this meeting until tomorrow morning. I will render my decision at that time." He pounded the gavel, stood, and left the room. The audience gossiped with excitement.

Henry led Jean-Marc to the stockade. Abigail pulled away from the priest and ran after her husband. Henry was removing Jen-Marc's shackles when she reached the stockade and pushed past him. Jean-Marc pulled her close. She tried to speak but could only cry into his shoulder. Henry stepped outside to give them some privacy. After several long minutes, Jean-Marc put his hands on Abigail's shoulders and gently pushed her back.

"The day has been long for you, and for our baby," he whispered. "You bring me every meal, and you stay for hours. You must go home and rest." Tears filled his eyes. He pulled her back to his chest. "Henry has yet to starve a prisoner. I love you, and I know that you love me. You've no need to prove it. Please go home and rest, for yourself and our baby." He kissed her and moved his hands to her hips. She started to say something, but he held his hand up, "There's naught to be done. I worry about you. We need you and the baby to be strong. It comes any day."

Abigail began to argue but stopped. She kissed him and turned to go. Reaching the door, she stopped, turned and said, "John, I can't, I won't live without you. Run and I will follow you."

"We did that once. Now we know. We would never be free." Jean-Marc backed into the cell and sat on the cot. "Henry," he called, in a loud voice, "You'll have to feed me from the inn tonight. Abigail goes home to rest. She'll not return this night."

*****

"On the surface, this case appears more complicated than it is in reality." The crowded office was silent as Governor Hamilton read from his decision. "The town of Burlington has benefitted from the many and varied contributions the man, known to its residents as John Rider, has made to the community. His value to the town was made clear by many impressive witnesses."

Abigail sat, wringing her hands in her lap, afraid to look up. Jean-Marc's jaw, which had been clenched, began to loosen. This sounded hopeful. Putnam's face reddened with anger.

"I have known Monsieur Bompeau for several years and have seen the results of his many good works, however," the Governor paused, apparently for dramatic effect. In fact, he was steeling himself for what he was about to say.

Abigail's eyes shot from her lap to the Governor's face. Jean-Marc's jaw clenched again. He sat bolt upright. Putnam's eyes narrowed, trying to read Hamilton's mind.

"However ... the facts presented reveal this to be a clear case of servile insurrection."

Abigail shrieked. A dozen whispered conversations filled the room.

Hamilton waited for quiet. "Servile insurrection that cannot be countenanced anywhere in British America. The base and violent nature of John Moore's character is apparent. This is a matter which should have been addressed by the magistrates in Massachusetts Bay. That they did not so do is to their shame. The failure of the officials of that colony to act in defense of its subjects, including Goodman Moore's family, his servants, and even a free employee who worked for room and board, is to their shame but not germane to the questions at hand."

Tears streamed down Abigail's face. Putnam grinned. John's head dropped. His eyes were closed. Henry Gaunt stared straight into Hamilton's face with a look of fury that shook the Governor. The crowd's noise rose to an uproar.

Hamilton hammered the gavel and shouted "Quiet." He banged his gavel again. "If I don't have quiet, I'll have the bailiff clear the room." He slammed the gavel into his desk three more times, leaving deep dents in its polished surface.

When the room quieted, he began again. "As I said, this is not germane to the questions at hand. First, does there exist a circumstance in which an indentured servant may lawfully leave his indenture, without serving the full term of said indenture and without leave of his master?"

The room erupted again. Putnam pumped his fist in triumph. Abigail buried her face in her hands and cried. John's manacled hands covered his head. Henry seethed with unholy anger, such as he had never experienced.

The gavel slammed into the desk.

"Order!" The bailiff shouted in vain.

"Order or I'll have the bailiff clear the room!" Hamilton tried to make himself heard above the uproar. Hammering the gavel again, he shouted, "Bailiff, clear the room!"

The bailiff's head spun toward Hamilton. Over the din, he cried, "How am I to do this?" He tried pushing people toward the door but was pushed back.

Hamilton hammered the gavel several times more, then looked at Henry. "Remove the prisoner!" Henry glared at Hamilton and did not move. Hamilton stood and left the room. He would not tolerate such insolence!

The turmoil continued for several minutes. It only calmed when the crowd realized the governor was gone. One by one, the bailiff convinced people they had to leave. Henry led Jean-Marc back to the stockade. Abigail sat sobbing in her seat. Elsie, who was seated beside her stood and helped her to her feet. She led Abigail to her house. Putnam stood motionless.

*****

Three hours later, Hamilton reconvened the hearing behind locked doors in the stockade. Jean-Marc stood behind the bars of his cell. Hamilton sat at Henry's desk. Only Abigail, Henry, Putnam and the bailiff were in the room with them.

Scowling, Hamilton banged a gavel on Henry's desk and began, "As I have stated, whether the magistrates of Massachusetts Bay acted with propriety or no, we have but two questions to address. One, does there exist a circumstance in which an indentured servant may lawfully leave his indenture, without serving the full term of said indenture and without his master's leave?" Pausing, Hamilton narrowed his eyes. One by one, he looked directly at each person in the room. "And two, does there exist a circumstance in which an indentured servant may legally take the life of his master in order to defend a free person who is under assault, but whose life seems not in jeopardy?"

Hamilton again paused. The small audience stood in stony silence, eyes fixed on the Governor.

"To these questions, I am forced to conclude, first, there does not exist a circumstance in which an indentured servant may lawfully leave servitude without serving the indenture's full term.

"I am certain that Monsieur Bompeau, who as John Rider did himself purchase such a servant, would be forced to concede this point. As such, it is the duty of this colony to return Jean-Marc Bompeau to his late master's heirs to serve the remainder of his indenture."

Abigail gasped for air. Henry's lips tightened. A smile flashed across Putnam's face. Jean-Marc stepped backward, dropping to a seat on the cot in his cell.

Hamilton looked toward the ceiling, took a deep breath and went on. "Second, I must conclude that there exists no circumstance in which an indentured servant may legally take the life of his master, even in defense of a free person being assaulted, but whose life is seems not in jeopardy.

"As such, without regard to my personal feelings for the servant in question, it is the duty of this colony to remand the servant in question to a representative of the Massachusetts Bay colony for judgment under the laws of that colony.

"May God have mercy on his soul."

Hamilton stood as he hammered the gavel down on the desk. Without another word, he left the stockade. Abigail cried. Jean-Marc buried his head in his hands.

Putnam said to Henry, "I'll leave at once for Philadelphia to arrange transportation to Boston. I'll inform you when to have him ready to leave. See that nothing happens to him while we wait for our ship."

Henry looked away but said nothing.

*****

Putnam was back by nightfall. He had arranged passage to Boston on a coastal freighter leaving Philadelphia in two days. He wanted Henry to have two armed men ready to escort them to Philadelphia at dawn that morning.

Chapter Nineteen
Fire

**"Grief has its limits, whereas apprehension has none. We grieve
only for what we know has happened, but we fear all
that may possibly happen"**

Pliny the Elder

CLANG! CLANG! CLANG! CLANG!

"Fire! Fire!"

Terror filled every soul in Burlington as the fire bell wrenched them awake. Men pulled on their breeches and boots, then ran into the streets. Women ran to their children, rousing and dressing each, wondering if they would have a home that night.

The southern sky glowed red/orange, telling each man where to find his bucket team. Running into a south wind, men knew fires like this destroyed whole families, whole towns.

Fire, hundreds of yards long, was consuming the town's southern edge. It raced north.

Someone shouted. "Those buildings be already lost!"

"Move back! We'll have to soak what's not burning. Mayhap we can save them."

Crews formed. Buckets passed from man to man. Ladders were thrown against houses. Roofs were soaked to stop flying sparks from igniting them. Men shouted unheard directions to each other over the roar of a ravenous beast intent on consuming everything in its path.

Children soiled themselves and screamed. Women grabbed what few possessions they could carry and ran as they herded their children, many paralyzed with fear, to the river's edge, north of town. Then, telling the older children to watch the younger, many ran back to their homes to release the animals they could, some too terrified to leave the safety they felt in their stalls.

In the middle of this melee, Putnam somehow managed to find Henry Gaunt.

"Gaunt! Gaunt! I'll take Bompeau now. I'll not have him die in this fire and deprive Massachusetts of justice."

320

Henry ran to move a bucket crew back. Another block was lost.

"Damn thee, Putnam. My whole town is burning, and thee're worried that John might die before thee get to hang him?"

Putnam ran beside him. "The fire's yours to tend to. Bompeau is mine. Give me the key, and I'll see to him myself."

"Will! Daniel! Move your crew! Fall back! We can't hold this line. Send a man down to move Silas' crew!" Turning to return to his crew, Gaunt ran into Putnam, sending both to the ground. "Damn thee Putnam! Get away—"

"Gaunt, have you released him, or is he still locked in your jail?"

Henry froze. "Great God! I forgot all about that!"

"Give me the key! I'll free him before he burns."

"The key's in the cabinet behind the counter of my store. Free him yourself!"

Putnam turned and fought his way through the bedlam, pushing aside terrified women and children. The door was locked. With no time to see if another was unlocked, he kicked his foot through the store's small window and climbed through, slicing his arm on the broken glass. He found the locked cabinet by the orange light that filled the room. Looking around the store, he grabbed an ax, smashed the cabinet open and grabbed the key.

It was a short run to the stockade. Jean-Marc was on his feet, tearing at the bars. He saw Putnam rush in, the key in his extended hand.

"Good, you have the key! Open the door! I need check on Abigail and my bucket crew!"

"You'll come with me!" Putnam shouted, pulling a pistol from his belt, he tossed the key to Jean-Marc. "We leave for Philadelphia now!"

"We can't leave now. The whole town is—"

"Burlington's no business of mine! I'm here to see that you hang for murd— "

Putnam stopped and fell forward. Henry stood behind him, holding a bloodied club. "I'll rot in Hell for this, but I'll not help him hang a good man!"

Jean-Marc looked at Putnam, then up. "There's not a moment to lose. Where be my crew?"

"Thy crew be damned! This is thy chance to run. None will know what happened to him. We can say thee were lost in the fire!"

Jean-Marc ran out the door, toward the flames. "Do you know where Abigail is?" he shouted.

"I don't!" Henry ran behind him. "I'll see that she's safe! Go!"

Still running to the inferno, "I'll not leave my wife and friends to die, while I run!" He saw a woman. "Have you seen Abigail Rider?" She ran past without answering. He came to a bucket crew, running to a new water trough. "Have you seen my wife?"

A man stopped. Soot covered his face like a mask. "Most women are by the river, north of town!" He spun and returned to his crew.

Jean-Marc sprinted for the river, Henry at his heels. Just past the northern edge of town they found a barge loaded with women and children, tied to a tree, but floating well off-shore. A rowboat was tied to the same tree. The men jumped in the boat and rowed to the barge.

"Has anyone seen my wife? Is Abigail Rider on board?"

There was movement on the barge as the boat neared. Abigail pushed her way to the edge.

"John!" she called, reaching to him. "John, you've come for me! This be our chance to run!"

The boat pulled up to the barge. He stood and leaned to kiss her. "Thank God, you're safe!" Touching arms, they kissed again.

"Help me in!" She saw Henry. "Henry, I knew you for a good friend! Where are we going?"

"We're not going anywhere. You're safe. I feared you were lost. I go to my crew. I'll not run while my home burns."

Henry shouted, "The brewery's lost. Abigail's right. This is thy chance. Take it!"

Jean-Marc kissed Abigail again, then pulled free.

"John, no! Take me, no one will know!"

He sat and pushed the boat away from the barge. "You and the baby are safe. Naught else matters. I love you." He pulled on the oars. Abigail shouted something, but he couldn't hear her.

Henry tried to pull an oar from his hand, "Don't be a fool. God sends not miracles twice. Run, John and Abigail can both die in this fire."

John pulled on the oars, "How far would I get with Abigail due any day? How many women just saw you, in this boat with me? You'd be jailed for helping me escape. I can't run. Besides, my home's on fire!"

"I told you, the brewery's already lost. "

"Burlington's my home, and my home's on fire. I'll not desert it while it burns."

He rowed to shore, tied the boat and ran to the flames, getting separated from Henry in the confusion. Jean-Marc found his crew and joined the bucket line. Men could only stay at the front of the line for a few minutes before the intense heat forced them to fall back. No one stepped forward to fill their place. The fire won another yard. Everyone's clothes had burnt holes. Blistered hands were covered with charred flesh. Buckets passed from hand to hand, water sloshing over their sides as men fought off exhaustion. Frightened men struggled in vain to lead terrified animals away from the fire to safety. Step by grudging step, the fire fought its way forward. Brave men fought in a losing cause. Minutes became hours.

With the sound of an explosion, a wall broke loose from a large building, falling on Jean-Marc's bucket line. Men screamed in pain. Most of the crew broke and ran from the flames. Trapped men cried for help. Jean-Marc joined a few who ran into the flames and disappeared.

Others shouted, "Come back. They're lost."

"You'll be killed!"

"There's nothing to do for them."

"The line needs to form up again, farther back."

The soot covered men running into the inferno had no idea who went with them. Using a bucket, Jean-Marc pushed aside burning timbers that pinned down a screaming man. Another man tore off his shirt, wrapped it around his hands and came forward.

Jean-Marc shouted. "I've got my bucket over the end." He pulled at the smoldering rope handle, trying to lift the timber. "Can you help lift it?"

The other man grabbed the timber and pulled, shouting in pain, his hands burning through the shirt. Together they strained against the timber. "It's moving. Just a little more."

The fire's roar and the trapped man's screams were deafening.

CRASH!

Burning timbers thundered down.

The rescuers disappeared.

The trapped man stopped screaming.

The bucket line fell back again.

Block by block they fought the fire. Men died from exhaustion after fighting for hours. A defensive fire break was set on the south end of the town green.

"We'll try to hold the line here."

The wind turned, first to the east driving the fire inland, away from the town. Then it shifted to the south, blowing the fire back on itself. Spent men dropped to their knees and sobbed.

A gentle rain began. Then it fell harder. The fire engulfed whatever was left south of town. Wide-eyed, trapped animals bellowed in their pens. The men at the green were too far away to hear them.

By mid-day, drenching rains drowned most of the flames. Smoke rose from rain-soaked ashes covering over half of what had been Burlington. Exhausted, soaked to the skin, thirsty and hungry, survivors of the great fire struggled to address their most basic needs. They crowded into the inn and any other building left. Men who had fought the fire all night struggled to make temporary shelters in a driving rain.

Women and children came from the barge and out of the woods. Soaked women searched for husbands and children; children for fathers and mothers. Too many were never found. Wives looked for anything they could find to feed men who were too tired to eat.

Families were destitute. Many were missing. Grieving, newly-made widows and orphans, huddled together and cried.

Abigail went into labor.

Chapter Nineteen
Going On

"The principal act of courage is to endure"
Thomas Aquinas

"Has anyone seen my husband?" Abigail cried into the overcrowded barn.

No one responded, or even seemed to hear. So many people crowded into the small barn that they turned the animals out into the rain. Unhappy animals packed into the corners of their pens.

Men lay in any open space they could find. Panicked women, children in tow, came and went, searching for missing children, missing husbands. Soaked to the skin, this was the fourth building Abigail had fought her way into, hoping to find Jean-Marc.

Then she felt a gush of warm water between her legs. The baby was coming. Looking back and forth, now she was as interested in finding Sarah or Elsie as she was in finding her husband. The barn was packed with a moving horde of women. Every one of them overwhelmed with cares. Abigail was alone in a frightened crowd.

"John!" she called. "Is Sarah Gibbs in here? Elsie?" Abigail managed to work her way to a rough-hewn wall. She leaned against it for support, as her first severe labor pains began. Crying, she sank to the floor, more from desperation than from pain.

"Dear God!" the young girl shouted, shoving her way to Abigail. "Are you having your baby right now? Here?"

Abigail looked up and nodded.

"I'll get my mother." The thin girl pushed through the crowd. A few minutes later, she returned with her parents. Abigail recognized Elizabeth and Edward Meadow from church.

Elizabeth bent over, pushed strands of soaked brown hair away, first from her face, and then from Abigail's. "Has your time come?" she shouted above the bedlam.

Abigail nodded.

"Who's your midwife?"

"Sarah Gibby, Elsie Longstreet!" Abigail shouted.

"I saw Sarah, looking for her husband, at the inn. Tillie!" she called her daughter. "Run you to the inn and see if Sarah Gibby's there. We need Sarah or Elsie Longstreet to help Mrs. Rider deliver." Tilly turned, pushed through the crowd and ran into the rain. "Edward," Elizabeth pointed at a small stall. "You have to clear that stall, to make room for her to deliver."

He wiped a burned and blistered hand across his sooty face. His filthy shirt, filled with holes, clung to his wet skin. His head and shoulders dropped. He sobbed, "How?"

"You walk over, say a woman is having her baby right now, and we need the stall for her. She can't have her baby leaning against this wall!"

Edward broke. Still sobbing, he pushed his way the few yards through the crowd. Elizabeth could see desperate men and women refusing to yield the small, over-crowded stall. They had nowhere else to go. She smiled with pride as her husband stood his ground and saw them out. One of the women Edward forced from the stall came over. She and Elizabeth helped Abigail through the crowd. By the time they reached the stall, Edward had found some dry straw and spread it on the manure-covered, mud floor.

As they helped Abigail past him, Elizabeth leaned up and kissed her husband on his filthy cheek. "You're a good man, Edward." She looked around the barn, still filled with women, many leading children, searching for their husbands. "'Tis my good fortune to have you." She kissed him again. Edward tried to smile, but instead sobbed, leaned his back against a post, and slid to the ground, his knees forced against his chest, in the crowded barn. A small boy sat beside him.

Tilly burst through the crowd, rain-water dripping over her small face and blue eyes. On a better day, people would say she looked just like her mother. "I can't find Sarah or Elsie, but some of my friends are looking. They'll bring them here. What can I do?"

"Can you find something to tie up against the front, so Mrs. Rider can have some privacy? Can you find her something to eat and drink? I'm sure she's had neither all day."

Without a word, Tilly disappeared again. In less time than anyone could have expected, she and another girl returned with a muddy quilt that they hooked to nails over the front of the stall, creating a more or less private space for Abigail. Then the girls left again. This time they returned with a scorched fire brigade bucket filled with water, a cup and a thick piece of black bread.

"Have you had anything to eat today?"

"No," Abigail said, shaking her head.

Elizabeth crouched and handed her a cup of water and the bread. "Here, eat this."

"How can I eat? I don't even know where John is? I have to go—"

"You have to go nowhere. You be no good to John or your baby if you take not care of yourself. My Tillie and some friends are looking for Sarah and Elsie." She turned to the small, bedraggled woman who had helped her bring Abigail to the stall. "What's your name?"

"Martha Ward."

"While Tillie looks, Martha and I will be here with you. John will be looking for you. He's a better chance to find you if you're not moving."

Uncertain, Abigail raised the cup to her lips. First, she sipped, then drained the cup of water and ate the bread. Elizabeth refilled the cup. Abigail drank that one, too.

"You've your fam… family to see to"

"My whole family is safe. My husband sits outside the stall with our little boy. My daughter got us the quilt, bread, and water. Now she's off to get your mid-wife. I've naught but time. Martha and I just met, but she's with us, too."

Martha looked over the privacy blanket and said, "My family's safe, but our house burned. We've no place to go anyway. We be here to help." She sounded less convincing.

"I hear south of … most south of town be gone. Is that true?" Abigail managed.

"So, I've heard," Elizabeth agreed. "Our farm was there. Edward thinks…" Elizabeth's brave front cracked. She sobbed, took a deep breath and started again. "Edward thinks all is gone, house, barn, even the ... the animals."

"Our house is, was there, too. John must be with Amos and Hans. They're our men. Must be looking to see what can ... can be saved."

"Of course, that's where John is. He's checking your house."

The blanket opened a bit. Elsie looked in. "Elizabeth, a word."

Elizabeth stood. "Martha's here. I'll just be a minute." She turned and left the stall.

Water dripped down Elsie's face. Her gray hair hung in strings around her hatless head. Wet clothing clung to her. "George tells me he thinks John dead. He and others ran to help trapped men but were themselves trapped when the barn fell. They've found bad burnt bodies. Her house and brewery be both gone, too," she said, in what passed for a whisper, in the barn filled with exhausted, hysterical people, as first one, then another cried out in pain after learning of the fate of a home or loved one.

"Lord have mercy! She needs to know none of that as she labors."

"Agreed. Most have lost some. Abigail's lost all. She needs to attend to her labor and baby. Recall, she lost her first while still a babe. There'll be time enough to tell her after."

Elizabeth nodded, and pulled back the quilt.

"Elsie!" Abigail managed a smile. "Have you seen my John?"

"I've not, but George will see to that. I'm here for you and your new baby." While they were talking, Martha looked, first right, then left, and slipped out of the stall.

Abigail sobbed, "When John gets here... we'll be, be fine. We've lost the house and brewery, but we've saved some money. John, will take care of every ... everything. He always does."

"Of course, he will." Somewhere, Tillie found a clean cloth. Elsie dipped it into the water bucket and wiped Abigail's face clean, just as her next contraction began.

*****

"You've a beautiful baby boy!" Elsie exclaimed, just before dawn. Tillie had managed to find a dry blanket. Elizabeth held it as Elsie handed her the baby. She wrapped it in the blanket and handed him to Abigail. She held him to her breast.

"He's sucking! He's healthy! John will be so excited! Where is he? He needs to know."

"I still haven't seen him, child." Elsie turned to Elizabeth and whispered, "Can Tillie find the priest?" Elizabeth nodded and stepped through the blanket.

"It's a boy!" Elizabeth smiled as Tillie's face lit up, then darkened. "Does she know?"

"Not yet. You've been so good all night. Do you think you can find Father Farnsworth?"

"I think so. I don't think the church is burned. I'd think him there."

"Good. Go get him. Be sure he knows about Mr. Rider. He should be here when we tell her."

Tillie struggled to her feet and disappeared into the night. *At least it stopped raining.*

As she expected, the priest was in the overcrowded church. People were sleeping in every available space. When she told him why she came, his tired face somehow fell even more.

"A day such as this should be visited on no one," He muttered as he followed Tillie out the door and to the barn.

Stepping through the opening and into the stall, the priest managed a smile. "Good morning, Abigail. I'm told you've a beautiful and healthy baby boy."

"I do!" Abigail beamed, "John will be so proud."

The priest knelt on the muddy straw, next to Abigail. He put his hand on her head, looked away, drew a deep breath and began. "Abigail, I need to tell you about John—"

"You know where he is! Send someone—"

"I know where he is Abigail, but he's gone. He—"

Her scream woke even the most exhausted man in the barn. The baby cried. Abigail shouted, "No! You're wrong! I know!"

Father Farnsworth put one hand on her head, and one over his eyes. He said a silent prayer and waited for Abigail to calm. Then he stood. Elizabeth reached down, took the baby and closed Abigail's bodice. She had cried herself to sleep.

"There'll be room in my house. We can move her there when she wakes and the barn clears enough to get the baby through the crowd safe," Elsie said.

"That's good. I'm needed at the church. We have to see about trying to feed the people there. Then there's those here with nothing. We face another fearsome day."

"That we do." Elsie turned to Elizabeth. "What will thee do?"

"I know not. Edward has always, always provided, but … I think we've lost all. How will he provide?" She began to cry, allowing herself to deal with her family's loss.

Elsie looked down. She could not remember when she felt so tired. "I think our animals can stay in the pen. We can let thy family stay in our barn. We'll share as we have."

Elizabeth bent her face into her hand and cried. Tillie took her hand. "Mrs. Longstreet, can I take my mother to your barn now?" She looked at Elsie with heavy eyes.

Elsie put her hand to Tillie's face. "Child, thee are a treasure. This night thee were a hero. Take thy mother to our barn. Tell George I said he should help thee move the animals into the pen, and he should bring thee a quilt for thy mother. I'll stay here with Mrs. Rider and her baby."

"What about my father?"

"When he wakes, I'll send him along."

By the time Elizabeth and Tillie reached Elsie's home, George had already moved the animals into their outside pens, shoveled out the barn and laid down fresh straw. He was burned, blistered, and slouched with fatigue, but tried to smile when Elizabeth and Tillie came through the gate in his unpainted wooden fence. A pitcher of beer, several mugs, and a loaf of bread were on the porch.

"Elsie send you?"

"She said we could–"

"I thought Elsie would send some. So many have lost so much. Thee're welcome to stay, but know, half the town's gone. My guess be others'll join thee."

Elizabeth thanked him. She and Tillie went into the barn. Elizabeth lay down on the straw. Tillie left and soon, she came back with two quilts. She covered her mother with one, then she curled up in the other beside her. They did not wake when Edward joined them about noon.

Elsie brought Abigail and her baby into the house at about the same time.

Chapter Twenty
Starting Over

"Now, God be praised, that to believing souls gives light in darkness, comfort in despair."
William Shakespeare in Henry VI

There was little activity that day. People needed to recover before they could rebuild. The town was in shock.

Quaker fellowships in Philadelphia sent wagon loads of food, beer, blankets, clothing, and promises to help rebuild. No one in Burlington went hungry.

When not sleeping, Abigail busied herself caring for her baby. When not busy, she cried. That afternoon, Father Farnsworth visited. Elsie put a pot of tea on the small table in their plain parlor and seated them on wooden chairs. She poured two cups and left the room.

Farnsworth looked around. The smell of smoke drifted through the open window in the small, undecorated, white room. Only the small shelf with a Bible and five other books hinted at the Longstreets' wealth. He took a sip of tea before speaking. She did not touch hers.

"Abigail, I've a hard task, in hard times... You know we lost a good many men yesterday."

She nodded, wiping at her tears, looking at anything but the priest.

"We need to bury them."

She kept nodding, still looking away.

"We know who most are." He paused. "John's one. There's no need for family to identify them. But I think the families need to see them... to say goodbye."

"I... I'd like that."

"You have to know, John was burned bad. Seeing him will be hard."

Tears flowed down her face. She looked at him for the first time. "Not seeing would be worse."

"I understand. I have to see the other famil–"

"Who were they, the others?"

Farnsworth looked down, then back at Abigail. This was painful. "We lost so many. Your John, Tim Hawkes... and Guy Iron, Will Burke, Sam Smythe." The priest touched a finger with each name, as if counting, "Tom Barre, George Wooley and Richard Kingsman. Good men all. The Friends lost more. Some we can't identify, we think them travelers from the inn who rallied to the alarm. Did you know any of them?"

She managed to say, "I knew all you named... But for Tom Barre, who wasn't married, I know their wives and children... Too much loss in so small a town."

"It is." The priest's eyes filled with tears. "And we must baptize your son. His soul's at risk."

"What need I do?" Abigail sounded exhausted.

"Under the circumstances, there'd be no common celebration. Have you picked godparents?"

"Elsie and George house us," Abigail said.

"But they belong to the Society of Friends. They could not make the pledges a godparent must make. What about people from our congregation? You must—"

"Elizabeth Meadow helped Elsie deliver my child. Mayhap she and Edward—"

"They would be perfect. If they agree, we can baptize your baby in private here."

Abigail could only nod.

"'Tis important we act soon, but I think 'twill be too difficult before the funeral. I can come the next day?"

Abigail nodded.

"I have to see Caroline Hawkes and Martha Iron. I could come back and walk you to the church."

"That won't be... be necessary. I'm sure Elsie will go with me... or Elizabeth Meadow."

"If you're sure–"

"I am."

Wiping at her tears, Abigail stood. The priest stood and took her hand. Before leaving, he said a tearful prayer. Then Abigail sat and cried. After a few minutes, Elsie came into the room.

"My heart weeps for thee, child. What can I do?"

"I need to go to see John…To show him his son. Will you come with me?"

"'Twill be my honor." Elsie tried to force a smile. "He'll be dirty. His clothes burned. We can take some of George's things. Thee will feel better if thee clean him."

"Thank–" Abigail slid from the chair and wept. Elsie knelt and wept with her. After many minutes, Abigail stood, and wiped her face. "We should go."

"We should. Wait a moment." Elsie stood and left the room. She returned with a burlap sack filled with clothing and towels. They walked the mile to the church in silence.

The priest was sitting in a pew, praying with Martha Iron when they arrived. The women waited, at a respectful distance, for them to finish. Abigail's baby slept on her shoulder. Elsie felt ill at ease in the ornate church. It was far different from the simple meetinghouse she attended.

The prayer ended. Farnsworth stood, helped Martha to her feet and walked her to the door. When he turned, Abigail blurted out, "Where's John?"

"We have them in the yard. This will be difficult ... We should talk first." He paused. "The burning is severe. Would you rather remember him as he was?"

"No. I need to see my husband."

He nodded and led the women to the church yard. The bodies, covered with gray woolen blankets, lay in a row between the church and the cemetery, in the shade of a large elm.

He's not far from our Mary. She turned to the priest. "Will you see that he's buried next to Mary?" There was a pleading quality to her voice.

"We thought you would want that. It's been arranged. The other men will rest nearby. John is third from the front." Together, they walked to the body. Elsie pulled a small blanket from her bag for Abigail's baby to lie on. He fell asleep in the shade.

The women stood at the John's feet. Farnsworth knelt by his head, and pulled the cover back, revealing only a face burned beyond recognition.

Abigail gasped, staggered back, and dropped to her knees. The priest replaced the cover. Elsie knelt next to Abigail, hand on her shoulder, but said nothing. Farnsworth said a silent prayer.

Abigail whispered, "I need to clean him. Change his clothing."

"You're sure?" the priest asked.

"I am."

Father Farnsworth had two men carry John to a table behind the church, so she would not have to kneel in the dirt. "You don't have to do this, Abigail."

"Yes, I do."

He pulled off the blanket.

"Look at his clothes," she cried. His blackened shirt was almost burned away. The fire had burned into his broken chest. His breeches were burned. Stockings no longer covered the charred flesh on his legs. "He's so dirty." She looked at Elsie,

"Then we'll just clean him."

Elsie pulled cloths, towels, and clothing out of the bag. Then she went to the well for a bucket of water. Abigail lifted a charred hand to her cheek, then gasped and stepped back, releasing the hand, "'Tis not John!"

Farnsworth said, "He was found where the barn fell, with two others. His injuries make it hard–"

"'Tis not my husband." Words tumbled from her mouth. "This be a laborer's calloused hand. I know not this man."

"Abigail, John was so burned, his hands so charred. Don't torture yourself. We're certain–"

"Then be uncertain. This be not my John."

Elsie put a hand on her shoulder. "Are thee sure?"

"'Tis this man George?"

"No. He's smaller."

"And neither is he John." She rinsed her hands in the water Elsie had brought to clean John's body, dried them on the towel, and picked up her baby. "Don't bury this man next to Mary."

"Are you sure, Abigail?" the priest asked.

"Don't you do it! This be not my John. We need to find my husband. Who looks for him?"

The priest lowered his head, and said, just above a whisper, "The whole town was searched for the injured or lost until they were too spent to look further."

"And now they've rested a day–"

"Abigail," Elsie said. "They found John. They've found them all."

"They haven't!" she shouted. "They missed my John. Hans and Amos will help me look. Where be they?"

Farnsworth looked up and shook his head, "None have seen either since the fire."

Tears welled in Abigail's eyes. "No one told me they were lost." She turned away from the priest, then looked back, wiping a tear. "I'll miss them, they were loyal servants, more friends—"

"Perhaps not so loyal." The priest moved closer and put his hand on Abigail's arm. "They're not among those hurt, or the lost. None have seen them. And John's ox and cart weren't at your house. They were taken, before your house burned."

"Then they be with John. They've gone for help."

"They weren't with John. He was in the jail, then ran to the fire. Hans and Amos are nowhere to be found."

Abigail's eyes widened. "They ran? The town burned, and they ran?"

"I fear so."

"Then damn them both. If none'll help me, I'll look for John alone." She turned to go. "Don't you bury that man next to Mary!"

The priest called, "Abigail."

"Don't you do it! Don't!"

Farnsworth turned to Elsie, "They found him right where John was lost."

"I'll talk to her." Elsie hurried after Abigail.

When she caught up, Abigail asked, "Will George help me look for John?"

"I'll ask him."

One of the men staying in the barn was helping George rake out wet straw when the women reached the Longstreet house. Elsie asked her husband to come behind the barn and told him about what happened. "Will thee help her look?"

"Elsie, the town's been searched. There's real work that needs doing."

"I know. Will thee help her?"

"Elsie–"

"Can thee not do this mercy for a grieving widow?"

George lowered his head. "I thank God daily for his mercy. I'll not deny it to another."

George and Abigail searched the devastated area for days before Abigail was willing to stop. George stayed with her the entire time.

*****

Henry Gaunt woke up exhausted. He had set up an office in his barn, where he tried to access the damages and plan for recovery. About half of Burlington was gone. While he was busy in the barn, his wife ran the store. That day, she gave away as much as she sold.

Henry swore under his breath when Putnam walked in. The wound on the back of Putnam's head was visible through his hair. Bruises covered his face.

"Gaunt, 'tis your duty to find out who attacked me last night. Whoever it was helped Bompeau escape—"

"None helped John escape. When **thee** let him out of jail, he ran straight to the fire. He died trying to save a trapped man." Henry sounded disgusted. He had no interest in dealing with Putnam. "I know it upsets thy plan to hang him, but John died a hero—"

"You expect me to believ—"

"I care not what thee believe. John's body is at the English church, waiting his funeral–"

"Then who attacked me? I demand—"

"Thee demand what? Thee released John. None would be surprised that thee were injured in such a fire—"

Putnam's face reddened. He spat as he shouted, "You'll not get away with this! I'll go back to the gover—"

Henry stood to his full height and leaned down, nose to nose with Putnam. Henry's Quaker beliefs taught him to hate violence, but for the second time in his life, he wanted to hit another man. Again, that man was Putnam. His voice sounded threatening, "Thee are going to go to the governor? And what will thee tell him? That **thee** let thy prisoner out of jail? That he then died trying to save another? Get out of my sight, before I..." He let his voice trail off.

"Before you what?" Putnam balled his fists. Despite his injury, he was ready for a fight.

Henry turned his back and walked a few steps away. In a quieter voice, "Get out of here before I forget who I am and do something I'll need repent later. Go to the church and see for thyself. Thy prisoner's dead. Then leave my town. There's work to be done here and thee have naught to do with it."

Putnam smiled when Henry backed down. He hated Quakers and enjoyed forcing another to show what he considered to be cowardice.

Convinced Henry was lying, he went straight to the church. He walked up to a large man sitting in the bed of a small wagon, keeping watch over the bodies.

"I'm Isaiah Putna—"

"I know who you are."

"Then you'll know why I need to see the bodies. Gaunt wants me to believe Bompeau died in the fire. A bit convenient."

The man walked to the bodies and lifted the blanket covering Jean-Marc's. "Seen enough?" He lowered the cover and spat. "Now get away from here. You dishonor brave men."

"How am I to tell from that? The face's gone."

The man stepped toward Putnam. "John was found where he died, trying to save others. You'd know naught of that. Leave here now!"

Putnam spat and walked away. He decided he would leave for Philadelphia in the morning. Maybe he could find someone to treat his wound.

*****

Elsie convinced Abigail to sit at the graveside, "With time, you'll regret not being by John when he's put to rest."

Abigail's compromise was to leave space for her to be buried between the man the others believed to be Jean-Marc and Mary. *At least I'll be next to my Mary, not some stranger.*

Holding her baby, she sat, dry-eyed at the graveside. Elsie and George, Henry and his wife stood behind her. Abigail smelled the freshly dug earth. *I remember this from Mary's. You smell dirt at funerals.*

She looked to the crying women sitting beside the other holes. Children stood near them, crying as they tried to be brave. Abigail paid no attention as the priest droned through the funeral service. After he finished, she wondered at men jostling around the widows.

Moses Dunbar, holding his hat at his waist approached her, "Widow Rider–"

"Leave her alone, Dunbar." Henry pushed between them.

"I was just–"

"I know what thee were doing."

"I–"

"Go. Abigail's not ready. Bother the others." Henry glared at Dunbar, who nodded, and backed away, before joining the queue around another widow.

Will Reed shook his head as he walked up to Henry. "The bachelors be like vultures."

"They are," Henry nodded.

Will looked around the crowded church yard, then said, "I waited until the funeral was over, but we need thee by the river. A body's been found."

"Not another." Henry looked down. His voice sounded like a much older man's. "I thought we'd found them all."

This one's not from the fire," Will looked around again and lowered his voice, "A body was found floating in the river, his head bashed in."

"Highwaymen?"

"Don't think so. There's a purse full of silver on his belt."

Henry turned to George Longstreet. "Will thee see after Abigail?"

Without waiting for George to reply, he trotted away after Will. Three other men were standing over the body when Henry reached the river.

"'Tis that Puritan, Putnam," the biggest of the men said. "Like as not the work of Indians. His head looks to be crushed by a tomahawk."

"Why would an Indian kill him, and take neither his silver nor gun?" Henry asked, looking at the pistol still pushed into Putnam's belt. He pulled the pistol from the dead man's waistband. "Still loaded. He never knew what hit him." Henry walked to the river and looked upstream, in the direction of the ferry to Philadelphia. "The Delaware bother none. Why would one kill a man and take not his money or gun? This had to be personal. What Delaware even knew him?"

None of the others could answer his questions.

*****

Leaving the funeral, Abigail said to Elsie, "I need to do something until I find John. I can't stay with you forever. Will you walk with me to my house? John and I saved well." She tried to sound determined. "There'll be enough for a small house. More will come from his agent."

"Of course. George, there's porridge over the fire for those in the barn. Will thee see to them?"

He nodded. "I've fed 'em afore. Tilly'll help."

George walked across River Road. Abigail and Elsie turned south and walked to the wreckage of her house.

At the house, Abigail said, "Oh, Elsie, I never dreamt 'twould be so bad." She turned to Elsie and cried on her shoulder.

"Now, child, we knew 'twould be terrible." She hugged Abigail, around the baby, and patted her back.

When the baby began to fuss, Abigail straightened and wiped her eyes. "Let's do what we came to do. Here." She handed the baby to Elsie, "You hold him while I get the purse."

Elsie held the baby while Abigail picked through the remains of her home. She stepped to the right of the fireplace and reached around its side.

"It's gone! The stone's moved and the silver's gone!" She looked around the burned-out room. "I don't even see the stone we hid it behind! That cur Amos must have come, even before the house burned, stole our silver and ran. I've lost all!"

"Not all child."

"I've lost all. How will we eat? Where will we live?"

"First, remember, you have your son. You said John's agent would send money for a few months. There's that. Thee can stay with us a while, but thee will want thy own home soon enough. 'Tis hard to say, but Moses Dunbar's not alone. There still be more men than women in this colony. Many a widow, especial those with a little money, marry quick. There's certain to be a good man to provide for thee, and thy baby."

"But I'm no widow. I told you, that man wasn't John. I can't marry another—"

"Speak not too quick, child. The fire was days ago. None have seen John."

"But we will."

*****

The ceremony for the private baptism of a child was brief. Edward and Elizabeth,

speaking for Abigail's son, renounced Satan in all his forms. They promised he would receive proper religious education and that he would be confirmed into the faith at the proper age.

Father Farnsworth took the baby from Tillie and said, "Name this child."

In a clear voice, Abigail said, "I name him Benjamin William Bompeau."

The priest dipped his fingers into a basin of water. Making the sign of the cross on Benjamin's head, he said, "Benjamin William, I baptize thee, in the Name of the Father and of the Son and of the Holy Ghost."

Benjamin cried when the small drops of water hit his head. He was still crying when the priest held him up and said, "Behold, the world's newest Christian!" He handed the infant back to Tillie, told everyone to kneel and he read a final prayer.

The brief service over, the priest sat at the kitchen table, took out his quill, ink well, and church record book. He opened it to the bookmarked page and said aloud as he wrote, "Private Infant Baptism of Benjamin William Rid—"

Abigail interrupted, "My son will know his father's name. Jean-Marc Bompeau."

"I am corrected. Benjamin William, how do you spell Bompeau?"

"I have no letters." Abigail cried. "I neither read nor write. I know not how to spell our name."

Farnsworth smiled, "Then I shall instruct you. Your name is spelled B-U-M-P-P-O."

He looked at the baby and said, "It is a hard world you enter, Benjamin Bumppo."

*****

That night, pounding at the front door brought George Longstreet to his feet. He expected no one this long after dark. He opened the door.

"I come to see Abigail." Three large Indians stood outside.

"I'm sorry, Friend, but she sleeps and cannot be disturbed." George stepped forward, trying to fill the doorway.

Tamaqua pushed his way in. "I will see Abigail. What room?" The others stood at the door, facing the street, as if on guard.

"Tamaqua, is that you?" Abigail called. "I'm in here. Have you found John?"

He walked into the tiny room. "Tamaqua hear. I come see you and baby are good."

Abigail sat up in bed. She wiped away her tears and lifted her baby. "See, John has a son. We named him Benj—"

"Baby not have name yet. He not earn name." He leaned close to Benjamin. "Parents call him Son. Village call him Boy." Tamaqua straightened, "One day he will do great deed. Then he earn name. All will know him by his deed. That be his name."

Tamaqua leaned in close to the baby again. He put his hand on the baby's head and said, "This vow I make to you, Son. You never be alone, as long as Tamaqua, or any of his clan live. Your friend be our friend. Your enemy, our enemy. No one will hurt you." He straightened and held his hand out to Abigail. "John was my friend. He is gone. You are not alone. I will see no one hurt you or your baby."

She took his hand with both of hers. Tears ran down her cheek. She struggled to say, "John's not gone. I'll find him. He will know his son."

Tamaqua seldom smiled but smiled now. "It is good to believe."

He turned and again pushed past George. Closing the door behind him, Tamaqua was gone. George hurried to the door and opened it. There was nothing to see. George and Elsie looked at each other in wonder.

"What do thee make of that?" Elsie asked.

George just looked at her. He had no idea what to say. He bolted the door, then followed Elsie into Abigail's room.

"Tamaqua is an old friend," Abigail explained. "I know not why, but he has been there for us, for years."

"What did he want? What did he say?" Elsie asked.

"He wanted me to know he was sorry to hear about John, that the baby and I aren't alone. He's still our friend."

"How did he know about John or that you were here?"

Abigail smiled through her tears. "That's the thing about Tamaqua. He just knows." She held her baby close to her face and said, "That's the thing, Son, Tamaqua just knows." She kissed him, held him close to her and lay back down. "He just knows." She closed her eyes.

CPSIA information can be obtained
at www.ICGtesting.com
Printed in the USA
BVHW04s0728140518
516067BV00002B/2/P